The Dragon Thief

Rowena Tylden-Pattenson

For Michael, who should read more books.
And for my parents, who nearly found out I was writing a
novel- It was supposed to be a surprise!

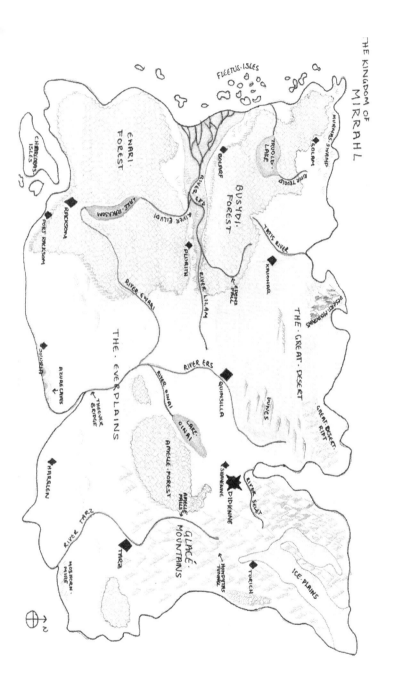

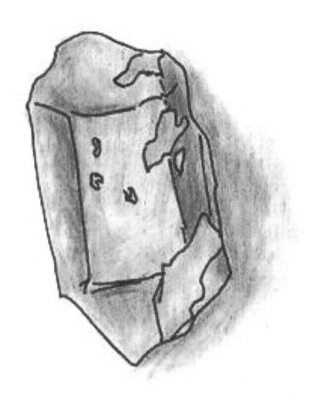

1
QUINSILLA. THE START OF SOMETHING.

On the edge of the great sand plains stood the city of Quinsilla, its white walls shining in the golden afternoon sunlight. To one side the vast desert stretched into the horizon, its sands rolling and twisting into restless landforms that none but those who knew the desert best could even begin to fathom. On the other side the sand gave way slowly to the green of fields and the dark shifting shades of a thick river that meandered its way calmly towards the ocean that lay many leagues to the south.

Quinsilla was bustling with people meandering around the fashionable shops that lined the streets or picking up their daily necessities in the sprawling northern quarter market. It was just after noon and trade was reaching its lunchtime peak, each stallholder trying to gain attention from the nearest passer by.

Out of the window of a tall building a young man reclined on the window ledge, resting his head in one hand as he stared down at the busy street below. A faint smile played across his lips now and then as he watched someone jump out of the way of a speedy wagon or slip on the muddy cobblestones underfoot, speckling their clothing with dark muddy splashes.

After a few minutes of watching out of the window he gave a sigh and turned away, rolling down the sleeves of his shirt. He pulled off a chunk of bread lying on a small table, pulling it to bits before eating it pensively. His belongings lay around the room; a blue coat tossed over the edge of the bed, a small bag of collected items spilling onto the floor. A feathered necklace peeped from below the fabric of the bag and he picked it up, running the smooth decorated stones under his fingers.

A knock came at the door, accompanied by a cheerful voice.

"Will you be wanting anything today, master Lutis?"

The man slipped the necklace into his pocket and hurried to the door, the stiff lock juddering in his hands as he forced it upwards. "No thank you Laurie, I'm fine."

"All right then, if you need anything, just ask downstairs and someone'll bring it up," said the cheerful girl that stood outside the door, giving him a smile before heading back down the corridor to the wide stairs at the end.

Lutis shut the door with a click, then pressed his back against the wood with a sigh, pushing his long brown hair out of his eyes with one hand. He would miss being in Quinsilla, even though he knew he was only there for a job, and then he would have to be out of the city again. Maybe if he was paid all he was promised he could go back to Kaionar and live handsomely in a place of his own, instead of the little flat that, by now, had probably been wrecked by his friends.

He gave a snort of derision. As if that dream would ever come true. People of his profession were not looked upon lightly, even when they were rich and had given up thievery. He shook his head and busied himself about collecting up his things.

As he exited the tavern he had been staying at he was hit by the buzz of the market. "Apple pies! Meat pies! Perfect lunchtime snack, will fill yeh up good fer the rest of the day!" called one stallholder, brandishing a pie in front of Lutis as he passed close by the stall. "Yeh look like you could do with a good meal, why not try one o' ma's pies?" She beamed, nodding assertion at a purchase, but he shook his head, holding up a hand.

"No thank you, kind miss," he replied quietly, continuing to move swiftly through the market and looking away from her gaze. *Any other day…* he thought to himself, *but not today*. He had important work to do, work that might buy him more than one pie if he was quick and clever about it.

He exited the market quickly, ducking down a less populated side street behind a stall selling glittering trinkets to a squall of squabbling girls who cooed over each item that was produced with a flourish by the stallholder. Immediately the noise receded and, while the street was still busy, it was nothing like what it had been in the Northern Square. He quickly glanced back at the sunlit crowds then turned into the darker shadows cast by the looming buildings. A small smile crept across the corner of his mouth as he made his way down the street, turning with purpose towards the heart of the city. Lutis blended well into the hustle and bustle, his dark clothing nonchalant and unassuming like many of those who thronged around him on their daily business. His pale skin was a bit of a giveaway to the fact he wasn't from the city, but he was slowly browning under the hot desert sun and would soon be as tanned as the true residents of Quinsilla. Normally they were fair game for a skilled pickpocket such as he was, but today he had his eyes on a bigger prize.

As he turned into another wider street, walking south, the sight of the Jewel Tower filled his view. It was the tallest building in Quinsilla. He lifted his eyes to the top, shadowing his gaze slightly with one hand from the sun that blazed in the west. Although the tower looked formidable from the ground, its windowless walls stretching high above the buildings around it, unassailable from any direction, at the top a room opened wide to the elements, its roof held aloft by thin twisting metal designs shaped like plants reaching up to the tip of the tower. It was the perfect entrance to the tower for any that could fly. Or the perfect exit, if you could get to the top of the tower by other means. Lutis tucked a hand into one pocket of his long coat, checking for the small bag of gold coins that rested there and continued towards the tower.

Once he reached the bottom of the tower he stopped again, looking at the gate that separated the tower from the street. It was patrolled by two guards, one male, one female, heavily armoured in gleaming silver plate. It was very decorative, but wouldn't be at all practical when it came to fighting, especially in the thin streets. As he watched the woman turned to the man and nudged him, pointing to a nearby cart where hot food was being sold- obviously the two hadn't had their lunch yet. Lutis narrowed his eyes, outlining a short scene in his mind before stepping closer to the tower. He was hailed almost immediately by the man.

"Hey, you there!" The guard gestured him closer with a wave of a hand. "Fancy earning some coins?" He reached into a pocket and withdrew a half-handful of bronze, showing them to Lutis before closing his hand tightly around them. Lutis nodded his affirmation, drawing closer to the guard.

"Get us some o' those wraps an' you can have the leftover coins." He handed Lutis the money, patting his hand reassuringly. "I would go meself, but I'm not allowed t' leave me post an' neither's Emi." He gestured to where the other guard stood. She gave a smile and a nod before entering the tower, no doubt to patrol the staircase or take a rest from the hot desert sunshine. Lutis nodded again and drew away, heading directly for the cart from which the spicy scent of Quinsillan wraps was drifting, a specialty food that was popular in the city. He bought two, giving the young girl selling the food a cheeky grin with the coins before heading back to the bottom of the tower. *All going to plan so far...and I haven't even used any of my own money yet.*

The guard was waiting expectantly at the bottom of the tower, watching him eagerly. He took the wrap gratefully, biting into it with apparent relish. Lutis himself found them rather bland without adding extra spices, but voicing such an opinion when there was work at hand probably wouldn't be the best idea. He pointed towards the doorway of the tower.

"I'll take this up to your friend- Emi was her name, right?" He stepped lightly towards the door, giving the guard a smile, who nodded thickly back through a mouthful of wrap and turned back to watching the hustle and bustle of the street. Lutis headed towards the dark entrance, a glitter of excitement betraying his real emotions behind the mindless smile on his face. It was almost too easy getting into the tower.

It was dark and cool inside. The hard stone that made up the thick walls kept the air cold and pleasant. A staircase twirled up the centre of the building, rough and worn, a complete contrast to the splendour and spectacle that the tower boasted on its outside walls. Lutis could hear a hollow thumping of boots as Emi walked back down the staircase and he knew he had to act quickly, before she reached the bottom of the stairs, if everything he had planned was to go accordingly. Holding the food tightly in one hand he leapt up the steps two at a time, his soft boots making little noise on the stone. The staircase spiralled dizzyingly and he had to rest his spare fingers on the outside wall. The sound of footsteps got louder, clumping in a regular rhythm, then suddenly they met around a bend, the height of the steps making Emi taller than Lutis. He gave a smile.

"Brought you some lunch," he said, holding out the wrap invitingly.

"Why would you bring it all the way up here?" she asked, hesitating before reaching out to take the food.

"Why, to see you of course!" he replied quickly, smiling disarmingly. She blushed and looked away, dipping her eyes to the steps they stood on, distracted. Lutis suddenly lurched on the step falling forward against her, as though he had tripped, grabbing hold of her arm as they fell to the ground. She gave a cry before she hit the steps, her armour clanking loudly, then it was cut short as her head cracked against the stone. A few echoes reverberated down the staircase. She slid a couple of steps down, lying limply like a rag doll, and Lutis was forced to spread himself along the wall to avoid being dragged down the staircase after her. He pulled a face- it had been his best idea to get rid of her, but he didn't like it all the same. At least it had been quiet. Well, relatively. She was definitely unconscious, but for how long, he didn't know.

He carried on up the staircase, a little slower now, pausing for breath. It was a long way up to the top! As he got higher and higher the staircase twisted closer on itself, getting thinner as the tower narrowed, but it was brighter than the semi-darkness of the lower staircase where only torches set into the walls gave a little light. A shard of sunlight glowed on the wall in front of Lutis and he knew that he had reached the top of the tower. He paused for a breather, looking back down the staircase for any sign of movement from the guards. Any moment now the man was bound to come and look for his friend, and then all hell would break loose. Taking a deep breath he stepped into the top room, not looking to conceal his figure any longer. There was nowhere to hide in the open-sided space and he would be revealed in an instant.

Lutis' eyes glittered with excitement as he stepped towards his prize- the ruby jewel that sat on a small table in the middle of the room. He didn't spare a glance for the view, not the intricate streets that wound their way below him, nor the fields around the city, nor the sweeping, ever-changing sands of the desert that lay to the north-east. He stretched out a hand, fingers held wide to envelope the gem completely… but stopped. No, there was one more thing. He reached inside a pocket, drawing a pair of leather gloves from its depths and slipping them over his fingers. He was already wearing fingerless gloves, but according to the person who had given him the job they weren't enough.

"Do not touch the ruby with your bare hands," he had been instructed, and as that was part of the deal, he had to comply. If he didn't then he wouldn't get his payment, and that was the only reason he had taken the job- the reward would set him up with gold for the rest of his life! Once again he stretched out his hand and this time took the gem from its nook in the table, a wide smile spreading across his face.

An unearthly shriek filled the air, unbearably loud. With a cry Lutis dropped the gem, covering his ears with his hands to try and block the noise. It had come from the gem, no, the whole tower itself. Releasing his ears he dropped to his knees, grabbed the stone and slid it into a pouch in his belt, swearing under his breath.

"Oh, you're definitely rumbled now Lutis!" he muttered to himself, scrabbling with the pouch to close it before straightening. The noise sounded again, alerting everyone in Quinsilla that something was wrong. In the streets below a panic erupted, guards flooding from every post in the city towards the tower, startled citizens scrambling to get out of the way. Already he could hear the thumping of boots on the staircase. He took a deep breath, trying to calm his nerves, following the movements he had practised for days in the little room of the inn he had been staying at. He shrugged off his coat, piling it on the floor, the contents of his pockets clinking. Next to go was the heavy mechanised wings that his coat had concealed, which he placed carefully on the floor. He pulled his coat back on (he wasn't going to leave all his gear behind for some nosy guard to rummage through) then bent back over the wings, unwinding the complicated mechanisms that held them shut- something, he realised belatedly, that he should have done before he had touched the ruby. The heavy sound of footsteps on the staircase slowly grew louder and a shout of concern echoed round the stone walls as the male guard discovered Emi lying on the staircase. Lutis pulled the wings back on. Now that they were open dark green sails were revealed, pulled tight between the thin struts that kept them in place. The wings were enchanted with magic to keep the wearer in the air, for the length of the wings alone wouldn't keep a human aloft for more than a moment.

Lutis patted the ruby in its little pouch to reassure himself it was still there then stepped towards the edge of the tower, a wind already beating at his wings, making them vie for take off. He hoped that the wind was as strong as it felt. More guards enter the door at the bottom of the tower, cutting off that route of escape completely.

Lutis took a deep breath and threw himself forwards into the air, letting the wind catch him. The wings billowed reassuringly beneath him, the straps pulling tight around his shoulders and torso. His arms shook slightly from the unnatural strain but he had to keep them straight to guide his flight away from the tower, towards the desert. Behind him the guard who had made it to the top of the tower yelled in frustration as he flew away, slipping out of his grasp. He laughed into the air, adrenaline racing through him. The wind whipped the noise away for none to hear. He was free, and with a prize too!

~

As Lutis escaped into the air, chaos and disruption were not only occurring inside Quinsilla. Two leagues to the north, in the Great Desert, distinctly more sinister plans were at work. The edges of the sand dunes that lay along the eastern side of the desert blew a little way out onto the flat barren Hamada plateau, thin tendrils of sand curling over the ground like wraiths. A collection of pale tents gathered on the edge of the rocky flats, seemingly deserted by their inhabitants, but they were really just hiding from the scorching afternoon sun.

At the top of a sand dune, overlooking the makeshift camp that the men below had set up at his last command, a man sat looking towards the dark shape of Quinsilla in the distance. His black hair ruffled slightly in the thin wind that scuffed the sand below the hooves of the horse he sat upon and he flicked it out of his eyes. The horse shifted uneasily, the sand slipping under its hooves but the man took little notice, his eyes boring into the horizon. His name was Zartear, and he led the band of mercenaries that made camp in the desert nearby. Despite the fact that they were under his command he wore heavy armour, the metal stained black to camouflage him against the night, the edges rimmed with bright silver.

As he watched the city a sudden noise screamed out across the land, echoing across the empty desert and breaking the silence. Even across the distance it was loud, but bearable. Zartear's cold, dark grey eyes hardened at the noise, watching the skies around the tower carefully for any sign of the thief. He had said he was good, but was he really skilled enough to get away with the prize he had boasted he could retrieve? It seemed so- a tiny black dot appeared in the blue sky, moving swiftly away from the tower. Well, at least that part of his plan had gone as ordered.

He turned away from the sight, trotting the horse down the side of the dune. It was only too happy to move, lifting its legs high and clear of the sand as it made its way carefully down the bank. Zartear knew the horse could find its own way down the dune best so he let it be, content to scheme silently to himself.

Down in the campsite a little movement started to come from inside the tents as the sound drew people into the open. As Zartear approached the camp the men who had emerged retreated back into their tents or stood to attention, watching their leader ride through the camp in silence. Zartear steadfastly ignored them; their lives were unimportant to him, they were just mercenaries. He continued his path through the camp, heading for a slightly larger tent on the outskirts of the site, the side closest to where Quinsilla stood in the far distance. A small fire burned outside it, a spit of roasting meat turning slowly above it. A woman crouched nearby, turning the spit slowly without stopping. She looked up as he approached, her golden eyes betraying no emotion.

"The thief managed it then?" she asked, not expecting an answer. Zartear leapt down off the horse giving her a look that confirmed her question, then tossed its reins to one side before entering the tent, pulling the fabric door shut behind him. She turned back to the meat, prodding it with the end of one finger and licking it before taking the spit off the fire and pulling the meat off the metal spike with her sharp teeth. She murmured thoughtfully to herself. "I'll take that as a yes."

The woman was Nox Arise, known throughout the camp as someone not to be crossed, her temper flaring up at any moment. She had been part of the party of mercenaries since the beginning and her loyalty (and lack of mercy) had been justly rewarded as Zartear recognised her talents. She was his second in command, the army's femme fatale, and feared by some just as much as Zartear was. She played the part well; although she was small in stature she was by no means someone you could miss, strange as she was. Her features were distinctly feline, her olive skin patterned with pale speckles that gathered in towards the corners of her eyes like a cheetah's markings. They might have been mistaken for decorative war markings, but they weren't- she had been born with them. Her parents were members of the race called the Felixis, a race of powerful beings that were feline in figure. She had been told her mother had been the most beautiful woman in the village and, as such, she had had many suitors. However it had come to grief when one of her suitors started to kill the others, driven to enragement that the others even dare look at her. That had been her father.

Nox had suffered under the hand of her father, punished when she spent time with her mother and stealing her away from him and punished again when she was not as beautiful as her mother was. Nox had chopped her black hair short like a man's and ran for freedom from the Felixis clan that she had lived with all her life when she turned seventeen, and had never once looked back.

Nox finished her mouthful and pulled another bite of meat off the spit, licking her lips like a cat. If the thief had come away with the ruby then they would soon be on the move and there would be little chance for sating human needs on the way to the city. She hurried eating- there was no way of telling when Zartear would give the order and she would have to abandon her meal. At least she would cope better than most of the army, being a Felixis. She had enough problems with just being accepted by the other mercenaries to be dealing with hunger too.

When Zartear reappeared from the tent he was wielding a huge double handed blade. It was nearly as long as he was tall, it's edges shining viciously in the desert light. She stood, stamping the embers of the fire out with the heel of her boot and bearing her teeth at him in a feral smile.

"It's time to go," he said, looking out over the quiet camp. "Ready the army, we have to strike quickly." He walked back to the horse that stood pulling strands of hay from a bag. It looked up at his approach, flicking his ears back against its skull. It had no wish to go back to where the sand shifted under his hooves.

Nox immediately started to make preparations, gathering the bow and quiver of arrows that were laying nearby and slinging them over her shoulder before setting off through the camp, shouting at the top of her voice.

"Let's be having you boys, it's time to move out!"

Half an hour later the army was on the move through the desert, the heavy tramping of their feet blowing up dust in a wake behind them. Quinsilla grew in size with each passing stade. Each and every member was armed to the teeth, mercenaries brandishing long swords, shields, pikes or maces, sneaking bandits filling the gaps, their clothing hiding daggers and bows beneath the folds. Quinsilla was still in a state of panic for the ruby had still not been found, and every guard in the city was combing the streets searching for the jewel- bar Emi, who was having her head bandaged and being heavily questioned as to who had stolen it. Nobody expected an attack, especially not one coming from the Great Desert. As such it was only when they were half a league from the city that the army was spotted, causing even more panic amongst the guards of Quinsilla.

In the covered city battlements that faced out across the Great Desert, one bored guard rested his elbows on the parapet, staring out at the desert. He was watching the advancement of the army with interest. Normally there was nothing interesting to watch on the desert side of the city and it was considered a punishment rather than a duty to take a shift there.

Another guard joined him at the crenelle and the first pointed out the army.

"Who do you think they are?" he asked, watching the marching throng tramp closer. He wasn't very worried- it was probably just a band of desert nomads coming to collect supplies or trade their wares.

"I don't know," said the other guard. "Isn't it a bit strange that they don't have any animals with them? Nomads normally have camels."

"You sound worried," said the first guard. "They've probably just left them back in the dunes or something. Would you want to bring all your animals to Quinsilla if you've got business?"

"I suppose not," replied the second again. "Well, better be off looking for that ruby again. I don't know why they're making such a fuss about it, it's only some old artefact."

"Have fun with that," smirked the first guard, continuing to watch the desert. As the mercenaries got closer though, he started to feel a little uncomfortable. It was true, there *were* no animals, and it was quite a large group too. He waited until they got closer then leaned out of the crenelle, hailing them with a shout.

"What do you want?" he called, pulling off his helmet so he could hear a reply. One of the women at the front pulled the bow from her back and fired an arrow, catching the guard in the throat and sending him toppling forward onto the ground far below.

Chaos suddenly erupted on the wall, the other guards who had been talking nearby running towards where the guard had fallen then throwing themselves to their knees when more arrows started flying towards the walls.

"Attack! We're under attack!"

The army charged the gatehouse that lead into the Great Desert, swarming through it in a torrent before the guards on the ground had time to react to the warning shouts coming from the ramparts. Nox was one of the first to enter the city, a loud banshee-like cry issuing from her lips.

"Leave no guard alive, take the rest as prisoners! Burn everything!"

In a matter of hours Quinsilla was a smouldering mess, burning buildings setting those around them on fire too. In many quarters of the city, particularly those nearest the northern edge of the city, empty smouldering wrecks leaned perilously over the streets which they had lined before succumbing to their wounds and crashing to the ground with an explosion of embers and dust. In the heart of the city more houses were left intact but had been looted by bounty-hunters for extra treasure. The inner streets were lined with shackled, scared prisoners of war, some only children, blackened from soot and bruised by the harsh beatings those who had fought had taken from their captors.

At the very top of the Jewel Tower, the only building left completely untouched, Zartear stood looking over the city. A smug smile flickered over his face as he enjoyed the carnage and pain that reined below. It reminded him of his homeland, Surahnia- that was a land bruised and bloody too. Ha, if the Surahnites could see him now, king of a whole city, an army behind him- and nobody would ever believe the plans he still had in store.

2
THE SUMMONING. XAOC. A SECOND ESCAPE.

Lutis landed clumsily outside the city, tumbling head over heels as strong gusts of wind whipped over the tops of the sand dunes in when he had landed, blowing him a distance before dropping him again.

He had easily cleared Quinsilla's walls, gliding like a bird of prey over the incredulous faces of the guards that still patrolled the outer boundary. But as elegant as he had been whilst flying, coming in to land had been an entirely different matter and he was ungainly as a baby bird in the fickle winds.

He touched down on the top of a dune momentarily before one of the unpredictable winds picked him up again, flipping him upside down and throwing him down the dune. He rolled over and over in the sand, the thin struts of the wings snapping as they bent beneath him. He finally came to a stop at the bottom of the dune, his right arm tangled in a complicated mess of wires and strings, the other shielding his face from the sun and the sand. He lay on his back for a while before groaning and sitting up, spitting sand from his mouth in disgust and wincing at the pain that lanced up his arm. It was broken. He let a stream of loud curses accompany his fumbling attempts at untangling the wires that had wrapped themselves in knots around his arm, the only sound apart from the whistling of the wind. It was no good, they would have to be cut. Sighing, he reached into his coat with his good hand and withdrew a dagger, pulling the sheath off with his teeth before starting to saw at the strings that bound his arm.

"That's going to be a pretty mess to fix later," he mumbled to himself darkly, replacing the dagger from where it had come from and groping at the scarf around his neck. It would have to do as a sling until he found something better to make one out of. Luckily he had fixed cuts and bruises himself before (broken bones not so much, but he might be able to get someone to fix him up back in Quinsilla, if there was anyone left after Zartear was done taking over). When he was finished he climbed to his feet, the wings flopping at bizarre angles from his back. He left them how they were as it was impossible to even start trying to fix them when he probably wouldn't even be able to get them off without jarring his arm.

"They may be broken, but I'm not leaving these beauties behind." He kept talking to himself as he turned in circles, trying to catch his bearings. A little sand trickled out of his hair and down his neck as he rubbed at the back of his head. Quinsilla would be the best direction point- not only was it large enough to be seen clearly from the desert, it was where he wanted to go. A thick black pillar of smoke billowed into the sky, marking the direction in which he should head.

"Well I wonder if that's where Quinsilla might be then," he said ironically, heading off across the dunes in the direction of the smoke. "Not doing things by half, eh Zartear?" He suddenly scrabbled in one pocket frantically, searching for the bag he had put the ruby in. His fingers closed around it firmly and he breathed a sigh of relief. It would be a cruel fate indeed for him to get away from the city with the jewel only to lose it on his escape into the desert.

Lutis walked slowly, his boots filling with sand at every step. When he reached the top of the first sand dune he stopped and looked at the distance he still had to walk. He gave a sigh, then he looked down at his boots, wiggled his toes and sighed again.

"I hate sand," he moaned quietly, pushing off one boot with the opposite foot then pulling the other off with his hand. He turned one upside down and a stream of the golden stuff slid onto the ground. The other boot held as much, if not more- it was a depressing outcome. Lutis picked them up off the ground, deciding that it would be better to just walk barefoot than try and plough on with them on and risk filling them up again. In front of him the soft sand of the dunes blew across onto the rocky Hamada, making it look like waves on a beach. It would be a long walk all the way to Quinsilla, and miserable too, as it was hot underfoot from the scorching sun overhead, and there was no shady respite in the shadow of a bush or tree.

Three hours later found Lutis almost at Quinsilla's northern gate. It was wide open and unguarded, most of the mercenaries that had taken Quinsilla too occupied by revelry or chasing down the last free citizens that hid in the secret places of the city to stick to the monotonous task of guarding a gatehouse. A thick black smoke hung low over the city, fires from still-burning buildings belching even more up into the sky. Lutis coughed at the ashy taste that pervaded the air, dropping his boots to cover the sound with his hand. If he got caught by someone now he would have a hard time not getting thrown into chains with the prisoners of war! He looked a mess, dirty, hot and sandy from his escape, his hair falling out of the short ponytail at the back of his neck and, of course, he had broken his arm, none of which would help him convince any mercenaries that he might come across that he was the thief that had initiated the events that had let them invade the city in the first place.

He picked his boots up again and headed for the wall near the gate, trying to avoid being spotted from the gatehouse as he pulled them on. They were still gritty with sand inside but he had to look at least a little respectable. Taking a deep breath to focus his nerves he crept around the corner to see if anyone was lurking under the gatehouse then entered the city at a jog, trying to not shake his broken arm too much. He knew that to find Zartear he had to head once again for the Jewel Tower, for that was where he would be- *probably gloating over his victory*.

Lutis kept to the shadows, avoiding any noise that came from nearby- no doubt many of the sources were taverns, where a free flowing run of ale would be found. It was tempting to join them but he decided against it- he should patch himself up a bit more first and give the jewel to Zartear, before he came looking. Luckily for him there was lots of shadow cover and they were getting ever longer as the sun started to dip low in the sky. He sneaked his way through the streets, cutting down the smaller alleyways to avoid any risk of being seen. They were so different from earlier when they were teeming with people- now they were barren of life. The difference was shocking; Lutis had never seen a city with so few people around, even with his many years of living in cities, and sometimes keeping quite inhospitable hours. He slipped into another large street again and was met with the sight of the Jewel Tower, just as it had been before, tall and elegant, pale against the buildings around it. He stopped briefly to take in the view, a little out from the side of the nearest building. It was a mistake. Behind him he heard loud arguing voices heading his direction. Mercenaries! There was nowhere to hide so he sprinted towards the tower, not turning to look back, not caring if he was seen. If he could get to the Jewel Tower he would be safe. They wouldn't dare enter it with Zartear waiting at the top.

A loud shout came from behind him. "Hey you! Stop where you are!" He ran faster, his coat flapping around his ankles. He couldn't get caught!

"I said STOP!" The voice came again, angrier now. Something came flying out of nowhere, catching him between the shoulder blades and sending him sprawling on the ground. He gave a cry of pain as he landed on his broken arm. A harsh laugh came close behind him but he couldn't see who it came from- there was mud in his eyes and the wings still attached to his back flopped limply in his vision. He pushed himself to his feet, stumbling into a run again. The wings flapped back behind him, the broken struts snapping with a series of loud cracks, but a shout from the men behind him was much louder.

"Stop or I'll shoot!" The second mercenary had removed a small crossbow from his back and was pointing it calmly at Lutis. There was no good in running now. He slid to a halt, turning to face the men. He felt a knot of defeat in his stomach.

"I think you should let me go," he said quietly, looking the armed mercenary. "I've got important business with Zartear."

The man snorted disbelievingly. "Why would *you* have business with Zartear?" he sneered, swaggering up to Lutis. He was a little shorter than the tall thief and he frowned in annoyance. The man stepped around to the side, looking Lutis up and down in scorn before suddenly driving the shaft of the crossbow into his shins. Lutis fell to his knees, wincing as the movement jerked his broken arm. A spray of mud splashed up his legs.

"You look like nothing more than a slave to me," the soldier mocked, crouching down to stare into Lutis' face. "Your escape attempt wasn't very good, was it?" Behind him, his friend gave a laugh. Lutis resisted the temptation to spit in his face- that was something a slave would do.

The friend spoke up. "I think we should kill him, here and now, for trying to lie to us."

"Good idea." The nearest mercenary straightened and rearranged his crossbow so that the bolt lay flat along the stock. Lutis gulped- this was not going well.

"I really do have business with Zartear!" A note of panic crept into his voice. "If you kill me, he'll not be happy with you when he finds out."

"Shut up," came the curt reply. The unarmed man stepped forwards and gave him a hard kick in the side which made him double over, gasping. "You're nobody, just admit it. Zartear wouldn't even think to look at you." He gestured to his broken arm. "Our leader has no use for the injured, which makes you useless."

"It wasn't broken when he gave me my instructions last week!" squeaked Lutis, fearfully watching the end of the crossbow. "I only broke it today! Please, you have to believe me!"

The armed man gave a sigh and pointed the crossbow at Lutis once again. "I'm bored of your pleading." Lutis closed his eyes, not wanting to see the crossbow fire. There was nothing he could do; fate was out of his hands.

"WAIT."

The strident command came from behind Lutis. The two mercenaries looked up, confused at the order. Nox Arise strode towards them, a look of barely contained anger contorting her face.

"What do you think you are doing?" she stopped in front of the two men, glaring at the armed one. Lutis peeked an eye open, wondering why he was still alive- *how* he was still alive. He slowly opened the other eye and turned to see who had saved him.

Nox pulled the crossbow out of the man's hands, running a finger along the smooth wood before holding it loosely in her hands.

"This is a good weapon," she said, looking up at the man. He started to stutter his thanks but she just raised the crossbow towards him and fired off the bolt. He gave a small "oh!" of surprise before dropping to the ground, the bolt lodged firmly in his chest. Nox looked suitably pleased, and reloaded the stock. She fired the bow again and the second mercenary dropped to the floor.

"Well, they won't be making that mistake again, eh?" Lutis said shakily, climbing to his feet and stepping out of Nox's way, just in case she decided that she wanted him dead after all.

"Shut up. Be thankful that Zartear wanted to save your sorry behind. This time." She tossed the crossbow away with a look of disgust and spun on her heel, heading back to the Jewel Tower. Lutis hurried after her, not wanting to be caught alone again by another self-righteous mercenary. Nox wrinkled her nose in disgust.

They entered the bottom of the tower, Nox heading up the steps without waiting. Lutis paused briefly before entering after her, steeling himself. The carvings on the outside of the tower leered down at him and he shuddered, moving into the soft gloom of the tower quickly. Nox was already climbing the stairs, her footsteps smooth and rhythmic. He followed her slowly, tugging at his wings to try and make them look more presentable. The wires that remained had tangled together, pulling the once-green sails into strange shapes.

At the top of the Jewel Tower Zartear still looked out at the city, a red sunset bathing the room in a bloody shade. When he heard the sound of footsteps on the staircase he turned and strode towards it, waiting impatiently until Nox's head appeared.

"Have you got him?" he asked, having watched the confrontation below.

"Yes, he's following behind," she said.

As Lutis stepped up into the room he contemplated how it was strange what a difference a few hours had made: Quinsilla was now in ruins, when it had been alive and bustling; he had been a fugitive on the run from the Quinsillan authorities and now he was in league with the new ruler of Quinsilla; he had broken his arm, when it had been perfectly well only hours before! He looked around the room and out at the city, ignoring the others and trying to act supreme. After all, he was the one with the prize.

"Do you have the ruby?" Zartear broke the silence, watching the thief closely. Lutis nodded at the shorter man and reached into his pocket, withdrawing the little bag that held the jewel. He took a couple of steps to the edge of the table and pulled the string of the bag, tipping the gem onto the table. It glittered in the red light of the sunset.

Zartear stepped up to the table, pushing past Lutis to lean over and look closely at the jewel. He didn't pay attention as Lutis asked for his payment. Here was cold power, right in front of him, right in his *grasp*. Lutis huffed in irritation but Zartear ignored him still, reaching out a hand and taking hold of the jewel, a smile creeping over his face.

The ruby started to glow a bright red, growing hot to the touch- too hot to hold, but Zartear couldn't let go, it was like the jewel was attached to his hand. He gritted his teeth at the pain, his eyes fixed on the ruby. It shone brighter and brighter, the scarlet colour bleaching out of the stone into a burning white. Then when it couldn't get any brighter the jewel disappeared completely into the air. Zartear opened his hand, surprised- he hadn't known what would happen when he touched the jewel. His palm was blackened with soot.

A sudden roar boomed from beyond the tower then a huge black shadow swept through the air... a massive dragon! Come out of nowhere! Zartear reached for the broadsword strapped to his back; Nox hissed; Lutis gasped, taking a step backwards and almost falling down the staircase. The beast dived down the side of the building then banked sharply, cutting its descent before beating its wings laboriously to reach a level with the open room. Its claws scratched the stone of the tower as it settled on the edge of the building, scoring deep white scrapes into the rock. It was a monstrous beast, bright scarlet runes interspersing the black scales on its flanks, legs, wings; its face was ringed by viciously sharp horns and its eyes glowed with untended evil. It gripped the side of the tower with sharp claws, its spiny head snaking into the room and observing the three bipeds with a haughty air.

"I am Xaoc," he rumbled before crawling up the side of the building into the room. He hardly fit, his long tail sweeping around the outside of the tower. "What do you want with me, human?" Xaoc growled threateningly, his dislike for even the most corrupt of humans obvious.

"I think you'll find that I am your master now," Zartear said, his hand still on his sword. It was true but there was no knowing how the dragon might react to this information.

Xaoc gave a snarl, his head flicking out to strike at the man but he stopped before the hit, growling. "So it seems," he said begrudgingly.

"Good," said Zartear. He turned to Lutis. "You wanted payment?"

Lutis nodded, his eyes flickering towards the dragon. "A thousand gold daraks, just like you promised."

"Hmm," said Zartear. "I think not. You were late getting the ruby, and now, well, you've seen too much." He sneered. "I think that it would be better for us all if you were dead. Xaoc, kill this thief."

Lutis' eyes widened in shock, then as the dragon swung his head round in his direction he fled for the stairs. His wings flapped behind him as he turned the first corner, banging against the low ceiling. There was a scalding flash of heat as Xaoc shot a tongue of flame at the staircase, blackening the stones.

"Get out and kill him, you can catch him at the bottom of the stairs!" shouted Zartear. There was a crash as the dragon exited at speed, smashing through the delicate latticework that held up the roof. Lutis ran faster, sliding his good hand down the inner wall to keep his balance. He was never going to reach the bottom in time to escape! He tripped forward on a worn step, the stone uneven underfoot and started to tumble out of control down the staircase. He gave a yell of pain as his broken arm thumped on the wall, then was cut off as one of his wings slapped him in the face as it bent under his weight. He flung out his good arm wide, pushing against the wall to stop his tumbling and jerked to an ungainly halt, jamming himself into the width of the staircase to stop himself from falling further. He climbed to his feet again, breathing hard, and started down the stairs again, feeling the wings pulling at his coat where they had twisted almost upside-down. There was a loud thump outside- Xaoc was waiting for him already?

Lutis panicked, searching frantically in the gloom for some alternate way of escape. There was no other way out! Behind him he heard light footsteps as Nox started to descend the stairs, trapping him between Nox's sword or Xaoc's fangs and fire. He chanced Xaoc, hoping the dragon was worn out from being trapped in its jewel for many long years, lurching down the final few steps. As the wall straightened he banged against it, head spinning from the twisting of the staircase, then broke into a run, swerving through the outside door at a tight angle to avoid being burnt to a crisp. He just missed the dragon, diving underneath him. Xaoc roared, tearing at the ground beneath him in the thought he might catch Lutis with his claws.

Lutis back-pedalled with his feet, sliding along the muddy cobblestones and out from underneath the dragon. He rolled over onto his front, pushed himself to his feet and set off running, dashing around the first available corner. Xaoc gave a snarl and leapt into the air, beating his wings hard to get the air beneath them. Lutis gave another yell and pelted down the street he had entered, his flapping coat flicking mud everywhere. The street was filled with lines of chained slaves and he had to weave this way and that, leaping over one cruel chain, ducking under the swinging sword of one of their captors. He couldn't do anything to help them, and most of them looked terrified at the sight of him anyway! He looked frantically this way and that, trying to find a suitable place to hide or an escape route, but with so many people filling the street it was hard to search. He dived into the nearest building, a ransacked house whose door hung from the frame at a perilous angle. Xaoc swept across the street, sending a sheet of fire towards the house and setting the dry timbers alight. Lutis slammed the door shut, feeling the wood heat up underneath his palms. A blood curdling scream came from outside, followed by more as the nearby slaves panicked, running this way and that as the chain that had held them together melted in the scorching heat.

The house was in ruins, chairs overturned, crockery smashed, even a cabinet overturned and broken into large pieces across the floor. If he was in any other situation, Lutis would have leapt at the chance to raid the house. Instead he headed for the door in the opposite wall, hoping it led out to another street. Behind him there was a snapping noise as the metal hinges of the door sprung under the heat of more fire.

Lutis pulled the door open, shielding his face as a wave of heat and ash billowed into the room. There was a staircase at one side, the top steps licking with flames, another door and a window, showing another street through the warped glass. He gave a dry cough, covering his mouth before running through the room towards the next door. There was a crash above him as the roof collapsed onto the top floor. The ceiling started to bend dangerously as Lutis yanked the next door open, running into the street as the house finally crashed to the ground. There were more crashes as Xaoc started to rip through the remains of the house, looking for him.

He ran down the street, trying to stifle his coughing. An layer of ash had stuck to the thick black mud on his coat, turning the blue fabric to a dirty grey. He worked his way towards the north gate of the city, knowing the Great Desert would be the last place anyone would look for him. Wordlessly he thanked his lucky stars that he was still alive as he snuck out of Quinsilla and not buried under rubble or fried to a crisp by Xaoc. He started out across the desert as the sun settled underneath the horizon, alone under the bloodstained sky and the faint stars that were just starting to peep at its furthest eastern edges.

Lutis walked through the night, leaving his boots on even when they were full of sand. Twinges of pain started to shoot up his broken arm after a few hours walking as Quinsilla dropped out of sight. The rising of the sun found him parched and exhausted, his hunger turned to nausea long hours before. The desert ran flat and rocky in every direction, barren of every form of life.

As the sun started to burn hotter, climbing high into the sky, Lutis made slower and slower progress, his path weaving this way and that until he fainted with exhaustion, topping onto his side to lay inert.

3
DESERT DRAGONS. MORE REBELS.

"Why ista sky blue?"

"I don't know."

"'Ow likely ista I'll be struck by lightnin'?"

"When did you last see lightning out here Hone?"

A patrol of lash Elites walked steadily through the desert, its bright guardians. Aeron's patrol was made up of six dragons and was one of the many that looked after anyone travelling or living in the desert. The lash dragons were lean but strong, made for running through the desert sands and surviving on the sparsest of foods. They had wings but they were useless- most lash dragons you saw were missing feathers from where they had yanked them out or broken the flights. They made for good blankets, but that was about it. Built for fighting, they had long curving spines up the front of their back legs, a spine behind their neck that stopped any surprise attacks from above and a wide, sharp blade on the end of their tail made from separate plates that could cut through any wood and sometimes soft metal too. They came in a range of colours, but the most common was Hone's purple and red colouration.

"Well I thought I saw some las'night, but it might'ha jus' been a dream," said Hone, looking thoughtfully at the sky. The sandy coloured dragon she was talking to shook his head in exasperation.

"There wasn't any lightning last night," he said, trotting a little faster to catch up with the rest of the patrol. They had fallen behind the others.

"How-ee Doan, wait up!" called Hone as the taller dragon dashed away, picking up her own feet in a jog. The lash dragons ran on their back legs, their front paws, wings and tail acting as balancing rudders. "I've got more questions!"

"More?" asked Doan, sounding phased. "Why don't you go ask Tekek?"

"I would, but she's still tryin'a decide between pirates or ninjas," Hone pointed one of her purple wingtips towards a small scarlet and purple dragon wandering along the edge of the group and muttering furiously to herself. Doan gave a laugh.

"What about Aeron?" volunteered Neby, the second sandy coloured dragon of the patrol, who had overheard their conversation. "He's in a good mood today, maybe he'll give you some answers?" Neby gave a small smile, looking at their leader, who was listening to his son, Echai. The two were quite similar looking, Aeron having green scales and blue wings, and Echai having both colours on his scales with purple wings. Aeron looked like the elder dragon, the pale blade of his tail scored with white streaks from years of fighting and one of his four ears shredded where he had taken on a jackal as a youngster. Despite their similarities there were obvious differences- to hear the two talk it would never have been assumed they were related, Echai having none of the desert mountain accent that Aeron had. He had grown up in a different part of the desert with his mother and it was only by chance that he had found his father's patrol when he signed up to become a lash Elite.

Aeron turned at the sound of his name, a questioning look on his face.

"Are fish sad 'cause they cannae live in t'desert?" asked Hone. Doan laughed at the nonplussed look Aeron gave the apprentice Elite.

"I've no idea," said the blue and green dragon, tapping a claw to his lips. "I'll think 'bout that'un. But first, it's time f'some trainin'!" He slowed his pace to let her catch up. Hone gave a bugle of excitement and leapt forwards, fluttering her head fans.

Aeron chuckled at her enthusiasm, flicking his head fans back at her.

"Djur see these tracks 'ere?" he asked, tracing a faint trail across the rocky ground. "They lead to a gila monster." Hone's eyes lit up with interest. Gila monsters were the largest type of lizard you could find in the Great Desert and made for a good snack. "Djur think y'can track it?"

"Sure can!" Hone said, putting her nose to the ground and snuffling at the long sweeping tracks. She looked along them in either direction, working out which way the gila monster had gone. The other Elites milled behind her, waiting for Hone's judgement on which way they should go. She hesitated for a moment before starting off towards the east, her eyes fixed firmly on the sand.

The other dragons stood where they were, Aeron giving Neby a wry look. After a few steps Hone stopped and turned back towards the group.

"I'm gaarn t'wrong way, ain't I?" she asked, then gave a sigh. Neby gave a small giggle, covering it with her wing before Hone laughed back at her.

"I knew that," she said, backtracking. "It's hard t'tell which way he's headin'."

"It's important t'learn which way tracks lead. After all, if you gar t'wrong direction, y'end up with no dinner!" said Aeron, padding next to her as she started out the right way. "Make sure y'don't step on t'tracks, y'need to leave them there in case y'wanna return t'where y'started."

The tracks led through the rocky Hamada towards the south. The gila monster had travelled a long way searching for food, but if it had finally found prey the patrol would eat well. It wasn't easy to follow over the dusty ground, with the traces of its passing sometimes only a shifted pebble or a claw print in the dirt.

"I've lost it," she said quietly after a while, her voice bitter with frustration. The ground had become too rocky to hold any tracks.

"No wait, it's just off to the left," came an even quieter reply from Echai. Hone slowly turned her head to look, her eyes narrowing when she saw a low shape moving slowly across the desert. The other lash dragons came to a halt, letting the young apprentice make the kill by herself. She locked her sights onto the reptile and took off towards it, pulling her wings close to her body.

The lizard spotted her and opened its mouth in defence, hissing and showing its short fangs. Hone took a leap and landed on top of it, digging her claws into its body. It writhed, trying to sink its venomous fangs into her leg but it bit her claw instead and she quickly finished it with a bite to the back of its neck. She squawked with satisfaction, lashing her bladed tail this way and that. Aeron bugled back followed by a call from Tekek, the patrol running over as a pack.

"Harreet Hone, tha' was fantastic! That'll be a meal f'you an' me," said Aeron. "Echai, take t'rest of the patrol south until y'find whate'er this lizard wherst hunting for. We'll catch up with you after we've eaten."

Echai nodded and started to lead the rest of the pack away, but Tekek hung back briefly before following.

"I think pirates," she said to Hone, nodding.

"What?" asked Hone, confused.

"Pirates or ninjas. I would say pirates. So much more variety in costume," said Tekek, giving a grin.

"How-ee! Finally, someone who agrees with me!"

The lash Elites headed south, walking in a flat line until Neby found a set of tracks. They started to follow them, keeping close to the light slots until a small herd of gazelle came into sight. When the lead animal saw the lash Elites it bolted, the others splitting into two groups, cantering this way and that with long strides, trying to escape the dragons. They were quick on their feet, skidding at strange angles when the dragons came at them, but the lash Elites were faster. Doan brought down a large doe and Tekek and Echai worked together to bring down a similar sized buck. The young doe that Neby was chasing got away and she returned to share Doan's catch with him.

The Elites took their time eating, knowing they wouldn't be back on the move until late afternoon, when the hottest part of the day had passed. They gorged themselves like lions until they were full and then stretched out on the ground to snooze off their meal.

When Aeron and Hone had finished their shared meal they had no difficulty finding the rest of the patrol, just following their tracks through the desert until the bright colours of their scales showed up on the horizon. They walked the distance slowly, Hone's full stomach stalling her questions for a time. She looked sleepily into the distance, daydreaming about what it would be like to be a full lash Elite. She couldn't wait until the day she finished her apprenticeship.

"What's tha' over yonder, on t'horizon?" said Aeron after a while, pointing with one turquoise claw. Hone shook her head to clear her dreams and squinted into the distance, trying to make out what he had seen.

"I dunno," she said, "Mayhap humans?"

He looked across at her. "Mayhap. Might be a cookin' fire, but it must be big if we can see it from all t'way out 'ere. They're not geet suited t'this sort o'climate though, it ain't good for 'em t'be in the heat."

"Canst gar an' investigate? Please?" asked Hone, looking at Aeron beseechingly. "They migh' be in trouble."

Aeron sighed. "Aye, they migh' be in trouble."

"An' we're supposed t'protect all travellers in t'desert," prompted Hone, nodding her head. "I think we should gar."

"Well, if y'think somebody *is* in trouble, we can see wha' t'others think," he reasoned. It wasn't just his decision where the patrol went.

"Please? They might be in trouble, if there's fire gaarn up." She looked back at the horizon, finding the smoke easily now that she had seen it before.

"We'll ask t'others," he repeated, a smile flashing across his face. "Come on, I'll race you!" He flicked his tail up into the air, putting on a burst of speed. Hone grinned, dashing after him with wings outstretched, pretending she was flying over the land like a bird.

When they reached the other lashes they came to a stop, panting slightly from their exertions. Grinning, Aeron turned to Hone.

"Beat you!" Before she could protest he turned to address the sleepy group. "Up an' at 'em. There's summat funny over on t'horizon an' Hone wants to gar check it out. Anyone wanna protest?"

Neby opened one eye, focussing on Aeron briefly before flicking her wing feathers over her face. "No?" he asked again, amused. Tekek wriggled onto her back in her sleep, kicking Doan and making him snore.

"Well Hone, seems like y'got your way. But I think a nap is mayhap in order afore we gar rushin' after smoke that may or mayn't actually be there. Ahreet?"

She nodded as Aeron settled down on the ground next to Neby, humming in delight as the sand started to warm his scales. Hone grinned, giggling with excitement as she sat down on the baked ground too, rolling onto her back and shuffling her wings in the dust before closing her eyes to sleep.

The lash Elites slept as the sun burned out the afternoon, enjoying its warmth and the fullness of their bellies, content to just enjoy the day in a lazy fashion. Now and then Echai stirred to roll over and find a more comfortable position or Neby shifted closer to Aeron with a smile on her lips. The two were very close. Hone woke up a couple of times, her dreams of what they might find at the source of the smoke so exciting they seemed real, but always drifted off into another dream after looking far into the distance and finding the smoke that still rose high into the air.

~

Nox threw the plank of wood she held over her shoulder, straightening up and taking a deep breath to try and cool her rising anger.

"He got away," she said, turning to smoulder at Xaoc who was digging slowly through the remains of the house he had destroyed. The dragon looked up, bored. Zartear had instructed them to search through the rubble until they found Lutis' body, to make sure he was dead- but they hadn't found it. She stalked towards Xaoc, clambering over the pile of discarded wood and brick that they had tossed aside. "You imbecile!"

Xaoc gave a snarl, rearing his head up out of her reach as she swung a fist in frustration at the end of his muzzle. "That's as much your fault as it is mine," he growled, puffing a roiling ball of smoke at her.

Nox coughed, blinking as the smoke stung her eyes. "You said you had killed him." Her words shook with barely concealed anger.

"Well it seems I was mistaken," replied Xaoc, looking at the short woman in disgust before turning his head away to preen at a wing. Nox gave a screech of frustration, picking up a nearby rock and throwing it at the dragon. It bounced off his flank and he gave her a dirty look, snaking his head down to her level.

"Do you really think you control me, Felixis? If it wasn't for Zartear ordering me not to kill you, I would have done it long before now," he rumbled, his scarlet eyes fixed on her gold ones.

Nox gave a feral snap of her teeth, turning away from his unwavering gaze. "Keep searching, I have other things to do today." She stalked back over to where she had been digging before, kicking at the smaller rubble with her feet.

He laughed, a triumphant look on his features, and then went back to digging. Nox plunged her hands back into the mess of debris, grunting as she pulled a large flat piece of wood free and threw it to one side, returning to the spot. She stopped, picking something small out of the mess. It was a picture frame, a small painting of a girl with big wings and long black hair smiling out of the simple wooden border. An avian.

She ran a finger over the girl's lips, feeling the ridges of paint underneath her fingers. A layer of dust came off leaving a set of clean lines where she had run her fingers. She took the corner of her sleeve and cleaned the rest of the dirt off, turning the picture in the light when she was done.

"Reminiscing are we?" said Xaoc, his voice scathing as he looked up from his digging.

"No," replied Nox, breaking the frame in two and pulling the painting out of it. "This'll come in use." She rolled up the little canvas and slipped it into a pocket.

"Why would a picture of a slave come in use to you?" he scorned.

"That's for me to know, and you to find out," retorted Nox, starting to scoop through the rubble again. Xaoc shook his head, rolling his eyes and restarted digging too, his claws gouging at the debris that lay all around.

They dug for a few more hours until it was unbearably hot in the midday sun. Nox hailed a passing mercenary and ordered him to bring some food and water. When he returned she sat at the edge of the road in a patch of shade, taking a long draught of water before starting on the food he had brought. It was quiet in the northern quarter of Quinsilla, most of the soldiers that had invaded either still drunk or organising the huge numbers of slaves they had captured in the west of the city. She had ordered the streets nearby cleared of people too, trying to keep the fact that Xaoc's quarry had escaped out of public knowledge. The dragon had gone off hunting over the fields around the city so it was just her left in the area. A bird started to sing on the edge of a nearby rooftop, trilling a simple melody before improvising on the tune.

Nox pulled the picture she had kept out of her pocket, smoothing it on her knee before studying it carefully. "Okay, brown skin, long hair..." she muttered under her breath. She pulled up one of her sleeves, studying her spot-patterned skin before frowning in concentration. Slowly the spots darkened, as did the rest of her skin until it was the same colour as the girl in the picture's skin. Nox was a shape changer. If she concentrated hard enough and had a reference she could change her appearance to match that of someone else. It was difficult, especially the first time, but after a few tries she could shift with ease into another guise. She had just started on growing a pair of wings like the ones in the picture when she heard a clatter of swords from around the nearest corner, jolting her from her concentration.

She reverted back to her normal appearance and got to her feet, tucking the picture back into her pocket for later practise and pulling her sword from its sheath. There was a shout then a be-cloaked figure on horseback cantered into her view holding a bloodied scimitar. The rider's face was hidden by a hood pulled high up around her face.

"Stop!" shouted Nox, stepping into the path of the woman. She pulled her horse to a halt, its dark hooves skittering on the cobblestones, and pushed back her hood with her sword hand, revealing dark brown wavy hair, white streaks crisscrossing the strands next to her cheeks and green eyes, her brows drawn down in a scowl.

"Do I have to kill you too?" she snarled, looking down at Nox and gripping her scimitar a little tighter.

"You won't if you know what's good for you, rider," replied Nox, eying up the woman's strange appearance. She was clad in green, apart from plate armour on her body, which was a shiny black. Her horse snorted in agitation, flicking his ears back and shaking his head. He was just as strange as his rider, his pale coat speckled with dark flecks of black like Dalmatian jasper.

The woman gave a laugh, but it didn't reach her eyes. "Why would that be?"

"Because I'm Zartear's second in command, and there's a dragon on the way back here at this very moment," said Nox. Xaoc had been gone long enough and he should be on his way back by now. Although, knowing the dragon, he would be late just to irritate her.

"Well that makes us on the same side then." The rider lowered her sword, cleaning it on the side of her saddle before sliding it back into the sheath that hung from her belt. "I figured there might be some work going."

"There might be, for the right mercenary," said Nox cautiously, lowering her own sword too. "Depends on whether you have the right skills."

"I think you'll find I do," said the woman, giving Nox a hard smile.

Nox folded her arms. "So what makes you so special then?"

"This." The woman held out one hand, her palm upright. Suddenly a small crackle of electricity played around her fingers and shot out at Nox, striking her in the chest. The Felixis flew back into the air, all the air huffing out of her lungs as she crashed to the floor a few metres back. She shook her head, dazed.

The woman dismounted, striding over to Nox and bending down next to her head. "Think about it. The name's Static, I'll be… around." She straightened, took hold of the horse's reins again and mounted, kicking the stallion into a canter and riding past without a sideways glance.

Nox took a deep breath of air, putting a hand to her forehead. Black stars danced in front of her eyes and she rubbed the back of her head. When she pulled her hand away it was sticky with blood.

"Static…" she mumbled, looking at her hand before slowly climbing to her feet and heading off to get a bandage.

4
DANGEROUS CURIOUSITIES.
RESCUE.

Once the hot midday sun started to cool, sinking slowly across into the west of the sky, the lash dragons began to stir. Hone woke quickly once a small conversation started to break out, Neby insisting that she had heard Aeron say they were going to go and investigate something. Hone was all too eager to tell them, shaking the dust from her feathers as she wandered over.

"We're gonna gar see what tha' big plume o' smoke over there is. Aeron said we could, an' nobody disagreed…" She preened at her wing feathers, running her teeth through a few that were grey with dust. She was impatient to be off as quickly as possible- the smoke looked like it was a long way away and it would be much harder to follow it when the sun set. She bounced over to where Aeron lay sleepily on the ground.

"Canst gar now Aeron, please? We won't be able t'see the smoke when it gets dark later," she said, bending down to his ears.

He tried to ignore her, batting her away but she persisted, knowing how hard it was to get the big dragon to wake after a meal and a sleep in the sun. "Come on, you're t'las' one asleep!" She pushed at him with a paw, trying to get him to move.

He grumbled and sat up, shaking away sleep. "Fine, fine."

"I'm sure there's more smoke now than there was earlier…" Hone mused, looking into the distance where the smoke was still visible as a thin pillar in the sky. Echai wandered over to her.

"Yes, there is quite a lot of smoke," agreed Echai, gazing in the same direction. "I didn't notice that before we ate, although we were pretty pre-occupied."

"Ahreet, let's gar." Aeron's weary voice interrupted their musings, already setting off towards the smoke. The lash Elites could walk many leagues in a day, being built for long desert journeys- and it was a good thing too, for their curiosity could never be sated.

They walked for a long time, the landscape hardly changing beneath their feet. At one point they took a short detour to the west to visit a nearby oasis, a small pool of water surrounded by hardy green shrubs that looked out of place in the washed out yellow of the rocky ground. Hone walked in the middle of the group, asking the odd question when they came to her.

"Where do turnips come from?" she said to Echai, looking at the blue and purple dragon with interest. He always offered an interesting explanation.

"Well, I've always been told that they grew underground, but I don't think that's true. After all, where does the soil go that they grow into? They're big; I don't think that they would be able to grow underground without hitting a stone. No, I think that they come from floating plants in the sky. I've never seen one growing on the ground, and if they don't grow on the ground, and they don't grow *under* the ground, the only option left *must* be in the sky!" He pointed upwards, gesturing at the blue expanse above them. "I bet they hide above the clouds. I bet there are big crops of turnips hiding on top of them just waiting to drop out of the sky and whack you on the head!" He covered his muzzle with one paw to demonstrate his point. "All right if you like eating them though, isn't it?" he laughed.

Hone listened intently, drinking in every word.

Unexpectedly, a shout came from Neby.

"Hey, what are those things moving around in the distance?" she called, squinting at the desert to the left. The other dragons looked and sure enough there were tall, thin creatures walking in a squiggly line across the desert.

"They look like...well, they look like humans," said Aeron disbelievingly.

"Humans? Really?" squeaked Hone. "What wouldsta be doin' in t'desert? I thought they dinae like t'heat like us..."

"No, they don't," replied Aeron, altering their course slightly so that their paths would cross. "Humans don't like being out in t'desert at all. Let's gar an' check it out, see if they're ahreet."

The other Elites changed their courses at Aeron's suggestion, following their leader's command and increasing their pace too. Once they were close Doan counted eight humans in total, his maths being the best. They stopped a little way off, not wanting to scare them- most humans they met in the desert weren't used to dragons- but even from the distance they could tell they were in a bad way. The woman who was leading them had a thick bandage around her head and was leaning on someone else, who was covered in dust and heavy black ash. Behind them a pair of children had linked arms and were pulling each other along, trying to keep up with a short woman who walked nearby. Three teenagers walked in silence behind them. The leading pair stopped when they saw the Elite patrol, watching them fearfully. It was clear they didn't mean to be in the desert and hadn't any experience of being in one either.

Slowly, leaving the rest of his patrol where they were, Aeron made his way towards the group of humans.

"Hoo'ista, y'ahreet?" he called, stopping before he got close. Although he didn't believe it, they might have a sword or two between them and he knew that when humans were frightened they were prone to doing strange things, even if you wanted to help them. "We don't want t'hurt you, I jus' thought y'might need some assistance, being out in t'desert an' all."

The humans looked at one another in surprise, the leading woman exchanging a few whispered words to the man she leaned on. The two young children peeped out from behind her legs, staring at the dragons with wide, curious eyes. She nodded to her companion after a moment's consultation then stepped forwards, letting go of his steadying arm. She wavered, getting her balance.

"What do you want?" she asked defensively, narrowing her eyes. "Why would you want to help us?"

"We're lash Elites; we make t'desert safe f'travellers, an' help the lost." Aeron kept his words measured. "Djur need some help?"

Visible relief flashed across the woman's face, and she gave a sigh of relief.

"Oh thank goodness!" she cried, taking a wavering step towards Aeron, a smile on her face. Her legs buckled and she dropped, her knees scraping on the ground. Her trousers had long rips where she had obviously fallen before. The man who had been helping her ran forwards, helping her to sit instead. He took over speaking.

"We've come from Quinsilla- that's the smoke on the horizon. An army invaded, we only just escaped." The woman on the ground nodded, her face ashen. "We don't have any supplies, we didn't have time to find any while we were escaping and we had to come straight into the desert; there's a dragon destroying all the fertile land to the south of Quinsilla."

"What's your name?" asked Aeron, beckoning the rest of his patrol forwards with a wave of his wing while he stepped closer to the woman. She was dehydrated, badly- they all were- but when she looked up into his face, she could hardly focus her eyes on his.

"Emi," she said, taking hold of the man's hand and trying to pull herself to her feet. He introduced himself as Deltan.

"Well, you're all in safe paws now." He called over Tekek, who was snuffling at the two children. "Canst carry Emi? She don't look like she'll be able t'walk much further."

"It's fine, really." Emi waved a hand, taking a step forwards but she stumbled again, even with Deltan's help. Aeron gave her a withering glance.

"Come on, you'll slow us all up walking," said Tekek, walking over to her side and offering a paw to help Emi onto her back. She finally accepted, crawling between the lash's wings and holding tight onto the spike at the top of Tekek's neck.

"Oh, this feels strange," said the dragon, shuffling her wings around Emi's legs.

Aeron meanwhile had been organising the other lash dragons. The two children climbed onto Doan's back while another boy rested on Echai's back, his eyes closed. The two teenage girls were patting Neby and stroking her feathers.

"Echai, will y'take these humans t' Eden's Fall?" asked Aeron, pointing across the desert to the west where the sun was starting to graze the horizon with the bottom of its glowing sphere.

"Of course Pa, but why aren't you coming?" said Echai, confusion written on his face.

"I want t'gar an' see what's happenin' in Quinsilla meself. An' if there's more escapees runnin' 'round t'desert it's no good all o' us gaarn off an' leaving no-one for spare." He looked in the direction of Quinsilla, the thick pillar of smoke marking it easily visible now they were close.

"That's true," said Deltan, stepping forwards to stand by the two dragons. He was the average height for a human but still stood shorter than them and had to look up to meet their faces a head taller than he. "We only escaped because a dragon melted our chains, and I managed to grab the keys off our guard as we escaped. But there may be others back there that have escaped since."

The boy on Echai's back interjected, "There was one man; he seemed to be running from the dragon… it was after him… he may have escaped too but the dragon seemed pretty pissed…" he tailed off, drawing on the memory.

"Well, if he's somewhere in t'desert ne'er fear, we'll find him." Aeron nodded then turned to his Elites, gesturing for them to gather around.

"Y'heard; they need help. Echai, you're in charge 'till I get back. Head for Eden's Fall, it's t'closest water source, an' out of t'desert too. Hone, you'll be comin' with me t'scout nearer to Quinsilla."

Hone nodded, waving to the others as they set off towards Eden's fall, then started after Aeron.

The two made fast progress towards Quinsilla, leaving a dusty trail behind them. The smoke darkened as they got closer, growing into a thick band staining the sky. Hone had a passing thought that a huge crop of turnips might be hiding above it and frantically scanned the outer edges of the smoke for any sign of the notorious plants.

As they got closer to Quinsilla the desert changed from a dry dustbowl, littered with hundreds of small pale rocks, to having a few rolling hummocks with rocks more spread out, but larger. They crested a small rise and all of a sudden Quinsilla came into full view before them.

The setting sun behind them cast a bloody view over the city, making its ruined buildings look even worse. Aeron gave a sigh, his ears drooping.

"Nobody'll else'll be gettin' out o'there," he murmured, looking down at the ground. It was so different to the Quinsilla of before- he had only visited the city once or twice, but then it had been full of life and elegance. The complete opposite to the empty shell that lay before them now. "Come on, if we run fast we'll make it t'Eden's Fall afore midnight." He turned away, looking towards the west and to the sinking sun.

Hone looked at the city for a little longer, her eyes scanning the city. A glitter at the top of a tower caught her attention but she couldn't work out what it came from. A dark draconic shape flew upwards out of a hidden street, coasting low over the city before gaining height to climb to the height of the tower.

"Come on Hone!" called Aeron impatiently, stopping to let her catch up.

"Ahreet…" she replied absently, taking one last glance at the city before turning and following Aeron back the way they came.

They headed quickly back the way they had come, following their own tracks for a while before turning more westerly to cut across a shorter portion of the desert. The sun shimmered on the horizon, sending long gold streaks in every direction across the sky. The desert flattened out again, making the going easier for the two dragons.

After a while they slowed from a run to a walk, taking a break. Although they were made for coping with the heat of the desert, running for leagues on end without stopping wasn't easy. Hone broke the silence.

"Djur think tha' man 'scaped from Quinsilla?" she asked, her voice quiet.

"I don't know," replied Aeron. "I don't think so. T'city was in a pretty bad state, an' only a big army could'ha done tha'."

"Hmm." Hone gave a sigh. "Well, I hope that he 'scaped." She looked out across the desert, taking in their position before it got too dark to see properly. In the desert, when it got dark you stayed where you were, unless you knew how to read the stars to continue walking the right direction.

She frowned, coming to a halt and squinting into the distance.

"Aeron…" she started.

"Aye? Wotcher see?" He looked back, stopping too.

"There's summat stickin' up over yonder, it's not a rock, it's summat else," she said, trying to make out the strange shape she had seen. "It's gettin' too dark t'see, canst gar an' look?"

Aeron tapped his tail, thinking. "Well, I suppose we could. How far away is this thing y'saw?"

"Oh not geet far at all, it'll hardly be much o' a detour. Quick, afore t'sun sets and we cans't see where t'gar," she said, pointing off into the distance with a claw before heading out at a run. Aeron followed her, trusting her judgment.

"Look, there's summat 'ere!" she called as they closed the gap to the object, squinting. The ground was black now, the sky a deep mauve. Aeron couldn't see at all well, but Hone was right- there *was* something sticking up out of the ground. He pulled a feather out of one of his wings, holding the quill in his claws before letting out a huff of hot air and setting the tip of the feather alight. It burned brightly for a moment then settled down to a gentle glow, its waxy covering making it burn slowly.

Meanwhile, Hone had reached the strange shaped object. It was a wing made from wooden struts and dark fabric, sticking up into the air like the sail of a ship. Hone bent down to the ground, snuffling at what -who- it was connected to.

"Ista human," she breathed, her eyes widening in surprise. She nudged at his head, blowing his hair out of his face with a puff of air. He was unconscious and didn't react.

"Aeron, ista 'nother human, an' he's unconscious!" she said, looking up with worry at the larger dragon as he walked over holding the feather to light his way. He ran the last few steps, bending close over the man.

"He's still alive, but I bet he ain't had any water for a while." He stuck the homemade candle into the ground and started to roll the man over. Hone flattened the wing with a well placed paw, squashing it under the man.

He looked barely alive from the front, streaked with dust and ash all over and his right arm bound across his chest in a sling. Hone stifled a gasp, batting one wing across his face to try and stir a breeze. A few spirals of dust lifted into the air, making the man cough dryly.

"Stop, stop! He's alive, we gotta get him t'Eden's Fall," said Aeron, moving around to the man's head and putting his paws underneath his shoulders before pushing him into a sitting position. The man's head lolled forwards.

"I can carry him on my back." said Hone, lying down on the ground next to the man and stretching out her wings to make space for him between them on her back.

"Are y'sure, he looks heavy…" started Aeron but Hone silenced him with a stubborn look. "Ahreet, but if y'get tired, tell me an' we can swap." He hefted the man onto Hone's back, pushing his legs behind her wings so he didn't fall off. The man slumped against her neck, the wings attached to his back flopping down her sides. Aeron fixed them over her neck spine through the tears in the fabric before she stood.

"Fine, no problem," she said, folding her wings down against her sides. "Let's gar."

Aeron nodded then turned back to where the sun had set, checking where the North Star was to make sure they were heading the right direction. "This way."

They ran at full speed for the western edge of the Great Desert, not stopping even when they grew tired. The man on Hone's back was lying at an uncomfortable angle but she didn't complain. His pockets clinked with hidden objects and Hone was sorely tempted to investigate what treasures he kept on him.

"Djur think this is t'same man from afore?" she asked at one point, drawing deep breaths between her words.

"Aye," replied Aeron, not slowing his pace. "Come on, we're nearly there."

The desert started to become less rocky underneath their feet again, sparse bushes speckling the ground. Even under the darkness of the night the two dragons could see the change as the yellow of the desert was covered by the green of tough desert grass and saltbrush. Beyond the scrublands a wavering line of trees showed the end of the desert and the start of the great forest that lay to the west.

A snake slithered from under Aeron's feet as he disturbed its slumber, hissing defensively.

Aeron came to a stop at the edge of the trees, slowing his pace and walking along its length. "Somewhere 'round here there's a path that leads straight t'Eden's Fall..." he said. "'Ere it is." He pointed into the forest where a sandy path wound through the trees. "Stay close, don't wander off t'path, whate'er y'djarn."

"Why?" asked Hone, following him down the path. It was easy to see, the pale sand bright amongst the dark of the forest floor.

"'Cause you'll ne'er find your way back to it, an' there are things out there that won't let y'get back t'the path either," he snapped, waving her in front of him with a flick of his muzzle. "Stick t'the path."

"Ahreet, ahreet," she grumbled, rolling her eyes. The forest was exciting and new and every little thing beckoned for her to go and investigate. Strange wavy-leaved plants hung down over the path, stroking their heads as they passed beneath them. The air was busy with animal calls, a hoot from a bird, a twitter of harsh notes from a mouth hidden below two round glowing eyes.

"Aeron, how far ista?" asked Hone, her words suddenly silencing the sounds around her. She gulped, looking around with wide eyes. "I don't like it here."

"Not far, we'll be there soon," he replied, his voice comfortingly close by.

"What's tha'?" asked Hone, frightened. Bright dancing lights had started to appear underneath the trees, swaying this way and that. The lights called to her- *come this way, come and see us.*

"They're pixies, don't look a' them. They can't hurt you if y'stay on t'path," said Aeron. He had seen them too and recognised the tiny mischievous creatures. One darted close to him and perched on his nose for a moment before he shook his head and it darted away, leaving a trail of sparkling lights in its wake. "Hurry up a bit, will you?"

Hone nodded and picked up her pace, keeping low to avoid the creeping plants that twisted down towards the ground. One caught her ears and she tugged free, the plant scratching her with its sharp thorns.

The pixies started to disappear after a while, the forest turning dark once again. The land sloped gently upwards to the right. Soon a new sound filled the air, slowly growing louder than the animal sounds around them.

"Are we there?" asked Hone hopefully.

"Aye. Welcome t'Eden's Fall." Aeron pushed past her, drawing back a veil of plants that hung over the path in front of them and revealing a large clearing, a river winding away from the base of a short cliff and the waterfall that poured over it.

"Oh, it's wonderful!" cried Hone, stepping out from the edge of the forest, her fear forgotten. Soft downy grass pushed up between her claws and she lifted them in surprise, used to having hard ground or sand beneath her feet.

Aeron stepped into the clearing next to her, letting the vines swing back into place. "Come on, t'the water." He started out towards it, taking Hone's paw and pulling her after him.

"They're here!" A shout from nearby made Hone look up in surprise as she crouched down next to the water, Aeron pulling the man off her back. He laid him on the ground, dunking one blue wing in the water and shaking it over his face. Hone shook her head, thinking she was imaging things- it had sounded like Echai- and started to dip her feathers in the water too, flicking them over the man's face to try and revive him. He didn't move, his head flopping to one side.

"Hone, Aeron, over here!" came Echai's voice again. Hone looked up, trying to find the dragon. This time she saw his head looking out from the side of the waterfall before the rest of him appeared. "We're all in the cave behind the fall."

"We found someone, bring one o'the humans, quickly!" shouted back Aeron, not looking up. Echai disappeared back behind the waterfall briefly before returning with a woman and a man, the three picking their way down the invisible path that wound down the side of the cliff.

"What's wrong?" asked Echai when he reached them, jumping off the cliff path and dashing over the distance to Aeron's side. The woman threw herself to her knees by the man's head, sitting him up in her lap and checking his breathing. It was shallow and only a few strands of her hair wisped out of the way.

"Get some water, quick," she said, fumbling with the straps that held the man's wings to his back. Hone gave her a hand, slicing through them with a deft stroke of her tail blade and pulling them off his back. "He's in a bad way."

Lutis felt flicks of water drip down his face, waking him from a deep sleep. A headache pulsed behind his eyes, preventing him from entering his dream world again. He felt warm hands underneath him sitting him upright, but it felt like reality was a dream and his dreams were the reality- until a torrent of water flooded across his face.

He spluttered, the water going up his nose. It tasted sweet against the dryness of his mouth. He coughed as he swallowed, his throat like sandpaper.

"He's alive!" said a voice from nearby. Lutis opened his eyes to see who it came from, recoiling when a strange draconic face looked back at him. *He had been captured by Zartear and it was Xaoc!* He gasped, trying to scramble backwards out of the way but someone held him still and his arm seared with pain when he pushed on the ground.

"Woah, woah, stay still." A different voice came from behind him- the person holding him- her tone commanding. "Go away, you're scaring him."

The dragon in front of Lutis disappeared from his view. He tried to move again, noise roaring in his ears as he pushed against the ground.

"I said stay *still*, I think your arm's broken," said the person behind him and he felt himself being lowered a little. Someone else pulled his arm back over his chest. Of course, he had broken it when he landed in the desert. He nodded, looking up to see he was half sitting, half lying in a woman's lap. *This is awkward.*

She took a flask of water off a man, putting it to Lutis' lips and letting him drink slowly. It tasted just as sweet as before and he drunk greedily. "Not too much now." She took the flask away, handing it back to the man.

"Please…" he croaked, his voice sounding strange.

"Not for the moment, you can't have too much at once. Hold still, we're going to try and fix that arm a bit better." Her voice was firm and Lutis knew he wouldn't get any more out of her so he closed his eyes again, savouring the taste the water had left behind.

He felt his broken arm being moved around as she untied his makeshift bandage, talking quietly to the man who was helping her. There was a ripping sound then he felt his coat sleeve being pushed up his arm. He winced, biting back a cry. She tutted under her breath as her fingers poked at his arm.

"He's definitely broken it," she said. "Look, it's bruised all over and burnt too. What were you doing?"

Lutis peeked open an eye, wincing at the state of his arm. Bruised was an understatement, his whole arm various shades of green and purple. "Uh…"

She shook her head, dipping his scarf in the river and laying it over his arm. It was deliciously cool, soothing his hot skin. He closed his eye again, listening to the rustling of the trees nearby and the rushing of the water.

The man who had been helping returned after a while with a range of short, rod-like sticks and an armful of cloth strips, putting them in a pile next to his companion.

"Thanks Deltan. Can you hold his arm still while I bandage it?" she asked quietly, taking one of the longer rods and laying it alongside Lutis' arm. "Try and hold still, this might hurt. What's your name?" she asked, trying to distract him.

"Lutis." He gave a dry cough, his throat sore from even a little talking.

"I'm Merac. It's nice to meet you Lutis. This is Deltan," she said, starting to wind fabric around his arm, the stick keeping his arm straight. He yelped, the fabric rough.

"You've got some nasty burns and scrapes. Were they from that dragon that was chasing you? You must have had a lucky escape."

Lutis nodded, keeping quiet.

"Well, you shall have to tell us how you escaped another time." She finished wrapping his arm, tying the fabric in a neat knot at his elbow. "There, that should hold tight for a while. Now, try and get some more rest Lutis. You've taken quite a battering these few days it seems."

He nodded again, closing his eyes and turning his head to one side. He dropped off to sleep quickly, still fatigued by the desert heat and the lucky escape he had had. Merac sat quietly by while Deltan fetched Echai again, helping Lutis onto the dragon's back so he could be carried up to the waterfall cave. Hone looked up in interest as Echai returned, laying Lutis on a soft bed of ferns in the corner before curling up to sleep himself. She padded over to the man, lying down close by to watch him sleep.

5
RECOVERY AT EDEN'S FALL.

Lutis woke to the hushing sound of the waterfall rushing over the cliffs at the front of the cave. He lay for a moment with his eyes closed then opened them and looked up, seeing long fronds of fern hanging from the rock ceiling above.

"Hello," said a voice from next to him and he turned to see a dragon sitting close, her face bright and eager. He gave a wordless shout, scrambling into a sitting position and pushing himself back against the wall.

"Oh no, don't be frightened, I jus' wanted t'see hoo'ista," said Hone, taking a step backwards. She slipped on a patch of damp moss and crashed to the ground, legs flailing. "Oops. Tha's the second time today."

Lutis watched her suspiciously, wrapping his good arm around his knees. Someone had taken off his boots the night before, and his wings too. Hopefully they hadn't gotten rid of them though- his boots at least weren't in *that* bad a shape...

"I'm Hone," said the dragon, rolling onto her stomach and watching him curiously. "Whista your name? We found you in t'desert yesterday."

"Lutis..." he said slowly. "What do you want?"

"Nothin'!" said Hone, her head fins flickering in surprise. "I wanted t'see howzah."

"A little thirsty," he said, his eyes flicking to the water rushing past the entrance of the cave. He could see light behind it- it was day, but more than that he couldn't tell.

"Here, I'll get y'some water. I bet you're hungry too, I think one o' t'other humans left some food for you..."she said, climbing to her feet and pottering off down to the entrance of the cave. Lutis watched her go, uncurling and rifling through his pockets while her back was turned. His fingers closed around the hilt of a short dagger and he swapped it from one of his inside pockets to a different one he could reach faster if needs be. Although Hone didn't seem aggressive, the last dragon he had met was Xaoc... and that had ended *really* well.

Hone picked up a flask off the floor that someone had left behind in the cave for drinking from, filling it absentmindedly from the running waterfall. Through the gaps in the water she could see out into the meadow below where the other humans they had found were resting in the shade, getting to know each other and the lash Elites. Doan and Aeron were missing, no doubt off investigating the forest or hunting for prey.

Water spilled out the top of the flask and Hone quickly jerked it back out of the flow, slopping some onto the cave floor.

"Oops…" she said, backing away carefully and heading towards Lutis, holding the flask steady so more water didn't spill over the top. "'Ere, it's very full."

Lutis took the flask, swigging a long draught. It tasted just as good as it had the night before but Hone was right, he was hungry too. "Thanks. Is there any food?"

Hone nodded eagerly, fetching a plate that had been left to one side when the others had eaten earlier. "It's fruit an' some sort o'bird," she said, putting it on the bed beside him. "I dunno what type, I've ne'er been t'the forest before an' all t'animals are different here. I saw something in t'trees earlier with hard armour all over an' a long snuffly snout!"

Lutis hummed in agreement, taking a small bunch of orange fruits from the plate and eating them slowly. They were slightly tart but still delicious. "Sounds like a pangolin."

"Wotcher say?" asked Hone.

"A pangolin. They're little animals that live on the forest floor and eat insects," said Lutis, picking up the plate and sniffing at the meat. It smelled good and he took a hesitant bite.

"How djur know tha'?" asked Hone, sitting down and watching him with interest.

"I saw one once in Kaionar. Someone had it as a pet," replied Lutis through a mouthful of food.

"Wowee, tha's cool. Djur come from Kaionar?" asked Hone. Lutis nodded. "What were y'djarn in Quinsilla then? Fraiz said he had seen y'bein' chased by a big dragon there."

Lutis blanched at the mention of Xaoc. "I was in Quinsilla because that's where I was being chased by a big dragon. Who's Fraiz?"

Hone laughed. "Y'weren't doin' anything else there?"

Lutis shook his head, and Hone laughed again.

"Fraiz is one o' t'humans we found in t'desert, before me'n Aeron found you. I think he's down at t'riverbank. He has sunburn," said Hone.

"We? Are there more dragons like you here?" asked Lutis.

"Aye, there are..." Hone counted on her claws "Six of us." She held up both paws, one claw pressed down.

"That's seven!" said Lutis, pointing at her claws and counting them out.

"Ah... I'm not geet good at maths." Hone looked ruefully at her paws as though they had betrayed her then linked them together. Lutis gave a laugh.

"Oh, you're awake," said a different voice from near the waterfall, the head of another dragon appearing around the cave's entrance. A sandy coloured Elite stepped into the cave, shaking her orange feathers free of spray.

"Aye," said Hone, climbing to her feet. "Lutis, this is Neby."

Neby gave a little wave, turning towards Hone. "Aeron and Doan are back from hunting, and Aeron wants to show you how to deal with the birds they caught. Will you come down to the meadow?"

"Ahreet," said Hone, then gave a worried glance at Lutis. "But... are y'gaarn t'be ahreet on your own?"

Lutis gave a smile at the dragon's concern. "Of course, I'm used to looking after myself. Anyway," he slid to the edge of the makeshift bed, capping the flask he still held. "I'm not an invalid. Maybe I'll come down to the meadow too?" He climbed to his feet, hanging on to the ferns that hung from the wall to steady his balance. "Remind me not to go back into the desert any time soon."

"T'desert ain't so bad, y'just had a bad time o'it," said Hone, hopping over to his side to help. He rested his hand gently on her neck, taking a few steps forwards. "Y'can meet t'others."

They left the cave, Hone slowly helping Lutis down the thin path that led along the side of the cliffs to the meadow. He was surprised at how wobbly he felt- the desert had taken more out of him than he thought. Neby followed behind, shrugging at Aeron when he shot her a bemused look. Hone led Lutis over to the edge of the riverbank near where the other humans were bathing then went for her training session with Aeron. Neby stayed close, having little else to do.

"Good to see you awake again," said one of the men lying on the grass, sitting up to look at Lutis. "I'm Deltan."

"Yes... I remember you now. And Merac patched up my arm a bit better, didn't she," said Lutis, nodding as he remembered. "Thanks for that."

"It's quite alright," said Merac, resting her elbows on the edge of the riverbank. She had been swimming and her pale hair was damp. Deltan grinned at her, leaning across and linking hands.

"So... how many escaped Quinsilla then?" asked Lutis, shrugging off his coat and making it into a pillow. It was hotter outside than it had been in the cave, and humid too.

"Eight of us, plus you," said Merac, looking at Deltan with soppy eyes. "And I'm so glad that Deltan was part of that."

Lutis shook his head and lay back on his coat, looking at the sky. *Urgh, lovey-dovey stuff.* There wasn't one cloud marring the blue, the sun burning bright yellow a little to the west. It was afternoon already- had he really slept through the whole morning?

There was a giggle behind him and a small shadow passed over his head then two pairs of hands dropped a wreath of flowers over his head. He sneezed, yellow pollen speckling his face, prompting more giggles. Lutis sat up and turned to see who it was, the flowers falling around his neck.

Two small girls grinned cheekily at him, their fingers dark with sticky pollen. One stuck her tongue out at him before running off, the other one following after, their tufty pigtails bouncing. He sneezed again and pulled the wreath off, laying it in a neat circle on the ground next to him. More giggles came from wherever they were hiding and he looked around, trying to find them.

His eyes settled on a woman sitting dabbling her feet at the water's edge, her head bandaged up with white cloth. "Oh no..." he whispered under his breath, turning quickly away as she bent to look at him. *Why would it have to be Emi that was amongst those who escaped?*

"The girls' seem to like you," said Neby, who had been watching everything going on. She sniffed at the flowers, smiling at their perfume. "I think you might be getting a lot of attention from them for a while."

Lutis gave the dragon a small smile, trying to calm his nerves. Emi could spoil everything with her knowledge of him being the one who had stolen the ruby from the Jewel Tower in Quinsilla... he would end up in jail, and there would be no way out of it.

"Who's that over there with the bandaged head?" he asked nonchalantly, pointing to where Emi had returned to splashing her feet in the water.

"That's Emi, she was a guard in Quinsilla," explained Neby. "Apparently she was in the infirmary when the city was invaded, so managed to escape." Neby's voice dropped. "She doesn't remember much what happened though."

"Oh, that's a shame," said Lutis, his heart soaring. Maybe he would get away with it after all? "Although, it looked like they were treated pretty rough as slaves."

"Weren't you a slave?" asked Neby, surprised.

"Nope. I hid in a house when they came raiding. I had just come out of hiding when a dragon spotted me and decided he wanted me for his dinner," replied Lutis, thinking fast.

"Lucky escape then eh?" said Neby, rolling onto her side. She started to fiddle with the flower wreath, twisting the plant vines around her claws absently. It was clear she had taken quite a liking to it.

"Very," agreed Lutis, laying back and closing his eyes again.

~

Nox sat on the edge of the Jewel Tower looking out onto the bright city below and twisting one of her short dark locks in her fingers. She had cut her hair short after brushing with Static, when the blood from her head had matted her hair into untameable spikes. She wished it would rain- the never-ending sunshine was so... *monotonous*. At least there was the army's departure to look forward to- unlike if you actually lived in Quinsilla, when you would have to put up with the sun day in, day out for months on end.

She climbed to her feet, bored of blindly staring, and started down the staircase, hoping there was some form of entertainment to be had in one of the taverns, even if it was only getting completely drunk and finding someone to spend the night with.

Down at ground level the air was hot and sticky, shadows cast across the street from the towering buildings. Nox headed down the street for the southern quarter where most of the buildings were still in one piece- or thereabouts. It was quiet, the slaves they had captured confined to the eastern edge of the city to make armour and weapons for when the army moved on and the mercenaries that belonged to the army either guarding the slaves or taking time off.

The southern quarter was a little more populated than the rest of the city and she started to pass soldiers heading the other direction or skulking outside seemingly destroyed buildings. She ignored them, knowing that whatever treasures they were guarding were nothing in comparison to what she had hoarded. Being second in command of the army definitely had its perks.

The first tavern she reached was eerily quiet so she kept walking. There was nobody around, so the alcohol had obviously run out. A lone drunk sat bawling out a song by the door, swaying towards her as she passed. Nox jumped back, snarling in disgust. There was just no respect these days.

Around the next corner the scene was a little different. A creaking sign hanging from a top floor read "The Rusty Oak" and noises came from inside. She headed for the door but before she could enter a woman came flying through it, knocking her to the floor.

"And stay out, we don't want no women in here!" shouted a voice from inside the inn, followed by a round of laughter. The door swung shut with a bang.

Nox growled and shoved the woman off her, jumping to her feet, her sword already halfway out of its sheath. Her eyes narrowed when she recognised who had been thrown out of the tavern. It was Static.

"You," she said, drawing her sword. "I've got a bone to pick with you."

Static huffed and picked herself off the ground, brushing the mud off her green cloak. "Hey, lots of people have bones to pick with me, but do you think I've got time for them?"

"You have time for me," snarled Nox. "I had to cut my hair short after last time."

Static gave a harsh laugh, her hand straying to her own scimitar. "Is that all? You should think yourself lucky then."

"Think yourself lucky for me not hunting you down before now," replied Nox.

"You really think you can take me?" Static's voice was scornful.

"I know I can take you. Swords only, no powers." Nox tightened her grip, starting to circle the electric sorceress.

"Fine, but you'll still lose." Static pulled her sword and leapt towards Nox, the blade flashing.

Nox parried it easily and slid a counterattack under her sword, the blades clashing together as Static parried back. The woman leapt out of the way as Nox started a flurry of feints, flicking the edge of her cloak under the Felixis' feet before pulling it back, which made her lose her footing. Nox felt herself falling but used the motion to flip backwards, landing on her feet again like an acrobat.

"Nice move. You should have been a clown," said Static, running forwards to engage blades again. "Oh wait… you already are!"

"Funny," replied Nox. "Too bad your words are faster than your sword." Nox took her sword in two hands for a moment, driving the hilt into Static's hand. Static dropped her scimitar, shaking her bruised grip and backing up to make some space but Nox kept coming, twirling her sword this way and that with ease. She stepped over Static's blade, leaving it in the mud before aiming her point at Static's heart and driving it forwards.

Static had been anticipating the move and leapt backwards as Nox's sword came for her, even though she knew her plate armour would protect her. She landed awkwardly though, her feet slipping on the thick mud underfoot, sending her crashing to the floor. Nox gave a laugh as she stepped forwards again, angling her sword at Static's throat.

"You've lost, amateur," she said, a malicious grin on her face.

"I don't think so," replied Static, raising her cupped hands to point at Nox. A green ball of electricity pulsed in her palms.

Nox's eyes widened in horror as the energy sparked, throwing herself out of the way as it shot towards her. It just missed but she felt the heat of it as it flew past her face, smashing into the tavern behind her and exploding across its front with a crack.

"Oops. Oh well," said Static, climbing to her feet and collecting her scimitar. Flames started to lick at the front of *The Rusty Oak,* the sign swinging limply from one chain. Surprised shouts came from inside as the tavern's patrons noticed the commotion. Nox climbed to her feet too, rubbing the mud off her hands.

"Nice move," said Nox, raising an eyebrow at the carnage she had dealt the tavern. "I think you'll find I won that one though."

Static gave a snort, pulling her hood back over her face. "Hardly." She spun on her heel, dismissing Nox.

"Hey!" shouted Nox after her, but Static ignored it, disappearing down a side street. Nox frowned then murmured to herself, "She'd be an interesting ally to have." Pulling the picture of the avian out of her pocket, she set out after her.

Static headed further into the southern quarter, getting far away from the scene of the fight. If any drunkards escaped they would head for the next closest inn and, as good a swordswoman she was, she wanted to have a bit of fun that didn't involve drunken brawls. Fighting Nox had been amusing enough; it was good to have a worthy opponent, but she was looking for something more downbeat for the rest of the evening.

She arrived at the southern market square, which was much smaller than the northern square but was one of the best places for taverns. The square bustled with people even at the early afternoon hour so she headed for an inn tucked in the corner of the square, the brightly coloured hanging baskets outside deterring most of the passing trade. Just how she liked it, although she wasn't surprised why most people were put off- with a name like "The Court Princess", there couldn't be much trade.

Inside the inn was just as bright as outside- if Static had to admit it, she thought it rather pleasant. She walked towards the bar, winding her way through the long tables and dropping onto a stool in the corner.

"Strong cider," she asked the barman, pulling her hood further around her face to shield it from the few others in the bar- a couple of other female mercenaries and a small group of goblins that she had caused interest among with her arrival. He set a cup down in front of her without a word, going back to his slow waiting game. Static took a long draught out of the cup, savouring the bittersweet liquid and the relative quiet. She traced her finger around its edge, lost in her thoughts.

Nox had followed Static to the inn, changing into the avian's form quickly when they passed down a deserted street. She had perfected it after her last brush with the sorceress and now wandered in the southern square for a bit, putting a few minutes between their entrances to the tavern- it looked like a quiet sort of place and entering so soon after would make the woman suspicious. When she deemed it long enough Nox pushed open the door and sat down near Static at the bar.

"What do you recommend?" she asked the barman, tapping her fingers on the countertop. He set down a small cup in front of her.

"Pear cider, we make it ourselves," he said quietly, trying not to attract more attention than needed. Although he was a free man it was only because he had to run the tavern, and annoying his customers would surely get him thrown back into chains with the other slaves.

Nox nodded and took a sip. "Tastes good."

Static took a look at the newcomer, raising an eyebrow. "I didn't know there were any avians around."

Nox looked back at Static, surprised that she had commented. The woman didn't seem like one for talking, apart from the odd ironic quip. "I was undercover in Quinsilla. They only just realised which side I was on down in the slave quarters an hour ago." She shook her head, looking at the ceiling.

"Useless mercenaries," she said with a snort, sliding along the bar closer to Static.

"It's not like their commanders are any better," replied Static, taking another swig from her cup. "You met the second in a command? She's a right cow."

Nox coughed into her glass, biting back a comment that would have revealed her true identity. "You're brave for talking about a commanding officer like that."

Static gave a harsh laugh. "What's she going to do to me? I'd like to see her touch this." She gestured to herself. "She's nothing special."

"Have you got something special going for you then?" asked Nox, knowing the answer already.

"Wouldn't you like to know," she said, putting down her cup and offering a gloved hand. "The name's Static."

"That your real name?" said Nox, shaking her hand. "Uh… Xion. Nice to meet you."

"No, its not. Don't ask for my real name," replied Static, her face stony. "So, undercover work. You got anything interesting?"

~

A strange birdcall caught Lutis' attention, the quick, fluent notes tempting him off the rocky stream path he was following. The forest was full of new and exciting things to see and more than once he had caught one of the others that were staying at Eden's Fall- Hone in particular, and Tekek too- wandering through the forest following a brightly coloured butterfly or a long-tailed bird that flared its blue-streaked wings when disturbed. Water bubbled along beneath his feet, the odd stone turning over under his booted foot. It turned out that Merac had saved his boots for him, but his wings had strangely gone missing...

As he turned a bend in the stream a shrieking sound went up from the trees and a group of tamarins swung away through the canopy, their black eyes watching him from within a frill of gold and black fur. Lutis came to a stop, locking eyes with a short brown capybara that had been drinking from the stream. It gave a squeak of fright and dashed away through the trees, its short thin legs looking ridiculous under its thick body.

Lutis smiled and turned off the stream, heading a little way into the forest. The undergrowth crawled with life, huge beetles fighting with their spined heads underneath a bush, a long line of ants tramping inexhaustibly across the floor, carrying the jagged edges of cut leaves high above their heads. He followed their trail, watching them clamber over the obstacles in their path until they headed up the side of a tree, defying gravity as they twisted around its trunk. He looked higher into the tree, trying to see where they were heading. An upside-down face looked back at him and he jumped.

"Ahreet marra?" squeaked Hone, her blue head fans hanging down. Lutis looked back at her, turning his head to look at her properly.

"Y'alright Hone?" he asked, used to the lash dragon's strange tendencies. She tried to nod, pulling a pained face instead.

"Blood... gaarn t'my head!" she said, trying to sit up the right way again but fell from her precarious perch instead, landing on the ground in a heap with a crash. She sat up woozily, shaking her head.

"You're so elegant," Lutis commented dryly, pulling her to her feet and out of the line of ants that were dithering around her feet. She sneezed, flicking her ears.

"I think I got ants up m'ears," she said, looking at the tree trunk carefully before settling against it and looking up into the green canopy that arched over them. Lutis shook his head despairingly and sat next to her, pulling an ant out of her feathers. There was probably no reason for why she was up the tree.

"Wotcher thinkin' about?" Hone snuggled against his side, her warm feathers pressing against him. She looked at him but he didn't look back.

"Nothing."

"Sure y'are, I can tell!" She watched him trustingly, her blue eyes wide and unblinking. "You can whisper it in m'ear," she whispered, wigging them. He looked at her, unimpressed, but let out an explosive snort of laughter at the intensity of her gaze.

"You're silly," he said, rubbing behind her ears with his fingers. She collapsed in a purring heap, twitching with contentment. Her head fans flickered with satisfaction, knocking against his broken arm. He yelped and pulled it away. "Ouch."

"Sorry." She sat up, looking at him in concern. "Did I whack it accidentally?"

"Just nudged it. Don't worry, it's not your fault." He rubbed at the rough bandages with his thumb. "It's getting better, slowly. At least my arm's not just one giant purple bruise now, eh?"

"How… how *dids'eh* break your arm?" she asked tentatively. She had avoided the question before now, but she couldn't hold the question forever. In fact, she had a lot of questions she had wanted to ask Lutis. He looked at her fiercely for a brief moment then the light died from his eyes.

"I tried to land after flying and misjudged my landing. I fell down a sand dune, and when I woke up my arm was broken." He twisted the fabric holding his arm in place with his fingers, stretching the material.

"Flying? But y'don't have any wings…" said Hone, confused.

"I had a pair of enchanted wings, but I broke them when I fell." He frowned. "I'm sure I was wearing them… Do you know what happened to them?"

"What? Oh, tha' mess o'fabric an' strings we found attached to your back? Aeron wanted t'throw it away, but I thought it migh' be important, so I kept it safe."

"You did? Really?" His eyes lit up with excitement and he spontaneously pulled her into a one-armed hug. "Where did you put them?"

"Up yonder!" she said, looking up into the branches above them, a smile on her face.

"So that's why you were up there!" he laughed, peering into the canopy too.

"Aye, djur want 'em down?" she said.

"Yes! Yes please!"

"They're in a mess an' a half, y'know that, don't you?"

"I don't care!" Lutis jumped to his feet, trying to see where Hone had hidden the wings.

"Ahreet… Don't say I dinae warn you…" She got to her feet, padding a few steps away from the tree before turning to face it. "Y'might want t'move over a bit. I don't wanna whack you on the way up," she said.

Lutis stepped out the way, avoiding the line of ants that was slowly reassembling itself. Hone took a running jump, hitting the trunk and clawing her way up the tree. She paused on the first branch, balancing herself before leaping further up the tree like a monkey, her tail swinging wildy to steady herself.

"Can you see them?" Lutis called eagerly, watching her progress.

She leapt a few more branches then reached into a clump of leaves that Lutis had thought to be the nest of a bird or a squirrel. "Aye, I've got 'em. Shall I chuck them down?"

"No! They're very delicate. Can you carry them down and not fall out of the tree at the same time?" he said.

"Aye, don't worry 'bout me." She took the pack in her teeth carefully, scooping the dangling strings and fabric into her jaws too. She didn't need them tripping her and sending her plunging out of the tree. She carefully climbed back down the tree again and leapt the last few metres, landing with a thump clear on the ground. The dragon turned to grin at Lutis through her mouthful of wings, offering them to him.

He stepped forwards and took them, regarding the soggy broken mess sadly.

"They are in a sorry state, aren't they? It's going to take ages to fix them." He stroked the dark green fabric with one hand. They weren't even recognisable as the same wings he had had a few days before. "They've never been in a condition like this..."

"How long have y'had them for?" asked Hone, picking up one drooping edge off the floor and brushing a wandering ant off.

"Oh, I don't know. A year or so maybe? They've gotten me out of a lot of scrapes." He turned the wings over, the wood holding the structure creaking as it bent in all the wrong places. "They can't be fixed, can they?"

"O'course they can!" said Hone brightly, taking the wings off Lutis. "Come on, we'll gar back t' Eden's Fall an' start fixin' them now." She looked around, suddenly confused. "Whista way?"

Lutis laughed and pointed to the direction he had come, the stream still gurgling away under the singing of the birds and the incessant buzzing of invisible insects. Hone gave a laugh and set off towards it, chattering merrily. "What do we fix first?"

He gave a sigh and started after her, picking up a scrap of fabric she had dropped. "I suppose the strings need removing first, then the struts need replacing... are you sure you want to help?"

"Aye, there's nothin' much else to do, an' Aeron always says t'find out 'bout new stuff." She stepped into the stream, giggling as she felt the current turn the stones under her feet. "What's tha'?" she asked, pointing to a huge-beaked bird that watched them from a tree overhanging the stream. It eyed them haughtily before turning its head and pulling at a bright fruit tucked in a crook of branches. A toucan.

They followed the stream slowly back to Eden's Fall, watching their steps on the slimy bed. Insects droned persistently around them in clouds, attracted by their heat and the humidity of the stream and it seemed that they only grew in number as the light started to fade from the day. The night came fast in the forest and soon they were walking in the dark.

"Are we nearly there?" asked Hone after a while, sounding bored. "Dinae know we'd come so far."

"Yeah, I can hear the waterfall. Listen," said Lutis, pointing downstream. The water glittered in front of them, curving around a bend to meet with another larger river. A dark shape swept down over its surface- it was a bat taking advantage of the plentiful supply of insects they had attracted.

"Aye, I can hear t'water too now," she said, following Lutis as he turned along the main riverbank. The ground started to slope away, the trees suddenly stopping where the waterfall made cliffs of rock.

"I would have thought you would have heard it before now, having four ears," remarked Lutis, shooting her a long sideways glance.

"Well I did... but I dinae know what it was. I can hear f'long, long distances. Seeing prey in t'desert is hard, so y'have t'listen for it, or track it. Elites are the best trackers and listeners out of all lash dragons, that's why we do wha' we do!" she said.

"What do you do?" Lutis felt himself being pulled in by Hone's excitement.

"We guard t'desert!" she flashed him a smile, her teeth white against the shadowy forest around them. "If someone needs help, or is lost, or jus' wants a travelling companion, Elites are always ready on hand. We're not t'only patrol in the desert, that's why we can leave it for so long; there are lots of us. You're still lucky I spotted y'though, any further off and we migh' have missed you completely."

"Well I thank thee wholeheartedly then, my friend." Lutis turned to the dragon, bowing low before her with a cheeky smile. She looked away, blushing beneath her scales.

They wound their way slowly down to the dark plunge pool below the waterfall before cutting across and up the other side of the cliff along the familiar path to the cave behind it. Light flickered behind the water from a cooking fire and they hurried up the path at the welcome sight.

"Do you want something to eat?" asked Merac when they entered, sitting by the fire and poking at a set of fish on a hot cooking stone. "There's plenty."

"Please," said Lutis, taking a flat leaf from a pile next to the fire. The smell of cooked fish was mouth watering and he suddenly discovered he was ravenous. He took an extra fish for Hone and they made their way to the back of the cave, eating before they started fixing the wings.

Hone put them on the floor, settling onto her side as Lutis smoothed them into the shape they were supposed to be, wide and batlike. They were poor to behold, the fabric of the wings ripped in a dozen places and two struts broken, making them lay lax on the rocky ground. The wires that ran along them to hold them in place were hopelessly knotted and even the straps that used to hold the wings to his back were sliced through. Lutis lent back and regarded them sadly.

"Sorry, I had t'cut the straps t'get y'out," said Hone, flicking a claw at one of them. It was bound tightly in a tangle of strings, and hardly moved.

"Don't worry about it," Lutis said, rustling in one of his coat pockets and taking a small dagger out, as well as a roll of string he found. He started to saw at the strings where they met the main pack of the wings, pulling them loose when they snapped. Hone went off to report to Aeron on her findings of the day. When the strings had been removed he pushed the wings flat onto the ground and pulled a scrap of paper and a charcoal pencil out of his pocket, making a list of all the things he needed to fix.

Hone returned to find him hard at work, bent over the wings in deep concentration, cutting the fabric around the struts carefully. She stood at a distance, not wanting to break his control over the knife and disturb his concentration. Without looking up he waved her over, pausing to look at the wings for a moment before removing a wooden strut, picking the wing up to shake the other piece out of the hole he had made.

"It's going to take forever to fix them, look at the list I made of everything we need to fix," he said, passing her the scrap of paper he had been writing on. A long list wound its way over both sides.

"I cannae read," said Hone, peering at the scrawled letters closely for a moment before giving back the paper. "What's t'first thing on t'list?"

Lutis looked at Hone in surprise before reading off "fabric tears" from the list. "I need something long, thin and sharp to thread the fabric together."

Hone thought for a moment, then extended a wing and pulled out one of her thicker feathers. "Will this do?"

"Ouch." Lutis winced, taking the purple feather gingerly. "You didn't have to do that."

Hone waved away his protestations. "Will it do?"

"Yes. But don't pull out any more feathers," said Lutis, turning his knife to the feather and shearing it to a point. Hone prodded at the wings before taking her tail blade and slicing along the fabric holding the remaining broken struts like Lutis had been doing previously.

The two worked on the wings for a few hours, talking little as they concentrated. By the end of the session the two were working well together, mutually helping one another where they couldn't do it on their own: Hone lifted the wings when Lutis couldn't manage with just one arm; he used his dextrous fingers to fix the fiddly mechanical parts. When the fire started to die down, throwing the wings into sharp relief against the black of the cave, they started to pack up.

"You know, if you weren't going to be a lash Elite, and wanted a job- if I wanted a job- we would make a great team fixing things." He pushed the wings together, one side at a time, smiling when they fit cleanly into their casing. "Would you look at that."

"Whista do before y'got caught out in t'desert like tha'?" Hone asked, taking hold of the wings in her front paws and standing up.

"Oh, you know, this and that," he replied, stretching and lying back on the nest he had made.

"No, I don't know really. You humans always seem t'be djarn strange things. Your way o'life is so different t'ours." Hone dropped the wings into a neat pile by the bottom of his bed and lay down against the wall, resting her head on a pile of leaves.

"I've done lots of things. I'm mostly a freelancer- what needs doing, I'll do." He avoided her gaze, not wanting to tell her his real past as a thief. Just that knowledge in the hands of others had gotten him into more trouble than the money and the thrill of it was worth.

"Sounds like fun," said Hone through a yawn, closing her eyes. She flicked a wing over her eyes, drowning out the last light from the fire. Lutis hummed back his assent quietly, turning onto his side and tracing a finger down the side of his bandages, his smile for the past few hours fading.

6
DEEP TROUBLE.

Lutis surfaced from under the water, taking a deep breath and pushing the hair out of his eyes. He floated on his back momentarily before turning and diving again, his good hand raking the bottom of the pool for hidden treasures. If there had been something dropped upstream, the likelihood was that it would eventually end up down in the plunge pool. His fingers closed around a smooth object and he kicked off the bed towards the surface, tracing its strange smooth, curving sides.

He turned it in the faint morning light, treading water. It was a shell as big as his palm, lined with shiny pearl. It was useless but Hone might like it. He started towards the bank, feeling a plip of water on his face as it started to rain.

When he reached the bank he saw a bent figure sitting near his pile of clothes, ignoring the persistent patter of rain. He slid onto a low ledge, dropping the shell onto the bank and pulling his shirt towards him. At the movement the figure looked up, her eyes misty.

"Do I know you?" she asked, lifting a hand to her head. "I don't remember…"

"You're Emi," Lutis said, his voice guarded as he pulled the shirt over his head. It drooped into the water.

"How do you know my name?" she said, turning away as Lutis clambered onto the bank and tugged on his trousers. "Have I met you before?"

Lutis pulled a hurt face, wringing out his shirt. "Are you likely to forget a face as handsome as mine?"

Emi pulled a slight smile, fiddling with a twist of hair. "Who *are* you?"

"I can be a friend, if you want." He tugged his coat on, looking up at the miserable clouds. He blinked as a raindrop fell in his eye. "I'm going back up to the cave, dry out a bit." He picked up the shell, thinking for a moment before giving it to Emi. "Here."

Emi frowned at the shell, turning it in her hands. "I do know you..." she started, then paused. "I... I think I might stay out a bit longer."

"Don't get too wet," said Lutis quickly, getting to his feet and heading for the cave at a jog. He was going to get into trouble if Emi started remembering who he was. He ducked inside the cave, squeezing water out of his hair. Great snores from Aeron reverberated around the cave, the dragon lying upside down in a pile of leaves. Lutis sat down by the ashy remains of the fire, stacking up the remaining wood ends and rustling in his pockets for a match. He heard a few footsteps behind him then Tekek huffed a little hot air at the sticks, setting them alight.

"Can't sleep?" he asked as the dragon settled across from him, yawning.

"Aeron's snoring's enough to wake the dead in here," she grumbled, dragging a claw through the ash and making swirling patterns. "Why are you up so early?"

"Ah, you know, this and that." He pulled his fingers through the knots in his hair as it started to dry out by the warmth of the fire. "It's raining outside."

Tekek shuddered, wrapping her tail close. "I hate the rain."

Lutis gave a short laugh, trying not to wake the others in the cave. "Is that the reasoning for living in the Great Desert then?"

Tekek smiled, nodding her head sincerely. "Yep!" she said, snuffling at Lutis' coat which he had abandoned to on the floor to dry. "Have you got anything to eat?"

"Not on me." A grin crept across his face. "There is something here though…" He reached out to one set of her ears, plucking a mushroom from the thin air. "What's this?"

"Wow, that's cool!" said Tekek, taking hold of the mushroom and sniffing it to see if it was real. "How did you do that?"

"Magic," he replied, sitting back with a grin at the purple and red dragon.

"Can I eat it?" was the next question.

"If you want, but I didn't think you dragons ate plants."

Tekek shrugged and pushed it to the edge of the fire, letting it cook. "I've eaten them before, but they always taste better cooked."

Lutis nodded and poked the fire, embellishing Tekek's ash patterns with a stick. After a while Hone wandered over too and plonked herself next to the lash Elite, yawning.

"Why ain't we outside?" she asked.

"It's raining," said Lutis, shuffling over and scratching the dragon behind her ears.

"Is rain cold?"

Lutis shot her a questioning look. "Yes... don't you know that?"

Hone shook her head. "No, I've ne'er been in—"

She was suddenly interrupted by Emi, who ran into the cave soaking wet and with a furious yell launched herself at Lutis. He crashed backwards under her weight, catching at her flailing fist with his hand.

"I know who you are, you... you monster!" she cried, punching him in the chest. He let out an "oof!" of air, pushing her off backwards onto the floor. She spun to her feet, her hair whipping in dark strands across her face as she made to leap at him again.

"Oh no you don't!" said Tekek, catching hold of Emi and curling her tail firmly around her. Hone had leapt to her feet and stood in front of Lutis, both protecting and preventing him from retaliation. He sat on the floor dazed and catching his breath.

"What... do you mean?" he huffed, trying to keep worry out of his voice. *This was bad...*

"You pushed me down the Jewel Tower stairs, then you stole the Quinsilla ruby!" she cried, tears springing to her eyes as her voice cracked.

There was silence for a moment, the two dragons turning to stare at Lutis in dumb horror. Tekek's grip on Emi loosened and the woman threw herself at Lutis again, not giving any heed to the nearby fire. They tussled briefly before the two dragons wrestled them apart. Emi burst into even more tears, drooping in Hone's grip until she slumped to the floor, all her fight gone.

"Is this true?" Doan's strong voice cut through the scuffle, the larger Elite coming to stand behind Lutis like a sentry. The man pawed at his face, rubbing gently where Emi had just given him a crack to the cheek- it was already bruising a dark purple.

"What?" he asked, still trying to sound nonchalant.

Doan's voice got dangerous. "Is. This. True?" he asked again, snaking his head round to stare close into the man's eyes. He rested a front paw lightly on Lutis' broken arm, pinning him in place.

"Leave him alone!" shouted Hone, launching herself at Doan. She bore him to the ground, the two rolling in the fire before sliding dangerously close to the edge of the waterfall. Ash and burning sticks scattered everywhere and in the madness Lutis jumped up, grabbed his coat and boots from the floor and ran for the cave exit, his feet sliding on the wet stone.

The rain pounded down ferociously outside, soaking him in moments. He ran down the path tugging his coat on before leaping off the side into the grassy clearing below, tumbling over with practised ease. He leapt to his feet, heading for the closest path he knew. The waterlogged ground squelched beneath his bare feet but he didn't put his boots on- that would save for later, when he was in less danger. There was a yell then a huge splash behind him, then an even louder scream and another splash. He slid to a stop, squinting through the rain to see what had happened- Doan's sandy coloured head popped up in the pool underneath the waterfall, then Hone and Aeron's heads too.

"Crap!" he swore, turning on his heel again and starting forwards, pushing the leaves that fell over his path out of the way. A splash of water fell down his sleeve, running all the way to his elbow and he shook it out, momentarily distracted. Shouts came from the clearing behind him, the three lash dragons setting immediately on his tail. If they found his trail fast then he would have no chance- even in the crush of the forest, they would outrun him easily. A path wound its way through the trees in front of him, dark against the bright greens of the forest plants and he was sorely tempted to follow it, as it was the easiest route. But the dragons would find it easier too... he could already hear Aeron crashing through the bushes behind him.

Lutis took a chance and turned off the path, silently cursing his stupid plan as he hurtled through the undergrowth as fast as he could. Ferns pushed wet against his legs, leaving dark patches on his trousers where they deposited rainwater but he pushed on, heading in as straight a direction as he could. Discarded leaves from the trees crunched under his feet and there was a sharp stab in his heel as he was bitten by something living in a hidden crevice but still he kept running, his arms outstretched to either side so he kept his balance. A tree trunk balanced perilously between two others and he ducked under it, one of the twisted vines that dangled from it snagging on his coat. Another tree trunk lay hidden on the ground, half rotten through, and he tripped on it, flailing as he lost his balance and fell to the floor. His yelp of pain at crushing his broken arm was muffled by the face full of earth he got. He spat out a mouthful of dirt and sat up, cradling his arm with the other hand. His boots hung absurdly from a branch where he had thrown them accidentally into a bush.

The clatter of the three following lash dragons suddenly paled into insignificance. In front of Lutis, dancing like a dying sunbeam at the end of the day a tiny glowing pixie fluttered in the air, wafting and pulsing like seaweed in the tide of the sea. It looked at him with huge dark eyes, blinking, then shimmered closer to his face, reaching out a tiny hand. It stopped before it touched him. He looked at it in confusion, the reason for why he was running suddenly spirited away by the creature's magic. The pixie left a little trail of sparkles in the air as it fluttered in front of him, its six translucent wings visible as it dipped before turning back into a blur of purple-blue.

The pixie held him spellbound, a bright light amongst the dark of the rainforest. It drifted closer to him, its frills fluttering gently up and down on the breezes from its wings, reaching out its hand further to touch him on the cheek.

A heavy branch suddenly shot through the air, catching the pixie and sending it tumbling to the ground. A high-pitched screech rang through the air and Lutis clapped his arms around his ears, trying to block out the noise. A lash dragon leapt over his head- his eyes were screwed shut so he couldn't see who it was- whirling and snarling at the other pixies that had closed in. There was more noise and the scrabbling of footsteps then a heavy weight fell on him, squashing him to the ground. He gave a yell, trying to shove the dragon off but they were too heavy and kicked out in surprise. He saw a flash of red and purple before a paw came out of nowhere, whacking him hard around the face. His head whipped back, he hit the tree trunk behind him and everything went suddenly black.

~

"Yer got somewhere t'sleep?" slurred Static, holding on to the side of the tavern she and Nox had just stumbled out of. After three or four more mugs of cider she had lightened considerably.

"No, ha'you?" mumbled back Nox, swaying.

"Yeah. See y'tomorrow." Static pushed off from the wall, her path wobbling from side to side down the street.

"Wait!" Nox stumbled after her. "Can I stay w'you?"

Static lurched to a halt. "What? Yeah, fine."

The two walked through the city, laughing hysterically at each other's drunken swaggering in the moonlight. Static finally turned towards a tall dark house tucked between two shops, their ruined finery bleak in the cold moonlight. She kicked open the door, a clatter coming from inside as whatever was holding it shut broke under the pressure.

"Welcome home," said Static, pulling off her sword and throwing it without heed into the room. She pulled her boots off next, stumbling against the wall as she tugged at each in turn, a stream of curses hissing from her lips as she banged her shoulder.

Nox followed her into the room, fumbling in her pocket and striking a match to give some light. The room was long and thin, a table and chairs shoved at one end and another door leading off to one side. Static headed directly for it, disappearing through the black gape. There was a thump as she dropped onto a bed in the next room.

Nox chucked her bow into a corner of the first room before trailing into the bedroom and falling back onto the spare bed, waving the candle out before it set the place on fire. Static groaned into her bedcovers, fumbling at her shoulder before there was a click and she pulled off her armour. She kicked it off the bed and wrapped herself in a pile of blankets, pulling them over her head.

Nox watched her blankly, smiling a little- had she just found an ally?- before she too tucked down in her own blankets, feeling strangely relaxed.

It seemed like only moments that Nox had been asleep when she was suddenly jerked awake by a loud scream. She sat up in the bed, fumbling for the bow that was no longer across her back. Her fingers caught at warm feathers and she panicked, wrenching at them with an iron grip. They came away in her hand and there was suddenly a sharp pain in her shoulder; belatedly she realised the feathers were her own and she was still in the avian's form.

There was another scream and she pushed the hair out of her face, squinting into the darkness to see who it was. A dark figure writhed in the bed next to her, throwing a blanket off the bed, then the figure followed it, thudding onto the floor with a crash. It moaned weakly.

"Static?" asked Nox blearily, rubbing at her eyes. Her mouth felt strange and dry. There was a incomprehensible mumble from the floor and Nox slid reluctantly out of bed, kneeling by the woman slumped on the floor. "Y'alright?"

Static looked up, half her face lit by the weak moonlight. Tears ran down her cheeks and she suddenly grabbed hold of Nox, pulling her into a hug and burying her head in her shoulder.

Nox resisted the urge to push Static away, grimacing instead and patting her awkwardly on the shoulder. "What's wrong?"

Static stayed quiet then straightened up and wiped her eyes furiously, pushing Nox away and crawling back onto her bed. She wrapped the blankets around her, tugging her cloak straight where it had pulled askew. "Nightmare. Thought the cider might get rid of them." She rubbed at her eyes again.

Nox padded back to her own bed, confused at Static's sudden shifts in emotion. "You… wanna talk?"

Static gave a sigh, trying to resume her stoic mask. She buried her face in her crossed arms, shoulders shaking as she started to cry again. Nox shook her head and crossed beds, putting an arm around the woman. She was useless when it came to emotions but she couldn't have her only true ally falling apart on her.

"Sorry," sniffed Static. "Damn nightmares."

"What about?" asked Nox.

Static frowned, her voice sharp. "Why are you so interested all of a sudden?"

Nox kept quiet. Static looked at her haughtily then her face cracked. "Bad memories."

Nox gave a wry smile. "We've all got those, but most of us don't wake up screaming in the middle of the night."

"Every night," she sighed. "I… There was this guy…" She tailed off.

"Huh. What did he do?"

"It wasn't as much as him as me. I ruined everything. Again." Static shook her head in frustration. Part of her wondered why she was suddenly opening up to this stranger.

"Human men are crap anyway." Nox leaned back against the wall, closing her eyes against the moonlight. She had more than enough experience with men to decide that.

"He's an elf. Armeno. We lived in Racksom for a while together."

Nox gave a low whistle. "It was like that then?"

"No! Ack, why am I even telling you all this? If you must know, he played the stupid hero and tried to kill a dragon that was after me. It crushed his arm and I spent two months looking after him." She pulled at a corner of her cloak, running the green fabric through her fingers as she thought over the time she had spent with Armeno. Not only had she looked after him, he had looked after her too as she recovered from the shock of the accident. A lot of her memories were blurry but she remembered how much time they had spent together... enough time for them to get to know each other *very* well. That was, after they had got over disliking each other over a "practise" fight on the beach- which had turned out to be not much of a practise, considering he had shot her in the shoulder with one of his arrows. Granted he had healed it quickly after, but it hadn't been a good first meeting.

"A dragon? Was that the nightmare?—"

"That obvious is it?" huffed Static. "Damn thing's been after my blood ever since it set eyes on me."

"Why?"

"It said we're too alike." She waved a hand languidly. "Her powers are too similar to mine. They jar." A spark crackled across her fingers and she clenched them in a hard fist.

"Hm. So, an elf? Bit different to the normal."

Static gave her a friendly shove and a weak giggle. "Bit nicer than the normal too."

"What's he like?" asked Nox, her interest peaking. It sounded like Static had quite a past.

"Brave, stubborn, overprotective… that was one of the reasons we split ways…" She gave another sigh.

Nox waved her hand, dismissing the information. "No, not like that, was he handsome?"

Static gave a laugh, her cheeks reddening. "Just because I'm a mercenary, doesn't mean I don't have good taste!"

~

"I think I knocked him out," said Hone anxiously, snuffling at Lutis' head. She poked him with a claw but he didn't respond.

"Good," replied Aeron, who had been scanning the forest around them for the malicious blue glow of more returning pixies. That was all they needed. "Means he can't run 'way 'gain." He walked over to Lutis, who was slumped half on the ground, half across the log. "Back t'Eden's Fall."

Doan hefted Lutis in his front paws, dropping him unsympathetically onto Aeron's back without much heed for whether he was hurting the man or not. He lolled to one side, his face bruising purple and blue from the beatings he had taken from both Emi and Hone- albeit the second accidentally.

"Careful!" said Hone, pushing him more securely onto Aeron's back. The Elite huffed indignantly.

"From what little I heard o' what went on in t'cave, seems like he ain't worth carin' for." Aeron started back along the path they had forged through the rainforest, his claws digging into the rotten log as he clambered over it.

"He's still t'same person as he was afore..." muttered Hone to herself, taking a look around the little flattened patch of undergrowth they had made. She giggled in astonishment as she saw the pair of boots hanging tangled in a bush, then shivered as a splosh of rain landed on her nose.

"Come on Hone, we're going to head for Plurith today," called Doan, stopping and turning to wait for the apprentice. Aeron was less forgiving.

"Hurry up, I don't want 'im waking up afore we're back in t'cave, that way he cannae 'scape again," he said, not stopping.

"Ahreet..." replied Hone, plucking the boots from the tree with her teeth and hurrying after the pair.

Their trail through the forest was easy to follow and they were soon back at the main path, then the clearing of Eden's Fall. The rain still hammered down from the clouds, turning the whole meadow a dull shade of grey.

"Are you sure it's wise to set off today?" asked Doan quietly as the three lash dragons started up the winding path to the cave, their paws slipping on the muddy trail. "It'll be very hard going..."

"Aye. The faster we get out o'ere, t'better." Aeron's voice was set and Doan knew better than to probe further when he was in such a stubborn mood.

Aeron dumped Lutis down on the hard ground unceremoniously when they got to the cave, giving him a narrow look despite the fact that he couldn't receive it. Emi was hiccupping in a corner and looked up with a tear-stained face as they re-entered the cave. She didn't say anything as the dragon ordered Deltan to bind Lutis around the middle with a length of rope he found, watching with wide child-like eyes until Echai came over to her, crouching in front of her view.

"What's the story?" he asked quietly, looking around at Lutis, who had been sat up against the wall of the cave, his arms bound tightly to his sides. It seemed like Aeron was taking no chances.

Emi hiccupped again then wrapped her arms around Echai, pulling him close. The dragon was warm like a hot water bottle.

"I was guarding the ruby at the top of the Jewel Tower with Rathe, another guard. We were hungry, so Rathe asked him to buy us some wraps- when this man came to give me mine, he... he..." she shuddered, tears starting afresh down her cheeks. She took a deep breath, trying to control her tears. "He pushed me down the stairs. I don't remember anything else, but I think he was the one who stole the ruby. I let him steal the ruby..." She buried her face further in Echai's feathers, clutching at them with a frightened, vice like grip. "I let him!"

Echai folded his wings around her, enclosing her in a purple cocoon, trying to comfort with his warmth. "It's not your fault."

Hone meanwhile had been hopelessly protesting against Aeron's vendetta against Lutis.

"Honestly, why are you djarn this? He's harmless, I've been out in t'rainforest with 'im loads o' times afore." She tried to block Aeron as he stepped closer to the man, thinking to wake him from his dead sleep. The larger dragon shoved her out of the way.

"Aye, well y'won't be gaarn out alone with him ever again." His voice was harsh and he nudged his head against Lutis', growling between his teeth when the man didn't wake. "You shan't even be talkin' t'him."

"What? Y'cannae do tha'!" she protested further, fluttering her head fans in anger. "I can tal-"

"I can do it, an' I am doin' it." Aeron rounded on his apprentice, stepping close to her, his features twisted into an angry frown. "Y'ain't t'talk to him again. Ever!"

Hone's wings drooped at Aeron's anger, shocked by his tone. He had never been cross like this with her before.

"I mean it Hone, if y'talk to him again I'll send you back to t'desert with another patrol, you won't even get t' Plurith."

"What?" This time Hone's voice wavered, fear showing in her eyes. Aeron didn't give her any respite, pointing to the back of the cave where there was a small pile of meagre supplies they had collected.

"Gar an' pack that lot. We're gaarn. You're t'carry the two girls." He turned away, stationing himself close to Lutis, far enough away that he didn't have to touch the man. His face was stony and closed.

Choking back her dismay Hone nodded and started to pack, blinking away the frustrated tears that threatened to spill over her eyes. The two children danced over to the pile, being wholly unhelpful, pulling out a cloth here to twirl around themselves in a spontaneous ribbon dance or tugging on the dragon's feathers to show her some other little item that caught their attention.

Lutis gave a moan as he came to, opening his eyes blearily. They felt sore, especially his left eye and when he tried to open it he hardly could, his face puffy from the black eye Emi had graced him with. He found his arms were tied when he tried to explore with his fingers.

"Good, you're awake." Aeron turned towards him when he heard his signs the man starting to wake, a judgmental look on his face. "Means I don't hafta carry you all the way t' Plurith."

"Plurith?" Lutis mumbled, trying to reach his face again. "Wha' is thiss?" his words slurred together.

"You tried t'run away. Don't think you'll succeed a second time neither," said Aeron, watching Lutis closely.

Lutis' face paled as he remembered what had just happened.

"Aye, you're in geet trouble now," hissed Aeron, his teeth bared as he anticipated the man trying to make another break for it. Suddenly Lutis realised how dangerous even lash dragons could be. They had behaved very civilly to the humans over the past week but it was obvious they could behave equally as threatening. "Who are you?"

"Lutis!" he said, trying to keep the fear out of his voice, leaning against the wall behind him to try and make space between the pressing of the dragon.

"Lutis who? What 'bout t'Jewel Tower?" pushed the dragon, eyes flicking up and down the man with mistrust.

"Passal. Lutis Passal. The Jewel Tower, isn't that the big one in the middle of Quinsilla?"

"Don't play t'fool with me, y'know I'm not talkin' 'bout t'tower itself," growled the dragon, his eyes narrowing.

"What do you want to know?" Lutis asked, breaking the dragon's gaze for a moment to look for some sort of respite from the interrogation. There was none- although he noticed one of the others had thought to pick up his boots again. He had a sneaking suspicion that it had been Hone.

"What happened t'the Quinsilla ruby?"

"It was stolen, that's all I know!"

"That's a lie, I can tell." Aeron's nose wrinkled in anger. "Wotcher bein' hunted by tha' dragon in Quinsilla for?"

"I don't know why! I hid when the mercenaries came, then made a run for it when I thought the coast was clear. Turns out it wasn't."

"Why would t'dragon pick you specifically?"

"I don't know!" Lutis' voice rose a pitch.

"Aye y'bloody do!" Aeron snarled in his face. "You're lying, it's plain t'see."

"You're not listening to anything I say!"

"'Cause I know they're lies. But t'truth'll be out when we get t'Plurith, Lutis Passal." Aeron straightened to his full height, towering above Lutis. The man gave him an angry stare, his eyes flicking to Echai who had been hovering at the edge of the standoff.

"Aeron." He sounded grim. "We better hurry, Emi has some very… interesting… information."

Lutis swore inwardly to himself. How did he let himself get into a position like this?

7
TRANSFER TO PLURITH. DRAGON
AND GRYPHON.

The rain beat down monotonously on the small
group, battering them into the smallest shapes they
could take. Although the grey of the clouds had
lightened a little they were still heavy with rain and
every plant in the rainforest was shiny wet. For Lutis

it had been an especially miserable journey, stumbling after the lash dragons as fast as he could walk- the other humans had been allowed to ride but Aeron hadn't let him, and hadn't untied him either. The female lash dragons thought it was a little harsh but after Aeron had snapped at Tekek for forgetting some of the fruits they had collected the day before they decided to keep quiet, not wanting the Elite to round on them next.

Hone winced as Lutis stumbled over a tree root but kept her distance. She didn't want a repeat of what had happened back at Eden's Fall, which had hurt her more than she showed. Aeron had never shouted at her like that before... a little hand patted her neck and she turned to see the small smile of the younger of the two girls she was carrying. The girl was watching her intently.

"He be all'ight," she said, hugging the dragon. Her body was warm and damp against Hone's scales. "His flower wreath will protect him."

Hone gave a sad smile, putting her head down to walk again. Water dripped from her nose and she sniffed, shaking off the droplet. The rain had crept under every scale, in every feather, every crease of clothing and it was making walking difficult- the ground underfoot was waterlogged and at every step mud either sucked at their paws or leaves sent them sliding out of control.

"Do you know what it's like in Plurith?" The older girl broke the silence after a while when Hone winced as Lutis tripped again, dropping to his knees as a vine tangled itself around his feet. Her ringlets hung straight and limp across her shoulders.

"No, I dunno what ista like," said Hone quietly, averting her eyes as Aeron pulled Lutis to his feet. "Echai, djur know what Plurith is like?"

The dragon turned at the sound of his name, slowing down to walk side by side with the apprentice. "Apparently it's not like many other places in Mirrahl. I've heard that dragons and humans live together there."

"Together? How does tha' work?" asked Hone, trying to distract herself.

"Well, the humans run smaller places like the tavern- I've heard it's very good- and a blacksmith and the bakery, and the resident dragons look after the land around and keep raiders at bay."

"Raiders?" the girl on Hone's back piped up again.

"Yes, Plurith's quite isolated, so they look after themselves." At the girl's worried expression he waved a paw, trying to dispel her fears. "Don't worry, the village hasn't been invaded for years now."

The girl didn't look very relieved.

When it should have been midday they stopped under a huge tree for some lunch, its thick canopy protecting them mostly from the storm above. Tekek and Echai wandered off into the forest to hunt, returning after a while with a pair of dull coloured birds. They were different to the ones that had been at Eden's Fall- as they had walked further south the rainforest had started to change, the trees shifting in shape and the animals they had crossed paths with becoming less exotic.

Hone was set the task of plucking one of the birds, the ground around her quickly becoming heavy with grey feathers. She frowned, spitting fluff from her mouth.

"I hate eatin' birds," she grumbled to herself, her attempts at plucking the bird with her claws failing even more than her teeth had.

"Do you need a hand?" whispered a nearby voice. Hone looked up to see Lutis propped against the trunk of the tree watching her make a mess of herself.

"I'm not supposed t'talk t'you," replied the dragon sadly, shaking her paws to try and dislodge some of the feathers.

"Who made up that rule? Aeron?" asked Lutis, looking around to see if there was anyone close enough to overhear their conversation. Hone nodded.

"Blow Aeron," he said, trying to shuffle closer. He fell over onto his side, groaning when his arm got caught under him. Hone abandoned the bird and nudged him back upright. "Look, if you untie me I'll help."

"I cannae, y'know tha'." Hone went back to the bird, picking it up out of the mess she had made. Tiny feathers and mud flecked the meat where the rainwater had made it sticky.

Lutis shrugged, pulling a wry grin through his black eye. "Ah well, it was worth a shot." He looked up into the green umbrella of leaves above their heads, scrunching his nose when a droplet of water fell on it.

"Hone, what are you *doing*?" Neby's normally mild voice was distorted by surprise. "I thought you knew how to pluck birds!" The Elite cocked her head to one side as she saw the two alone, but didn't make any comment.

Hone shrugged, suddenly ignoring Lutis. She would get into innumerable trouble if Neby told Aeron the two had been talking.

"Come on, I'll give you a hand. Aeron's still in a bad mood, and he'll have a go at you if he finds this is the best you've done." The lash Elite took hold of the bird Hone was holding, looking at it critically before setting to with her claws and stripping it of its feathers. When she had finished she gave it back to Hone, turning to look at Lutis with a half-smile on her face.

"Come and eat with the rest of us. Just because Aeron's suddenly holding a vendetta against you doesn't mean the rest of us dislike your company."

"Are you sure?" he asked, warily meeting the dragon's eyes.

"Of course! And I don't know why he's tied you up like this, it's very unfriendly." Neby stepped over to his side, angling the blade on her tail before slicing through the ropes and cutting him loose. "Come on."

Lutis pushed the broken ropes off him, climbing to his feet and rubbing at his stiff arms. Being trussed up for so many hours had left his broken arm particularly sore. "You trust me?"

"Just as much as I did before," said Neby and turned to Hone, who had been skulking at the edge of the conversation. "I'll talk to Aeron. Now, come on!" She took a skip forwards, beckoning to the two. "You'll miss out on lunch if you're not quick!"

Hone grinned in delight, bouncing around Lutis before tugging him along to where the others had set up a little fire under the tree, the damp wood they had collected billowing black smoke. She dumped the plucked bird by the edge of the fire before they settled down together with a pile of fruits. Aeron was nowhere to be seen and Lutis guessed that Neby was trying to convince him to let him have some freedom, but he still received a pair of dirty looks from Emi and Echai, who were also sitting together eating. She had started to depend heavily on the dragon now he knew what had happened in Quinsilla, and the two were rarely far apart.

When the two dragons returned Neby looked supreme- she had managed to convince her partner after all. They didn't stay under the tree for much longer, Aeron announcing they were going to walk a bit further before it got dark. "Less ground to cover tomorrow that way," he said. The fire had dropped to a weak smoulder, giving out little heat, and there was no other benefit to staying under the tree- the ground underneath it was now as waterlogged as everywhere else.

The dragons swapped which humans they were carrying for the next leg of their journey, Deltan taking pity on Lutis having to walk twice as far as everyone else and offering his ride. As the daylight began to fade they made their next camp. The rain had slackened off a little but the canopy above them had grown thinner, so they were still soaked to the skin when they turned in for the night. Hone wrapped herself around Lutis and folded her wings over them both, forming a purple-feathered tent.

The next day the weather had improved but the sky was still grey with clouds. Hone kept looking fearfully up at the sky, the gap between each look growing shorter and shorter until Lutis asked her what she was looking for.

"Echai said tha' turnips grew on top o' clouds. I don't want one t'fall on my head!" she said, checking the sky for the fiftieth time.

"What?" Lutis laughed, patting the dragon on her side. He was back to walking again. "Turnips don't grow on clouds! Turnips grow underground."

Hone huffed in derision. "They can't grow underground, there's not 'nough space. Where does t'ground gar tha' they grow into?"

"They do grow underground- remind me when we get to Plurith, I'll show you there. I'm sure they'll have turnip crops."

"if your still free when we get there," growled Aeron, who had been walking nearby and overheard their conversation. There was a silence.

"Well that put a damper on the conversation," said Merac from Hone's back, trying to laugh off the Elite's comment, but it was hollow. The dragon gave a sneeze.

"Are you getting a cold?" asked Lutis, trying to turn the conversation back to a more light-hearted subject.

"I don't think so," sniffed Hone. She was starting to sound snuffly and sneezed again. Lutis wasn't convinced by her optimism but kept quiet, the conversation lapsing into silence again.

The forest started to thin out, the trees becoming shorter and less varied, their branches no longer decorated with vines but brown and bare. The path thickened as the wild undergrowth diminished to a layer of tame ferns, although their leaves were still sharp ridged. It started to rain again, pattering unceasingly onto the ground, the sound only broken by the odd sneeze from Hone- they were getting increasingly more frequent as the time passed.

After another hour the forest in front of them started to lighten, its edge in sight. They sped up, hoping Plurith was close by as they came to the end of the rainforest.

A grassy plain stretched before them, bending around the rainforest to their right and out of view. A flock of long-legged white birds took to the air from a hidden spot as they stepped into the grass, their wings clattering as they beat at the air.

There was a dent in the long grasses where a thick river meandered slowly all the way to the sea in the west and the village of Bolarf on its edges.

Plurith lay on the other side of the flood plains, the complete opposite to the white buildings of Quinsilla. It was surrounded by high wooden barricades, designed to keep intruders at bay. Behind them hid the low dark buildings, only two guard towers raising their heads to watch over the land. To finally see the ugly wall of the village was a relief-only a short distance separated them now from the village and safety.

The travellers set off across the floodplain, watching their every step. The river split off into little distributaries all across the meadows, turning it into a series of little islands, rough meadow grass covering the deep-dug stream channels so it was hard to distinguish whether it was grass and ground below or a hidden dip. The only person the sight of the village wasn't a relief to was Lutis.

He walked between Aeron and Hone, his eyes firmly on the ground. The Elite kept shooting him dark looks and it felt like he was walking to the gallows and his death. A raindrop dripped from the tip of his ponytail down his back and he shivered. He could feel someone's eyes on his back and he turned to meet Emi's reproachful stare. Her eyes were haunted as she held her gaze for a moment then looked across at Echai, halting to let him catch up.

Lutis frowned, looking back to the village in front of them. Now it was closer he could see there were little flurries of action behind the gatehouse, the silhouettes of humans flitting through the grey of the rain. Shouts echoed across the floodplain towards them then the gate to the village swung slowly shut. Aeron breathed a sigh of frustration.

"Who do they think we are, an invadin' army or summat?" he snorted, pulling a face.

Lutis suddenly tripped down a hidden stream as he looked up, plunging wildly into the dragon. "Oops, crap, sorry." He tried to regain his balance, wobbling on the edge of another hidden dip. The meadow grass was slippery with rain and he slid into another stream, huffing at the indignity of it all.

"Well, maybe we are an invadin' army?" said Hone, giving a mock snarl, trying to show how fierce she could be. "We will triumph!" The dragon flared her head fans in excitement, taking a little hop and a jump into the air, then knocked off balance by the uneven ground she crashed to the floor, laughing.

"Uh Hone, that's not funny..." said Lutis. She laughed harder.

"Aye Hone, try an' refrain from the 'invadin' army' jokes for a while, ahreet? We do actually need t'get into Plurith, so it would 'elp if you weren't pretendin' y'were trying t'invade an' all." Aeron looked around at the rest of the group tailing behind and, wisely, came to a halt. "Come on, it's cold out 'ere. Maybe t'Plurithians'll have a nice dry inn or summat we can stay at for a couple o'days?"

The travellers came to a halt outside Plurith's main gate, huddling together in a cold wet group. The village gate was firmly shut, the tall spikes on top of it unwelcoming. Aeron took a look at the sorry band and, as nobody else looked up for representing the group, he stepped forwards, slapping the flat of his bladed tail sharply against the gate. It rung metallically against the wood.

"Canst come in?" he called, projecting his voice as much as he could.

"Why are there so many of you?" shouted back a hard voice, worn by years of guarding. Plurith had fought its way through many small skirmishes in the area and they weren't about the let their guard down for even such a meagre group of humans and dragons. For all the Plurithians knew, they could be raiders posing as refugees.

"We're a rescue party for those who escaped t'war in Quinsilla," Aeron called, his voice sincere. "The city has been overrun with raiders!" He flashed Lutis a haughty glance, the man trying to keep his relaxed demeanour under the dragon's penetrating gaze. "Will y'let us in?"

The sound of muffled voices drifted over the wall as the guard who had spoken discussed with others, then a strange beaked face appeared over the top of the wall. It was a dragon, her wings visible as she hovered in the air, her claws reaching for a grip on the top for the barricade. As she landed on the wall Hone regarded her with interest. Her scales were dark brown and shiny with rain, two-toned chocolate and white feathers running down the back of her neck and ending her tail in a tuft like a lion. Two pale curving horns twisted from the sides of her head under her ears and a stripe of white ran along her throat and belly. She tucked her big wings to her sides, hiding the pale undersides from view as she inspected them closely, her face impassive before she turned to look at whoever was inside the village and fluttered out of sight again.

"Djur think they're gaarn t'let us in?" Hone asked quietly, leaning over to whisper in Lutis' ear. He shrugged, waiting.

The gate finally creaked open, the dragon peering out at the group with a friendly expression.

Come on then, it's wet out, said a strange voice from nowhere. Hone looked all around for where it had come from, her face the picture of confusion. The voice gave a laugh. *It's me, Ink!*

"Who's Ink?" asked Hone aloud, following Aeron and Lutis inside the gatehouse and shaking the rain off her feathers.

I'm Ink. The new dragon stood inside the gatehouse too, her bizarre beaked mouth open in a smile. *Welcome to Plurith!*

Ink led them through Plurith towards the council hall at the heart of the village. The street they followed would have been pleasant in the sunshine, lines strung across its width for washing to be hung on and brightly coloured bunting decorating a corner where two other streets met. However, it was bleak in the rain, the low buildings stained dark brown with water and the cobblestones beneath their feet slicked with mud.

Now they were in the village spirits had suddenly lifted. The two young girls danced down the street, kicking and splashing in the puddles, and Merac and Deltan were walking arm in arm down the middle, laughing at their antics. There were two whose spirits had dampened though- Lutis' mood matched his bedraggled appearance and Hone was worried about him, despite the tempting desire to talk to Ink. The dragon was skirting along the edges of the buildings, shaking herself dry of rain every so often as a waterfall gushed from the eaves above onto the road below.

Where are you from? asked Ink in her strange mindspeak, waiting underneath the overhang of a building in the hope the rain might die down a bit. It didn't.

"Well I'm from t'Great Desert, but t'humans are from Quinsilla, an' Lutis is from Kaionar," said Hone, nudging at Ink's wing to try and make her move. The dragon flared it, showing the white feathers underneath.

Nice. I've been up to the Great Desert before once. Interesting treasures you get if you're lucky.

She poked her muzzle out into the rain, frowning in annoyance but stepping out anyway, the feathers along her neck flattening. *Who's Lutis?*

Hone pointed to Lutis, the man looking miserable stuck between Echai and Aeron. "He knows lots 'bout everythin'."

Ink gave a smile and a laugh, leading them at a trot to a set of double doors set in a wide, flat building the opposite side of the road. *This is the council hall.* She reared up on her back legs, pushing with her front against the door. It swung open easily and the black and white dragon dived hastily inside.

The council chamber was just one long room, a semicircular table at the opposite end to the doors and a ring of chairs behind it. A fire burned brightly in a grate halfway down and Ink headed immediately for it, leaving behind muddy prints on the wooden floorboards. Hone sneezed at the sudden warmth, leaving her own line of mud as she headed for the fire too.

"Is that you Ink?" called a voice from another room. It was followed by a crash and a string of stifled curses.

And some new humans, and… what sort of dragons did you say you were? replied Ink, projecting her speech to the person in the next room.

"Lash dragons," said Echai from the entranceway, pushing the heavy door shut.

"Oh, lash dragons. Guardians of the Great Desert," said the new voice, growing suddenly louder as the person moved out of the next room and into the council chamber. It was a gryphon, dark blue all over. His head was like an eagle's, a bright red beak open in a smile and long fluffy ears twitching with interest at the thought of new company. His back legs were like a lion's and covered with fur as his feathers ran out across his chest. His tail was like a lion's too, with a tuft at the end. And of course, as his breed determined, he had wings, big and curving from behind his shoulder blades, the feathers almost black at the tips. As he saw how many newcomers stood in the hall his burgundy eyes widened in surprise then he beckoned a wing, brushing one of his front claws on his chest feathers. They were stained green with paint- the crash had been his easel falling over as he tried to scrub paint off one corner where he hadn't wanted a certain colour. The gryphon was quite the artist, when he had time to spare. "Come in, you're all wet! I'm sorry, I haven't anything to eat or drink, but if it stops raining for a bit, we can go to *The Red Rock* and get something."

Hone sneezed again, lying down close by the fire and opening her closest wing wide to try and dry off a little. The others started into the room a bit further, most heading directly for the hearth too. The gryphon retreated into the next room and there were clattering sounds before he returned holding a pile of brightly coloured blankets in one of his front paws.

"Here, it must be atrocious outside. I haven't been out in two days," he said, dropping the blankets in a pile and shoving them towards the closest gathered.

Is that why there's no food? said Ink sardonically. The gryphon huffed.

"Thank you…" Aeron hovered for a name.

"Oh, of course, I haven't introduced myself. I am Ebon," he bustled, regally indicating himself with one wing and a smile. Hone couldn't hold back her giggle of laughter at his formalities.

Aeron started introducing himself and the others but Ebon cut him off before he was even halfway around. "Don't worry, I won't remember everyone's name anyway. Now, tell me, where have you all come from?"

The two wandered off into the next room while Aeron outlined the events of the past few days in the Great Desert and at Eden's Fall. The others arranged themselves close to the fire, sharing the blankets that Ebon had provided. Hone kept sneezing.

"I think you *have* got a cold," said Lutis glumly, squeezing his ponytail to dry it out. Hone sniffed, rubbing at the end of her snout with one paw. Her scarlet scales were pale.

"I've ne'er had a cold afore," she said, curling her tail around and over her nose. "I don't think I like it."

Lutis took pity and rubbed behind her ears, unwrapping the blanket from round his shoulders and tucking it over the dragon instead, pulling her wings away from her sides. Hone grumbled, trying to lay them flat again.

"Come on, you'll warm up better if your scales aren't all wet with those feathers," he said, stretching out her wings. They were still slick with rain.

"How djur humans stan' this cold?" huffed the dragon as Lutis started to rub feeling back into the ends of her wings. The man laughed.

"Ah, it's just because you're not used to it. If you want adventures, you'll have to stand up to harsher cold than this!" he said, tugging off his sodden fingerless gloves and lying them on the hearth of the fire. They steamed in the heat.

The windows of the chamber fogged up, making outside seem like a dark cloudy dream world. The warmth of the room lulled Lutis into a doze after he was finished warming Hone's wings, the low murmurs of the others like a lullaby in the background. He tugged one of the dragon's wings over him, making a tent like the night before. He hadn't had much sleep and now things were starting to catch up with him...

He had just dropped off to sleep, his head resting back against Hone's flank, when he felt something nudge his boot. He flicked it, hoping it would go away but there was another, firmer push this time. He gave a yawn and pushed the lash's wing off him, blinking in the firelight.

Emi sat at his feet, her face twisted with guilt.

"Why would you steal the ruby? Why?" Her words were soft and Lutis hardly caught them. "Why, why?" She gave a sniff, burying her head in her hands.

"I didn't steal your ruby," replied Lutis, trying to look innocent.

"You did!" The woman's voice was squeaky with tears. "And I... didn't do a thing... to stop you..." Her voice was cut off by another sob. Lutis gave a sigh and wriggled out from under Hone, wrapping an arm around Emi. She gave him a horrified look and scrabbled away from him, backing up until she hit the hearth. Lutis tried a sympathetic look but she had got to her feet and was heading for Echai, shooting a frightened look over her shoulder.

The look died from his face and he shuffled back next to Hone, pulling her wing back over himself again and tucking his legs up. He tried to go back to sleep but her words had made him feel guilty and he couldn't for a long time.

After an hour or so Aeron and Ebon re-emerged from the other room, the dragon looking determined.

"Time t'gar find someplace t'gar an' get some food," he announced, poking Hone awake. She gave a sneeze and sat up, blinking sleepily.

"Food?" she asked, pulling her wings back to her sides. Lutis stirred as the warmth from the cocoon she had made around him evaporated, dragging him back to the unpleasant present. "Come on Lutis, I'm hungry."

"Lutis is gaarn t'stay here for a bit Hone, we've got some things t'discuss. You gar on ahead though," said Aeron, pushing his apprentice with his nose to make her get up.

"Ink, can you stay too?" asked the gryphon.

Sure, is this business or fun? questioned Ink, untucking her wings from underneath her paws. The gryphon gave her a look that said, *bad question to ask.*

Alright, because it's you, said the dragon, rolling her eyes. *But you better let Terrowin out of prison early.*

"Deal," replied Ebon, nodding his head and speaking to the whole group. "The tavern is called *The Red Rock*. It's easy to find, just follow the road to the left all the way to the square. There is a sign outside with a dragon on it."

Aeron ordered Doan to make sure everyone got there in one piece then turned back to Ebon, waving Emi over with one of his wings and launching into a whispered conversation.

Lutis, who was still sitting on the floor, raised an eyebrow at their secrecy and slid closer to the fire, turning his back to it to try and dry out the rear of his coat. Something was up- something bad.

8
A TRIAL.

The chair scraped loudly as Lutis pulled it from behind the table, its legs squeaking on the floorboards.

"There, that's a good place for it," said Ebon. Lutis dragged it to a stop in the middle of the hall. The gryphon sat on a long chair behind the table opposite him, Ink, Emi, Aeron and Echai flanking him on one side.

Can we have cake? asked Ink, looking slightly put out that she had to be in the council chambers and not in the tavern with the others.

"We could if I had some," replied Ebon, looking slightly morose. "Remind me again another time."

When am I suppose to know when the next time is? said the black and white dragon, her innocent expression distilling the pointedness in her remark. The gryphon huffed.

"Look, if you're going to ask questions like that, you can make the cake." He licked his beak. "The last one you made was delicious."

Ink gave a cheeky smile, looking coy. *I got Gerty to make it.*

"I knew that it tasted too good for you to have made it!" exclaimed Ebon, ruffling his feathers in disapproval.

I'd like some more of that cake... Or strawberries... mused Ink, looking off into the distance as she started to daydream.

"Shall we start?" asked Echai.

"Fine. Aeron's told me what's happened in Quinsilla. I think you," he turned to Aeron, "Should take the survivors you rescued on to Racksom- they won't want to stay in a little place like Plurith. You can stay here for as long as you want though, I'm sure Gerty in the tavern will be happy to have you all." He gave a friendly smile and the dragon nodded.

He turned and looked straight at Lutis. "But now I'm interested in the Quinsillan ruby. Aeron tells me that Emi accused you of stealing it."

"I don't know why, because I haven't even seen the ruby, let alone stolen it," Lutis replied, keeping his voice measured.

"Hmm. Well, let's start with easy things. How did you end up in the Great Desert?" asked the gryphon, a smile on his face.

"I escaped from Quinsilla on my own- I was in the far south quarter when Quinsilla was invaded, so I managed to avoid the mercenaries for long enough to escape," said Lutis smoothly.

"Really, how interesting." Ebon nodded his head. "And Aeron tells me that another of your group- Fraiz, you might know him- said that he saw you in the city being pursued by a dragon. How did that happen?"

"It saw me, how else?" Lutis' face turned ugly at the memory of the black dragon. "Tried to fry me alive for its tea..."

"Hmm, and how come it saw you, and there were no mercenaries around too?"

"I thought that they had all left, so I made a break for it."

"Very well. How did you break your arm?" Ebon quickly changed topic.

"Um... Well... I..." Lutis faltered for a moment, confused by the sudden change of topic. "I fix things. I have a workshop- had a workshop- back in Quinsilla. Someone brought in a cart that needed fixing, the axel was broken at the back. Anyway, so I was fixing this cart and, of course, my little brother decides to come along and sit in the cart while I'm working on it- he didn't know there was no axel. The cart collapsed and I broke my arm. Bloody hurt too," he finished, looking down at his bandaged arm. The cloth was dirty from not being washed for a couple of days and streaked with mud from when he had fallen.

"Really." Ebon nodded slowly, his eyes flicking to Aeron. The lash Elite shuffled on his seat, not used to it, then spoke.

"I have a question. If y'broke it afore you 'scaped from Quinsilla, then why wherst it so badly bound when y'scaped? Merac had to bind it afresh, with new splints too. Why hadn't y'splinted it afore?"

"Because when your only way of living is fixing things, money is infrequent. I didn't have the gold to go to a healer in Quinsilla, they're really expensive, you know?" said Lutis, his fingers running unconsciously over the fabric of his bandage.

"What about the payment for fixing the cart?" Echai butted in. Next to him, Emi gave a sigh of frustration.

"I was getting paid after I had fixed it," replied Lutis.

"How old is your brother?" Ebon took back control of the conversation with a new question.

"He's eleven, just at that sort of age, you know?"

"And how old are you?"

"Twenty four."

"Hmm." Ebon tapped his beak with one wingtip, pondering all that Lutis had said. He turned to Aeron. "You're right. Lutis is lying."

"What?" exclaimed the man, leaning forwards in the chair where he was sitting. "How can you say that?"

"Your story all seemed very plausible, except from just one small thing. You don't have to pay to see a healer in Quinsilla. In all cities, healers offer their services free, because they are paid by the ruling body in that city." The gryphon saw Lutis open his mouth to interject, but he continued, "Don't try and tell me I'm wrong, I've been to Quinsilla myself many times before, and it's been like that for many years. And if you had a brother (which I highly doubt) I would have thought that considering the city just got invaded by rebels, you would have been a little more concerned for his fate, annoyance to you or not."

Lutis slumped back into the chair, a frown on his face. He stayed silent but he was inwardly cursing his stupidity. There had never been a system like that in Kaionar... and of course, he should have thought of that other little loophole. Damn it.

"Now we need to find out what's true and what's not," decided Ebon. He turned to Ink, who had been sitting quietly, her face looking more and more surprised with every turn. "Ink, could you go and see if the mage is available please?"

The dragon nodded hastily, looking at Lutis with wide eyes before jumping off her seat. *I'll be back sooner that you can say!* She swept towards the door, grimacing at the weather but taking off at a run down the street anyway.

"Hmm, some cake would be quite good now," said Ebon, preening nonchalantly at his feathers with his beak. "By the way, how did you get that black eye?"

Lutis sunk deep into the chair, flashing dark looks at the two lash Elites. His eyes met Emi's and her mouth widened into a vengeful smile. "Emi punched me," he muttered, unamused.

"Ouch."

Ink returned shortly, followed by a man wearing dark red robes that trailed all the way down to the floor. As he entered the council hall he pushed his hood back from his face, revealing short black hair. He looked disgruntled at being disturbed, folding his arms in irritation.

"What is this about?" he asked, directing his question at Ebon. The gryphon looked up at his entrance, ruffling his feathers back into place.

"Ah, hello Sepi. We have just had a very interesting meeting following the arrival of a large group from Quinsilla. This young man here-" he pointed towards Lutis, who looked away, "has just told us some very interesting stories about escaping the city, however I fear that he is not telling the truth, as does Aeron here, a lash Elite who escorted the group from Quinsilla."

"So you want me to read his mind?" The man was straight to the point.

"Precisely."

Lutis looked up, sudden fear showing on his face. "Wait a minute, what do you mean, read my mind?"

"Well, Lutis, if you won't tell us the truth, then we shall have to get it out of you another way. Sepi, if you please?" Ebon sounded saddened, tipping his head.

The mage stepped forwards, pushing the cuffs of his sleeves back from his hands. "Stand up please," he asked, looking down at Lutis in the chair.

"Why would I co-operatate?" said Lutis, still trying to get out of having his mind read.

"Because if you don't, I shall have to force you to. Stand up please." The mage sounded annoyed.

Lutis remained sitting, his face twisting into an ugly scowl.

"Very well then, I *shall* have to use force." Holding his hand open, the mage seemed to beckon Lutis. He didn't respond but immediately felt himself rising from the chair, despite not wanting to. It was as if a giant hand had taken hold of him and was lifting him from where he sat.

"There. Now, this will not hurt, but it might feel a little strange." The mage moved his hands to either side of Lutis' head and closed his eyes. Lutis immediately felt something odd, a bit like a headache. He shut his eyes too, not enjoying the sensation. Memories of the past week flickered in front of his eyes: running through the rainforest with Aeron, Doan and Hone on his tail; being hit by Emi;

fixing his wings with Hone; having his arm bandaged; collapsing in the desert- the memories flicked past as the mage discarded them one by one. Then he was being chased by the dragon. Xaoc. The name flickered in his mind. Then he was running down the stairs of the Jewel Tower, talking to Zartear, almost being killed by the two mercenaries who had spotted him. He shuddered involuntarily. The mage went further back into his memories: escaping the Jewel Tower for the first time; stealing the ruby. Sepi took particular interest in that memory and Lutis fought against him to try and hide it but it was no use. He had no experience of magic and there was nothing he could do, nothing in the slightest.

The mage replayed the memory again, watching him steal the ruby over and over until it drove Lutis mad. Then, as if he wanted to spite Lutis he re-watched the memory of him escaping Xaoc. He could feel his feet pounding on the staircase, then he slipped...

Lutis' eyes flashed open, a cry breaking from his lips. He pushed the mage away from him with both hands, making the other man stagger. Pain lanced up his arm, this time real, searing up the whole of his arm and shoulder. He gasped, his sight dulling and black spots dancing before his eyes.

He staggered backwards, pain flashing up his arm with every heavy step. The spots in front of his eyes grew in size, linking together like ink spreading over a carpet. There was a roaring in his ears, loud like a roaring dragon, then he fainted into oblivion.

Ebon leapt over the table as Lutis staggered backwards, catching Sepi carefully with his paws as he stumbled too. The mage shook his head, looking dazed. Ink had jumped over the table too and was crouching beside Lutis, fanning him with one wing.

He's fainted, she said, nudging him with her nose.

Sepi leant against Ebon, getting his balance. "I'm...I'm okay. I think I may have pushed him too far, he has never been exposed to magic before."

"Did you get what you need?" asked Ebon, looking across at Aeron. The lash Elite hadn't moved and looked shocked at the turn of events. He shook his head suddenly and padded around the table to where Lutis lay, crouching by his head.

"Yes, I have enough." Sepi said, sitting down in the chair Lutis had previously occupied. Ebon nodded and paced back to his side of the table, his tail swishing in interest. He banged a claw on the table, catching everyone's attention.

I think he's waking up, said Ink, stepping away from Lutis as he groaned.

"Good. Can you prop him against the chair?" asked Ebon. Ink took hold of one of Lutis' upper arms, tugging him upright against the side of the chair. He groaned again, opening his eyes and blinking blearily through his black eye. "Are you listening?"

"Ugh, my head..." he mumbled, covering it with his arms. It felt like he'd been up all night drinking and now it was the next morning's hangover. His head pounded.

"Well. I have discovered some interesting things about this man," said the mage, starting despite Lutis' evident disrepair. "First of all, his name is *Errol* Passal. He is a thief. But that is the least of his crimes. If I have divined correctly- and I expect I have, for I watched his memories more than once, and that is why is he is in this state now- then he is not just a thief, but a traitor to this land." He cast a scathing glance downwards, tugging his robes away from Lutis.

"What do you mean?" Ebon's voice cut through the others' exclamations of surprise and horror.

"This thief, it seems, was the downfall of Quinsilla. A man named Zartear ordered him to enter the city and steal the ruby that was held in the Jewel Tower, which he did. He then proceeded to escape, during which he broke his arm, and Zartear invaded with an army of mercenaries. When the thief re-entered the city to claim his reward Zartear betrayed him and sent the dragon he had summoned from the jewel- a tribal battle blood dragon that goes by the name of Xaoc- after him. He escaped again but collapsed in the Great Desert; that's when you found him." The mage gestured to Aeron and Echai as he finished, then placed his fingers together in a pyramid.

"Hmm." Ebon's face was grave as he looked at Lutis. The man had looked up as Sepi outlined his past but now his head sunk back down onto his chest, his fight gone. "I think the best thing to do is take Lutis to Racksom. This is much bigger than I ever imagined." The gryphon's words were frank. "I can't be the one to deal with a problem like this. Until then, he needs to be kept under watch. Ink, fetch some guards to escort him to the prison."

Lutis had kept still as Ebon outlined his fate but at the mention of prison he suddenly leapt to his feet, making a desperate run for the door. The mage gave a heavy sigh, flicking a hand idly in the air and Lutis suddenly found himself upside down, suspended in midair by his ankles.

"Please, don't think you can escape," said Sepi cynically, rolling his eyes and not even turning to look at his catch. Lutis floundered, his coat flapping around his face. He swore violently from within its folds, trying to reach for his ankles.

Ebon watched him sadly then turned away towards the little adjacent room to the council hall. "Thank you Sepi."

 "Wait a minute…" Aeron took a step after the gryphon, suddenly concerned. "Are y'sure 'bout this?"

"Are you doubting my magical ability, dragon?" asked the mage, annoyance flickering across his face. "I assure you, everything I have said is true."

Guilt worked its way onto Aeron's face, and the lash Elite looked down, wracked. What had he done?

9
INK AND TERROWIN. IMPRISONED.

The Red Rock was the only tavern in Plurith
and attracted a lot of trade whatever the weather.
With the miserable never-ending rain it was packed
full with customers and the growl of many voices
could be heard from the street.

Doan found the tavern easily enough, pushing open the unusually large door with both his front paws and waving the others over the threshold with a wing. They attracted attention as they filed in, a few customers shuffling closer together to make room for the newcomers.

"Are yeh new in town?" called a young woman from over the bar, resting her arms on the countertop. Her copper hair was tied back in a messy ponytail and her skin was speckled with freckles all over. She had a friendly smile on her face, and not just because of the extra custom.

"Yes... we spoke to the gryphon in the council hall... he said to come here?" ventured Doan, stepping further into the tavern. It was big and roomy, the roof twice as high as a normal building and would easily fit a dragon much bigger than a lash Elite.

"Ebon? I don't suppose he offered anything to drink or eat, did he?" The woman shook her head in disbelief and started rustling behind the counter. "Sit down, I'll get yeh all something to eat. Make yehselves comfortable!"

Doan turned to the others, shrugging. "What she said, I suppose." He headed for a long table near the fire that had been thoughtfully cleared, the others following. Hone went straight for the fire, lying down almost on the hearth and resting her head on the hot slates, her eyes slitted against the heat.

The rain battered at a slant against the window panes, streaming down them unendingly. The woman who had been behind the bar returned with plates piled high with steaming food, distracting Hone from worrying why the others hadn't found their way to the tavern yet.

The dragon didn't see Ink slip in the door half-way through her meal, or she would have cornered her to ask where the others were. The food on her plate was new and exciting and Hone had never eaten anything so strange- she was particularly interested in vegetables, although when she tried a carrot, it didn't agree with her.

Ink crept through the tavern stealthily, avoiding the bar and the travellers from Quinsilla. After the tension of the council hall, what she really wanted to do was hide in a dark place and eat strawberries. She knew there would be nowhere quiet to sit in the tavern on such a dull afternoon but there were definitely strawberries out in the back storeroom... she scanned the room to see if she was being watched then slipped behind the bar, padding nonchalantly into the store cupboard. Long shelves ran around three walls, boxes and cartons stacked perilously in lines. There were huge barrels of ale and mead lined underneath the shelves, each neatly labelled with a small slip of paper but Ink ignored them, her eyes ranging around the room until she caught sight of the box she wanted- a shallow tray of strawberries on a high shelf. She licked her lips and reared up on her back legs, reaching for the strawberries. The shelves wobbled as she leant against them.

Suddenly the shelf underneath her paw cracked as she lent on it, sending the stacked boxes on it tumbling to the floor with a crash. The dragon scrabbled for the tray before someone came to investigate. She caught it with one claw and strawberries tipped all over the floor. She looked up, her eyes wide with the fear of being caught, then raced after the strawberries rolling around, munching on them with relish.

"Ink! How could you?!" Her private feast was interrupted by Gerty the landlady's appalled exclamation. The woman grabbed hold of a nearby broom, brandishing it angrily at the dragon. "Out of my cupboard!"

Ink gave a squeal of mock fear and cheeky glee, scooped another strawberry into her mouth and dashed through the doorway, pursued by Gerty still waving her broom. She clattered into the bar, leaping over the counter and dashing across the floor. There was a cheer as Gerty waved the broom triumphantly at Ink, shaking her head and giving up on the mischievous dragon. Ink bounced onto the table where the lash dragons were, sticking her tongue out at the landlady.

"Ink?" Hone sounded surprised to the see the black and white dragon.

Hello again, said Ink, licking her beak clean of strawberry juice. There were plenty more back there, maybe she could sneak in and get the rest when Gerty's back was turned…

"Where's Lutis? An' Aeron… an' Echai an' Emi?" Hone was straight to her questions, taking a quick look around the room to see if she had missed them entering. After all, Ink had been sneaky enough for her to miss her…

Ink looked out the window, avoiding Hone's intense gaze. The end of the day was drawing close and the sky was starting to darken, despite it being the summer months. She looked back at the lash dragon, her words dragging. *Lutis kind of got thrown in prison...*

"What?" Hone's eyes widened.

He's um... in prison... mumbled Ink, averting her eyes again.

"What? Wotcher mean Lutis is in prison?" Hone's face was a mask of disbelief.

Our mage read his mind, and he said that he was a thief... and a traitor... replied Ink, wishing she was somewhere else.

"No he's not, he's my friend!" she shrieked. She was starting to attract attention from the other customers. "He's done nothin' wrong!"

It came from his memories; Sepi's never got it wrong before. Ink tried to reason with Hone, but it seemed only to infuriate her further.

"But tha' was t'past!" she squawked, suddenly leaning forwards and narrowing her eyes. "Where are y'keepin' him?"

In the village jail, by the pond! squeaked the smaller dragon fearfully. She flicked a wing over her mouth to silence herself. *No, wait-*

Hone ran for the door, pulling it open with a paw and disappearing into the rain without another word. Ink shook her head slowly, watching the lash dragon go then slipped off the table, sitting between the two young girls who had escaped from Quinsilla. They giggled and started fussing with her feathers. Only a few hours ago everything was rosy bright, and now everything was falling to pieces all over the place.

The lash dragon ran through the streets of Plurith, splashing her way blindly through the puddles that speckled the road. She turned down street after street, frantically trying to find Lutis' prison. She ran past darkened houses, bright houses, past closed off shops until she was sure she was going in circles. She couldn't find a pond anywhere!

~

Lutis had hung from his ankles, furiously trying to free himself without success until a pair of guards had arrived at the council hall. He lashed out at one with his good hand but his swing fell short. The mage had sighed, muttered a few words underneath his breath and everything had gone black around the thief. The two guards had no more troubles with Lutis after that, clamping a pair of manacles around his wrists and tugging him out of the council chambers.

He tried to run as they led him down the streets to the prison but the mage had cast some spell on him that dropped a black fog across his eyes and he couldn't see a thing. The two shorter guards dragged him along unwillingly, his feet slipping on the mud underfoot. When they came to a halt he heard a clanking noise as one of the guards fitted a key into the lock of the prison and Lutis tried to make another break for freedom, getting his arms free, but almost as soon as he started into a run the ground disappeared underneath his feet and he found himself knee deep in pond water.

The guards laughed, catching him easily again. There was a rustling noise from inside the prison as the key turned in the lock, then a strange voice.

"Oi, are ye goin' tae let me out yet?"

"Not yet Terrowin," said one of Lutis' guards. "You have to stay in there for at least another couple of days, that's what the council decided."

"Aw comeon, Oi wasn't *that* drunk," protested the man inside.

Both guards laughed again. "You tried to kiss Ebon. If I were him, I'd make you stay in there for much longer!" The lock clicked a second time and the door swung open. "Anyway, we brought you some company."

The guards pushed Lutis through the doorway, shutting the door quickly behind him. The pitch black suddenly lifted from his eyes and although it was still dark inside the little prison he could just make out the shape of another man sitting on the floor.

"The mage said his name was Errol Passal." The shorter of the two guards said through the tiny grill in the door. "Have a good night boys!"

Lutis huffed, sliding down the wall to sit on the floor. "It's *Lutis* Passal actually."

The other man nodded slowly. "Oi'm Terrowin. Nice t'meet ye mate… Oi think… wot did they chuck ye in here fer then?"

"Oh, this and that," replied Lutis, skirting around the question. His wrists were still locked together with the manacles. "Hmm…" He thought for a moment then reached clumsily into a pocket, fumbling around before he pulled out a long lock pick. He tried reaching the lock with his fingers but it was at an awkward angle, so he took hold of it in his teeth and jiggled it in the lock, wriggling it with an expert's touch until it clicked open and released his wrists. The manacles dropped to the floor.

"That's better." He rubbed his bandaged arm, making the splint shift slightly. He frowned before he reached into his coat pocket and pulled out a stumpy candle and a match. He struck it and a little light flared into existence, lighting the tiny room.

"Wot happened to ye?" Terrowin exclaimed, his face lit by the flickering light of the candle. His wide teal eyes were framed by a shock of blond hair, dark stubble grazing his chin. He was wearing green, but it was a little marked by the mud that lay in a thin film over the bottom of the prison. "Did ye get into a fight with a dragon or somethin'?"

"You could say that…" replied Lutis, pulling a face. The man gave him a sympathetic smile. Although Lutis didn't normally trust people he met in jail (it wasn't his first time in one, sad to say) Terrowin had something… friendly about him, in a roguish way, that was instantly likeable. "Actually it was a couple of fights."

Terrowin gave an admiring whistle, leaning back against the wall. Lutis gave him a wry grin, shrugging his coat off and pulling up his sleeve to reveal his bandages.

"Ye really did get into a fight with a dragon, didn't ye…?" Terrowin sounded incredulous. He hadn't actually thought that Lutis was telling the *truth*.

"Yeah, I did. It's a long story," replied Lutis, tugging the knot that held the bandages around his arm out with his teeth and slowly unwinding them. He gave a sigh of relief as the last folds fell off and the splint clattered onto the floor, feeling a cool breeze blow over his skin.

Terrowin picked the splint up as it rolled against the tip of his boot and passed it back. "We've got all night. Unless those lock picks o' yours can open the door?"

"They might." He picked up the candle and held it close to the door, squinting. Lutis shook his head and put it down again. "No, there's no lock on the inside of the door, and the frame's too big to get something around it."

"Got anythin' else in ye pockets that might get us out o' here?" asked Terrowin hopefully.

"Only a string of firecrackers, but they'll do more damage to us than to this pit," shrugged the thief, pushing together a little pile of the straw on the floor and resting his arm on it as Terrowin gave a sigh. "Looks like we're stuck here for the night."

"Great. Why do ye have firecrackers in ye pocket?"

"Don't *you* keep firecrackers in your pocket?"

Terrowin laughed. "No!"

~

Hone ended up at one end of the village sniffing furiously as her nose ran, tears starting to prick at the corners of her eyes. She couldn't find the pond anywhere! Her wings drooped as she splashed her way through another puddle and around a corner. Plurith was like a maze, and the thing she was looking for was nowhere to be found- and it was still raining, so she was soaked through again. Cold raindrops slid down her muzzle and before she knew it, hot tears were following them.

Hone! Hone, you're going the wrong way. Ink had tracked the lash dragon after she had left *The Red Rock*, heading for the prison- the lash dragon was nowhere near it, so she had started to search the streets. *Look, if you're that desperate to find it, I can take you.*

Hone sniffed again, turning to face the black and white dragon, who had finally found her. "Really?" Her voice was squeaky.

Of course, come with me. It's not far. Ink gave a smile, patting the lash dragon with one wing as she caught up. *Don't cry.*

Hone gave another sniff, rubbing at her eyes with a paw and following Ink. She really had been close- they turned a few more corners and the street suddenly widened, snaking around a dark pond. The place was strangely calm, the surface of the water rippling with raindrops. Across the pond stood a small curved dome, the pale stone shining amongst the darkness. A lone human languished outside it, leaning against the rounded wall.

Here we are, said Ink, pointing to the dome with a claw. Hone sprung into a run around the pond.

"Lutis, Lutis?" As she got closer she saw there was a door, set into the stone, the only entrance.

The guard stepped forwards as Hone approached, his hand moving towards the hilt of his sword.

"Stop there!"

Hone kept running, a desperate look on her face. The man drew his sword, stepping forwards to deter her. She gave a shriek and leapt at him, bearing him to the ground. His head cracked against the stone of the path and he lay still. Ink gave a huff of dismay as she bounded off him and to the doorway, thrusting her head against the tiny grill set in the doorway.

"Lutis? Lutis are y'there?" Her voice was panicked. There was a shuffling noise inside.

Lutis jumped to his feet as he heard Hone's voice, peering through the grill of the door. The candle blew out, leaving Terrowin blinking in the sudden darkness.

"Who's that?"

"It's Hone!" said Lutis, pushing his fingers through the grill to stroke the dragon. They just grazed her nose.

"Lutis, whista they done wit' you?" asked Hone, pushing her nose closer. Ink had caught up with her and was sniffing at the guard.

You knocked him out Hone, she said, flicking his face with one claw. The man didn't move.

"They put me in prison?" A note of cynicism entered the thief's voice, his face twisting into an ugly frown.

"But...why?"

"They didn't tell you? I thought they'd be gloating all over town by now."

"Ink said that y'were a traitor an' a thief!"

"Is that what they're calling me?" He looked down at his feet, muttering under his breath. "Well, I suppose it fits well enough..."

"Wait, wait, wait, wot's this about a traitor? Was that Ink?" asked Terrowin, getting to his feet and trying to see out of the little grill too. Ink bounded to the door, pushing Hone out the way briefly.

Hi Ter! How's prison? The black and white dragon's voice was chirpy. Terrowin grimaced. Hone pushed her back out of view again.

"She's lying, righ'?" said Hone.

Lutis didn't answer.

"Righ'? Righ'?" Panic entered Hone's voice again, more tears creeping down her muzzle.

"You believe what you want to believe."

"Whista tha' supposed t'mean?" Hone's voice wavered.

"I'm saying that if you don't believe that I'm a thief, then believe that, but I don't think you'll find many other people with the same view as you."

"What djur *mean*?"

"I mean they're right!" Lutis shouted finally, his voice cracking at the end. "I'm sorry Hone." He turned away, rustling in his pocket for another match to light the candle.

"I don't believe you," she said, shaking her head slightly. "No, no, I don't believe you."

"Well that's your choice then." Lutis moved out of view and Terrowin quickly took his place.

"Hello lass. Hey, don't cry." He poked his fingers through the bars too, catching the tears that ran onto them. "It's not so bad in here."

That's the biggest lie you've ever told Ter, you moan for days every time you get chucked in there, said Ink from out of sight. Terrowin gave a huff.

Hone sniffed, rubbing at her tears. "When are they gaarn t'let you out?"

"Me?" asked Terrowin. "Guard said another couple o' days."

Actually, Ebon's going to let you out early.

"Oh good. Now?" said Terrowin.

Tomorrow morning he said, replied Ink. Terrowin looked slightly put out, but still pleased that it wasn't as long as he thought.

"Will they let Lutis out tomorrow mornin' too?" asked Hone, her eyes raking the little space around Terrowin to see where the man was. He obligingly moved out of the way.

"I don't think so," said Lutis bleakly from his dejected seat on the floor.

"If you're a thief, are y'gaarn t'scape? Y'must have 'scaped from places afore…" Hone sounded hopeful.

"No, there's no lock. I'm stuck here good." He rested his head in one hand.

"Will you try an' 'scape when they let Ter out?"

"I expect that mage'll come back so I can't. And there's nowhere I can go," replied Lutis. Terrowin shot him a sympathetic look.

"Sepi's a bloody monster, isn't he? Did he read ye mind?" asked the man.

"Yeah, that's how they came to the conclusion I'm a traitor. Gave me the worst headache too. He watched over me breaking my arm again and again. It's not something you want to happen more than once." As if it reminded him, Lutis picked up the bandages and splint again and started wrapping his arm back up. Hone sneezed. "Is it still raining?"

"A bit." She sniffed, looking up at the sky. The clouds raced along, clear patches revealing the glittering stars here and there. There was a damp feel to the air that clung to her scales.

"Your cold'll get worse. You should go back to the tavern."

"No, I'm gaarn stay out 'ere all night!" The lash dragon pushed her face back against the grate. Ink gave a sigh behind her. She couldn't just leave the other dragon on her own in such a state.

"No you're not. Go back to the tavern with Ink," Lutis said sternly, knowing that she wouldn't listen to him if he gave her any opportunity to protest.

"But you'll be lonely!" She tried a different tack.

"Ter here can keep me company."

Terrowin gave a smile, pushing Hone's nose away from the door with his fingers. "Yeah, don't ye worry lass, Oi'll look after ye mate."

"I don't wanna gar though… an' I screamed at Ink in the inn, t'others'll think I'm horrible."

"Well that was a well-to-do-action then wasn't it?" said Lutis sarcastically.

I don't mind that, said Ink.

"I wanted t'know where y'were." Hone sniffled, tears welling up in her eyes again.

"Hey, hey, don't cry." Lutis climbed to his feet again, leaning against the door. "It'll all work out eventually. Now, why don't you go curl up in front of the fire in the inn, and come and visit me again in the morning?"

Hone sniffed then nodded slowly. "Are y'sure you'll be ahreet?"

"Yeah, don't you worry about me, I've been in much worse scrapes than this before. I'll have to tell you about escaping that dragon in Quinsilla properly one day."

"Well I'll see you in t'morning then?"

"I'll be waiting."

Hone turned away from the grill of the window, nodding to herself before heading back to the inn. Ink poked her nose against the grill, speaking with Terrowin briefly before trotting after her. Lutis sat back down again, pulling his coat close around him. He took a puzzle box out of one pocket, fiddling with the shape. It was too cold to sleep and his fingers were starting to go numb as Terrowin sat down too and immediately asked about what dragon he had escaped from in Quinsilla.

"Lutis, are y'ahreet?" Hone had returned to the prison early the next morning, trekking through the puddles left from the rain the day before. Low-lying mist swirled through the streets, turning everything a shade of murky grey.

"Yeah, I'm all right." The thief had been fiddling with his puzzle, Terrowin having dropped off to sleep a couple of hours before, but now put it away and stood up to peer through the grill of the door. "How are you?"

"I caught a cold," sniffed the lash dragon. "But I brought you an' Ter some brekkist, look, bacon!" She pushed two packages through the bars, dropping them into his hands.

"Is it just bacon, or something else too-?" He unwrapped the package eagerly, the smell of hot bread and bacon wafting into the little domed room. "Ooh, that looks good." He sat down opposite the door, poking Terrowin awake and tucking into the food, chewing with obvious relish. "Thanks."

Terrowin gave a yawn, looking at the package in his lap in surprise before unwrapping it. "Mm, are these from Gerty?"

"Aye, she gave me extras f'brekkist so I thought y'might like 'em." Gerty had made extra rolls that morning, but she hadn't intended on them being eaten by Terrowin and Lutis. Hone wasn't going to admit she had *borrowed* the extras without asking though.

Terrowin gave Lutis a shove in the side with his elbow. "You made a good friend here mate!" He grinned at Hone. "Ye have very good taste."

Hone smiled back, biting one of her claws in modesty. "Is t'guard meant t'be sleepin'? 'Cause he's not djarn a geet good job if he ain't."

"If he wasn't sleeping, you probably wouldn't be talking to us, and we probably wouldn't be eating Gerty's finest bacon rolls," replied Lutis, taking another huge bite of the roll. "Talking t'prisoners isn't usually allowed y'know."

"Really? I dinae know tha'." Hone looked across at the guard, who was sitting up against the stone wall of the prison, his eyes closed. He had woken up after Hone had hit him with an almighty headache and had immediately decided to take a voluntary nap.

"He's right," said Terrowin. "Is Ink around today?"

"I think she was gaarn t'see Ebon t'get summat to get y'out o'here, then she was gaarn t'come down too," said Hone, sitting down by the door and curling up like a cat. She watched the mist drifting spectre-like over the black pond water, hiding the other bank from view. As the next couple of hours passed it lifted slightly, revealing the green reeds sticking out in explosive tufts along the pond's edges, here and there wrapped together by the webs of raft spiders that lurked low on the water and hunted the buzzing insects that laid their eggs in the thick mud. The sun peeked woefully through the fog, a pale cream ball that was nothing like the hot desert sun that Hone was used to. They talked idly, the door hardly forming a barrier to the three's conversation.

As the day wandered on to a more hospitable time than the early hour Hone had rose at there started to be a little activity, a few inhabitants of the village beginning to stir. Hone attracted odd glances-it wasn't unusual to see a dragon in Plurith, but one sitting by the prison was not an everyday occurrence.

A throng of chattering schoolchildren marching past in pairs after a fussing hobbit dragon made Hone look up to watch, her head fins fluttering in interest. They giggled and pointed, the lash dragon a novelty. Their talking jolted the sleeping guard from his slumber and he stretched, yawning widely before he saw Hone curled up nearby and leapt to his feet.

"What are you doing here?" he cried, fumbling at his sword.

"I'm talkin' t'Lutis an' Ter," Hone replied brightly, looking up at the fuming human. Inside the prison the two men looked at each other then jumped to their feet, peering out of the grill to try and see what was going on.

"She's not causin' any harm!" called Terrowin. "All we've been doin' is talkin' tae the lass."

"Well you can't be doing that, talking to prisoners is strictly forbidden," the guard reeled off automatically.

"Aw come on, she was only talking!" said Lutis. The guard shook his head.

"Sorry, rules are rules…" He shrugged, stepping forwards to pull the dragon to her feet. Hone frowned, curling her tail around her tighter like a belligerent child.

"I don't wanna gar!" she complained.

At that moment Ink swooped in from overhead, her feet dangling above the ground before she folded her wings neatly to her sides and landed.

Hello, how's everyone doing today? asked the dragon with a smile, pushing Hone out of the way so she could stand up on her back paws and peer into the prison. The guard gave a sigh of frustration.

"You're not supposed to be talking to the prisoners!" he repeated, crossing his arms. "Now you have to leave, before I make you!"

Ink gave a huff, rolling her eyes and turning to face the man. *Oh shush, I've got a note from Ebon that says we can talk to them all we like. And Terrowin's to be let out too.* She flared one of her wings, revealing a bag slung round her neck. *Check in here.*

The guard grumbled but did as Ink asked, fishing in the pocket and withdrawing a short cream roll of paper. He unrolled it and read it quickly, his eyes flicking over the page.

"Very well then. But nothing else, you hear?" He reached into his pocket and withdrew a thick key, stepping over to the door and pushing it into the lock. Hone shuffled out of the way, rubbing at her sore nose with the tip of one wing. The guard unlocked the door and let Terrowin out, shutting it quickly before Lutis tried to escape again. Then he went back to sulking against the side of the prison, muttering about "wilful dragons" and "that pushover gryphon".

Terrowin stretched, a grin on his face. "Thanks Ink." He reached up and ruffled Hone's head fans familiarly then sat down next to her, pulling Ink down next to him and taking the bag from around her neck.

"Aren't you gaarn t'gar an' do whatever y'do?" asked Hone, shifting so that she sat close by. He seemed just as friendly on the same side of the prison and, she noticed for the first time, wearing both a sword and a bow over his green shirt.

"Nope, ye look lonely on this side. Anyway, nobody needs my services," he said, hunting through the bag and pulling out two apples.

"Oi, I'm lonely on this side," called Lutis. "Fancy coming to keep me company again?"

Terrowin gave a laugh. "No thanks mate! Have an apple tae keep ye company instead." He gave one to Ink, who pushed it through the bars for the thief before settling down next to Terrowin again. He threw an arm around her, chewing on his apple.

"What 'services'?" asked Hone, looking at the man.

"Oh, monster huntin', demon slayin', that sort o' thing. Anything with a bit o' danger in it's my sort o' job- ye ain't livin' unless yer on the edge o' death, eh lass?"

Hone gave a smile. "Sounds like fun." She raised her voice so Lutis could hear better. "Hey Lutis, mayhap y'should take up demon slayin' too?"

"No thanks!" he replied quickly.

"So Ink, what's there to do today then?" asked Terrowin.

There's another council meeting this morning. I think Ebon was going to call together the whole council to decide what's going to happen to Lutis, she said.

"I wanna come," said Hone immediately, a determined look creeping onto her face.

I thought you might. Will Aeron let you go?

"I dunno. I'll jus' come anyways," she replied, stubborn as her patrol leader.

You should probably check with him. He seemed pretty annoyed yesterday when he found out you'd run off to find Lutis, said Ink, sounding particularly sober for a moment. Terrowin looked surprised at her seriousness.

"Ahreet, fine…" complied the lash dragon, climbing to her feet and clambering over Terrowin. "Lutis, I'll see y'later, and I'll have t'key!"

Lutis waved through the grill at her, a less-than-optimistic smile on his face. "Get Ter to show you some turnips!"

"Ahreet!" grinned back Hone, turning to the other man. "Lutis says turnips grow underground, but they don't, they grow on top o' clouds, don't they?"

Terrowin laughed, getting to his feet too and setting off down the street with the two dragons. "He's right, they do grow underground. Who gave ye the idea they grew on top o' clouds?"

The three wandered around the village looking for Aeron, Doan or Echai for a good while before giving up and conceding that that were nowhere to be found, heading straight for the council hall instead. Even from outside they could tell it was busy, the sound of voices drifting out of the half open door. Ink cut Hone off suddenly, stopping her in her tracks.

Hone, you know 'Lutis' isn't his real name, right? she asked hastily.

"What? 'Course Lutis is his real name. Why wouldn't it be 'is real name?" Hone sounded confused, turning her head to one side.

His real name's Errol, Errol Passal. He really is a thief, the mage never gets these things wrong.

Terrowin nodded. "He never does get stuff wrong, an' Lutis... Errol... had lock picks in his pocket- who carries lock picks?"

Hone shook her head, frowning. "No, Lutis is nice! Why wouldsta be called Errol, tha's a silly name!" And with that, she skirted round Ink and marched in the door.

Inside the council hall it was very busy, humans and dragons (and Ebon too) mingling around before the meeting began. She craned her head to see if she could see Aeron and was rewarded with a glimpse of his blue and green head. She started to shove her way through the crowd, wriggling between the gaps. Ink and Terrowin followed her, the two shooting each other worried looks.

Hone zipped through a last gap, appearing close to Aeron. Echai was there too but he was shorter than their patrol leader and didn't stand above the rest of the crowd. The Elites did a double take at the apprentice.

"Hone! What are you doing here?" exclaimed Echai, fluttering his head fans in surprise.

"I'm here t'be part of t'council. I don't think Lutis should be locked up in prison," she replied.

"Tha's none o'your concern." A frown started to crease Aeron's face at his apprentice's stubbornness.

"Lutis is my friend, it's not right f'him t'be locked up in tha' stone prison. Hasta see what they're keeping him in?" Hone's voice was indignant.

"No. Y'shouldn't be hangin' 'round at the prison anyway, it reflects badly on us lashes, an' Lutis is a traitor."

"I don't care. Since when were y'so interested in reputation anyways?"

"Hone!" Aeron raised his voice slightly, incensed. "Y'ain't t'talk to me in tha' way." The younger dragon pouted, anger starting to cloud her features. "Now, gar back to t'inn where the rest of the Elites are. You're t'join a work party this morning t'repay the residents of Plurith for housing us las' night."

"I don't wanna. I want t'stay here." Hone wrinkled her nose in annoyance.

"Tha' weren't a request, tha' was an order. Now gar!" Aeron pointed a claw towards the door, silencing her protestations with a stern look.

Hone turned on the spot, swishing her tail in anger. "Fine. But y'were never mean like this in t'desert." She exited the chamber haughtily, huffing at Terrowin in annoyance as she passed him.

Aeron sighed. "It's for her own good."

"Mm, well that was sort of harsh…" shrugged Echai. "Can't do anything about it now…" He turned to the curved table at the far end of the hall as Ebon banged a paw on it to call for silence and start the meeting.

Hone stalked angrily through the village, splashing through all the puddles that were in her path, irritated enough not to divert around them. The cold mist swished around her, chilly on her scales. She sneezed once violently, and then again. It wasn't fair that she wouldn't be given a say on what happened! Where was the democracy?

She made her way towards the tavern, not knowing any better place to go. It was warm there, with company too, but she was still angry. As she swept through the door she sneezed again, the warm air making her nose tickle.

"Looks like yeh might be getting a cold Hone!" called Gerty from the bar. Hone ignored her, slumping down by the fire.

"Hey, what's up dragon?" She heard the sound of footsteps behind her then Gerty laid a warm hand on her shoulder.

"They won't let me into t'council meetin'," grumbled Hone, shooting the landlady a grumpy sideways look.

"Ah, well yeh'll find it boring anyway. Don't yeh worry, yeh'll find out soon enough what they discuss. Ink's as big a tattletale as they get." The woman bent down beside the lash dragon. "My, you're all damp and chilly-like!"

Hone sneezed. "I caught a cold."

"Well no wonder, walking through the rain for two days, and sitting out in it all morning too! I know you were up early with that thief this morning, yeh stole the extra bacon rolls." The woman nodded decisively then bustled off to the bar. "I'll get yeh something hot, an' we'll stoke up the fire. Yeh'll feel much better tonight."

"Thank you," said Hone, sniffing as her cold grew. Gerty brought her a hot, spicy drink a little while later which helped, warming her insides, but she still didn't feel... right. Not well enough to go out back into the mist and sit with Lutis, even though she felt guilty about not doing so. Instead she stayed inside and listened to Gerty's gentle banter with her customers, adding the odd injection every so often. Now and then she gave an explosive sneeze.

After a couple of hours Aeron and Echai returned to the tavern talking animatedly between themselves. When Aeron saw Hone by the fire a look of surprise crossed his face.

"Hone! Wotcher doin' here? I thought y'were gaarn out with t'work parties?"

"I got a cold," said the apprentice stuffily, rubbing at her nose.

"Hone's been helping me in here," called Gerty, leaning over the bar top to hail the two dragons. "She's been keeping a good eye out on the fire, makin' sure it don't get too low, an' she's been tastin' some of me finest cold syrup. How's it taste Hone?"

"Geet nice, thank you," replied Hone, taking another sip from her tankard. Its spicy aroma did seem to lift the heaviness from her face, she had to admit.

"Well… good t'see y'making yourself useful then." Aeron seemed to dither before turning and heading for the door, perhaps to see where the rest of the lash Elites had got to. "Oh, Hone, we'll be leavin' in mayhap a week's time, so try an' get rid o' tha' cold by then."

"Will Lutis be comin' with us?" she asked hopefully.

"Aye. We'll be takin' 'im t'the big prison in Racksom. Cannae keep him safely in t'little prison here f'ever," he replied as he pulled the door open, disappearing into the mist.

A wide smile crept across Hone's face and she leapt to her feet.

"Eh eh eh, where do yeh think yeh going?" asked Gerty, blocking her path as the dragon headed for the door.

"I'm gaarn t'tell Lutis he's comin' with us!" crowed Hone, flickering her head fans in excitement.

"Oh no yeh're not, young lash dragon. Yeh're going to stay right here for the rest of the day, and not visit that thief once. If yeh're leaving soon, then yeh have to get rid of that cold sooner!" She waved the spoon she held vigorously, shooing her back towards the fire. Hone protested but a raucous sneeze interrupted her. Her eyes watered as she rubbed her muzzle with one wing, Gerty taking a firm hold of one paw and leading her back to the fireside.

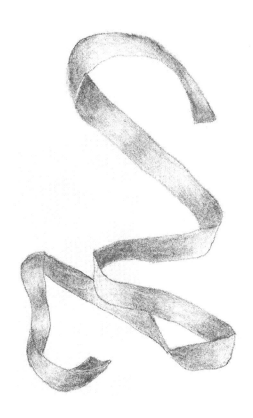

10
THE TRAINING GROUND. A RIBBON.

There was a loud crash and tinkle of glass as a jar fell out of the cupboard Nox had just opened, shattering and spilling porridge oats all over the floor. She swore and hopped up onto the countertop, shuffling along it till she was out of range of all the glass. A shard in her foot was the last thing she needed right now. She jumped back down again, pulling her boots on before searching for a broom.

"What was that?" asked Static, yawning as she wandered out of the bedroom. Her hair was tussled in knots and she dragged her fingers through them, getting them tangled. Some days she just wanted to cut it short and not have to deal with those sort of problems on top of everything else.

"I dropped a jar," said Nox, starting to clear up.

"What did it have in it?"

"Porridge."

"Ugh, good thing you did. Tastes of nothing," said Static, hunting down her boots and pulling them on before giving Nox a hand. "Did you find anything else for breakfast?"

"That was the first cupboard I checked."

They worked in silence until the floor was clean again, sweeping the mess into a box they found. Static started to raid the cupboards, pulling out everything that looked edible and heaping it on the sides. A fair pile of stores quickly built up- it was obvious the house had been lived in shortly before they had claimed it after invading Quinsilla.

As they tucked into almost-fresh fruit and half a loaf of bread at the table they heard loud noises outside, shouting and bangs.

"More escaped prisoners I suppose," said Nox, not even bothering to look out the window. It was becoming an all-too frequent occurrence.

"Mm," agreed Static, rolling an apple around on the table. "Look, about last night... sorry I just dumped all that on you."

Nox waved a hand. "Don't worry about it. Can't have my only ally falling to bits on me now eh?"

"I'm not falling to bits!" said Static indignantly, her eyes flashing with anger. Then she sighed. "Okay, I am a bit... you consider me an ally?"

"Sure, you're the first person that's not tried to take advantage of me, or tried to kill me," Nox replied, withholding a hidden smile. That had a kind of irony about it...

"Huh, well I can see how that makes me an ally then." She leant back in her chair and took a bite of the apple. "So, what were you thinking of doing today? Got anything to do, or are you at a loose end too?"

Nox thought for a moment- she should really report to Zartear, but she really didn't feel like it, and he hadn't given her any duties for a few days- he had been saving them all for Xaoc, a fact that brought a bitter taste to her mouth. Although she might be able to glean some information off him if she went to report- something like *when they would be getting out of blasted Quinsilla*. "Just one thing, I gotta report to Zartear and see if he's got any missions lined up for me."

"Great. Well, I won't be coming with you, that deputy of his has got it in for me," said Static. "I'll meet you just outside Quinsilla to the south- there's a training ground set up there, I'm going to get some sword practise in. If you want some armour, they'll probably have some that fits you there, there's a couple of armourers stationed nearby." She got to her feet, heading for the bedroom again to get her own armour.

"Okay, hopefully he won't have anything too major planned," replied Nox, standing too. She had picked up her sword when she had got up, and now buckled it to her belt before heading for the door.

She walked briskly towards the centre of Quinsilla, knowing that she would find Zartear either at the Jewel Tower or the city hall, which he had styled as his royal palace. The streets were a little busier than the day before, chained slaves working in regimental rows to strip the city of its finery and prepare for war. She hurriedly morphed back into her normal form when she started to get suspicious looks from the mercenaries that she passed, tipping her chin challengingly for a fight.

She tried the Jewel Tower first but, contrary to her expectations, he wasn't lording it over the rest of the city in the room at the top. The tower looked bleak and abandoned, its formerly splendid white marble blackened with soot at its head and feet from Xaoc's fiery rage. Nox kicked a piece of carved stone that had fallen off the building in frustration, sending it spinning across the street with a clatter.

Her ire grew as she headed for the city hall, a headache from the night before throbbing behind her eyes. The growing heat of the sun did nothing to brighten her mood and once again she found herself longing for the cool shade of the trees where she had grown up.

The city hall was not an unassuming building, made of the same regal stone as the rest of Quinsilla, but it was overshadowed completely by Xaoc sitting outside, haughtily watching the few that dared to walk past. As Nox slipped out from a side street his face stretched into a predatory smile and he ran his tongue across his teeth.

"What have we here then, a little kitty who's lost her way?" he hissed, eyes glinting.

"Get lost Xaoc, I'm here to see Zartear," said Nox brusquely, stalking past him and starting up the steps to the building. He swished his tail in her path, pulling her to a halt.

"Oh really. What if he doesn't want to see you? You've not been making yourself very useful over the past few days." His eyes glinted maliciously. "Zartear doesn't need you any more."

Nox folded her arms, trying to keep calm despite the dragon's taunting words. "I hardly think *you're* useful for anything more than being a large guard dog."

Xaoc gave a growling laugh at that, tossing his head up into the air. "Is that the best you can do?"

"Get out of my way," snapped back Nox, laying a hand on Xaoc's tail and vaulting neatly over. The dragon flicked his tail at the touch, trying to throw her off balance, but she had as much poise as a cat and landed without more than a small wobble. "Nice chat."

The dragon laughed she made her way up the rest of the steps and into the building, his scorn echoing around the pillars. She sucked in a breath and turned towards the main chamber of the building, knowing Zartear would be in the room that seemed to hold most power.

He was sitting at a desk, maps and charts covering its every inch. Zartear leaned back in his chair, feet on the table as he read a torn scroll, his grey eyes skating over the page. When Nox entered, closing the door behind her with a quiet click, he looked up, a small frown on his face- he had instructed Xaoc that he was not to be disturbed. He looked back down at the paper, going back to reading.

Nox strode over to the desk, her eyes flicking momentarily across its contents. She didn't recognise the area the largest map showed, obviously a city, but the label was covered by an open book and she didn't dare move it. At Zartear's steadfastly ignoring of her she folded her arms, resting on one leg.

"Orders?" she prompted after a moment.

Zartear finished the sentence he was reading, making her wait until he was ready to speak, but even then it wasn't what she wanted to hear.

"I told Xaoc that he wasn't to let anyone in. That included you." His voice was cold and emotionless.

"Well, looks like the dragon failed then," replied Nox, meeting his stare. He took his feet off the desk and leaned forwards, rolling up the scroll so she couldn't see its contents. "Do you have any orders?" she prompted again.

"I would have, had you been useful and around. As it is, Xaoc has carried them all out." He could see the infuriation in the Felixis' eyes at the dragon's victory.

"I was collecting an important ally," said Nox, curling her fingers into fists in irritation.

"Important for you or for me?" replied Zartear.

Nox looked away, tapping the desk with one finger to change the subject. "Does this mean we're heading out of this hellhole?"

"You would know if you had been around." An edge of annoyance crept into his voice this time and he picked up another map, spreading it over the books. "Next time don't think you'll be so fortunate to live through Xaoc if you don't make yourself useful. Get out of my sight."

Nox turned on her heel, heading for the door without another retort. The new map had told her one thing- there were two lines drawn on, one to Racksom, another from Racksom to Tarz. That would have to be information enough for now.

Xaoc smirked as she stormed out of the building again, inspecting the slaves working down the street for which looked the tastiest. "He was pleased with you then."

"Damn you, dragon," spat Nox as she passed him, looking down the street to see how crowded it was. It was relatively clear and she would have a fast path all the way to the training ground that Static had suggested.

"Touchy." He leered, dismissing her in much the way Zartear had. She ground down her rage within her, saving it to beat out on some opponents later, morphing back into the avian's form as she stalked away.

Static was cantering her horse in complex patterns when Nox finally arrived at the training ground, her anger at Xaoc and Zartear little abated. The woman pulled up nearby, her stallion snorting and pawing at the ground. He shook his mane, trying to back away from Nox but Static held him in place with a firm hand.

"Stay *still* Tamarisk." She looked at Nox, frowning. "He doesn't seem to like you very much."

Nox shrugged, crossing her arms and steadfastly ignoring the horse. "They never do. Bit ostentatious, isn't he?"

Static gave a small smile at that. The spotted horse certainly wasn't the normal war horse that most other mercenaries rode. "Got any interesting news?"

"A bit. Are there any more horses around? Looks like I'll be needing some riding practise."

Static pointed to one end of the ground where a line of horses were tied to a fence, tacked up and ready to be ridden. "You going somewhere then?"

Nox didn't answer, heading for the horses with a determined look on her face. She never got on well with the beasts and she really didn't fancy getting thrown off after her earlier humiliation. She picked a steady looking mare, her chestnut coat shiny with health and rode back, fighting already with the normally-docile beast. Static gave her a look that said, *is that really a good idea?*

"What's the news then?" asked the sorceress, steering Tamarisk close as they headed for an open space. Nox gave a growl, twisting the reins between her fingers.

"No orders, his *ever-so-helpful* dragon's carried them all out."

"That's a good thing, more time for drinking and training," said Static.

"Hardly, he'll send the dragon after me if he thinks I'm a loose end." She tapped the side of her head. "Too much information."

Static nodded, understanding. "What's the latest news then?"

"Looks like we're heading for Racksom, then possibly Tarz," replied Nox before her horse suddenly bolted, separating the two.

A little surprise showed on Static's face but she quickly erased it, pushing Tamarisk into a canter and catching up to where Nox had finally pulled the chestnut to a halt. "You *will* be needing practise on a horse then, it's a long walk to Tarz." She avoided the subject of Racksom, which was irrevocably linked with Armeno.

"Never been to either of them," replied Nox, frowning at the horse before nudging her gently with her feet into a walk. The mare complied, but her ears were still flattened back.

They rode for a short while until the mare started to buck and kick, her dislike of Nox suddenly worsening. Static grabbed at the horse's reins, dragging her to a halt for just long enough to let Nox dismount, the woman hastily stepping away. The chestnut eyed her wildly until she moved out of sight, hiding behind Static's stallion.

"That's enough riding for me today," declared Nox, climbing over the fence that surrounded the field they had been riding in and leaning on its edge. Static gave a smirk, trotting the two horses across to the gate and knotting their reins together.

"Tamarisk's all het up too, I'll let them cool off a bit," she said, sliding off his back and giving him a pat on the neck. His speckled fur was slick with sweat. "Up for a sword fight instead? Last opponent I fought was much too easy."

Nox gave a fierce grin, her hand slipping to the sword at her side. "Well I hope you're not too out of practise, I could use a worthy opponent."

Static pulled her own scimitar out of her scabbard, swishing it twice through the air as she stepped away from the horses and beckoning with one hand. "Come on then."

Nox vaulted back over the fence, tumbling over on the ground like a gymnast before leaping to her feet and drawing her sword in one lightning quick motion. She gave a laugh as the two blades met, parrying the attack that Static sent her way. She backed up a little as Static pressed forwards, not wanting the scimitar to catch her- Static was wearing armour, whereas she was not. She dived to one side as the woman jabbed with the blade, rolling on the ground again.

"What sort of tactic is that?" asked Static as her blade missed, whirling around to try and catch Nox, who had gone into a series of tumbles around her. Not only was the woman fast, she made a tiny target so close to the ground.

Nox gave another laugh as Static spun, suddenly exploding into a jump and cutting forwards with her blade. The end snagged on her cloak and there was a rustle, a long piece of fabric coming away with the blade. Static swung her blade around, parrying Nox's blade as it sliced through the air then froze, her eyes widening at the length of green that stuck between the two blades.

It fluttered frantically in the wind before it slipped free, twisting in a long fold through the air and landing on the ground in a mess. Static dropped her sword and fumbled for the fabric, which Nox now saw was a long green ribbon. Nox plucked it from her grasp, dangling it in front of the woman's face.

"What's this?"

"Give it to me!" Static straightened up and snatched it away, her brows drawn in a scowl. The frayed end ripped into tatters as she wrenched it through Nox's fingers and she gave a little gasp, her face falling from its angry glare into a look of anguish. "You're ripped it…"

"I didn't rip it, you pulled it out of my fingers!" said Nox, stepping back as a little green electricity curled through the front of Static's hair.

"What does it matter, it's only a ribbon- is it a luck charm?"

Static twisted the ribbon between her fingers, shooting Nox a venomous look before spinning away, picking up her scimitar and mounting Tamarisk without looking back. She kicked the stallion into a canter past Nox, jumping him over the far fence and disappearing down a lane that wound between the two fields. The Felixis watched her go, sliding her blade back into its sheath and taking hold of the mare's reins to follow. Static's sudden leaps from anger to upset were really starting to confuse her.

Static pushed Tamarisk furiously on until the horse was bathed in sweat and panting, foam dripping from his lips. She slowed their pace, dismounting and leading him along the track until it ran along the meanders of the river that flowed all the way from the mountains. The horse took a thirsty drink from its waters as she stopped and pulled off his saddle, letting him wander free while she sat on the bank, gathering her cloak around her in folds. She pulled off her gloves and ran the ribbon through her fingers, regarding its frayed ends sadly. It had once been the same colour as her cloak but now it was hardly a shadow of that former beauty, stained with mud and dirt from the months she had worn it on her cloak.

She tentatively tied it in a loose bow, smoothing out the edges so it was perfect, but even then it didn't look quite right. *Of course it'll never look right,* she thought, pulling out the bow and threading it through her fingers again. It would only look right on Armeno's wrist, like when she had first gotten it and given him it as a present.

"I shouldn't have this," she sighed to herself. Tamarisk whickered gently, wandering over and nudging at her hands for a treat. She pushed his nose away, tucking the ribbon away in her hand so he wasn't tempted to try and eat it. His strange markings would always stand out amongst other horses. Which led her to a problem- if the army headed for Racksom and fought against the city, and Armeno was still there (she hoped he had left, he had enough reason to), he would recognise her immediately. The elf wasn't one to shy away from protecting the city if he had to, and they were bound to meet. She buried her face in her arms, clutching the ribbon like it was her last lifeline- what was she going to do?

After a while the sun started to burn the back of her head and she pulled the hood of her cloak up, looking up at the river running slowly past. A kingfisher perched motionless on a branch overhanging the water and she watched it, its electric blue and orange shimmering in the sunlight. There was a noise along the lane behind her and it started, twittering in surprise and flying off down the river with a curious bouncing flight.

Static turned to see Nox riding along the track on the same horse from before. She had leaves stuck in her hair and it was obvious the mare had thrown her. She hurriedly tucked the ribbon inside her armour, tying it around one of the buckles so it wouldn't come loose, then stood, grabbing the chestnut's reins when Nox pulled it to a halt.

"What are you here for?" she asked, irritated that the woman had followed her all the way to the river.

Nox climbed down off the horse, brushing at one of her wings to try and get the green stain out of the feathers. "What's the big deal about the ribbon?"

Static scowled and threw the reins at Nox before turning away. "Nothing. Leave me alone." She stalked over to Tamarisk and started pulling knots out of his mane.

"There obviously is something, you don't react like that about a ribbon if there's nothing in it. What makes it more than a trinket?" Nox dropped the horse's reins and it scooted away from her, whickering unhappily.

"Damn it, why do you need to know?" cried Static, rounding suddenly on Nox and closing the gap between the two. "Get your nose out of the way I live. I don't ask about your past, so why do you need to know about mine?" she gave Nox a shove, sending the shorter woman reeling backwards.

"Because if it gets me killed because you're thinking about bloody *history* between you and some *elf*, then we shut this alliance off right here," retorted Nox, giving Static a similar push back. A tingle of electricity shot up her fingers at their touch and she had to resist the urge to wince.

Static's face went red with anger and it looked like she was about to draw her sword for real against Nox when she suddenly stopped and turned away, kicking at the grass underneath her feet. Nox watched her, breathing hard.

"I can't go to Racksom," she finally said, sounding worn. "I can't fight if he's there fighting for the other side. I just can't do it."

Nox waited for a moment, keeping her distance. "The ribbon?"

"A few days after we first met, we got attacked by a dragon. Same one that gives me nightmares. I thought he was going to die, then a sorcerer healed him. Apparently I went into shock and gave him this." She pulled the ribbon off her armour and waved it in the air. "I don't remember much of it."

"Why do you have it now then?" Nox kept her voice neutral.

"The last time we talked- well, it was more argued- I took it back. I was so angry, I didn't want him to have it... it was the only thing of mine he had. I shouldn't have, it was his." She finally turned around to face Nox, and the Felixis saw that the woman looked close to tears. "He asked me once for it, but I left... I can't see him again, he must hate me." Her fingers closed tight around the whole length of the ribbon, hiding it from view, and she buried her face in her hands.

Nox couldn't think of a single thing to say for moments after Static had finished, watching the sorceress in discomfort. When she had first met Static the woman seemed impenetrable and cold as steel, but in truth here she was falling to pieces over a ripped ribbon and a relationship that seemed just as battered.

"You really loved him, didn't you?" she asked tentatively, sitting down on the ground and pulling up a handful of grass.

Static looked up and nodded hesitantly, sliding into a miserable heap on the floor. She pulled her cloak close, going back to aimlessly passing the ribbon through her fingers again. "What do I do? If we attack Racksom, he *will* fight."

"He could have left?" suggested Nox, discarding her handful of grass and ripping up another.

"I can only hope," said Static, staring across the water towards Quinsilla in the distance. "Only hope."

11
TRAVELLING TO RACKSOM. A CLOSE ESCAPE. THE MASSING OF ARMIES.

The dull weather that had been hanging around for the past few days had finally cleared up, leaving Plurith looking clean and new. The sun was shining, the perfect companion for the group of humans and lash dragons that were about to head for Racksom.

"Will tha' come with us?" asked Hone, trying her best pleading look on Ink and Terrowin. They had come to see the group off at the southern gate.

"Sorry Hone, there's been reports o' a demon near Bolarf. We're heading up there tae see if we can do anythin' about it," said Terrowin, shrugging regretfully.

We'd come in an instant otherwise, added Ink, wrapping her wings around the lash dragon in a hug. The two dragons had instantly become the best of friends, and the black and white dragon was sad to see Hone leave. *Maybe you can drop back into Plurith on your way back to the Great Desert?*

"Aye, I'll convince Aeron t'do tha'!" said Hone, smiling at the thought of returning. She looked across at the Elite, who was talking to Ebon- the gryphon had come to see them off too. Behind him stood Lutis, flanked by two guards.

"Ye look after yeself lass. Make sure that cold doesn't come back," said Terrowin, patting the dragon. Gerty's medicine had done the trick and Hone's cold was no more than a bad memory. "'Ere,

Oi've got somethin' fer ye." He dug in his bag and produced a long root vegetable, handing it to Hone.

"A turnip! They grow underground!" crowed Hone, taking the turnip and grinning. Ink laughed at her obvious joy at knowing the fact.

"Hone, ready to go?" Doan wandered up to the three, not bothering to comment on the unusual present. The apprentice had been getting up to all sorts of strange things while they were in Plurith, and this wasn't the weirdest. "I think Aeron was planning to try and get to the near edge of Lake Racksom by tomorrow evening."

"Ahreet," said Hone, wrapping her wings around Terrowin and Ink in another hug before following the Elite. "Bye Ink, bye Ter!"

They waved as the group set off, turning back to the village as soon as they had disappeared into the edge of the forest. They too had a long way to go, and there was no reason to hang around in Plurith.

Instead of walking at the front of the group like she normally did, Hone hung back in the middle, slowly sidling closer to where Lutis was walking between Tekek and Echai. Although he had promised that he wouldn't try and escape (and Hone trusted his promise completely) he was still under close guard and his wrists were locked together, despite the fact his arm was still broken. Aeron hadn't said anything to Hone about not being allowed to talk to him, so she decided that she would keep him company on the journey. She kept quiet for a while until she was convinced Aeron hadn't noticed.

"Whista they say they're gaarn t'do w'you?" she asked, turning her head. Her ears flopped at strange angles as she looked at him.

"Hm?" Lutis had been daydreaming, and hadn't noticed the dragon sidle up until she spoke. "You mean when we get to Racksom?"

Hone nodded, glaring at Echai when he gave her a look that said, *stop talking to him*. The Elite turned away, huffing under his breath.

"Ebon said Racksom council would have a meeting and decide what would happen. I haven't got much say in it- well, no say in it at all. Gotta sit and see what they say!"

"Wotcher think they'll say?"

"No idea. They could say anything I suppo-"

"Hone! Come up front, I want t'talk t'you!" Lutis was cut off by Aeron, who had noticed the two were talking. Hone pulled a face and trotted off, bracing herself for the chiding that was sure to come.

Two days later the little group found themselves on the shore of Lake Racksom, not far from the city. They had made camp for the night on its edge and had a roaring fire going, banishing the shadows. The group sat around it, finishing the last remnants of their meal. Hone poked at the fire with the end of her tail, stirring the cinders with the flat of her blade. Lutis sat nearby, fiddling with the chain of his handcuffs.

"We'll be at Racksom tomorrow, I think," Aeron announced with a smile, breaking the comfortable silence that hung around.

"Whista Racksom like?" asked Hone to nobody in particular.

"It's not like anywhere else I've ever been," said Merac, leaning forward to look at the dragon. "The buildings are in the trees, connected by rope bridges all through the canopy."

"T'buildings are in t'trees?" questioned Hone, not really understanding the concept.

"They're hard to describe. You'll see when we get there," said Merac.

"Hasta e'er been t'Racksom, Lutis?" Hone turned to the thief, who looked up at the sound of his name. He had been keeping a low profile since Plurith.

"Me? Yeah, I've been once or twice."

"No doubt t'thieve off the locals," muttered Aeron darkly, shooting the human a black look.

"Why do you always assume I'm doing something wrong?" huffed Lutis, frowning in indignation at the Elite.

"'Cause you're a thief, an' that's your nature." A hint of malevolence crept into the lash Elite's voice. "But now justice'll, make sure y'get what's coming t'you."

There was an awkward silence for a moment. Tekek, not used to tension, gave a nervous gulp.

"Whista your favourite, grass or circles?" Hone broke the silence suddenly with a change in topic. It earned her strange looks from the humans, who weren't used to her questions.

"What?" said Merac, laughing.

"Whista your favourite, grass or circles?" She repeated, looking at her earnestly. She laughed again.

"Circles," piped up one of the small girls, earning her a jab in the side from her friend.

"Circles are t'best! They're so much fun!"

"I've never heard circles described as "fun" before," Lutis said ironically.

"Grass or circles then?" repeated the lash apprentice challengingly.

"I think I might have to say grass. I like the smell," he said.

"How dids'eh they invent soup?" Hone changed the topic again.

"How does that relate to grass *or* circles?" Lutis asked, a smile creeping across his face. The young lash dragon asked some very strange questions sometimes.

"I dunno, I jus' wanted t'know. Djur know?"

"Maybe they had lots of things cooking, but didn't have enough pans so they just tipped all the ingredients in together?"

"No, it mus' be a more interestin' reason than tha'…" reasoned Hone, tapping a claw on the ground. "Mayhap they were throwin' fruit from t'trees an' it all got squashed in a pot, then there wherst a fire an' it cooked… then they ate it?"

"Or maybe they dumped water and food in a bucket and put it over a fire, then forgot to get it out when the food was cooked?" contributed Lutis, starting to laugh.

"What 'bout there wherst food in a bucket over a fire, then it rained an' turned into soup?"

"And then a bird came along and added herbs?"

"Aye! And then… and then another person came along an' mixed it all up!"

"And then the first person drunk it?!"

Hone burst into laughter, hiccupping ridiculously. She took a look at Lutis, who was also laughing, and buried her face in the dust, her wings shaking with mirth.

"I think mayhap it's time y'went t'bed?" said Aeron, looking over at Hone, who was gasping for breath. She shook her head slightly, laughing harder. A smile flickered over the Elite dragon's face as he tried to hold back his laughter at the pair but it erupted finally in an explosive snort, which made the three of them laugh even harder.

"Oh, this is gettin' us nowhere," the Elite finally gasped out, shaking his head and turning away from the laughing two to try and stop himself. "I'm gaarn t'bed." He got to his feet and wandered off to find a soft place somewhere under the trees to sleep for a few hours before he took the dawn watch. "If you're gaarn t'stay up, y'might as well take first watch."

The next morning dawned early, the birds trilling their morning chorus from the trees that surrounded the lake. A few clouds drifted across the sky and it looked like it was going to be another fine summer's day.

"Rise and shine, time to head for Racksom," called Aeron to the sleeping travellers, testing a paw on the cinders of the fire the night before. They were still warm to the touch, perfect for drawing on the markings of an Elite patrol leader. He covered his paw with ash, drawing swirling patterns onto his scales. He didn't have to redraw them very often but they had washed off in the rain of the past week. Normally he burnt sand and used that, but ash would do for now. He could always fix them properly when they reached Racksom.

"Come on now, let's make a geet start an' we might be there f'tea." He started prodding awake those who he knew best when he was finished, leaving ashy paw prints on whoever he touched.

Hone sat up blearily, scrubbing the sleep from her eyes with a paw. "Ooh, lookit t'sky, looks like it'll be a geet day!"

"Aye, it does Hone, why don't y'try an' persuade t'others o'tha' too?" Aeron smiled at the young lash dragon, who leapt to her feet and set about waking the rest of the group with a loud bugle. A bird exploded out of a tree nearby, fleeing into the air.

Lutis jumped in shock as he was rudely awoken, bolting upright.

"Shut up you noisy dragon!" he shouted, trying to cover his ears with his hands.

Hone gave him a wide smile, her tail swishing contentedly. "Mornin' Lutis! Sleep well?"

"I did until you just woke me up, yeah," he grumbled, yawning. Nearby Echai gave groan, pawing at his ears.

"Ugh, that was really loud Hone."

The forest was strangely quiet after Hone's cry, not one frightened birdcall breaking the silence. The sound of a horn suddenly echoed through the trees, a rolling bass note that sounded like nothing Hone had ever heard. Aeron's mouth dropped open in horror at the noise.

"Was that-" started Echai, dreading Aeron's answer.

"Aye! We've got t'gar, now. Now!" Aeron shouted, dashing to the packs they had been carrying and throwing them to the other lashes.

Echai cursed under his breath. "Get your stuff, leave nothing behind that might suggest we were here. We're in danger, and if we don't get to Racksom fast… well, it's not going to be good."

"Whista? What wherst tha' sound?" squeaked Hone, scrambling to her feet. She knew the two Elites weren't joking around. She pulled Lutis up too, ignoring his protests.

"Tha' wherst t'horn of goblins," Aeron replied quickly, dashing to the fire and scooping dirt over the ashes. "Come on, we 'ave t'gar! Hone, carry Lutis, we've gotta make fast time."

"Carry Lutis?" asked Hone in disbelief- they *must* have been in danger for the Elite to let Hone carry him.

"Aye. Tell t'other Elites that they'll have t'carry humans too. Do it now."

Hone nodded quickly, running to tell the others. The horn sounded again in the distance, sparking fear now she knew who blew it.

They hurriedly packed up camp and ran, each dragon carrying a human or two. There was no talk, the group laced with fear, and the stillness of the forest around did nothing to alleviate the tension. Blasts of the horn echoed through the trees every so often as the goblins started to pick up the tracks they had left inevitably in their wake. Goblins were formidable trackers, and once they got hold of prey they rarely let it escape.

It was easy running for the lash dragons underneath the tall pine trees, a dark canopy high over them preventing any smaller plants from growing underneath. A layer of dried brown needles from many past autumns lay on the ground, making their footsteps soft, but they were sharp-ended and sometimes caught up a claw, painful and uncomfortable until they were removed. They could see for a long way in all directions but that meant that when the goblins caught up they would have no trouble following them. The ground rose slightly in front of them and as they crested the small hill they saw there was some sort of blockade between the trees *here* and the trees *there*.

"Tha' must be Racksom!" said Hone, breaking the silence.

"Shh!" Aeron quietened her instantly, flapping his head fins to emphasise the danger, but the damage had been done. Behind them the horn sounded again, much louder and longer than it had been before, and when they turned to look behind the dark green of goblins could be seen swarming through the trees.

"Run!" cried Aeron, running as fast as he could for the city, the other lash dragons leaping right on his tail. The goblins swarmed over the crest of the hill that the dragons had just stood on moments after, their leering faces baying for blood.

The ground was thankfully free of obstacles, making running easier for the lash dragons who were used to flat unbroken desert, but it let the goblins run just as fast. A wide gate beckoned the pursued group into the city, offering sanctuary.

"To t'gate!" cried Aeron, swerving across towards it. Hone ran close to the front of the group, the young dragon's limbs coursing with adrenaline, fear and excitement. Lutis hung onto the spike on her back, fiddling furiously with a lock pick he had jammed into the cuffs around his wrists to try and free them. He jerked it with his teeth as Hone swerved along the wall and they clicked open. He shook his wrists free and threw his arms around Hone's neck as she swerved again.

There was a screech behind and they looked around to see who it was- a goblin had leapt at Echai, bowling him to the ground. The lash Elite snarled and sliced out with his tail, batting the goblin away. He leapt back to his feet, Emi (who had been riding with him), vaulting back onto his back and sprinting again for the gate. Hone slowed down to check if he was alright but Aeron shouted at her to keep running.

There were shouts from Racksom's walls as the guards mobilised, lining the walls and firing a steady stream of arrows over the heads of the lash dragons. The portcullis over the gate was already starting to close, drawn inexorably downwards by the guards who had seen the goblins advancing before they had seen the lash dragons.

"Wait!" shouted Hone, running through the gate as it creaked shut, ducking as the portcullis started to graze head height. The other lash dragons ran after her, Echai at the back diving under the spiked grille. A few of the fastest goblins managed to slip under just in time too, grinning menacingly as they realised they were inside the city, showing their pointed teeth, which made their ugly, flattened faces look all the more frightening. They had two thin horns on their heads in place of hair and long ears, longer than those of a human, but shorter than an elf's. Outside, the goblins that were left behind shrieked and screamed in wordless rage, jabbing their serrated blades through the portcullis to try and stab their escaped prey.

Chaos erupted under the gate, the younger humans leaping from the backs of the lash dragons and running for cover, a few guards advancing to kill the goblins, others fighting with the second portcullis. The green skinned goblins advanced slowly on the dragons, twirling their swords through the air.

"Duck!" shouted Hone to Lutis as a goblin leapt at them, snarling like a feral animal. The lash dragon pivoted on the spot, swinging her bladed tail around in an arc and hitting the monster full in the chest with the sharp edge. A spray of black blood erupted from the creature and it collapsed to the ground but they hardly had time for a breather as another goblin leapt in to take its place.

Lutis rolled off Hone's back as she spun round, landing on his feet and pulling a dagger from inside his coat. A goblin snarled and leapt at Hone while her back was turned and Lutis threw himself at it, pushing it to the ground and stabbing with his dagger. It thrashed and squirmed, gurgling more black blood. He ducked as another attack came his way, jumping over Hone's tail as it came swinging past to hit the goblin. There was the *shink* of arrows as the guards on top of the wall reloaded their bows, firing arrows at the monsters outside, the green beasts returning volleys of their own.

"Lutis, look out!" a strangled cry came from Neby nearby and he instinctively threw himself to the ground as a dark arrow sliced through the air where his head had just been. Scrambling to his feet he dashed through the second portcullis, which was starting to wind shut. Guards pushed a huge wheel just inside the wall, loosening a heavy chain that held the grille and closing the city off to the invaders.

"Come on!" he shouted to the others, who quickly abandoned their opponents and retreated through the second gate, leaving a path of carnage. The second portcullis clanged shut, locking the goblins between the two gates.

"Stand back," shouted a voice from the wall, one of the guards dragging Echai away from the portcullis. The dragon staggered, almost falling on the man. A rushing sound came from within the gatehouse, penetrated by unearthly screams. A little sand slipped under the portcullis, steaming.

"What was that?" gasped Lutis, catching his breath.

"Fire-heated sand." Lutis turned and saw a tall elf, looking grim and waving a strip of red cloth in the air to the guards on the wall before looking back at the group. His grey-blue eyes were hidden under the long strands of dark hair that hung over his eyes, his pointed ears cutting through and marking him as one of his race.

"Welcome to Racksom."

Now that the goblins were no longer such a threat, Hone could wonder at the city in its full. She suddenly understood why Merac couldn't describe the city, and why they had only noticed the wall from outside. Tall pine trees rose into the sky much like the ones outside of the city, casting a dark greenish light onto everything beneath. Between their huge trunks and branches ran hundreds of rope bridges, building up a huge many-layered network of roads in the sky. Buildings clustered around the trunks of the trees, in some places completely encircling them.

When she looked closer she saw that the bridges were bouncing gently, the smaller ones with the gentle wind, the larger with the pounding of feet. The city was teeming with people, snatches of music and voices drifting down from the canopy. Hone looked for some way of getting up to the remarkable city and saw that there were slopes running down to the ground here and there, the closest curling around the trunk of an ancient pine whose bark was blackened with age.

"Wowee," she breathed, eager to set off exploring the city immediately. She turned to Echai, her face glowing with excitement. "Look Echai, ista 'mazing!"

Echai mumbled an agreement, looking down at his front leg. His face twisted in pain as he moved it slightly.

"You ain't even looking!" huffed Hone, now admiring the towering stone wall that ran around the edge of the city. The guards that stood on it had been firing arrows but had now stopped, the goblins out of reach of even the best of shots. There was a strangled cry behind her.

"Echai?"

The dragon gave a moan, staggering before he dropped onto one side, curling up and biting at one wingtip. Emi rushed to his side, as did the elf and Aeron.

"What's wrong? Did he get hit?" asked the elf hurriedly, pulling the Elite's wing away from his side to reveal a long gash running across the top of his front leg. The edges were black and oozing with a poisonous substance.

"One o' t'goblins must 'ave caught him with a weapon," said Aeron, his voice worried.

"Yes, we got knocked down, but I didn't know that Echai had been hurt!" said Emi, her eyes widening in horror.

"Goblins poison their weapons, he needs a healer fast!" ordered Aeron, trying to pull Echai to his feet. "Comeon kiddo!"

Echai moaned again, closing his eyes. Aeron gave him a kick in the side, forcing the injured dragon to his feet. He swayed, his wounded leg hanging limply at his side.

"The closest healer is Liesk," said the elf, pointing up into the canopy. "I have magic, but I don't think it's strong enough for-"

"No, magic ain't gonna work." Aeron cut him off mid-sentence. "Where does this Liesk live?"

"Up this ascent to the fourth-" started the elf, but he was cut off again.

"Liesk? I know Liesk, the healer, right? Get him as far as you can, I'll get her," said Lutis, who had been listening. Before Aeron could stop him, he was running for the city, disappearing in a flap of his blue coat.

Aeron watched him go, torn between saving his son and stopping the thief from escaping. Hone took one look between Lutis and Aeron then ran after the man.

Lutis panted for air as he ran further up the path, dodging through the increasing number of people that started to get in his way. Liesk's house was a long way up in the canopy and he silently cursed the fact with every breath, but finally he made it to the house, her bright blue front door a welcome sight. Bending over and gasping for breath he banged on the door frantically until, after what seemed like an age, it opened.

"Lutis? What are you doing in Racksom?" A surprised Liesk greeted him, her sleeves rolled up to her elbows and her hands sticky with a half-mixed potion. Her black hair was tied back in a ponytail, keeping her long locks out of the way. She wore trousers and a white apron, orange splodges marring the fabric here and there.

"A friend… poisoned by goblin spit… you gotta come quickly," he puffed, pushing the hair out of his eyes and leaning on the doorframe. The woman's eyes widened before she grabbed a bag from beside the door, pushing Lutis aside. She ruffled light brown wings from her back, the same colour as her skin, opening them fully and beating them a couple of times. She was an avian.

"Where?" she asked quickly. Lutis pointed down to the ground.

"North gate. A dragon called Echai."

"Don't nick anything, I'll know it was you," said Liesk, gripping her bag tightly and running for the edge of the bridge. She leapt off, spreading her wings wide and diving down towards the gate.

Lutis staggered into the house and collapsed into a chair until he had got his breath back, taking a drink of water from the tap. A candle burned on the table and he snuffed it out with his fingers, heading for the door again and pulling it shut. The busy street called to him to flee, to escape while he had the chance but he ignored the temptation, heading back down the spiralling road to the ground again, this time at a much slower pace.

Echai wobbled as Aeron shoved him towards the ascent, blood dripping from the slash on his arm onto the ground. He took a few tiny steps then collapsed again, his head sinking onto the soil.

"Come on Echai," grunted Aeron, tugging at the Elite's wing with his paws but he didn't move. The elf stepped forwards, pushing the cloak away from his shoulders.

"Let me try magic, it'll help!" He rubbed his fingers together, summoning his power.

"No! Magic makes goblin spit worse!" shouted Aeron, pushing the elf out of the way. He scowled, picking himself off the ground.

"It's healing magic, it'll make him better."

"No!" cried Aeron, folding his wings across Echai to form a barrier. The elf glowered more, angry that the Elite wouldn't even let him try.

"The dragon's right. Armeno, go and tend to your men." Liesk fluttered down from the canopy, folding her wings as she started to hunt through her bag for the antidotes she needed. "Or be quiet and hold these." She threw the elf a handful of bandages, silencing his retort with a stern look. He stood still for a moment then knelt by her side as she pulled Aeron's wings away, inspecting the wound.

"Nasty." She uncapped a small bottle of dark liquid then poured it onto Echai's wound. It hissed menacingly as it touched the Elite's flesh and a rank smell filled the air.

"I need some salts," muttered the avian. Armeno dutifully rummaged in her bag, taking out a potent smelling bag and handing it to Liesk without a word. She waved them under the dragon's nose, and when that didn't work, took more drastic measures and rubbed the bag across his face.

Aeron stood back from the two, growing more worried with every passing moment, feeling useless. Echai finally gave an almighty sneeze as the smelling salts woke him from his sleep then groaned in pain, his eyes scrunched shut.

"All right, it'll be all right," crooned Liesk, taking a salve from her bag and the roll of bandages off the elf. She opened the tub, scooping out a handful of the white cream and covering the black wound with it, gently rubbing around the edges of his broken scales. Echai moaned, flinching away from her touch. The tip of his tail flicked weakly in protest but the woman took no notice, unwinding a length of bandage before folding the long piece of fabric around Echai's shoulder, over his wing and under his front leg. The white of the bandage stood stark against the dragon's darker blue and green scales.

Halfway through bandaging the Elite Hone and Lutis reappeared from the canopy, having met on the stairway. Hone's eyes were as round as moons at all the wonders Lutis had been pointing out but, as soon as she saw the others, she gave a pleased cry.

"Lookee Aeron, I told y'that Lutis can be trusted, he came back!" She flicked a wing around Lutis' shoulders, pulling him into a hug. Aeron gave a sniff, ignoring the man in favour of the dragon he was sitting by.

"Will he be alright?" Lutis asked slowly as the two joined the others by Echai's side, looking at the prone dragon, hardly moving apart from to take short breaths.

"He will, but that was a close call. Any longer, and he would have been dead. As it is, he's going to need some looking after, and that leg might not be quite the same again." Liesk looked across at Lutis as he sat down nearby, knotting the bandages as she came to the end of the roll. Next to her Armeno climbed stiffly to his feet, stretching after sitting on the ground for so long.

"I need to make sure my men are alright," he said, heading for the wall. The other lash Elites and the refugees that had fled from Quinsilla were sitting on the steps that led up to them and the elf stopped by them briefly, giving them directions to the closest place they could stay. Doan slowly got to his feet, encouraging the others and they started wearily up the slope, tired from their furious escape.

Liesk sat back on her heels. "So, what brings you to Racksom? Lutis, I didn't think you could come back here after… last time." She raised one eyebrow briefly, referencing some passed history. Lutis gave a laugh, shrugging.

"Not here by choice of my own, but not much chance of escaping when you're pursued by a hundred goblins, eh?" he replied. Aeron shot him a warning glance.

"So y'*were* thinkin' o'scaping!" cried Hone, giving the man a playful shove with a paw. He shrugged again.

"A hundred goblins? What are a hundred goblins doing this far south? I thought they only lived in the Great Desert Rift..." said Liesk, frowning.

"'Parently not," said Aeron, his eyes returning to watch his son's face. Echai had drifted into sleep, twitching with pain every so often.

"Are they still outside the gates?" asked the avian, looking up to where Armeno was leaning over the edge of the wall.

"Let's see, shall we?" said Lutis, getting to his feet and heading for the wall. Hone immediately followed him, bounding up the steps to the wall walkway two at a time. The cheerful look on her face died as she looked over the wall onto a scene of chaos, ranks of goblins swarming just out of reach of any arrows that the guards could fire from the walls. Armeno looked at her briefly, then back out at the army again his face bleak.

A rumbling chant started up as Lutis joined the elf and the dragon, a hundred guttural goblin voices screeching out a single venom-laced word.

"Zartear! Zartear!"

12
THE TWISTED BRANCH INN. THE THIEVES GUILD

"That'll be three gold coins." The tradesman crossed his arms expectantly, waiting for the gold.

"Three? I'll give you fifteen silver."

The man scoffed. "Three gold pieces, nothing less. You're asking me for a very specialised item here."

"I'm asking you for six cogs! I could make six cogs if I had the materials, they're not that difficult. One gold piece."

"But you aren't making them, you're buying them. Two pieces."

"One gold piece and five silver ones."

"Make it ten silver pieces and we have a deal."

"Fine." Lutis begrudgingly shook the man's hand, rustling in his coat to find the required coinage. The tradesman smiled and turned to take the desired cogs from one of the many drawers that lined the walls of his shop.

Lutis had seized the chance of freedom within the city while he had the chance after the group had split up at the gate of the city. He presumed that the other humans were somewhere close to the north gate, but he hadn't bumped into them yet, and was relishing the chance of some time to himself. Echai had been taken to Liesk's house, Hone and Aeron carrying him, and the Elite hadn't thought to check that Lutis was following after. The man had been abandoned on the wall with the elf and, after exchanging luck for what looked like a looming battle with the goblins, he had set off into the city to enjoy the little freedom he had before Aeron inevitably tried to throw him in jail again.

He had decided to stock up on the supplies he had used or lost since leaving Quinsilla, the most important of which were new cogs for his mechanical wings. Hone had kept them safe for him since Plurith, rescuing them from the council hall when nobody was around, but hadn't fixed them because the cogs that they needed were very specific. They were also the last thing he needed before he could fly again. Of course, he would have to find a mage to enchant them, but in a city like Racksom he hoped that wouldn't be too much of a challenge.

Leaving the shop with his new purchases Lutis wandered along the raised street, pausing to admire the view. Rope bridges were strung between trees in every direction, setting up a giant spiders' web that teemed with people. The road that he stood on was relatively quiet, but still swayed gently as people wandered between the shops that hugged the trees. Smaller stalls branched out along the streets, fixed using a network of cables to the edges of the bridges closest by. Even with these precautions it was still a precarious business and every so often there was report of one such stall coming loose of its cables and crashing to the ground below. Despite such hazards they were still a popular business in the city, supplying trinkets and food on many of the higher streets.

Lutis finally gave in to the tempting smell of roasted pine nuts, lingering near one stall until the owner was distracted and scooping a handful off the cart. He blew them cool when they started to burn his fingers, tugging his fingerless gloves further down his hands. A smile crept onto his face as he wandered further into the city, munching on his pilfered food. Even though Racksom probably wasn't the safest place for him, (especially since he wasn't on the best of terms with Racksom's thieves' guild) it felt good to be back in the treetop city.

His feet took him to the centre of the city, where the trees were the oldest and biggest. Wide concentric bridges circled a stone tower that rose all the way from the forest floor, through the canopy and out into the sky above. It was a sight to see, easily recognisable as the twin of Quinsilla's Jewel Tower. Lutis leant over the edge of the road, admiring the carvings etched into the stone- most of the figures were avians, with wings, not humans like the ones in Quinsilla. His eyes flicked up and down the tower, absorbed in the details, until he felt one corner of his coat twinge.

He twisted suddenly, catching out at the grubby hand that was reaching into one of his pockets. There was a squeak as the little child whose wrist he had caught protested, trying to pull free, but Lutis wasn't having that. He tugged the boy close, bending down to his height.

"It's dangerous business boy, stealing from a thief." He met the child's frightened eyes with a cold stare- the boy obviously hadn't been caught before.

"I wasn't doing anything mister, honest!" squeaked the boy, trying to wriggle his hand free. "I'm only trying to make a living!"

"We're all trying to do that. You'd do better selling information than nicking things." Lutis narrowed his eyes. "Unless you're as poor a listener as you are a pickpocket?"

The boy squealed, the fingers of his free hand trying to peel away Lutis' grip. "Just because you've caught me don't mean you don't have to pay, if you want information."

"Who's in charge of the thieves' guild at the moment?" asked Lutis.

"Ooh, if you're a thief, that's the sort of thing you should know. Classified information that."

Lutis grimaced, twisting the boy's arm so they were face to face. The child howled in pain.

"Narrat!" he squeaked.

"Thank you. They still using the old haunts?"

The boy nodded, biting his lip. Lutis gave a distasteful sniff, digging in one pocket quickly and pulling out a coin, which he pressed into the child's hand then released his grip, standing upright again. "Next time check who you're pickpocketing first."

The boy took a few steps back, his eyes widening as he saw the shiny gold coin in his hand. He grinned foolishly at it, then stuck his tongue out at Lutis and disappeared into the crowd, vanishing without a trace.

Lutis shook his head in disbelief and turned back to the view, resting his forearms along the edge of the bridge. He stood still for a moment then whacked the wood with one fist, earning curious glances from the people nearest. Why did Narrat, who had it in for him the most, have to be the one who ran the guild now? Being in Racksom had suddenly become very dangerous.

~

Aeron and Hone finally managed to carry Echai all the way up to Liesk's house, lugging the Elite inside and depositing him on a pile of blankets near the fire. She had then promptly kicked them out of the house, telling them to go and explore, and not disturb their friend. She had also told them the most likely place they would find Lutis would be at the *Twisted Branch Inn.*

The city was confusing for the two dragons, who had never been to Racksom before. The many layers of interlocking streets were mind-boggling, completely different to the towering buildings of Quinsilla or the winding streets of Plurith. They ended up on the circular streets around the Jewel Tower, stopping in a quiet viewing area to try and work out where they had come from, and where they were trying to go.

"Well this don't seem t'be gettin' us muchplace," said Aeron, trying to read a sign that pointed in every direction. His nose scrunched in confusion as he tried to read the squiggly writing, quickly giving up.

"No, I think we can safely say tha'," Hone laughed, a grin on her face despite the fact they were lost. "It's quite nice 'ere though, I feel like a bird."

"Mm, I've ne'er been so high up. Look Hone, I don't think tha' we're gaarn t'actually find Lutis…"

"Wotcher mean?"

"He's probably taken this chance t'scape an' avoid being thrown in prison 'gain, even if he did come back last time." Aeron looked down at Hone, ruffling his feathers apologetically.

"But he came back las' time, dinae he? An' he saved Echai's life, gaarn t'get Liesk, an' mine too, fightin' those goblins," she said, her eyes wide and sincere. "If he hadn't stopped tha' goblin, I would prob'bly be dead."

Aeron sighed. However much he wanted to deny it, Hone's words were true. Three weeks ago when they had first found the other refugees in the desert she would never have come out with something so plausible. "These good deeds cannae redeem t'fact that he gave t'Quinsillan ruby to Zartear. Because o'him, all those people we've travelled here with- Emi an' Merac, an' t'others-they've lost their homes, their livelihoods, their families, their friends. Can y'even start t'imagine what tha' feels like?"

"No, but I do know that Lutis'll try an' put those things right now. I don't think tha' he meant f'so much harm t'pass."

Aeron slowly shook his head. "I'm only tryin' t'protect you Hone," he said quietly, looking at her with a little despair in his eyes. "You're too young for him t'be good f'you. Even if he dinae mean for those things t'happen, he's still a thief. You can't take t'thief outta him."

"You're wrong, Aeron, I can look after meself. But... I know y'only mean t'best." A small smile graced her lips. "Maybe it's jus' your old age fussin'?"

"Are y'calling me old, whelp?" he squawked indignantly.

"Mayhap!" She replied with a laugh, throwing a wing around him. He protested briefly then wrapped his own wings around her, pulling her into one of the strange feathery hugs that the lash dragons gave. He held her tightly for a moment then let go.

"Come on, if you're so convinced he'll be where Liesk said he'd be, we'd best ask f'directions." He stepped out into the crowded street, stopping a friendly passer by and asking which way the tavern was.

The two lash dragons headed off through the city, winding their way along the streets. They attracted a lot more attention than they had in Racksom, dragons being much less common in the forest city than they had been in Plurith. They asked for more directions when they got lost again, confused by the meandering streets- in the desert you could run for miles in a straight line but in Racksom everything twisted and turned like the folds of a snake.

When they finally arrived at the *Twisted Branch* the city was starting to darken as the night crept in. True to Liesk's word, when they entered the tavern Lutis was sitting by the window, a half empty pint of cider on the table in front of him. When he saw the two dragons he half rose from his seat, his eyes flicking to the door.

"Relax, we were jus' wond'ring where y'had got to." Aeron waved a paw, pushing Lutis back into his seat. "Whista that?" he pointed to the drink, flicking the glass with one claw. It chinked.

"Err... cider?" he said, watching the dragon in distrust. Hone stuck her nose over the glass, coughing when she inhaled the fruity fumes. Lutis pushed her nose away, taking a sip.

"Whista taste like?" asked Aeron, trying to be friendly. Lutis raised one eyebrow from behind his glass.

"Look, I'm sorry I didn't think y'were gaarn t'come back. Guess I was wrong... I hafta thank you for saving Echai's life, an' Hone's too... I know I ain't been quite fair, but I thought y'were gaarn t'corrupt Hone an' put us all in danger..." gushed the Elite, making Hone roll her eyes. Lutis slowly put down his glass, staring down at the table.

"I know I did some bad stuff back in Quinsilla, but I didn't know what was going to happen. People keep making me out to be great pals with Zartear, but I was only in it for the job. I didn't know what was going to happen- and I wasn't going to just stand by and watch Echai die. Yeah, I was going to scoot, but you've always got a choice, right, and this time, I chose to come back." He looked up, a whisper of a smile on his face. "Did I pick right?"

Aeron grinned, nodding. "Aye. Thank you." He turned his head, beckoning a barmaid over with one of his wings. "I think I might like t'try some of tha'... whista?"

"Cider," said Lutis, passing his empty glass to the barmaid. "Another for me too?"

The barmaid gave a smile. "Would you like something too?" she asked Hone.

"Um... I think I migh' try some o'theirs first..." she said, chewing at one of her claws. "Mayhap after tha'?"

"Of course!" said the woman, turning and heading back to the bar to get their drinks.

"So, what were you thinking you were going to do with me then, eh?" asked Lutis, turning back to Aeron.

"Well, Ebon did give me a letter t'give to Racksom's council, but takin' into t'account tha' you saved two o'my patrol today, it don't really do justice any more..." replied Aeron. "If you tell us everythin' y'know 'bout Zartear's army, I'm startin' t'think tha' you should gar free... mayhap y'could be a useful asset t'takin' back Quinsilla?"

"Really? You would let me go free?" Lutis' words were eager. Aeron nodded.

"O' course, it's not jus' up t'me- the person you've hurt most is Emi, an' it's up t'her jus' as much as me."

Lutis sat back in his chair at the mention of Emi. She was going to be a hard one to convince... he shot the barmaid a smile as she returned with two fresh pints, taking a grateful sip. Hone poked a paw into the top of his drink, sucking off the liquid. She pulled a face, sticking her tongue out.

"Ugh, tha's 'orrible! How can y'drink that?" she said, pawing at her mouth to get rid of the taste. Aeron laughed and licked at his own glass, frowning at the strange taste.

"It's strange, but quite nice. Kinda like a smoky fire with spices." He took a longer drink, licking his lips with his black forked tongue.

Lutis gave a laugh. "The more you drink, the better it tastes!" He rustled in one pocket for a moment, pulling out a small wrapped parcel. "Here y'are Hone, try this instead."

"Whista?" asked the lash dragon, peeling the thin paper away from the block to reveal a flat, slightly shiny brown... something.

"It's chocolate, tastes sweet." He clumsily broke a corner off the chocolate with his good hand, giving it to the dragon. She licked it, smiled at the taste then took a bite, munching contentedly.

"Mm, tastes geet good," she said stickily. The man gave a grin and took another drink from his glass.

The conversation turned to lighter topics as the two drank and Hone ate her way through the chocolate bar, Lutis telling the others the best places to go in Racksom. Despite not visiting the city for a good few years, his knowledge of the place was still extensive. Outside the view of the city slowly faded as the light died from the day, but the city wasn't completely dark, lamplighters walking the streets and lighting the many lanterns that were strung along them. Soon it looked like stars had fallen amongst the trees, tiny floating lights stretching in every direction. It was one of the sights that attracted many travellers to the city, the famous fallen stars of Racksom.

A steady stream of customers passed through the door of the tavern, Hone's insatiable curiosity making her turn to look at every newcomer. When a group of young men with long black coats entered she gave an interested purr, flapping a wing at the other two to get their attention.

"Hey Lutis, them humans have coats like yours!" said Hone, not bothering to lower her voice.

It carried across the room and one of the looked over, his eyes narrowing suspiciously.

Lutis was chuckling at something Aeron had said, and only looked up when Hone gave him a poke, taking another relaxed drink from his glass. When he saw the men he suddenly choked, his eyes widening as he shrank into the shadowy recess of the window.

"Shh Hone, don't say a word!" His voice was instantly quieter and he put his drink back on the table, drawing the edges of his coat up to his face.

"Why Lutis, whista matter?" asked Hone, her ears twitching as she kept watching the men.

"Shh!" He waved a hand at the dragon to try and silence her, but it only attracted more attention. Pointing their direction, the man who had looked at Hone started over towards the three, frowning. One of the others noticed and he gave his companions a shove, following the first so that the whole group came over to stand in front of Hone.

"Wotcher lookin' a' us for?" he said gruffly, leaning forwards into Hone's face. His long black hair drooped over his eyes, covering them.

"You've got a coat like my friend has," said the dragon brightly. "Has it got as many cool things in it?"

The man leered. "Betcha he ain't got 'cool things' like this." He dug in his pocket, flicking out a long switchblade.

Chaos suddenly erupted as the other men stepped forwards, more blades appearing in their hands too. Lutis leapt to his feet, pushing the man's blade away from Hone's nose. The man wobbled, thrown off balance, then toppled over onto the ground.

Another man sliced his blade across at Lutis, who gave him a shove and sent him crashing to the floor too. Lutis gave a yelp as pain shot up his arm, grabbing hold of it with his good hand.

"You!" said another man, advancing around the table on Lutis.

"Time to go I think Hone, Aeron!" cried Lutis, leaping over the table and pulling Hone to her feet. The other people in the tavern were staring, some of the drunker people laughing as Lutis dived under the grasping hands of another of the men, tripping him with a well-aimed kick. Hone grabbed hold of Aeron and dragged him after her, the two dragons jumping over the twisted branch that threaded its way through the middle of the inn and gave it it's name. Aeron misjudged his leap and tripped, falling over the branch onto a heap in the floor.

He looked up at Hone with confusion. "What jus' 'appened?"

"I think you're a bit tipsy!" laughed Hone, tugging the Elite to his feet and pulling him towards the door again. Lutis slid over another table, wrenching the door open.

"Come on you two!" he cried, dashing out of the tavern. The two lash dragons followed him, leaving in a flap of bright colour. Lutis' head appeared in the doorway again as the door started to swing shut, a wide grin on his face.

"I'll be back to pay later!" he called before disappearing again, the door crashing shut before the group of men started after them, their exit applauded by the whole tavern- entertainment hardly ever got as good as that!

Lutis and the two lash dragons ran down the raised street that led away from the inn, the road bouncing underneath their feet. The man navigated the streets easily, familiar with the area, getting them as far away from the tavern as they could before they slowed to a walk.

"Whista all tha' 'bout?" laughed Hone, her head fins fluttering with excitement.

"Ah, those guys… don't like me," panted Lutis, leaning against the side of the bridge to catch his breath.

"Well tha' wherst pretty obvious!" said Aeron, his eyes twinkling with mischief.

Lutis gave a laugh, bending over the barrier at the edge of the road and looking down at the ground far below. "They're probably part of the current Thieves' guild. I didn't recognise them, but it looks like they recognised me alright."

"Whista y'do t'annoy t'Thieves' guild? You're a thief ain't you? I thought you lot stuck t'gether?" asked Aeron, who suddenly sat down in the middle of the street. It was deserted and the world was spinning genially around the dragon.

"Sure I'm a thief, but that doesn't mean I'm in with the Thieves guild," he said, sitting down next to the lash dragon. "Yeah, I was in with them once, but I didn't really like the whole 'share and share alike' business they'd got going on, so I took my fair share and a bit more, and lo and behold, they were after m'guts faster than you can say 'stop thief!'."

Aeron looked at him in astonishment, then gave an explosive snort of laughter. "Djur mean t'say that y'stole from t'Thieves guild?"

Lutis looked proud, a grin creeping onto his face. "Well, yeah, I suppose you could say that!"

Aeron laughed harder.

13
COMPLICATIONS.

Much to Static's dismay, the news that Zartear's army would be travelling to take Racksom spread through the city only days after Nox had heard word of it. In the week that Quinsilla had been under Zartear's command, mercenaries looking for a quick way to get rich had flocked to the city, attracted by the thoughts of gold. Despite the growing number of people in the city it still seemed empty in contrast to how it had been before, the white buildings slowly falling to pieces as they were ransacked, wrecked then finally torched.

A few days after the command that the army was going to be moving on, the house that Nox and Static had taken as their own was broken into in the middle of the day by a pair of looters. They were surprised to find the house inhabited, and even more surprised to find Nox taking a bath, but their surprise didn't last long, Static shocking one on the spot and Nox running the other through with her sword as he tried to escape. After that they kept the door firmly locked whether they were in the house or not.

It was only a week later that the army finally left Quinsilla. It was an ordeal, especially for Nox, who had to organise the mercenaries into what resembled ordered forces, a job that wasn't easy when most of the men who she was trying to organise were used to following their own agendas. Keeping her real identity from Static started to become hard and her temper grew steadily worse as she battled with stubborn mercenaries all day then spent the evening on edge, waiting for the woman to discover that she wasn't an avian, but a Felixis.

Nevertheless she coped, and things seemed much better when they were on the road heading out of Quinsilla. Nox had never got used to the scorching desert heat and was grateful to be heading to cooler climes, despite having to reassure Static countless times that she wouldn't run into Armeno. Racksom was a big enough place for him to be somewhere entirely different to where they would be attacking.

Three days after they had left Quinsilla, a party of nearly a hundred goblins caught up with the army, creeping up on its tail end. They hailed from the Great Desert Rift, attracted by the army's thought of war. The goblins were a bloodthirsty race and the only thing that stopped them from falling on Zartear's army was the thought of attacking Racksom. They hardly stayed with the army for two days before they forged ahead, killing and destroying the few animals and people they found in their path.

It was the same goblins who pursued the lash Elites and their companions to Racksom. Although a few died in the skirmish at the wall, most survived, setting up a crude camp just out of sight of the city and awaiting the rest of the army for another attack.

~

Hone, Aeron and Lutis decided to call it a night after the fiasco at the *Twisted Branch*, slowly heading back to Liesk's house. As they made their way down from the top layers of the city, where there were the most shops and taverns, the number of people they passed slowly dwindled. By the time they got back to the house Hone was yawning with exhaustion every minute or two, blinking blearily to try and stay awake. She gave a sleepy smile as she saw the blue door of Liesk's house.

The avian answered the door quickly, putting a finger to her lips for quiet as they filed in.

"Echai's sleeping, so don't make too much noise," she whispered, pointing to a shadowy form lying near the fire. "There are more blankets if you want to kip here tonight." She walked over to the table, picking up the pile of blankets that she had dug out of one of her cupboards. She passed a few to Hone and Aeron, then one to Lutis too. "You can sleep in the chair."

Lutis grinned. "Thanks darlin'."

Hone and Aeron picked warm spots by the fire, spreading out the blankets before wrapping themselves up in them and dropping off to sleep, Hone curled up in a ball like a sleeping cat. Lutis watched her, then slumped into the chair as Liesk disappeared into her bedroom, kicking off his boots and sinking deep into it soft fabric with a contented sigh.

The next day found Aeron with a terrible headache, Hone longing for chocolate and Lutis feeling rather stiff from sleeping at a strange angle. Hone woke first, stretching out across the floor and giving Echai a smile, who had been awake for a while.

"Mornin' Echai! Howzah leg?" she asked, shuffling across to his side. The Elite made room for her, spreading out his wings.

"Hot and sore. And my scales itch like crazy," he said.

"Ouch. I wonder what Liesk used yesterday, she put somethin' on your shoulder that seemed t'help," said Hone, looking around for the healer's bag. It was hanging on a peg by the door,but had an air of forbidden fruit, and she didn't go to take it down.

"Liesk?"

"Aye, she's a healer. An' she has wings, real ones, she can fly! Lutis fetched her yesterday when y'got hurt by them goblins," said Hone.

Echai blinked at her in confusion. "Lutis fetched someone to help? Did he come back?"

Hone nodded feverously, a wide grin on her face as she pointed to the sleeping man. Echai gave a low whistle through his teeth, the noise making him stir slightly.

"I would have thought that he would have run off."

"So did Aeron, but he came back, an' then we went to a tavern las' night an' Aeron drunk cider, an' then these mean two-legs came in, an' then we had t'scape 'cause they didn't like Lutis, 'cause he stole from t'Thieves' guild!" she crowed, her excitement from the night before returning. Aeron and Lutis woke as her voice suddenly rose.

"Ooh, I do 'ave a 'eadache today," grumbled Aeron, flicking his wings over his head and mumbling to himself. Echai laughed a little, wincing as the movement jarred his leg.

"Good mornin' Lutis! Djur have more choc'late?" asked Hone, climbing to her feet and nosing at the man's pockets. He pushed her away, sitting up and blinking away sleep.

"What? No, you ate it all last night. I'll get you some more today." he said blearily, pushing off his blanket. There was a light tinkle of metal as the cogs that he had bought the day before fell out of his pocket.

"Ooh, y'got t'cogs for your wings! Can we fix 'em today? Can we fix 'em now?" asked Hone, picking them up. "Please?" She ran her claw along the edge of one of them, a screeching noise coming from the metal. She quickly stopped, her ears flicking back in dislike at the harsh sound.

"Not right now, I've just woken up. Let's see if we can find some breakfast first, shall we?" said Lutis, taking the cogs off Hone and getting to his feet. He stretched, then padded into the kitchen, rustling in Liesk's cupboards without any heed for her privacy.

"What do you lot say to lemon pancakes?" he called through the doorway.

"Pancakes?" Hone mouthed at Aeron in confusion. He shrugged, as clueless to what they were as she.

"Ahreet, we'll try some 'pancakes'," she called back, following him into the kitchen. He had already found a basket of eggs, a lemon and milk, and was hunting though a cupboard for a pan. He grinned at her as he found it.

"Just you wait till you taste my pancakes, they're the best you'll ever get!"

The two busied themselves with the ingredients, Hone being more of a hindrance than a help, but they still managed to get a decent number of the flat cakes out the mixture they made, despite Hone accidentally mashing eggshell into the mixture. The smell of cooking brought Liesk out of her bedroom, who took one look at the mess they were making, told them *you're cleaning that up*, and went to check Echai's shoulder.

The dragon's scales were in a sorry state when she pulled off the last bit of bandage, dried blood marking their blue colouring, a few of them bent at awkward angles where the goblin's blade had sliced right through them. He winced as she washed the wound, bandaging it up again with clean fabric when she was finished.

"Well, you seem to be healing remarkably fast," she said as she worked. Despite looking bad, the wound wasn't as nasty as she thought it would be.

"It itches," complained Echai, trying to restrain from pushing away her hands and scratching at his leg.

"Well, itching is good, even if it doesn't feel good. It means that it's healing already." She looked across at Aeron, who had been watching her. "Do you always heal fast?"

"Aye. Livin' in t'desert means y'have t'be fit an' healthy all t'time, otherwise you die," he said matter-of-factly.

"Mm, I suppose," she replied, packing the contents of her bag again.

"Grub's up!" said Lutis, emerging from the kitchen with a plate piled high with pancakes. His hair was streaked with white where Hone had rubbed flour into it. The dragon followed him out of the room, carefully balancing a tray laden with a jar of sugar and a cup filled with sour lemon juice. She managed to make it all the way to the table without dropping the load.

The others made their way to the table, Echai wobbling slightly as he got to his feet. Lutis passed him a rolled pancake, making another for himself.

"Mm, these taste good," Hone said stickily, licking sugar off her nose as she took a bite. "An' they were geet good fun t'make!"

Lutis laughed, taking another pancake. "You're got to help me clear up yet."

"What happened to your arm?" asked Liesk, pointing at his bandage. He had rolled his sleeves up to keep them clean, revealing the white fabric.

Lutis pulled a face. "Broke it when I crashed in the desert. I was flying out of Quinsilla."

"I won't ask why you didn't take the normal *ground* route out of there," said Liesk, giving him a disapproving look. Lutis shrugged.

"Have you got anything to make it heal a bit faster?"

"I might, depending on what you're going to be getting up to once it's fixed again."

"Aw come on, Aeron and Hone are gonna keep me out of trouble now." He pointed at Aeron. "He's been watching me like a hawk since Eden's Fall. Think I can keep my old ways with that?"

Aeron laughed. "Hey, as long as y'don't get Hone stealin' things too, I'm still in debt t'you for savin' my son's life." He pulled Echai close, the two dragons looking remarkably similar.

Liesk gave a laugh and got to her feet. "Okay, I've got something that'll speed up the healing process, but your arm's going to hurt an awful lot while it heals."

Lutis grinned, giving Aeron a friendly shove. "Thanks mate!"

After Lutis had taken the potion Liesk offered, he and Hone spent a while replacing the cogs in his wings. They spread the wings out on the floor, pulling out the old cogs one by one and fitting the new ones in place. Aeron and Echai talked quietly together, the older Elite watching their work with interest.

When they were finished Lutis held the wings up, smiling as they held their shape perfectly.

"They're back to normal! I didn't think that they would be the same!" He pressed the edges of the wings and they folded neatly together. Hone grinned, the dragon's eyes lit up with excitement.

"Are you gaarn t'fly now?" she asked.

"I need to find a wizard to enchant them first. And I think I might wait until my arm's fixed too." He looked across to Liesk, who was mixing up more cures at the table. "You were right, my arm hurts like bloody anything."

"Let's gar an' find a wizard then!" said Hone, pulling Lutis to his feet. The man slung the wings onto his back, admiring them over one shoulder.

"We could gar an' find t'other Elites too, I wonder where they've got to?" said Aeron, rising to his feet as well. Echai had dropped back off to sleep, his sides rising and falling slowly with every deep breath.

"That elf told them where they could stay las' night. Mayhap he could tell us where they migh' be?" said Hone. Aeron nodded.

"Armeno's probably back at the city gate," called Liesk after them as they left. First they hunted down a wizard, who obligingly re-enchanted Lutis' wings for a small price then, taking the avian's advice, they headed down to the ground.

Sure enough, Armeno was keeping a watchful eye out over the forest, waiting for the goblin attack that he was certain would come at any moment. He was all too happy to point them in the direction he had sent the others, wishing them luck.

It didn't take them long to find the inn that the Elites had stayed at, but to their frustration, they had headed out to explore the city. Merac and Deltan had stayed behind though and, after exchanging friendly greetings, told them that they were heading for the top of the city. Tekek had decided that she wanted to know what it was like being a bird, flying high above everything else.

"I know where they'll be, the best place to see the city is a viewing platform up near Racksom's Jewel Tower," said Lutis, pointing up into the canopy.

"Ista what tha' big tower is?" asked Hone as they walked.

"Yep, like the one in Quinsilla, but I've heard there's an amethyst in it instead of a ruby."

"Don't gar gettin' any ideas," said Aeron, waving a warning claw at Lutis, but his eyes twinkled with laughter.

"What? I had no thoughts of the sort!" Lutis spread his hands wide, trying to look innocent. Aeron chuckled.

The bridge up to the top of the trees was wide and well-marked, travellers to the city wandering slowly up and down it and admiring the view. The sight kept distracting Hone and the dragon quickly fell behind as she stopped to peer over the side to the ground far below, or ask what a building was, or where a street led. Aeron gave up trying to make her keep up after a while, knowing the apprentice would catch up in her own good time.

The viewing canopy poked out above the top of the trees, with a view across the whole forest. In the midday sun the tops of the trees were a shiny green, stretching like a dark field in every direction. A flock of birds chattered in a tree nearby, its boughs alive with the tiny red creatures as they flitted from branch to branch, pulling off the bright berries that were just ripening between the spiked leaves of the pine. In the opposite direction lay the Jewel Tower, its top poking out into the sky, the black slates of the roof shining in the sunlight.

Aeron gave a pleased bugle as he spotted the rest of his patrol admiring the view, flaring his head fins and running over. Neby spotted him and gave an excited squeal of her own, leaping towards him and enveloping him in a feathery hug.

"Where have you been? How's Echai?" she flicked her tail back and forth, regarding Aeron at paw's length for a moment before hugging him again. The Elite gave a laugh, blowing her golden feathers away from his nose.

"Echai's fine, he's stayin' at a healer's house. Tha's where we've been- with an avian called Liesk. Armeno pointed us t'where y'had been stayin', an' Merac an' Deltan to here," he said.

"Howee, you *are* 'ere!" cried Hone as she made it up to the viewing platform, launching herself eagerly at Tekek, who had been staring out across the view.

"I think it would be nice to be a bird..." she said dreamily. Hone giggled- the Elite was fantasising as usual. She gave Doan a hug too, grinning happily at Lutis, who had been hanging back from the others.

"T'view's so cool up here! Is tha' t'top o' the Jewel Tower?"

Lutis nodded, his eyes flicking to Emi, who had accompanied the Elites up to the viewing platform. She narrowed her eyes at him, stalking over to stand in front of him.

"What are you doing here?" she demanded, looking up at him. He backed up against the edge of the viewing platform, holding his hands up.

"Look, I'm really sorry about what happened, I want to put it right!" he said quickly. She gave a snort of derision.

"That's all talk and no action. I know you're not going to do anything about the Quinsillan ruby!"

"Wait Emi, I'm gaarn t'gar an' talk t'Racksom council today," interjected Aeron, pushing the woman back with a soft push from his tail. "It's obvious Lutis wants t'fix what he's broken, an' with t'right punishment if he don't help, I'm sure he'll comply. Right Lutis?"

The man nodded feverously. "I don't like what's happened just as much as you, and I'll do anything to get back at Zartear."

Emi huffed, turning away. "Fine, whatever you say. Just stay away from me." She gave a frugal wave to the other Elites as she disappeared below the forest canopy, ignoring Lutis completely. He blew out the breath he was holding, relaxing against the barrier behind him.

"I mean it, y'better help sort out this mess you've made, o'erwise you'll be dealin' with me as well as whate'er punishment t'council think up f'you."

"Okay, I'll sort it out!" he said, wafting him away with one hand. How, he wasn't quite sure, but with a barely-veiled threat from Aeron, he would have to try.

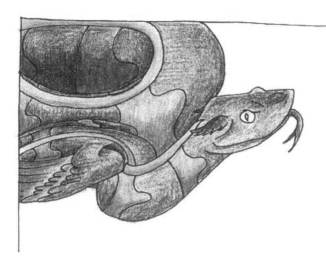

14
THIS IS WAR.

The group had stayed on the viewing platform for a little while longer, enjoying the view before they ventured back into the heart of the city. Aeron headed for the council with Neby, telling the others to meet back at Liesk's house later, so they could see Echai.

Hone was begging for chocolate and the others were starting to get hungry too, so they decided to find somewhere to eat, trailing the streets until they came across a large tavern, delicious smells wafting from its open door. They spent a noisy lunch eating their way through most of the dishes they offered, the dragons' antics greatly amusing the other customers.

As the day crept into evening they wandered further through the city, roaming through every layer. Despite the late hour that Hone had gone to bed at the night before, the young apprentice was still bright and eager to explore every corner of the city, even when it started to get dark again. They picked up more food on the move, picnicking on one of the quiet lower roads. Lights started to appear under the trees as lamplighters walked the evening streets.

"I quite like it here," said Doan suddenly, smiling as a lamplighter walked along the deserted street they were sitting in, touching his long burning taper to the wicks of each light that ran down the street.

"More than the desert?" asked Tekek, preening a few of her feathers free of jam from a sandwich she had just eaten.

"Can you compare somewhere so different to the desert?" he asked, waving a paw around them. "I think if I had to pick, I would choose the desert, but only because it's so busy here."

"I like the view, you can see for miles up in the sky, and all the way to the edge of the city from here, look," replied Tekek, pointing a claw into the distance, a smile on her face.

"Aye, strange how there are so many lights, an' then nawt a' all," said Hone. Beyond the city walls there was complete darkness, the silhouettes of the patrolling guards on the wall of the city faintly visible as they moved in and out of the light of the lamps that hung along its length.

Hone was just about to turn away from the view when a faint sound in the distance caught her ears.

"Hey, whista..." she said, cocking her head to one side, straining to hear what the noise was.

"What's what? I can't hear anything..." replied Lutis, tapping Tekek on the nose to quieten her as she rustled in a bag for more food.

"No, there's definitely somethin'." Hone wrinkled her nose as another sound came to her ears. "I'm sure I've 'eard it afore..."

There was a break, then a sound drifted through the air, this time loud enough for Lutis to hear. It was a long metallic note, lowering in pitch as it came to an end. With a shiver of realisation, he realised what the sound was, and what it meant.

"Goblin horns!" he gasped, leaping to his feet. Beyond the wall lights suddenly started to spring into view, dotting the forest with yellow. "Racksom's under attack!"

"What?" The others looked at him in confusion, then Doan suddenly realised what he was talking about.

"Quick, we have to raise the alarm! Those goblins that chased us here are back!" he said, his eyes raking the forest. "And it looks like they've brought back reinforcements!"

Abandoning their picnic, the four of them started for the wall of the city, running as fast as they could along the streets and making the bridges bounce with their heavy footsteps. Lutis quickly fell behind, the lash Elites built for speed. Hone slid to a halt, doubling back for him.

"Get on, you'll get left behind!" she said, spreading her wings wide.

"Are... you sure?" he puffed between breaths.

"Aye, comeon!" she flicked her tail, gesturing for him to get onto her back. He nodded, grabbing hold of her spine and pulling himself up behind her. She ruffled her wings around his legs and dashed after the others, shrieking a battle cry.

As they approached the wall of the city the sound of goblin horns suddenly ceased, replaced with the much quieter hushing sound of arrows being released from innumerable bows. The quiet of the night was suddenly broken again, this time by the screams of the dying guards who patrolled the city wall, their light armour useless against the deadly bolts.

The lash Elites made it to the ground, dashing across the gap between the bridge that they had descended down and leaping up the steps to the city wall. An almighty bang sounded from the gatehouse as a cannon fired, alerting the rest of the city to the attack. Doan gave a fierce war-cry, the other lash dragons answering his call as the army outside the city surged forwards to attack.

Groups of heavily armoured goblins ran for the wall, two at the front of each group throwing long grappling hooks over its edge. The ones nearest to the lash Elites caught and held firmly, the goblins pushing at the bottom of the ladder to straighten it up to rest against the wall, hanging onto it as it rose through the air. Below more goblins swarmed close, waiting for the ladder to set against the stone before they too started climbing. Behind them, human mercenaries bayed for blood. Horns sounded through the air as the avians who had been defending the wall started to attack, slashing out at the ropes that held the ladders in place.

"Cut the ladder down!" cried Lutis, sliding off Hone's back and running for the ladder. He pulled a short dagger from his belt, sawing at the rope feverously. A flight of arrows whizzed past him and he ducked low below the parapet, still trying to cut through.

"Outta t'way!" cried Hone, stepping forwards and swinging her tail in a wide circle. It sliced through the rope, making the ladder jerk backwards. Lutis flattened himself on the floor, sitting up again as a goblin leapt at the wall. It snarled, dragging itself onto the walkway and bearing its teeth.

Lutis yelled, slashing out with his dagger. Hone's tail came out of nowhere, shoving the goblin off the side of the wall into the void below, but the man's relief at the goblin's demise didn't last long as more swarmed over the battlements, the two having been distracted for long enough that another ladder had been set up.

"Run!" he shouted, scrambling to his feet and dashing off down the wall. Hone followed him, swiping a paw at a goblin who tried to leap at her, making it screech in pain. More goblins were appearing on the wall, the defending Racksom guards overwhelmed by the sheer number of ladders being put up, the clash of blades echoing through the air as men crossed swords with goblins.

Lutis leapt over a fallen avian, grabbing hold of a sword that lay abandoned on the walkway, dragging the blade up to parry an attack that came his way.

The furious, bloodthirsty face of a human looked back at him and he gave a yell, stabbing out with his dagger. The man staggered backwards, Lutis' dagger coming away scarlet, then collapsed, revealing Tekek fighting against a ring of goblins. Doan leapt in to help her, felling a goblin with a slash from his claws.

There was the *whoosh* of more arrows as another volley shot towards the walls, killing the invaders and the defenders alike. Lutis covered his head, dodging to one side as another invader lunged at him and thrusting with his own sword. The man parried the blow, forcing the sword out of Lutis' weak grip, his arm twinging as the blade flew out of his hand. The thief backed up, fear welling inside him.

The man smiled, bringing his blade back to slash Lutis in two, but suddenly stopped as a sword appeared through his middle, gurgling blood as he dropped to the ground. Armeno stood behind him, the elf bloody from fighting.

"Thanks!" gasped Lutis, reaching for his weapon.

"We need reinforcements, there are too many of them!" shouted the elf, turning to engage another opponent. "Get to the gatehouse, fire the cannon again!"

Lutis nodded, setting off at a run. The walkway was slick underneath his feet, the stone marked with the red blood of humans and the black blood of goblins. He tripped on a pike that came at him through the parapet, crashing to the floor. He screamed as pain shot up his broken arm, kicking away the weapon and scrambling to his feet again. Fire flared up out of nowhere to his right, lighting the battlefield for a moment. Chaos reigned upon the wall, people fighting and dying everywhere, and every invader that died being instantly replaced by another from the ranks that still bayed outside the city walls. Doan fought nearby, his orange scales bright like blood until the light died and everything was plunged back into darkness.

Amongst Zartear's troops, Nox and Static had hung back from the first wave of mercenaries that had attacked, knowing that they would quickly come to a sticky end. Behind them stood the huge form of Xaoc, every so often blasting a fireball into the sky to light the battle that raged.

A loud bang suddenly rocketed from the gatehouse, rumbling across the battlefield. Nox turned to Static, pulling her sword from its sheath and holding it high.

"Now or never!" she cried, running forwards into the fray. Static nodded, following the woman at a run.

The ground was peppered with the dead as they reached the wall, the two climbing quickly up the closest ladder they found with ease. Static went first, blasting away the closest defenders with a wave of electricity as she jumped onto the walkway, pulling out her scimitar. Nox followed her, diving at the nearest avian with a vicious snarl on her face. The man hardly recognised that she was an enemy before he fell dead at her feet and she leapt over his body, slashing at her next opponent.

Static stood back, watching the woman fight before she aimed a sparking ball of electricity at a guard, sending him flying. She ran forwards, using a combination of her electricity and sword to cut through each opponent that stood before her. Her heart raced with fear and adrenaline, ducking below a sword thrust before shooting a bolt of lighting out at the guard it had come from. The guard fell to the ground, the sword twitching out of her hand. Out of the corner of her eye she saw Nox battling a sandy coloured dragon, the woman leaping around the larger beast like a gymnast.

She straightened up, looking for the next attack that came her way. There was a loud war-cry from above her and she twisted, her sword cutting through the air to deflect whatever was coming her way. An avian dived down out of the air, his sword at an angle she could never hope to parry. She gave a scream, trying to run clear, but it was too late. The avian's sword hit its mark, driving into her shoulder at an angle, the blade screeching against her armour as the two slid past each other. Pain exploded across her chest and she staggered, lurching backwards and dropping her scimitar. The avian soared back into the air, releasing her from the blade, and she dropped to the ground, scarlet already blossoming across her green shirt.

"NO!" came an anguished cry. The sounds of battle were suddenly very loud as one hand crept to her shoulder, her eyes closing in pain.

"No, oh god, no..." said a voice, a sword clattering to the ground beside her before hands lifted her up. "Static, what are you doing here?"

The woman turned her head, opening her eyes to look into the face of Armeno. The elf looked shocked at seeing her, his eyes locked on her own.

"I'm... sorry..." she said, forcing the words out. Her cheeks scrunched with pain as fire seemed to sear through her body.

"I can heal you, you'll be fine, there's nothing to be sorry about," murmured Armeno, his fingers fumbling with the buckles that held Static's armour on. She caught at his hand, stopping him.

"It's too much, even... for you..."

Armeno shook his head, trying to free himself from her grip but she didn't let go, pulling his hand across to one edge of her armour. Slowly she reached for a hidden ring on the inside of the breastplate, tugging the long green ribbon that she had kept from him for so long free and pressing it into his palm.

Silent tears started to leak from the corners of his eyes as he pulled her onto his lap, tipping her head up to kiss her. She closed her eyes, laying limply against his chest as her own burned. His earthy smell was tainted with the taste of blood.

"You can't die Static," he said quietly as he pulled away, cupping her face in one hand. He dimly registered an avian crashing to her knees opposite him, but took little notice.

"Kassandra," she coughed, wincing. A little green electricity sparked between her bloodstained fingers. "Kassie, Kassie Lemaire."

"Kassie…" he whispered, kissing her again. More green sparked between her fingertips and she flinched.

"You… have to get out of here… can't control electricity… much longer…" she panted. Armeno shook his head, tears running along his cheeks.

"Go!" Her voice was strangled this time and her eyes flicked to Nox. The woman nodded.

"We've got to get out of here, now!" said Nox, climbing to her feet. Armeno protested noiselessly, laying his face alongside Static's. Nox's features twisted into an ugly scowl and she drew her sword, pointing it at Armeno's throat. "Move, now." She grabbed hold of his arm, dragging him to his feet. Static gave a wordless cry of pain as she fell to the floor, curling into a ball.

"Get the hell away from me, I'm staying right here," he shouted, trying to pull his arm from her grip, but it was like iron. She snarled, dropping her façade of an avian form to reveal her true one.

"I will kill you," she hissed dangerously, twisting his arm behind him and forcing him forwards. He wrenched his arm out of her grip, scooping his blade off the floor.

"Go Armeno!" screamed Static, green electricity crackling bright along her arms. His face creased in pain and he suddenly turned, running along the walkway. Nox followed him, giving the sorceress one last sympathetic look. The elf nearly stopped as he passed a lash Elite, the dragon lying on his side, blood oozing from a wound on his head.

Static curled further into a ball, feeling her electricity slowly seep out of control. Flashes of green obliterated her vision, each followed by a burst of pain that ran through her body, more painful than anything she had felt before, each worse than the last.

Nox forced the elf to keep moving, her blade hovering over his heart when he tried to turn back. His face was black and red with dirt and blood, thin rivers of tears washing pale streaks down his cheeks.

"Let me go back, I can save her!" he finally begged, crossing his own blade with hers and bringing them to a halt. The woman growled, batting his sword out the way with ease and drawing hers up to his throat.

"Can't you see she loves you enough that even the thought of you dying would kill her? She's not let that ribbon out of her sight for all the time she was in Quinsilla."

Armeno looked down at the green strip he was still clutching in his hand, running his thumb along its length. "No, if she dies, I'm going to die with her." He pushed her blade away with his hand, starting into a run back towards Static.

A green explosion suddenly ripped through the air, stone from the wall blowing high into the air. Armeno was stopped in his tracks, watching in horror as dust blew out from where they had been, the wall disappearing in a cloud. Rubble rained down from the sky, peppering the battlefield with huge rocks. The elf shook his head in disbelief, his sword falling from his hand as he took Static's ribbon in both hands and pressed it to his face, falling to his knees, his shoulders shaking with grief.

Zartear sat at the back of the army on a slight incline, perched behind Xaoc's wings. He had refrained from entering the battle so far, letting his troops exhaust themselves before he himself rode into battle.

"At this rate, we might actually win..." grated the tribal battle blood dragon, watching the battle with bloodlust in his eyes. It was obvious he wanted to join the battle, but his connection to Zartear prevented him from doing so.

"Winning the city is secondary in interest," said Zartear, his face impassive. "The most important thing is to get the next jewel from Racksom's Jewel Tower and free your draconic companion."

"Why would you want to free Botsu, she's a bitch..." said Xaoc, rolling his eyes in distaste. His grumbling didn't seem to make much impact.

"Time to go." Zartear's calculating voice cut through the sounds of battle and the dragon leapt into the air, his wings beating hard as he zoomed up through the trees and into the black night above. The battle disappeared suddenly beneath the thick canopy of pine trees, only the screams of the dying cutting through to them. Xaoc gained a little altitude, Zartear looking down from his back before directing the dragon towards the top of the Jewel Tower that emerged from the centre of the city.

Most of the defenders of Racksom didn't notice Xaoc and Zartear's departure, concentrating on trying to stay alive. Lutis had reached the gatehouse, stuffed the cannon full of firecrackers (they had finally come in handy) and fired it, sending out the alarm to the rest of the city. Hone had seen him go and fought her way after him, shredding the goblins and humans that dared to stand in her path without mercy.

Lutis ran out of the gatehouse again, his ears ringing from the noise of the cannon. Hone caught him on the way, pushing him to the ground as a Felixis leapt from the roof of the gatehouse, slicing out with his clawed hands and a screech. Hone snarled back, catching him in her claws and wrestling him to the edge of the wall. He scratched and writhed, one hand raking across her face and making her squeal. She shoved him against the parapet of the wall, pinning him in the middle until she had to let go, the momentum of his thrashing carrying him off the edge of the wall onto the ground below with an ear splitting shriek.

Hone stepped back, shaking the blood from her face as the scratches he had given her welled blood. Lutis climbed to his feet, catching her face between his hands.

"Hone, Hone can you see me?" he asked, wiping away the blood. She blinked, scrunching her eyes tightly shut as a long scratch just above streamed.

"No! My eyes sting..." wailed the dragon, waving her head fins in distress.

"Hold still, we'll go get you patched up." Lutis looked up from the dragon, searching for someone to hold their backs while they retreated. The purple and red scales of Tekek stood out in the warped light of fires burning below. "Tekek, Hone's hurt!"

The Elite looked up from where she was fighting, swinging her tail around in a final arc and deflecting her opponents, knocking one backwards off the wall and another onto the blade of another defender.

"Quickly, get her down to the ground, I'll block off any attacks! Go!" she cried, leaping towards them and sending a goblin sprawling as she raced over. Lutis took one of Hone's paws in his hand, tugging her towards the nearest flight of stairs. The lash dragon followed blindly, slipping on the blood that marred the stone of the walkway. Tekek followed behind, blocking off the attacks that came their way and screeching a loud war cry now and then, trying to call the other Elites to their aid. She didn't know that Doan was unconscious, blown aside by the explosion.

Hone fell down the last few steps, rubble from the destroyed wall tripping her. She pulled Lutis down too, the two rolling down to the ground, Lutis knocked half senseless from the heavy dragon falling onto him.

"Get up Hone, now!" grunted Lutis, shoving the lash dragon off him and dragging her to her to feet. They ran for the same ascent they had taken before, Hone's paw firmly held in his grip. The bridge bounced with footsteps and as they turned the first corner to head up into the trees they ran into Aeron, the Elite sliding to an abrupt halt.

"Whista 'appened? Whista gaarn on?" cried Aeron, the colour draining from his face as he saw the state of Hone's.

"I think it's only light," said Lutis quickly, wiping away more blood from the dragon's face with his sleeve.

"Let me be the judge of that." Liesk poked her head around from Aeron's back, sliding off the dragon and pushing him out of the way. She took the apprentice's face in her hands, running her thumbs along the dragon's cuts as she ordered Aeron to find bandages in her bag.

Xaoc landed on the side of Racksom's Jewel Tower much like he had with the Quinsillan Jewel Tower, his claws ripping into the decorated stone as he hung on. Zartear clambered into the building, taking an unlit torch from where it was attached to one of the pillars that held up the roof.

"I need a light," he commanded, holding the torch in front of the dragon. Obligingly (but with intense dislike) Xaoc lit the torch with a long tongue of flame, scorching the wall opposite. The man held the torch down briefly, letting it catch, then walked to the table at the centre of the room, pushing the torch into the holder that protruded from one side.

He pulled his armoured gloves from his hands, placing them to one side as he inspected the jewel. A little holder sat in the middle of the table, inside it an amethyst, a cold glitter flickering at its heart. The man eyed the jewel before he picked it up it in one hand. It grew icy to the touch and a piercing shriek ripped through the air, echoing across the whole of the forest. It faded for a moment before sounding again, unbearably loud. The amethyst in Zartear's hand glowed a bright white, lighting the tower room like a trapped star.

Xaoc looked away from the table, irritated at the show. The light flashed purple, the jewel disappeared, then Zartear stepped back from the table, holding up his hand. A small black dragon wound its way around his arm, a forked tongue flicking from her scaly mouth. Patches of deep purple decorated her scales, colour running in a long stripe along her spine. Two tiny feathered ears protruded from either side of her head, pitch black, the same colour as the mean blade that ended her tail. She took one look around the room, luxuriously stretching her wings.

"Fantasssstic," she hissed. "Here I am, back in the landsss of the living, and I have to ssshare it with Xxxaoc."

Xaoc growled. "Oh, I'm as displeased about this as you are, snake."

As the screeching noise filled the air, Lutis looked up from the lash dragon, dread crossing his face.

"The Jewel Tower!" he cried, breaking her grip. "This is only a diversion!" He shot Aeron a frantic look, dashing down to the forest floor without further explanation.

"Lutis? Lutis where are you?" squeaked the lash dragon, her voice becoming panicky as she heard his footsteps recede into the general sound of battle. She searched blindly for the thief, shaking her head from side to side to try and find him. Blood streamed from the cuts on her face, blurring her vision red as she cracked her eyes open. A cheer of victory came from the city wall, running through Zartear's ranks and swelling to a roar as Xaoc came soaring down through the trees, blasting a fiery trail along part of Racksom's wall, torching everything in his path.

The noise thrummed in Lutis' ears as he ran down the bridge, making a sharp turn around the bottom and heading for the base of the Jewel Tower. Its pale walls were easy to see in the darkness of the night, the city floor deserted. When he reached the building there wasn't a guard in sight. A thick wooden door was the only protection the amethyst had, all the city guards deployed to the wall to fight. Lutis tugged on the door handle in vain momentarily, then scrabbled inside his coat and retrieved a lock pick, the metal bent to open even the most complex of doors. He jiggled it in the lock, ear pressed close to the wood, breathing rapidly. It clicked and he wrenched the heavy door open, twisting his lock pick free before he bolted up the staircase. It was pitch black and the steps were uneven, sending him sprawling to the floor twice, but each time he pushed himself to his feet and kept on running.

The staircase ended abruptly as it reached the open room at the very top. Panting for breath, Lutis dashed over to the elegant old table that stood in the centre of the room. A torch burnt slowly next to the delicate holder that should contain the Racksom amethyst... but it was gone.

Lutis shook his head, leaning on the table to catch his breath. The amethyst was gone... Zartear had gained another dragon. A roar echoed quietly in the distance, tinged with success. They had lost more than just defenders and the city wall tonight; they had lost the second city jewel.

15
AFTER THE CARNAGE. TRAVELS TO THE LIBRARY.

"Lutis, where's Lutis?" wailed Hone, trying to find her friend. The city wall was in chaos, defenders trying to fix the huge hole that had been blown in part of its length and hold back the invaders that were still attacking. When Xaoc had entered the battle most of the army had fallen back into the forest, running from the dragon's fire that seared across the wall, but some of the more bloodthirsty goblins had decided to stay and enjoy the carnage.

"Hone, we'll find him, calm down!" Aeron ran after the young lash dragon, catching her and pulling her desperate hunt to a halt. Her eyes flicked over his face, fear shining through them before she pressed her face into his chest, whining as her wounds stung through the bandages Liesk had wrapped them with.

"Why ain't Lutis here, where's he gone?" gulped the distraught dragon, tears springing from the corners of her eyes. Aeron pulled her close, wrapping his wings comfortingly around the dragon.

"He's gone t'take care of somethin', he'll be back soon," crooned Aeron, scanning the area around them for an unexpected attack. It was starting to calm, the Racksom guards pushing back the invaders slowly but surely. His patrol was nowhere to be seen and he hoped that they were all alive and well, but he knew that in a battle as fierce as this they couldn't all have escaped unharmed.

Lutis had sat at the top of the Jewel Tower for a while, looking out bleakly over the treetops to where Xaoc had vanished with Racksom's amethyst. When a troupe of guards finally arrived at the top of the tower the sun was starting creep over the tree tops, blissfully unaware of the destruction that had taken place that night. Lutis explained what had happened, then, not listening to their frantic questions, silently unpacked his wings from under his coat, opened them to fly and leapt from the tower into the sky, gliding away like a hawk under the trees, ignoring the pull of the straps on his arm as it healed.

He landed by the city wall where the bodies of the fallen were being laid, walking past them in silence, his eyes hunting for the brightly coloured scales of a lash dragon. Relief filled him when he saw none, but he knew that there were still more dead on the wall that hadn't been retrieved yet, and someone still could have been lost.

He headed along the wall's length, hoping to find at least one of the dragons. As he walked past a huge chunk of stone that had fallen from the wall he spotted a pair of figures, Aeron's bright green and blue scales clashing with Hone's red and purple ones. Her broken voice reached his ears as she sobbed his name again, inconsolable. Inhaling a sharp breath he broke into a run.

"Hone, Aeron!"

"Lutis?" she gulped, looking up over Aeron's shoulder. Her face lit with happiness as she saw the man. "Lutis!" She leapt to her feet, ran the short distance between them and threw her front paws and wings around him in a huge hug.

"Lutis where did y'gar? I was scared an' you weren't there an' I thought y'might have gone forever an'-"

"It's okay, it's okay, I'm here now." The thief patted the dragon awkwardly, wincing as her embrace made his new bruises pound. "The city was in trouble and nobody really knew why- the jewel's been stolen from the Jewel Tower."

Hone didn't care, burying her face deeper into Lutis' shoulder. Her friend was back, and unharmed too, and that was all that mattered to the lash dragon.

"Come on, it looks like t'wall might come down more, an' I need t'find to find t'rest o'our patrol. I hope nobody else is hurt..." Aeron's wise words were strained as he worried about the other lash Elites. He looked up at the wall, his eyes scouring along its length for any sign of dragons, and caught sight of a purple wing fluttering desperately in their direction, Tekek obviously calling for them to "come quickly!", but they hadn't heard her over the noise of the guards who were holding the wall.

Aeron's stomach flipped in fear at her frantic look, and, without looking to the others to see if they followed, he ran for the wall, leaping up the staircase two at a time. Hone shot Lutis a frightened look, her smile fading, and pulled him after her patrol leader.

Tekek crouched next to the prone form of Doan, the sandy coloured dragon's breaths coming in short gasps. Aeron shouldered her aside, the Elite of little use when it came to looking after others, revealing Doan's wing. It was bent at strange angles over the rubble that Doan lay amongst, his yellow feathers stained scarlet with blood.

"I can't... feel my wing..." he gasped, his head fans fluttering weakly. Aeron laid a paw on his shoulder, horrified.

"Wha' happened?" he whispered to Tekek, looking up at the female dragon. She shook her head slightly, gulping.

"He was hurt... I couldn't move him in time, and there was a rockfall..." she rubbed away the tears that trickled down her face. "His wing got trapped underneath a big rock that fell."

Aeron nodded, stretching out a wing to take her shoulder. "I need you t'find Liesk, now, Doan needs her help."

Tekek blinked away her tears and nodded back, looking down to the ground for any sign of the avian. As Aeron let her go she raced off, urgently searching, the elder dragon looking back at Doan.

"Hang in there, you've gotta stick around for a few more years yet."

Hone tugged Lutis up the steps, her feet sliding on the slick stone. As the man saw the chaos of the walkway he paled, coming to a halt.

"Whista wrong? Come on, we have t'find t'others!" she urged, her eyes raking the walkway. They settled on Aeron and she gave a gasp as she noticed Doan too.

"You go ahead, I... I think I need a minute." He pulled his hand out of her grip, pushing back his hair from his face. Hone looked at him in worry, but her concern for her Doan overrode it and she reluctantly left, leaving Lutis to sink down onto the steps, his head in his hands. If this was the sort of carnage that just a *distraction* wreaked, then what was a full-out attack going to be like?

Hone made her way over to the others, crouching nearby. Aeron was whispering encouragement to Doan, trying to keep him awake, the sandy Elite grimacing as he battled against the urge to sink into unconsciousness for a second time. His eyes flicked to Hone then back again, alerting Aeron to her presence. He looked up briefly.

"Hone, gar an' join one o'the parties helpin' t'injured. They need your strength. If y'see Neby, tell her t'do the same, then come t'Liesk's when things are done." He pushed her nose away with a wing, hiding Doan's shattered one beneath his feathers.

She unwillingly drew away, passing Tekek and Liesk without a word as they went to help Doan. The Elite looked strained and scared. She found Lutis still sitting on the stairs. He looked up as she nudged at his shoulder, his hands leaving bloody prints on his face.

"Are y'ahreet?" she asked, standing still as he used her as a support to stand. "Y'look kinda pale…"

"Yeah… no… I feel a bit sick," he said. He curled his arm around Hone's neck as they started down the stairs, leaning against her.

"Right…" She watched him in concern, then something clicked. "Of course, you're a thief, not a warrior, you've ne'er been in a battle afore, hasta?"

He shook his head and reached for the water bottle at his waist, taking a long draught of the liquid. It made him feel a little better, but there wasn't much and it was soon gone. He hooked the flask back onto his belt, fixing his eyes on the trees as Hone led him over towards the ramp that led up into the city. She crouched nearby as he sunk to the ground again, his eyes skirting over her face as he took in the ruffled bandages that wrapped over her scarlet and purple scales.

"You need those bandages fixing, let me deal with them," he said, trying to take his mind off the aftermath of the battle.

"No, I have t'gar an' help, there might be more injured people back at t'wall," she said, twitching her head out of his reach. "Everyone's gaarn t'meet back at Liesk's house, I'll see y'there." Before he could protest she was gone, leaving him astounded. She had grown up in the past few hours, her thoughts entirely on everyone elses' safety.

He rested for a time then got to his feet, thinking to lend a hand too. However, at the first sight of the chaotic wall his nausea returned tenfold and he hurried away.

~

Zartear relaxed in a high backed chair, watching over his army under the rising sun. Xaoc stood behind him, looking displeased. The dragon longed for nothing more than battle and he hadn't even wetted his lust for blood during the short time he had been allowed into the fight. The army was looking battered but victorious, mercenaries celebrating in small groups. Zartear was pleased- out of the massed troops that had gone into the battle the ones that had suffered the most were the goblins that had come from the desert, and they would have been a hindrance to the next step of his plans anyway.

"Ssso, what'sss the plan?" hissed Botsu, the new jewel dragon. She was wrapped around the back of the chair, her coils slowly shifting as she slid over the dark wood, never pausing.

Zartear smirked. "You can't guess?"

"We go to Tarz, free Khaan from his jewel, then you take over this realm," came Xaoc's bored voice.

The smirk on Zartear's face grew. "Very good." His voice was laced with sarcasm as the dragon shifted, and he was even rewarded with a cynical clap of his hands. Botsu laughed as she saw Xaoc trying to restrain himself from attacking, then her head flicked towards the army, her eyes glowing with interest.

"What have we here?" she hissed as Nox came into view, holding herself stiffly. The feline markings on her skin were obscured by a sheen of blood that turned her a cruel scarlet in the light of the rising sun. She inclined her head slightly at the sudden attention.

"Most of the goblins have been killed, and around a fifth of the rest of the army. We also lost a mage and the other Felixis." She rattled off her report quickly, her voice hoarse.

"They were disposable," Zartear said emotionlessly, resting his elbow on the arm of the chair, his hand flat. Botsu slid from behind the chair, her reptilian scales rustling as she twisted across his palm. She opened her wings, fluttering the short distance between Zartear and Nox with a surprising lack of agility.

Nox recoiled as the dragon wrapped herself around her shoulders, Botsu's black tongue flicking in interest. The two eyed each other.

"This is the prize we attacked the city for?" Nox asked finally, not taking her eyes off Botsu. The dragon gave a malicious smile.

"Sssomeone'sss in turmoil over battle, hmm? Did sssomeone lose a friend?" she rasped, stroking the edge of her wing along the Felixis' cheek. Nox's face contorted in anger and she ripped the dragon from her shoulders, throwing her to the ground before stalking away without a glance at Zartear. No doubt she would pay for the action later.

Botsu gave a mocking laugh, uncurling herself from the floor and winding her way back to Zartear. He watched her impassively for a moment before leaning forwards.

"You can read the minds of others," he stated. The dragon flicked her tongue at him, confirming his thoughts. He narrowed his steely eyes at her, thinking. *A help, but also a hindrance... she needs to be kept at arm's length.*

Nox stalked through the camp, heading for the place she and Static had left their horses- the other woman wouldn't have need of her Tamarisk now, now that she was dead. The spotted horse flicked his ears back at her approach, snorting at the metallic scent of blood. She extended a hand, trying to convince the stallion that she was harmless but he pulled his head out of reach, snapping at her fingers.

She looked away, sighing as she sat at the base of a nearby tree. Tamarisk shuffled away from her, turning aside. He was still wearing his saddle, Static's belongings rolled neatly behind the cantle and tucked into saddlebags and the sight suddenly made her hurt inside. Growling angrily to herself she tugged off her gauntlets and threw them to the ground, making the horse shy. A droplet of water splashed onto her hand and she froze, staring.

Another drop joined it and she slowly raised a hand to her face, her frown melting away when she found her cheeks were wet. She looked at her damp fingers in surprise then her eyes flicked up to the horse. His dark spots were blurry as her eyes started to run with tears.

She rested her head back on the tree trunk and let them come, her shoulders shaking silently with heavy sobs.

~

Despite Lutis' detour to be sick, he was still the first one to arrive at Liesk's house. He took a drink of water from the tap and washed the grime off his face before slumping into an armchair. To his relief, Echai slept through the noise Lutis had made, letting him rest in peace for a while.

It was broken by Aeron and Liesk arriving with Doan strapped to a litter that they had fashioned and strung behind Aeron's shoulders. The injured dragon was out cold as Aeron dragged him through the door, the clatter waking both Echai and Lutis from their slumber. Liesk dashed around the room, collecting all the medical supplies she had and piling them onto the table as the Elite untied Doan from the stretcher.

"Oh god… what happened?" asked Echai, lurching to his feet and over to Doan's side. Aeron quickly explained, skipping over the details of the battle.

"What about the rest of our patrol, are they alright too?"

"They're fine, cuts and bruises," said Lutis, wincing as he stood, the movement stretching his bruises. "Can I help?"

Liesk shoved an armful of supplies into his hands, pointing towards the dragon. "Lutis, I couldn't save his wing. When that dragon wakes up, he's going to be hurting more than you can imagine. You have to help me get painkillers down him."

The man nodded hastily, dumping his armful into the chair and sorting through it. He picked out bandages and a bottle of black poppy seeds, handing them to Liesk. The woman took them without a word, pouring them into a mortar and grinding them down to make a paste.

Lutis turned to Doan, sitting down behind him. His eyes were closed, one wing tucked underneath him. Of the other only a few forlorn yellow feathers remained, a sad reminder of what it had been. Taking a deep breath, he started to wind new bandages around those that Liesk had already started with, wrapping them around his shoulder.

After a while, when the sun had risen and people were starting to walk the streets of the aerial city, unaware of the chaos of the night, Tekek and Hone stumbled in through the door, the two dragons looking exhausted. Tekek collapsed in a heap near the fire, not caring for the state of her scales as she succumbed to sleep. Hone mumbled a greeting to the others and pattered over to Lutis, inquiring about Doan as the man started to unwrap the bandages from her face, washing her scales clean with warm water. Five long red streaks ran across her face, three above her eye and two below. The sharp claws of the Felixis had cut a long way, but the wounds weren't deep.

"Lutis..." called Liesk as he was halfway through re-bandaging the lash apprentice, drawing his attention. She knelt by Doan, the dragon shifting a little. He gave a long moan, his face contorting.

Lutis jumped out of the chair, waking Hone from her dose as he stepped over her, grabbing the bottle of poppy juice Liesk had made from the table. He dropped to his knees next to the avian, pulling the cap off the bottle and giving it to her.

"Hold his head still. Dragon, this is going to make the pain go a bit." She tugged at Doan's ears to make sure he was listening as Lutis lifted Doan's head, resting one hand on the dragon's neck. The two managed to get a fair bit of the liquid into him, Liesk patting him on the cheek as she capped the bottle again and smiled thankfully at Lutis.

Doan licked his lips and relaxed as the medicine took effect, his pained expression fading. Aeron watched him, settling next to the big dragon and sharing his warmth.

When Lutis had finished patching up Hone she was half asleep, her eyes closed. The man leaned back in to the chair, catching some sleep with the rest of them while he got the chance.

It was late afternoon when Lutis woke again, the sun sending orange rays through the trees. One shone on his face and he sleepily tried to bat it away, before he realised what it was. Hone snoozed at his feet, her head in his lap. He picked her up slowly, trying not to disturb her as he slid off the armchair and wandered into the kitchen, stretching. Neby was lying on the floor next to Aeron, their wings twisted together. *She must have come back while he was asleep,* he decided.

Liesk was standing next to the stove, half lying on the countertop as she watched a pan of water slowly boiling. Lutis grinned, putting his hands on her shoulders. She jumped, twisting out of his grip.

"Oh, it's you…" she said, relaxing. She rubbed her face with one hand, blinking wearily.

"You look exhausted Liesk, go to bed. I'll stay up until one of the others' wakes," he said quietly, reaching around her and taking the boiling water off the heat. She started to protest but a yawn cut her off mid-sentence.

"Okay… thanks Lutis," she said, standing up on her tiptoes and giving him a quick kiss on the lips before ducking around him and out of the doorway, rustling her wings around her like a blanket. He smirked, his fingers brushing across his lips, before he poured the boiling water into a mug and stirred it with ground chocolate.

He carried the bitter brew into the other room, sitting at the table and pulling his shirt sleeve up. His arm had stopped hurting, which by his reckoning meant that it was time to take the bandages off. He unwrapped them eagerly, flexing his hand slowly, then more vigorously when it didn't hurt. Grinning, he picked up the mug of hot chocolate in his right hand and took a gulp, relishing the free use of his arm again. Finally, he was back in one whole piece.

The smell of warm chocolate woke Hone, the dragon stretching before she rolled onto her back and shuffled her wings on the floorboards. One wingtip fluttered over Doan's face but the dragon didn't move, sunk deep in sleep.

Lutis gave a wave as she sat up and she padded over to the table, dipping a claw into his mug and sucking off the liquid. He batted away her inquisitive nose as she liked the taste, hoping to steal more.

"Oi you, get your own," he whispered, covering the top of the mug with one hand. She pulled a hurt face, pouting. They sat in silence before he lifted his hand away and she scrabbled for the mug, tipping it over in her bid to get another drink.

Lutis stifled his yelp as he leapt out of his chair, the drink spreading across the table and pouring off the side in a little waterfall. The dragon gave a chirrup of pleasure and opened her mouth, letting the hot chocolate drain into it.

Lutis rolled his eyes and went to get a towel to mop up the mess.

When the table was clean again, and Hone was preening herself nonchalantly of the last few drips of hot chocolate, she asked whether they could go exploring. Despite it being nearly evening, the dragon was wide awake- but they had just spent the day sleeping, so that was understandable. Luckily for her the sound of voices woke Echai, who agreed to watch over the others while Hone and Lutis escaped for a few hours, on one condition- that Lutis made hot chocolate for him.

They headed out across the city, making their way towards the Jewel Tower. Turning along one of the busier streets, they were met with a crowd of people blocking its width.

"Whisa gaarn on?" asked Hone, craning her head up to see over the people. A man stood on a box to one side of the street, hailing the crowd.

"The amethyst has been stole from Racksom's Jewel Tower! This has never happened before, and neither has the wall of Racksom ever been breached. Is worse going to befall the city now the jewel has gone?" he called to his crowd, gesturing wildly. "What can we do to stop worse coming?"

Lutis shook his head. Scaremongers, had they nothing better to do? He tugged at Hone's wing, drawing her away.

"Djur think ista true?" she asked as they made their way down a different street, the dragon's eyes lingering behind. Lutis gave a snort of disbelief.

"No, 'course it's not. But... Zartear's stolen two of the city jewels now, and the first time, a dragon appeared. I wonder if the second was holding one too?"

Hone tapped a claw against her mouth, musing aloud, "Ain't there 'nother jewel in Tarz?"

"Yeah, there is... I wonder what he's planning..." he frowned. "It's a bit strange that there are three jewels in three different cities... and dragons appear if you touch them? What's the significance?"

Hone shrugged. "Can we ask someone?"

"I don't know anyone that might know about that sort of thing..." he said, thinking. "I've heard there's a library in Racksom though, we could try there?"

"Ahreet!" crowed Hone, grinning at the suggestion. "Whista library?"

Lutis shook his head in despair. "Come on, I think I know whereabouts it is."

They started down the city, away from the busy higher streets. Unlike most of the other public buildings of Racksom, the library was on the ground, too big to fit into even the largest of trees. It was easy enough to find once they got close, the building lit by many lamps strung around its entrance in the growing gloom of the evening.

They looked around in interest as they entered the building, Lutis never having visited before (going to the library was hardly high priority for a thief), and Hone not knowing what to expect. The entrance led straight into a huge room- or at least the two thought it must be enormous but, as it was, it was almost as dark as night, and it was hard to tell. Tall bookshelves stood in stiff rows like sentries, their tops shrouded in darkness, splitting the room into long rows. Here and there a tiny candlelight flickered, held aloft by someone reading or browsing the shelves.

"Wowee, this place is cool!" said Hone loudly, stepping forwards to peer up at the ceiling. "Look, t'books gar up fore'er!"

"Shh, Hone, you're supposed to be quiet in a library," whispered Lutis, trying to silence the dragon.

"Why?" Heads started to turn in their direction at the disturbance.

"Quiet please, some people are trying to study," said a new voice from behind a nearby bookshelf and a tiny dragon fluttered into view, one paw pressed to his lips.

"Sorry, Hone's never been in a library before," whispered Lutis, shrugging an apology. The little dragon huffed.

"Well, make sure she's quiet from now on." He turned to leave, shaking his head in despair.

"Whista *you*?" Hone blurted, stopping him.

"I'm a dragon of course!" he said indignantly, turning to face her.

"Not a *proper* dragon. You're too small!"

He flushed, fluttering close to Hone's face. "I am *too* a proper dragon."

As he moved closer, Hone realised the extent of his uniqueness. Not only was he tiny, hardly much bigger than her face, he was made from paper! The little dragon was a pale cream colour, the paper he was made up of folded into flat plates. Two pairs of wings, like those of an insect, beat furiously at the air to keep him aloft. His dark black eyes were framed by frills and a long tail twisted through the air behind him like the ribbon of a balloon, swinging this way and that as he adjusted his position in the air.

"You're made o'paper!" exclaimed Hone.

"So? That doesn't make me any less of a dragon. Please keep your voice down, this is a library." He crossed his paws one over the other, hovering.

Seeing they would get nowhere with the two dragons arguing, Lutis stepped forwards, silencing the lash apprentice.

"Good dragon, where's the best place to start research on the Jewel Towers?"

Immediately distracted the dragon turned towards Lutis, his quarrel with Hone forgotten. "Finally, a worthwhile question. Jewel Towers… hmm, maybe along at six hundred and ninety… or maybe seven hundred and twelve… I'm Zack by the way. Oh, maybe it's nine hundred and thirteen!" He flitted off into the gloom, leaving the other two to look at each other in confusion before following. There was a box full of candles by the door and Lutis ducked back for a few- they were the only source of light in the library, and from what Zack was muttering it looked like they were going to be there for quite a while, hunting through innumerable books.

Zack led them through the winding bookcases with ease, murmuring ferociously under his breath. He seemed to know exactly where he was, despite the bookshelves being hardly more than dark outlines and the books on them practically invisible.

"How does he know where t'gar?" whispered Hone, leaning in close so the little dragon couldn't hear.

"I have no idea," Lutis whispered back, handing her one of the candles while he hunted for a match. She licked the wick, then set it alight with a puff of hot air.

"Here we are," said Zack suddenly, coming to a halt in front of a bookshelf that looked no different from the others. "This is the shelf for city architecture. There's more on landscape architecture a few shelves that way." He pointed into the gloom, hovering in the air again.

"How do we get to the books at the top?" asked Lutis, holding the candle up high. The bookshelf stretched far above the little circle of light.

"There's a special seat system that you can use." He flitted over to the edge of the bookcase, where they saw there was a long rope tied around a small metal hook. Zack patted the rope and Lutis obligingly unwound it, letting it slip slowly through his hands as he felt a weight the other end. There was a creaking sound from above them and a flat bench slowly descended from the ceiling, wide enough for a human to sit on and pull themselves up to the higher books with ease.

"You can sit on the bench to get to the top books," explained Zack, "Sorry dragon, you're too heavy for the seat, so you'll have to stay down here."

Lutis gave Hone the other candles, telling her to light them and find a table for them to sit at while he started to scan the bookshelf for a title that looked useful. Not many were of interest, focussing more on the unique layout of the forest city and the way the buildings were held in the trees, rather than the Jewel Tower itself. Lutis quickly found the chair helpful, using it to get to the very top of the bookshelf. There was a basket attached to the side for the books he wanted, and the chair was soon swaying from side to side as it became unbalanced with the extra weight.

The top few rows were empty of books, for which he was thankful. As he made his way down to the ground again he passed Zack, who had wedged himself into a tiny space underneath the slump of a few books and was eagerly reading a long scroll that dangled down over the void below. He took no notice as Lutis dropped past, completely engrossed.

Hone was waiting at the bottom of the bookshelf. They carried the books to the table she had found, the dragon flipping over the cover of the top book. A cloud of dust puffed into the air and she sneezed, rubbing at the end of her nose.

"Do you want to take a few, and I'll scan through the rest?" suggested Lutis, dragging up a chair and opening the closest book. Hone bit one of her claws, suddenly anxious.

"I...I cannae read," she mumbled, looking at the floor. Lutis looked at her in surprise, then he remembered.

"Oh, you can't, can you?" He pulled a face, then clicked his fingers in solution. "I'll write out the word we're looking for, and you can look for it. Then, maybe when we've figured out what's going on here, I can teach you how to read." That would be an interesting task, considering how short the dragon's attention span was.

Hone nodded. "Ahreet!"

Lutis dug in a pocket, pulling out a scrap of paper and a charcoal pencil. He wrote the word "jewel" in big letters on it, spelling it out loud for the dragon before dropping a book into her waiting paws. She settled down on the floor with the book and the paper, opening it to the contents page like she had seen Lutis do and slowly started hunting down the word she needed.

They had little luck with the books they had picked, and soon there was a large pile of those they had discarded on the floor.

Lutis was close to giving up for the night when something on the page before him jumped out. He frowned, rereading the sentence before tapping Hone and reading aloud, "One of the first buildings erected in Racksom following *the beast* was the Jewel Tower. In Quinsilla and Tarz, Jewel Towers were also some of the earliest buildings established."

"Whista t'beast?" asked Hone, abandoning the book she was flicking through and peering over Lutis' shoulder at the book he had open in front of him. The word "jewel" stood out, but the rest was just squiggly lines.

"I don't know… maybe we could ask that little paper dragon- Zack. He might know where else we can look. Tidy up some of these books while I go and find him." Lutis stood, folding over the corner of the page before heading for the bookshelf and disappearing up into the darkness on the chair.

Zack hadn't moved from where he had been reading before, the only sign that he had been doing anything the fact that the scroll was dangling even further down the shelves than before. As Lutis arrived at the shelf he held up one paw, stalling his questions until he reached the end of the sentence.

"Did you find what you were looking for?" he finally asked, tearing his eyes away from the page.

"Not quite, we had one mention, but it was very vague. Something about a beast that destroyed the Jewel Tower?"

"I've never heard of something like that. I bet I know someone who does though- Foen."

Lutis looked quizzically at Zack. "Who's Foen?"

"He's the sorcerer who enchanted me," Zack replied, a smile on his lips. "He knows everything, I'm sure if there's anyone who knows about what you're looking for, it'll be him!"

"Do you know where we can find him?"

"I expect he'll either be here in the library somewhere, or in his house experimenting." He rolled up the scroll he was reading, gathering it in his paws before zooming off down the bookshelf. "Come on, I'll show you where he'll probably be!"

Lutis let the chair down to the ground again, knotting the rope back into its original place and picking up the book with the turned-over corner. Hone had piled the others into wobbling towers on the table but they had no time to sort them back onto the shelf as Zack was off through the library, his scroll tucked firmly in his paws for later.

They collected up the candles, blowing a couple out before following, the paper dragon a pale darting speck in the dark. He led them towards the front of the library (or at least it seemed like the direction they had come from, everything looked the same), where there were a few more people around, in comparison to back with the books on architecture. There was a steady source of light from a few thick candles placed in the middle of the tables, lighting the bookshelves around with a warm glow. From the glance Lutis got at a shelf he saw that they were in a section that dealt with magic and sorcery.

"I can't see him down here, so he might be on top of one of the bookshelves," whispered Zack, peering through the gloom for any sign of the man. He shook his head and headed up the side of one of the shelves, looking like a fluttering moth in the low light.

"Wait here, don't cause trouble," said Lutis, giving Hone a warning tap on the nose before heading over to a free seat and hoisting himself up after Zack. For his size, the little dragon certainly could move at speed!

When he reached the top he found Zack sitting near a young man, reading his scroll from before. He pointed at the man, not looking up.

"This is Foen."

Lutis tied the chair in place and slid from his perch onto the top of the bookshelf. It was lined with cushions, wide enough to sit on, with little rails either side to stop anyone too engrossed in a book from falling off. There were one or two avians sitting up in the little eyrie, but mostly it was empty- which made it an even more attractive place in Foen's view.

The man looked up as he slid along the shelf to sit nearby, peering over the edge of the bookshelf. It was a good thing Lutis was comfortable with heights.

"Can I help you?" he said, pushing back the brim of his beige pointed hat from where it had slumped over his face. A few blonde bangs of hair flopped over his eyes and he shook them away, puffing in irritation when they fell straight back into place. Lutis might have mistaken him for a wizard, with the pointed hat, but he was wearing just a simple shirt and trousers, not robes, like he would have thought a wizard would wear. And he was very young, maybe only nineteen or twenty- which immediately made Lutis doubt Zack's unwavering faith in the man.

"We were wondering if you could tell us about the Jewel Towers. Zack said you 'knew about everything...','"said Lutis.

"Just about the Jewel Towers? They're easy to research, why did you have to come and ask me about that, I'm very busy you kn-"

"No, not just the Jewel Towers," Lutis interrupted, sensing that Foen was about to go off on a rant. "More, the jewels *inside* them. And what's inside the jewels themselves too. Someone's been collecting the jewels."

Foen blanched suddenly, catching at Lutis' arm. "What do you mean, 'someone's collecting the jewels'?"

"That's exactly what I mean. Don't know if you noticed, but last night, there was an attack on Racksom. Two weeks ago there was one in Quinsilla too. Both times, the jewel has been stolen- the first time, a tribal battle blood dragon was summoned."

Foen now looked slightly green, his eyes flashing around at the nearest other people suspiciously to see if their conversation was being overheard. Zack took no notice whatsoever.

"And we read something in a book about 'the beast'," Lutis added as an afterthought.

Foen jumped at the Lutis' addition, his face twisting in worry. "I think you had better come back to my house," he said, sliding off the top of the bookshelf onto the seat and making it bob up and down. "Hurry now."

Lutis slipped back onto the seat next to him. He had hardly got settled before the young man had let the winding mechanism go, sending them whizzing towards the floor. Lutis gave a yell, grabbing onto one of the rails at the side of the seat and staring at Foen with incredulity. Zack hissed from the top from the bookshelf, shaking his head despondently. The man just tugged on the rope, bringing them to a jerky halt a little way off the floor, then let the seat down slower so they came to a gentle rest with their feet on the floor. He gave Lutis a grin and tied the rope to the bookshelf, jumping down from the seat.

"Did you think that was fast?" he inquired, a smile still on his lips. "I went slower than normal."

Lutis let out a breath and climbed off the chair, beckoning to Hone. "This is Foen, he seems to know something about the Jewel Towers."

"Ooh, canst tell us what t'beast is?" asked Hone, tipping her head to one side. Foen nodded.

"Not right here though, we'll talk back at my house." He beckoned them to follow, starting off back towards the exit. Hone gave an excited hop-skip, ruffling her feathers in excitement. She followed close after, nosing at the edge of his hat.

"Are you a wizard?"

"No, of course not!" Foen sounded offended and pushed back his hat again self-consciously. "I'm a sorcerer!"

"Why are y'wearin' that silly hat then?"

"Because I like this *silly hat*." He frowned, then flicked her on the nose. "Do you like this silly hat?"

"Aye, geet much!"

They took a different path to before, Foen leading them through the maze of bookshelves. They were all a mystery to Hone, the unintelligible writing making no sense to the young dragon, but something within the library compelled her to stay and explore further. As they passed by a set of books with dark green spines she suddenly halted, turning her head to look down between the shelves. It was like something was calling, *Hone, come and investigate…*

"Wait, I wanna see what's down here…" she said, taking a few steps into the gloom. The other two came to a halt, looking back.

"Come on Hone, there's nothing down there," said Lutis, beckoning her forwards, but she didn't move.

"One minute, I wanna see…" she mumbled, wandering down the gap between the two shelves. Lutis shrugged, rolled his eyes and started after the dragon, meaning to bring her back to the task at hand. She always got so distracted!

"No, let's see what she's after," said Foen, following Hone. The dragon had come to a halt at the end of the little path, her head turned to one side as she stared at the wall in front of her. It was a dead end.

"What is it?" asked Lutis, holding up his candle so he could see the wall. It was a creamy blue colour, and as the light hit it, it shimmered with every colour of the rainbow.

"The wall's covered in opal," said Foen, stepping close and adding the light of his own candle.

Hone laid one paw on its smooth surface, a shiver running down her spine. "It's a precious stone."

"I like it. It sings," said Hone, pressing her other paw against the stone and laying her nose along it. Lutis shot her a quizzical glance but she missed it, her eyes closed in hidden rapture.

"It's called a heartstone. Every breed of dragon has a special heartstone, this must be yours," said Foen, bending down to look at the base of the slab. There were two words written there in a strange writing. "This must say 'lash dragon'."

Hone stepped away from the opal, squinting at the words. Then her eyes widened in surprise.

"It *does* say 'lash dragon'!"

"But... you can't read!" said Lutis, shoving her out of the way to peer at the writing. "These are just forgotten runes, they're not the same letters *we* use."

"Maybe only a dragon can read these symbols?" suggested Foen, tracing one finger along the shapes. "Intriguing. I shall have to investigate this further. But for now, come, we have much to discuss."

They managed to tear Hone reluctantly away from the heartstone, only the thought of unravelling the mystery of the Jewel Towers drawing her away. Lutis made sure to remember the route they took back to the entrance, knowing the lash apprentice would want to come back and admire the stone more another day.

Outside it was dark, time having passed quickly since they had been in the library. It had been easy to lose track of time when there was no way of measuring the hours, and it could have been any time of night, from late evening, to midnight, to the unkind hours of the morning. The streets were deserted and they made their way quickly through the city, Foen leading them to a relatively large building set low in the canopy. He fumbled at his belt for a key, jamming it into the lock and twisting it firmly before the door clicked open.

"Watch yourselves, some of these experiments are very old," he said as he ushered the two in, shutting the door behind him.

The room was lit by the cosy glow of a fire in one corner, the light reflecting off all manner of strange objects. A table to one side of the room was covered in glass bottles and tubes, coloured liquids bubbling and steaming inside a few of the jars without any obvious source of heat, the tools of a sorcerer. The few chairs in the room were covered in stacks of paper and books, more lining the walls on long shelves. Foen hurried around the room, collecting up his belongings and shuffling them into piles so his guests could find a place to sit. He dumped an armful of books on the bottom step of the staircase that led up around the trunk of the tree, flattening a few stray papers under the cover of the top one.

Hone shot Lutis a quick grin and made her way over to the fire, flopping down in front of it as he gave Foen a hand lighting the lamps spread around the room. As she looked up, she gave a giggle, her eye caught by a glitter above. The erratic sorcerer had cutlery stuck to his ceiling.

When they had finished Foen cleared a space for himself and sat down in one of the armchairs near the fire, gesturing for Lutis to join him in the other.

"Quickly, sit. If someone is taking the jewels from the Jewel Towers, then it must be told what the consequences are. Let me tell you the story of the beast…"

16
THE BEAST. REVENGE.

"Many years ago, when Mirrahl was a land filled with chaos, and humans were a scarce sight, there were often wars between the different races that lived here, trying to gain power over the land. The smaller races- elves, avians and the like all had their separate battles (and a few shared ones too), but in the end, it came to be that the dragons ruled over the land as the others bickered.

"Dragons were a much more common sight than now. Of course, there were lashes, hobbits and magpies to name a few we know today, but there were also much larger, ancient breeds of dragon. Of these, the three most magnificent dragons were the sunblaze, the spined shadow and the tribal battle blood. While the sunblaze and the spined shadow symbolised the day and the dark, the tribal battle blood stood for the blood- and rightly so, for of the few things it coveted, spilled blood was its favourite. It was the fiercest, most terrifying dragon you could find, roaming Mirrahl looking for death and destruction, and when it couldn't find any, making its own. Whenever another dragon, or avian, or elf saw a battle blood in the sky they would run and hide, knowing that if they crossed paths, one would die, and it would not be the battle blood.

"Although tribal battle bloods were the dragons with the darkest hearts- despite their name, most spined shadows were surprisingly soft-hearted, and the noblest of dragons- other dragons also lusted for the darker things in life. Of these, the ones that are concerned with this story are the venomous serpent dragon and the hoarder dragon. They lived apart, wrapped in their own bubbles of death and lust and greed.

"It wasn't to last though. As the years passed the smaller races started to multiply, their settlements growing and their numbers increasing until they started to encroach on one another. Unlike the other times they had fought, the elves and the avians became allies, quickly gaining the support of the humans as they rebelled against the rule of the dragons. War broke out. Elves and avians are not warmongering races, but when they turn to it, it is a terrible thing. Many were killed, dragon and two-leg. Pain ruled.

"With the coming of war came the meeting of three of the dark dragons. The tribal battle blood had been rejoicing in the carnage that the land had become, its path followed by a hoarder dragon who took to pillaging the destroyed settlements that he left behind, taking anything valuable for his own. When the hoarder dragon became dissatisfied by the gold that he gained he joined the tribal battle blood, the two working together to meet their own ends. The names of these two were Xaoc and Khaan.

"Soon after they were joined by a third dragon, Botsu, the venomous. Her only interest was in manipulating others and gaining power. The two male dragons, while they knew that she was dangerous, kept her by their side as her charmed words started to earn them powerful followers, who were looking to take over Mirrahl once the dragons were done with its destruction. The sunblaze dragons and the spined shadow dragons could do nothing to stop them as they decimated the land, even going so far as to attack the few dragons that remained following the bloody war between the two-legs and themselves. These two ancient dragon breeds vanished from the land, many being killed, others fleeing to the mountain regions and the rainforests of the north, until Xaoc hunted them down and slaughtered them. It is not known if any more are in existence, but I expect they are all dead.

"One of their most skilful followers was a mage, one who practised only the darkest of magics, and followed the three dragons with a loyalty that was unrivalled. In his quest for gaining in the three dragon's view, he came to them with a dark proposition- in return for their promise that he would become the most powerful man in Mirrahl, he would make them stronger than they had ever been before.

"The three dragons were greedy for strength and finally agreed to his demands, if reluctantly. Botsu still managed to charm him into allowing them free reign of the kingdom that was about to become his- but he had little choice, even if he had not agreed, for his strength would not have been enough to control the beast that he now unleashed on the land. With all his talent in magic he devised a spell that bound the three dragons in one shape, forming a dragon stronger and more potent than any dragon that had been alive before- and since too. The dragon was huge, with tattered black wings bigger than a ship's sails and three snaking heads, each of which could blow red-hot fire. It was covered in red, purple and green runes, the colours of the three dragons that formed it. It was named the triblade dragon, and was always accompanied by certain death.

"The mage that created this horror couldn't look upon his own creature though, because it had blinded him with the brightness of its fire. The three dragons could swap between their own forms and their joint form at will, and when in her own form, Botsu seduced the mage with her cunning words, convincing him that he ruled over the whole kingdom, when there really was no kingdom left at all- the triblade dragon had destroyed everything. Xaoc eventually killed him in cold blood when he tried to command the triblade dragon to bring him all the gold in the land.

"It seemed like nothing could stop the dragon, with the few rebel groups that had survived now stamped from existence or chased to the icy glaciers of the far north. Many years passed, a tiny pocket of elves surviving in the forests to the south east and a few humans living on the desolate Charkoras Isles. The triblade dragon seemed invincible, and it looked like it would reign over Mirrahl forever.

"But unknown to the others on the island, the three dragons were growing discontent with one another. Botsu was forever trying to manipulate the others into playing her sadistic games, and Xaoc cared little for the company of others. Khaan was only interested in his treasure, and gloated at every opportunity.

"Their dissatisfaction made it harder for the three to stay in their shared form for very long, which made them weak to attack, when it finally came. The rebel groups from the north came in numbers, their population having grown since they fled many years before. The three dragons had ignored them, thinking that they would never dare attack. They had never found their stronghold either, which was buried deep under the ice of the largest glacier that ran through the mountains near what is known as Turich today. Despite their numbers, the rebels were nearly destroyed by the triblade dragon, but were saved by a sorcerer named Ferlan.

"Ferlan used a combination of sorcery and magic to defeat the triblade dragon, a combination that had never been used before. He created a potion that enhanced his magical skills, then cast a spell that separated the three dragons from one another. What he did next was magic that has never been seen since. He locked the three dragons in special heartstones- like the opal heartstone in Racksom's library- trapping them in the jewels so they could no longer terrorise the land. Xaoc was trapped inside a ruby, Botsu in an amethyst and Khaan in an emerald. The battle was finally won.

"The three jewels were separated. Although the dragons were now secured, their power was still strong, and with a single touch they could be released. Three Jewel Towers were built in different settlements across the island, which have now become known as Racksom, Quinsilla and Tarz. These were very small towns when the triblade dragon was defeated, but when the towers were built, people moved to be near them. The power of the jewels seemed to repel any evil that still lurked on Mirrahl and the cities flourished. Battered as the inhabitants of Mirrahl were, a peace was set between the many races that had survived, a peace that has lasted through to this day. Although, if what you say is true, and two of the three dragons have been released, and the third is threatened, then the peace will come to an end."

There was a pause as Foen finished his story, the two letting the new rush of information sink in. There was a sudden clatter in one corner of the room as a fork fell off the ceiling and they jumped, Hone giving a squeal of fear and burying her head underneath her wings.

"Don't let it get me!" she squeaked, shaking. Lutis patted her flank and she flinched, terrified.

"It's fine Hone, we're safe, nobody's going to get you," he crooned, rubbing her scales. "Relax."

"But two o'the dragons are free now, an' they took t'stone so easy, an' now they could head f'Tarz, an', an'…" Her voice got faster and faster, the words tumbling out. "What if they destroy t'island!?"

"That's not going to happen," cut in Foen, his voice calm.

"What about the sunblaze, or the spined shadow dragons? Could we could find them?" asked Lutis. Now they knew what Zartear was up to, it looked bleak on the defending side, with only small dragons to protect Tarz if it came under attack, which looked inevitable.

"There are none left, nobody's seen either for many years. The only reason I've heard of them is the oldest of legends, in the most obscure of books. The best lead I've ever gotten was a picture, one I found on a scrap of paper shoved inside an old book of myths, but I never found out where it came from," said Foen, shrugging. "I think its safe to say there are no more ancient dragons left on Mirrahl. You can see the picture if you like though." He frowned at the bookshelf then tugged out a tome, flicking through the pages until there was a rustle of paper and the drawing fell out. He looked at it wistfully for a moment before passing it over to Lutis. A hastily scrawled note identified the regal-looking dragon as a spined shadow, a name written underneath- it looked like 'Trukais', but Lutis couldn't be sure. It was lying on its side, looking out of the page, its bright eyes framed by curving horns, and down its back ran a thick set of blue and green spines. It was interesting, but of little use. Lutis passed it back.

"This Ferlan, the mage that trapped the dragons in their heartstones- can you do that?" was Lutis' next question, looking for any lead possible.

Foen laughed. "He was a sorcerer, not a mage. Big difference you know. I'm a sorcerer too. I can't think up the same potion; it took him years to do that- but it might have been written down somewhere. And I could try and duplicate it..." He tapped a finger to his lips, thinking. "Yes, that could work..." He suddenly jumped to his feet and ran to the bookshelf, tugging out a huge volume on the middle of the shelf, obviously well thumbed. "Well, if you're laying all the work on me, better start now, eh?"

"...Do you want help?" offered Lutis, watching the sorcerer as he started to scan the contents page.

"No, this is complicated stuff. Anyway, I don't need some nosy poking through all my books." He gave a small smile, not looking up. It was obvious he wasn't going to give up his search until the sun rose again at the least, already on the hunt for something, anything that would stop the triblade dragon from returning to the land.

"Come on you silly dragon, time to head out," Lutis whispered to Hone, prodding her in the ribs to make her move. She squealed and leapt to her feet, chewing on one paw when she saw Foen's amused smile.

"Whista time?" she asked, suddenly yawning. Nothing could be seen through the windows, the world completely black outside.

"No idea," replied Lutis, tugging the dragon towards the door. "Thanks for the information, you've been great. Uh... shall we come back tomorr-"

He was interrupted by a heavy thud on the other side of the front door, the noise sending Hone shrieking to hide behind an armchair. Foen dropped his book in surprise, cursing when a few loose slips of paper flew out across the floor. There was a scratching sound, then a click as the lock was opened by whoever was on the other side.

The person the other side was invisible as he dropped the bundle of keys that he held in one hand and leaned against the frame of the door, before staggering forwards into the light. The lamps flickered from the breeze that came through the open door, but were bright enough to reveal Armeno. The elf looked terrible- half his face was red with dried blood, his hair stuck down on one side, and sticking up on the other. His eyes flicked around the room, then he wordlessly headed for the staircase, swaying from side to side.

"Bloody hell Armeno, what happened?" exclaimed Foen, his mouth dropping open as he stepped forwards to catch hold of the elf and stop him in his path. Close up he looked even worse, his chain mail armour stained with mud and dirt, his dark cloak ripped all the way down from the shoulder and one ear bent at a strange angle, flopping limply down.

Armeno avoided Foen's gaze until the sorcerer gave him a shake, his eyebrows dipping into a frown before speaking.

"Static's dead," he said shortly, pulling his arms out of Foen's grasp.

"What? But... she's not in Racksom any more!"

"She was with the other army. I could have saved her... but that *bitch* stopped me. And then she knocked me out and ran for it." His voice turned into an angry growl and one hand curled around the hilt of his blade, his intentions obvious. He started towards the staircase again.

"Wait, what are you doing? You can't be thinking to go after the army, not looking like that!" Foen shot Lutis a look saying, *help!* before running after the elf again, trying to reason with him. "Please Armeno, think! Use some common sense!"

"Think? Think?" shouted Armeno, turning suddenly to tower over the shorter man. "Static just... died and..." His voice started to crack and he pinched the bridge of his nose. "She can't be dead..." he whispered, shaking his head.

"I'm so sorry..." started Foen, but the elf pushed him away.

"Just... leave me alone. I'm going after them, that Felixis isn't getting away with this." His voice was hard as he held back his pain and bolted for the stairs before Foen could catch him again.

"Fat lot of help you were," huffed Foen to the others as he returned to his book, picking it up and shoving it back onto the shelf. "He never did have much sense... suppose I'll have to try plan B." He headed for his chaotic desk, rummaging amongst the bottles and papers.

"What were we supposed to say?" protested Lutis, catching a scroll that the sorcerer knocked off the edge of his table. "That made no sense whatsoever to me!"

Foen clicked his tongue, holding up a bottle and inspecting the contents before giving a terse nod. "You could have told him to have stopped being so stupid- he never listens to me."

"And what made you think he would listen to me?" scoffed the thief. "Why, we've only met for a moment, and that was after a goblin attack!"

"Aha, so you *do* know Armeno! I thought you might. Well, you could have tried." He shook his head, picking at the edge of the bottle's label to try and peel it off. It half ripped and the sorcerer tutted again.

Hone had been investigating the rest of the room after she regained her composure and had come to a halt at the bottom of the stairs, looking up to see where the elf had gone. She was just about to start up after him when he reappeared, looking determined, but little improved. He headed straight for the door again, a bag slung over his shoulder, bulging with the few possessions he kept.

"Wait, you can't leave looking like that. Let me at least fix your ear, it looks terrible. And take some of this," Foen scrabbled for the bottle he had put down, "It'll help if you're really stubborn about leaving this instant."

Armeno looked as though he was going to turn down the offer, but at the last moment sagged. "Fine. Be fast." He sunk into one of the chairs at the table, resting his head wearily in one hand.

Foen cracked a relieved smile, dumping the bottle in front of him and rummaging around in a cupboard for his box of medical supplies. His cures were what allowed him such freedom with his time, and the comfort of such a large home- people came from all over the city to receive them. Armeno took a good swig of the bottle, looking at his hand in disgust as dark red blood flaked off his face in little speckles.

"I'm just going to fix your ear up…" said Foen, plonking his box onto the table and pulling out bandages and splints and sticking plaster. The elf took another swig of the bottle, grimacing at the taste.

"What is this stuff?" he asked, peering at the torn label. His eyes widened as he made out the faint writing. "Foen, I'm going to bloody kill you." He got to his feet, reaching out for the sorcerer, but he stumbled, his legs buckling.

Foen only just caught him in time, lowering him slowly to the floor with a grunt. "Heavy! Come and give me a hand here will you?"

Lutis obliged, pulling Armeno into a sitting position. The elf lolled to one side, eyes shut. "What did you give him?"

"Sleeping potion, he won't be going anywhere for a couple of days with the amount he just drunk," Foen chuckled, hooking his arms under the elf's armpits. "Come on, help me get him upstairs."

It was nearly two days later when Armeno woke to find himself in his bed at Foen's house. For a moment he didn't realise where he was, then he pulled the covers over his head, trying to hold back the wave of grief that hit him. He buried his face in his pillow as he cried, then scrubbed his tears furiously away, looking at his hand in surprise when he saw it was bandaged. In fact, there were a few bandages- Foen. That bloody sorcerer!

Armeno gritted his teeth in anger and sat up, pushing off the blankets and hunting for a shirt. Foen may have stopped him from leaving right away, but he wasn't going to get in the way again. He started to lump all his belongings together on the bed, concentrating on going through the motions rather on the memories that threatened to overwhelm him once more. Soon he had a tidy pile, everything packed into two saddlebags that he could attach to the saddle of his horse, his bow and quiver of arrows placed on top. There was only one thing missing...

"Foen? Where the hell's my sword?" he yelled down the staircase from the doorway, not caring to find the man. He could be anywhere.

There was a thump from across the hallway, then another door flew open and Foen emerged at speed, trying to conceal his surprise. "Uh... you're awake! Did you want some breakfast or something?"

"Where's my sword?" asked Armeno again, narrowing his eyes at the sorcerer. Foen bit his lip.

"It's in your room, like always." He pointed behind Armeno into his room, gesturing noncommittally.

"You've hidden it, where in my room?" He stepped aside as Foen came forward, watching the man carefully.

"I haven't hidden it! I'm sure it's here somewhere, just *look* for it." His gaze ranged over the room, flicking from the dishevelled bed to the cupboard and back.

Armeno folded his arms, looking down at the shorter man. "It's under the bed, isn't it?"

"Why would I put your sword under the bed?"

The elf shot him an unamused look and bent down to pull the covers up- lo and behold, there was his sword, under the bed.

"Well, would you look at that," said Foen lamely, fleeing out of the door when Armeno gave him another annoyed look. "I uh... if you really are going, you'll need some provisions."

"You're not stopping me Foen!" called Armeno after the sorcerer, buckling the sword onto his belt and scooping up the saddlebags in his arms. His bandaged hand twinged where he had cut it pushing Nox's blade out of the way, but he ignored the faint pain.

By the time he got downstairs (Foen had made the staircase practically impossible to navigate, putting books in perilous piles on nearly every step, obviously to deter Armeno from leaving), the sorcerer had wrapped up a pile of supplies for him on the table, and was sitting nearby reading another book. The room had become even more cluttered than before (if that was even possible), papers scattered wide as the sorcerer frantically searched for *anything* that might stop Zartear's plans. Armeno packed the food in the last empty saddlebag, giving his thanks. As he headed for the door, Foen looked up from the book, a worried look on his face.

"Armeno… don't do anything stupid. Revenge isn't worth it."

"This revenge is." The elf didn't look back as he pulled the door shut after him and started down into the lower levels of the city. He headed straight for the stables where he kept his horse, Velox. It was quite a large set of buildings, but he knew exactly where his black arab would be, and was soon tacking up the flighty stallion. He paid the stables for looking after his horse then left at a canter, heading for the north gate with a determined look set on his face. First he would follow and find Zartear's army, then he would kill that Felixis that stopped him from saving Static.

17
GATHERING OF MORE TROOPS.
BOAT TROUBLES.

"Get a bloody move on Foen, they'll leave without us!" bellowed Lutis up the staircase, shaking his head in frustration. The sorcerer was taking *forever*. The day after Foen had found out that two of the jewels had been taken from their towers he had left Armeno recuperating for a few hours on his own while he went to Racksom council, explaining his tale again and warning them that action needed to be taken. To his relief they had believed him and the city guards were readied, a few ordered to remain in the city to keep Racksom safe from another possible attack, the rest prepared to travel to Tarz and defend the city against Zartear's forces, who were bound to have plans to head for the city.

Armeno had left a few days before, heading out on his own vendetta. The word that there was a going to be a mass movement of troops was sent to nearby Port Racksom, and a fleet of ships were put in order to take the warriors to the next port along, Jiluria.

The first guards had left early that morning but the lash dragons had stayed behind, waiting for Liesk and Foen, both of who were also travelling to Tarz. The sorcerer was vital for stopping Zartear's plans, and the healer had refused to be left behind. Under her close watch Echai was recovering quickly, and was almost back to his old self. For Doan however, it was a different story. Although Liesk's quick thinking had saved his life, the dragon had lost his wing- and with it, his balance. While he now had enough strength to stand he was as clumsy as a newborn puppy, and despite all his attempts to regain his balance had fallen at every hurdle.

The others hated to leave him behind in Racksom, but the lash Elite saw that they had no choice and bid them farewell, despite Hone and Tekek's protests. He finally persuaded them, albeit reluctantly, and made himself comfortable at Liesk's, promising to keep the little house safe- and to try not to break anything. Liesk didn't hold much hope for it though- the dragon's attempts at walking had been invariably followed by the breakage of something or other.

"Okay, okay, I'm coming," huffed Foen, staggering down the staircase with an armful of scrolls. The short man could hardly see over his pile, and stumbled as he knocked against one of the towers of books he hadn't cleaned off the stairs. His armful went flying as he tripped, scattering papers into the air.

Lutis managed to catch two scrolls before they hit the floor, a book that had been hidden under the papers thumping him on the shoulder as he tried to retrieve it. "Ouch! Why do you need so many books?"

"This potion you've got me trying to find isn't common you know!" said Foen, rubbing the back of his head as he got to his feet and started clearing the mess. "Nobody's made it since Ferlan first used it."

"You would have thought someone would have written such an important potion down…"

grumbled Lutis, helping Foen shove all the books he needed into a bag. "Is that it?"

"Yes, I think so... quit hanging around, we're going to be late!" said Foen, shooting Lutis a grin before pulling open the front door. "Oh, and bring that bag over there too will you?"

The man muttered under his breath as he picked up more of Foen's gear, swinging it over his shoulder. The lash Elites had gone on ahead and were waiting at the south gate for them.

The pair wound their way down through the city to the ground. The place was busy, the last few guards that were leaving saying their farewells to their families, sharing hugs and plaguing those who were leaving with more supplies than they could carry. When Hone saw the two she gave a pleased bugle and ran over. The bandages that had covered the wounds on her face had been taken off the day before, revealing the pale stripes that cut through her purple scales.

"We thought you weren't comin'! What took s'long?"

"Foen decided he needed twice as many books as he had packed," said Lutis, handing the dragon one of the bags he was carrying. "Better go, before he's decided he's forgotten more."

Hone giggled, peeking inside the bag. "Cor, he does have a lot o'books!"

"That ain't even half of them."

They tagged onto the end of a group of guards that were setting off, Aeron making sure his patrol kept close together. After two of his patrol had been badly hurt, he wasn't going to let anyone else get hurt too. Hone kept the mood light in their little group as they walked, but outside the patrol spirits were grim, nobody really knowing what to expect for the journey and the battle ahead.

It was a day's walk between Racksom and Port Racksom, trekking through the forest on a relatively well-maintained road. Every so often they passed an inn, but they didn't stop, pressing on until dusk. They made camp by the track, eating a sparse meal before turning in for the night, knowing there was another day of walking ahead of them the next morning.

The weather the next day was dreary, a thin mist laying itself under the trees and drifting between the trunks. When they reached the small town at lunchtime the haze gave the place an aimless, dreamlike quality. In the harbour the huge sailboats, their masts pointing naked into the sky, wandered in and out of the sight, the fog turning the familiar shapes into dark, wraithlike objects. There was a faint clinking, slapping sound as the breeze stirred the ships' tack, sending taunt ropes banging against the masts or hulls bumping against the harbourside. There was little noise otherwise.

"Wowee! Are we gaarn on one o'those?" asked Hone, pointing to a ship. Liesk nodded, giving her a pat on the shoulder.

"Yes, have you ever been on a ship before?"

"No, whista like?" The dragon's eyes were bright with excitement.

"They're great, just you wait," chipped in Lutis, pointing to a large clipper resting in the harbour, its figurehead a great black leaping cat, face twisted into a ferocious snarl. "We're on that one."

"Cool!"

They headed up the ramp of the ship, walking slowly so the thin bridge didn't bounce and send them toppling into the water. The deck was busy with sailors getting the ship ready to sail. As Hone gawped at the mast that stretched high above them there was a shout from above and the dark mainsail was let down, fluttering in the breeze.

"Looks like yeh made it onboard jus' in time, we're 'bout tae set sail," said a man, stepping forwards to shake Lutis and Foen's hands. He was wearing a tricorn hat, the face underneath ruddy from years of the cold sea air, his hair dry and salty and his chin speckled with a layer of stubble. "Bes' get down t'the quarters, let ars do our job. Yeh can come back up on deck when we're out t'sea."

"Does a ship always move underpaw like this?" asked Hone, staggering slightly as the boat leaned on the waves.

"Aye it does dragon, an' this aye nobbut still," said the man, turning to the young lash. "Yeh just wait 'til we get out t'sea!"

"Does it gar up an' down more at sea then?"

"Aye. Ne'er put tae sea before, eh dragon?" he asked with a laugh, putting one hand on his hip as he viewed his crew. Seeing the mast flap in the breeze he barked an order and it was instantly secured.

"None o' us have before," said Aeron. "We're more… desert dragons than sea monsters."

"Aye, an' that's jus' the way I like it t'be!" he laughed again. "Go on, off with yeh." He waved them towards the hatch at the aft of the boat. "Aye, an' while you're aboard t'*Sleek Panther*, yer'll call me capt'n!" he shouted after the dragons as they descended the steps below decks, Hone already tottering this way and that.

They made their way slowly down to the hold, where they were sharing quarters with the other guards that had been put on the ship, as well as a lot of the supplies they were carrying. There was a jerk as the ship set off, moving slowly through the water while the crew rigged up the jib and topsails, then faster, leaning slightly to one side when they caught the fresh sea wind.

As they moved away from the coast the mist that had covered the port started to thin, revealing the fleet of ships setting off. The *Black Panther's* sails were dark, reflected in the water as an inky blot. The other ships drifted in and out of view, their own sails a myriad of colours- pale cream, sky blue, burgundy, one even green. The land disappeared from view as they sailed into deeper water, the mist clinging to the distant shore like a cloud and dispersing into thick clumps that floated low over the waves further out.

Aeron made his way up to the top deck after a while, checking to see if they were allowed up above the quarters again. The captain was standing at the helm of the ship and gave the Elite a cheery wave. Aeron waved back then wandered over to the side of the ship, curling his paws over the gunwale. The spray flicked in his face as the ship gathered speed and the Elite held on tightly, his face lit up with exhilaration. It was almost as good as speeding across the desert.

"How d'yeh like it?" said the captain as he walked over, leaving his duties to another member of his crew.

"It's… it's nice. I can see why y'sail t'seas Capt'n. Not sure I would pick it over t'desert, but it's nice."

"Y'should see 'er when t'stormwinds get up. Now tha's somethin' t'see." He leaned his elbows on the rail, grinning when he saw that his ship was catching up with the rest of the fleet. "How're t'rest of yeh dragons' doin'?"

"Tekek went very pale, an' said she felt sick. Echai dinae look s'good either, but tha' might be 'cause he ain't been on his feet for a geet long time…" said Aeron.

"They're prob'bly feelin' seasick. Go an' find t'ship's doc. He'll sort them out right an' proper."

"Thanks!" Aeron turned away from the side, meaning to go find the doctor straight away. From the way Tekek had been slowly turning a nasty shade of green (which was a strange colour, considering her scales were purple and red), she at least would be needing something to keep the sickness at bay.

He met Lutis coming up the steps, his coat (for once) tucked away elsewhere. His shirt sleeves were rolled up to his elbows and he was looking cheerful.

"Any dolphins yet?" he asked, a grin on his face.

"Whista dolphins?" Aeron cocked his head to one side, looking confused.

"What are- are you kidding? You gotta come up on deck and watch for them. They're like nothing else on Mirrahl."

"I have t'gar check on t'others first, but then I'll come back."

"You don't want to go down there. Seriously, it's not a pretty sight."

Aeron pulled a face, not liking the sound of what awaited him. "Patrol afore self, Lutis."

"Yeah, you keep telling yourself that." He waved a hand in dismissal and wandered over to the prow of the ship, leaning over the side to look for the dolphins he had mentioned. They tended to stick quite close to the shore near Port Racksom- the extra fish from the fishing boats made for an easy meal, and there was at least one pod that swum the seas near the little town.

As the ship picked up speed, cutting through the water like an arrow, dark shapes appeared near the clipper, featureless until they rose to the surface, leaping high through the air before splashing back under. The dolphins had pale white skin, dappled with dark patches of orange, black and red, each animal different.

The wind caught at their frilled fins, stretching them out like wings. Lutis watched them jump, grinning at their play. They were so carefree... You could almost forget the crazy things that were happening on the island. They suddenly turned off towards another ship as the *Black Panther* dipped through a patch of fog, leaping off in a big group.

"Y'were right 'bout not gaarn down there." Aeron appeared beside Lutis again, looking pale. "I got t'doctor. Let's hope his cures work on dragons as well as they do humans... Hone's not feelin' great either, 'though she won't admit it."

Lutis pulled a face, patting the Elite on the shoulder. "You're feeling alright though, right? You missed the dolphins by the way, they just left. They might be back later though."

"I'm ahreet, but... whista tha' then, if it's not a dolphin?" Aeron asked, leaning over the side and looking down into the water. A slimmer, faster shape darted past, twisting left and right with reckless speed. It suddenly came to the surface, flicking its tail once before pushing out of the water and leaping right over the bow of the ship. Its scales shimmered in the weak light for a moment before it dived back underneath the waves, disappearing deep into the water.

"That wasn't a dolphin!" Lutis exclaimed, running to the other side of the prow and leaning over to look for the animal again.

"Hippocampus t'starboard!" came a cry from the back of the boat, identifying the creature before it leapt again, throwing itself much higher into the air, alongside the ship this time. It was longer and lither than the dolphins, a dark frilled fin running down its neck from the back of its head. It was a mottled turquoise colours, patches of green and blue speckling its skin. It's finely boned face was startlingly similar to that of a horse- it even had front legs like one, but instead of hooves it had huge fins, curved like scoops to propel itself through the water.

As it hit the water again its fins collapsed, turning from wings into paddles as it sped away, its tail flashing from side to side as it dived. The pair leant over the side of the ship, trying to see where it went, but it was nowhere to be seen.

Suddenly there was a splash behind them and the hippocampus leapt over the prow of the ship again, its scales flashing. A strange *ponk* noise echoed through the air, dying for a moment, then reverberating once more. It was cut off as the hippocampus dived under the water again, abruptly silenced.

"Dids'eh hear tha'?" Aeron gasped as the creature disappeared, leaning over the side to try and see where it had went. Lutis put a warning hand on his wing, ready to pull him back if he lost his balance.

"Hear what?"

"There wherst a *pink* or a *ponk* sort o'noise…" He frowned, shaking his head and looking at the man. "It was prob'bly nothin'…"

"Right…" Lutis didn't sound convinced, watching the dragon for a moment. "Are you okay?"

"Aye, aye I'm fine… " He wrinkled his nose, checking the water again for any sign of the creature. "Actually, I think I might gar sit down, I feel a bit dizzy."

"Don't tell me you're feeling seasick too?" moaned Lutis, his face falling. Without anyone else to talk to, it would be mind-numbingly boring on board the ship. He might even be put to work by the captain!

"No, I don't think so… I'll be ahreet in a minute." The dragon slid to the floor, leaning against the side of the ship. Lutis hovered briefly, then sat down beside him, resting his head against the side and looking up at the masts that towered above them.

"Well, I'm staying on deck. I wouldn't go down below decks if you paid me."

It only took two days for the fleet of ships to get to Jiluria, making fast time with a strong wind helping them on their way. Lutis spent a lot of time with Foen, who had managed to persuade the captain to give him his own cabin to continue looking for the potion that he needed to trap the dragons in their jewels once more, and had quickly given into Lutis' offer of helping. All the lash dragons, apart from Aeron, got bad seasickness and kept below decks for most of the time they were at sea. Hone thought it all rather miserable, and her normally voracious appetite was sorely lacking.

The books that Foen had brought with him were full of obscure potions and Lutis found the lilting script that it was written in hard to read, more used to quick scrawled messages like the ones his thief friends back in Kaionar used to write. Nevertheless he battled through the books the sorcerer gave him, occasionally asking about a strange ingredient or effect that a potion gave. For all his knowledge of cities and underground networks, when it came to sorcery, he knew next to nothing, something Foen took great humour from.

After one such hard session, Lutis working through a tome that he thought would never end, they felt the ship turning, its tilt growing more pronounced as it leaned on the waves.

"Wonder why we're turning," commented Lutis, leaning back and stretching. He rolled his shoulders a couple of times, stiff from hunching over books for so long.

"It is?" mumbled Foen, his finger running over the potion he was reading. "Are you sure?"

"Yeah, that pile of books looks like it's about to fall over now." He pointed to a stack leaning perilously to one side. Even as he called attention to it, it tipped and tumbled to the floor, making the sorcerer jump and turn.

"Hmm, maybe we're stopping for the night?"

"Its still daylight," said Lutis, sighing and getting out of his chair to collect up the pile again.

"It is?" The sorcerer blinked and went back to the book he was reading, reaching out with one hand for the quill that he had handy for anything he thought might be important. Lutis rolled his eyes.

"I'm going up to see why, do you want anything?" he asked, nudging a book aside as he picked his way through the mess they had made. The little cabin looked as higgledy-piggledy as Foen's house had been- the sorcerer seemed to care little for it, and Lutis wasn't going to clear up his mess.

"Mm, something to eat would be good right now. Kiwi-fruit. Zack's favourite. I like it too. I think he got his liking for it from me."

Lutis laughed. "Not sure there's going to be kiwi-fruit on board. You'll have to have something a bit plainer." He disappeared out the door, letting it clang shut behind him. The pile of books fell over again as it made the floor shake.

Things were busy on deck, and it was instantly clear why. They had been travelling a little way away from the coastline, keeping it on their left, just in view. Now they were turning in towards it, a dark smudge a few leagues off showing the end of their journey by sea. It was Jiluria, the next harbour along from Port Racksom.

"Whista gaarn on?" asked Aeron, who had come up onto the deck like Lutis had to investigate. The man pointed into the distance.

"That's Jiluria, our next port of call."

Aeron gave a relieved smile, flicking his tail in pleasure. "Good. Will we get there today? I've nearly had it with the others' moanin'."

"Looks like it, we've still got quite a wind behind us." Lutis looked up at the sails. "What happened to 'patrol before self'?"

Aeron laughed. "There's so much moanin' an' groanin' you can take. Y'know, I don't see why they're complainin' so much."

"Well, seasickness isn't very nice… I've had it a couple of times, but only in bad weather. You're pretty lucky- being the only lash aboard not feeling green! Can't say the same for your scales though!" He grinned, making the dragon chortle.

"You've been on lots of boats afore then?" Lutis seemed quite knowledgeable about sailing, and the lash wondered why.

"Yep, back in Kaionar when I was a boy, my Pa used to take me out in a little sailing boat down the river whenever he could." He smiled at the fond memory. "Used to be great fun, sometimes when the wind was up we went real fast."

"Was he a sailor?"

"Nope, a thief." His smile widened into a grin. "Just like me."

Aeron chucked. "Runs in the family then eh?"

"Sure does."

They watched the land grow slowly bigger for a little while, then Aeron headed back down to tell the other lash dragons the good news. Lutis hung outside for a little longer, not wanting to go back to the stuffy little room, but if he didn't go and chide Foen to pack away all his belongings, he knew that the sorcerer would never get the place clean.

As it was, when he returned, the room was hardly recognisable, papers strewn all over the place, a few splattered with blue ink.

"What did you *do*?" asked Lutis incredulously. Foen looked sheepish, spreading out a blot of ink on the papers in front of him with one finger.

"I uh… got frustrated…" He gave a guilty smile, looking around at the mess before laughing. "These books are useless!"

"So you…"

"Threw them all over the place, yeah…"

Lutis burst into laughter at his confession. "Only you would do that sort of thing."

"Come on, you would have done it too!"

"Probably. We better start clearing up, Jiluria's in sight." He started collecting papers off the floor, patting them together into a neat pile. "I'll give you a hand."

"Thanks. Did you get any food?"

"Nope."

"Are you lying?"

"Yep."

"Where's the food?"

"Wouldn't you like to know?"

"I would."

"Better get on with helping me clear up then!" Lutis threw a book at the sorcerer, who was still sitting at the desk drawing patterns in the ink. The man huffed, rubbing his fingers together before getting to his feet and mucking in.

The room took the whole afternoon to sort out, by which time the *Sleek Panther* was heading into Jiluria to dock. Aeron had managed to coax his patrol up onto the deck, and he and Liesk (who had been looking after the dragons) tried to keep their spirits up for the rest of their voyage. The harbour was much smaller than Port Racksom, and could only hold a few ships at a time, forcing the others to dock outside the harbour and take it in turns to unload. By the time it was their turn to moor the sun was low on the horizon, sending red rays shooting across the water. Those on board the *Sleek Panther* would wait until the morning to leave the town.

They berthed easily, the captain guiding his clipper carefully between the other moored ships to a tight spot close to the mouth of the harbour. Dock hands helped make the ship secure as the cargo was unloaded.

The captain stood by the gangplank that was let down, occasionally calling out an order, but otherwise letting the crew get on with their work. As the Elites headed off the ship, thankful to finally be getting back to dry land, he stopped Aeron.

"Goo' luck with ever'thing. Come back alive, won't yeh?" he said, tipping his hat to the dragon.

"We'll try. Y'stay safe on t'seas too," said Aeron, but the captain laughed.

"Ah, half t'fun's t'danger." He waved his arm to the gangplank. "Yeh war awaits."

"Thanks... I think." He started down the plank, watching his step. The last thing he wanted to do was take a dip in the sea. There was a parting shout from the captain,

"Go kill some Surahnite scum!"

18
STEALTH COMES TO NOTHING.

Armeno quickly found the trail that Zartear's retreating army had cut through the forest, the thick swathe from hundreds of enemy feet crushing the undergrowth flat and making it easy for the elf to make fast time. Even he, a warrior, not a tracker, had no problem following their trail. His horse, Velox, was edgy from not being ridden for a couple of days and danced at every little thing that was out of place in the forest.

When the elf came to the place where the army had made camp a little way from the city he reined in the stallion, viewing the place with a growing anger. Signs of celebration lay scattered across the newly-hacked clearing, the cinders from campfires twisting into the air in little spirals as Velox's hooves stirred them. Bottles lay scattered amongst the undergrowth, along with darker items- bloodstained daggers and the gory trophies taken by the bloodthirsty goblins, here a clump of feathers from the wing of an avian, there the blood-splattered shield of a fallen elf, deemed too lowly to be admired for more than a moment.

Armeno shook his head slowly, resentment bubbling inside him. What sort of monsters did *this*? He hardened his resolve, making a vow that whoever was responsible would die, then spurred Velox into a canter, his eyes set on the trail in front of him.

He saw nobody else as he rode, the only signs of life the odd bird perched high in the trees, watching him with suspicion. They didn't sing, frightened by the cold steel of the army that had passed through only days before. He guessed that he couldn't have been more than two days behind- he was travelling fast, not having to slow down for a companion, and he had wasted no time once he had woken from his sleep.

The track led back north, heading towards Racksom Lake, so Armeno guessed that the army must be heading for the lake to stock up water supplies before setting out... wherever they were going. He camped a little way away from the lake that night, keeping his presence secret until the right moment, when he would strike. He ate a meagre supper, rationing the food that Foen had supplied him with before wrapping a blanket tightly around him and trying to catch some sleep.

The trail *did* lead to Lake Racksom, as he had predicted. He stopped to fill his water flask from the side of the lake, looking out across the sparkling water for a while, thinking. Velox took a long drink from the edge, sending ripples across the still water as he shifted uneasily, unnerved by the strange smells that hung around the abandoned camp. Armeno patted his side gently, waiting until he was finished, then pulled his reins over the stallions' head and started off down the trail again, walking to save the horse's energy for when he might need it when they got closer to the army.

The trail cut through the woods in a straight path, heading due east, towards the Everplains. It would be a long walk to the rolling meadows and open grasslands, but Armeno didn't doubt they were heading there- the Everplains were like a crossroads; from there, you could get practically anywhere else on Mirrahl.

As Armeno covered ground he started to become more wary of catching up with the army. A lot of the distance they had covered he had pressed on as fast as Velox could go, trying to keep his dark thoughts at bay, focusing on the fact that with every step, revenge was a little closer.

When it got to late afternoon, and Armeno was back to riding, the track crossed the thick river that wound from Lake Racksom through the Everplains and down to the sea. He rode alongside it for a while, trying to find a place to cross- where the army had crossed, it was wide and shallow, but the bed was dark with silt, and Velox's hooves would stir it up, which could give away his presence if the army was heading downstream. He tracked upstream for nearly a league, growing increasingly frustrated when the river deepened. He tried the other direction but he had little luck that way either- the trees that lined the river started to grow thicker along the banks, making it impossible to access the water.

The elf backtracked again, annoyed that he had wasted so much time with no gain. The water ran smoothly across the crossing-place, the mud dark and silky and deceptively smooth, but Armeno knew that at the first touch of Velox's hooves it would go swirling down the river in a dark cloud, giving him away instantly.

He dismounted, checking his saddlebags were secured and taking a drink of water before getting back into the saddle. Once he had crossed, if the army had moved downstream, they would surely know they were being followed. He gathered his reins, checked his sword was to hand, then spurred Velox into a canter across the river. Water sprayed up into the air, drenching Armeno's legs, but the elf sat tight, his face grim as the river blackened with mud and went spiralling down the river like ink in a pool.

~

Nox had abandoned the horse that she had ridden to Racksom, riding Tamarisk, Static's knabstrupper, in place of the haughty mare. Once he had gotten used to the fact that she would be riding him he quietened, keeping up a steady pace as she trotted up and down the ranks of the army, trying to keep herself occupied. She had abandoned the guise of her avian form, now she had no-one she had to hide her real identity from, but she missed the company, especially when they made camp at night.

At the lake she spent most of the night alone, eating a fast supper before reporting to Zartear- not that there was anything to report. Tamarisk had woken her sometime during the night when a brash mercenary took a fancy to having the stallion and tried to make off with him, but Nox dealt with him quickly, not listening to a word of his attempted excuse before she slew him with her blade.

Despite the length of the army train, the venomous dragon Botsu always managed to find Nox. She was like a bad penny, turning up in a whisper when the Felixis least expected it, dropping her purple twists over her shoulders with a smile and a hiss.

"How are we, misss?"

It was during one such encounter with the dragon that a mercenary rode up on a battered-looking horse, kicking the beast mercilessly with his heels. He hailed her with a shout, earning himself a narrowed look.

"What is it?" she snapped, brushing Botsu off her shoulders like she was a pesky fly. The dragon sniggered and fluttered away, her body trailing through the air.

He gave a half bow, pulling his horse up to a walk. "Saw a load of mud drifting down the river, thought it might be worth checking out."

Nox watched the man, then suddenly pulled her sword out of its sheath and angled it at the man. "Do you know who I am?"

"Yes! You're second in command," he said, eyeing the blade cautiously.

"So, if you know that, where's your respect?"

"Oh! Sorry miss… I mean commander." He tugged his horse away a little, hoping to escape with just a verbal warning.

"Better. Swap your horse for one that you haven't ground into the dirt, take a group of nine others and backtrack, see if we're being followed."

The man nodded. "Yes commander." He turned towards the rear of the army, where a train of free horses had been roped together to replace those which were exhausted, but Nox halted him for a moment more.

"Capture them alive, bring them to me. I want to know why we're being followed."

He nodded again, this time with a coarse salute, and rode off down the ranks, leaving Nox to ponder on who might be following. Who could be foolish enough to follow the army that had just destroyed a good part of Racksom's defences?

Her interest aroused, she eventually decided to turn and investigate herself, tugging Tamarisk around in a circle before heading back along the troops at a trot. She couldn't hope to catch up with the little group that she had sent off, but she would reach them faster if they were heading for each other.

The end of the army tailed off quickly once she reached the supply carts, leaving only their messy wake behind them through the trees. It was quite hard for the Felixis to see the devastation they had left, after she had lived most of her life amongst the forests of the west, but she quelled the sorrow that tried to prick at her, telling herself that it was stupid, and that there were bigger things at hand.

The scream of a horse echoed through the quiet forest, then the faint clash of blades- so, there had been someone following them. Nox kicked Tamarisk into a gallop, leaning close over his neck to keep her balance.

~

Armeno had only just seen the small group of enemy soldiers riding back before they were upon him, his sword catching the first blow that came. Velox, trained for battle, instantly held his ground, leaping forwards when the elf squeezed his knees against his sides, the reins free. His opponents outnumbered him ten to one, quite literally, but he didn't give up, slicing his blade this way and that. He managed to dispatch two as they tried to control their horses, reluctantly slicing out at a mount and making it scream in pain as the blade cut and it crashed to the ground, throwing its rider.

His good luck could never hold out though, as the others approached slower, their blades drawn and ready. Armeno made Velox back up a little, taking hold of the reins again.

"Come on, I'll take you one by one, or all at once, your choice!" he growled, his eyes flicking from man to man. When none moved he spurred Velox's sides, making the arab jump forwards to close the gap between them. There was a flurry of swords as the mercenaries hastened to defend themselves against the surprise attack, those on the edges pulling their horses around to trap Armeno in a circle.

He spun Velox, looking for a way out, then swore violently in elvish, the stallion rearing with a whinny as swords jabbed out at him. He leaned into the horse, grabbing at the pommel of his saddle as Velox kicked out, felling another of his opponents. As he dropped to the ground again, snorting and pawing, one of the men pushed his horse forwards and threw himself at Armeno, knocking his sword aside as they tumbled from their horses onto the ground. Armeno snarled and elbowed the man aside, reaching for his sword, but Velox danced backwards into the way and he had to avoid the stallion's sharp hooves.

He scrambled to his feet, reaching for the bow slung across his back, but the other riders had gathered themselves in the time that Armeno was down, and had their swords pointed at him, each an instant kill at the first hint of resistance.

"Drop your weapons!" shouted one man, jabbing forwards with his blade to indicate the bow pulled halfway in the elf's hands. He glared then threw it away to one side, raising his hands slowly into the air as he surrendered.

Still keeping their swords on him, the man who had spoken quickly dismounted, stepped forwards and forced Armeno to his knees, his sword at his throat. With the other hand he unbuckled the elf's quiver of arrows, throwing them to one of his comrades.

"Don't move an inch, or I'll slay you on the spot," the man barked, clicking his fingers at another man. "Come and search him, I bet he's got more weapons on him."

The other dismounted, muttering under his breath about assumption of power, and knelt before the elf, searching through his pockets. Armeno had to restrain the urge to lash out at the man, contenting himself with a narrowed look, his face going white with anger when he started to relieve him of the few daggers that he had hidden about his person.

The man chuckled, holding up one to show his comrades. "Heh, looks like he was expecting a fight." He waved the dagger in front of Armeno's nose, grinning maliciously. "You won't need this any more."

"Get a move on. Grab some rope and tie him up, before he starts getting ideas." said the first man.

"Keep your hair on, what's the big deal? There's nobody with him, he can't do a thing with you there." argued another, coming forwards with a length of rope and binding the elf's wrists tightly together, tying them with a complex knot that he had no hope of working free. Someone else had managed to catch Velox and had tied him behind another horse, the arab tossing his head in distress at being treated like a mule.

Armeno was pulled to his feet by his bonds and tied behind another horse, the mercenaries remounting their own steeds. The two men that he had slain were left behind, the man whose mount he had injured catching hold of one of the spares and mounting at a trot, forcing the elf to run behind.

They had barely started when Nox came crashing through the trees, dragging her horse to a halt. A wave of cold pain washed through Armeno at the sight of Static's horse claimed by another, his face hardening into a black stare as they stopped too.

Nox regarded him then dismounted, stalking over to stand in front of him. The elf was much taller, and she had to look up at him.

"So, look who we've caught. If it isn't Static's pretty boy, come to see if we've stolen his girl away from him, hmm?" she took on a mocking tone, folding her arms over one another. "Well sorry honey, she ain't around any more."

He glared at her, his face set in an angry glare, then all of a sudden lunged out, kicking her legs from underneath her and trying to wrench his hands free of their bindings. She went down with a yell, landing in a heap on the ground before hooking her own arm around his legs and dragging him to the floor too. He thumped onto his side, rolling to try and get back to his feet, but she had a dagger at his throat, pinning him to the floor before he could move.

"How dare you? How *dare* you?" she hissed, fuming. Armeno tried to push her off his chest, wriggling backwards in the dirt, but she grabbed at his face, digging her sharp nails into his cheeks. "I don't care if she loved you, for that, you'll be punished."

The horse that Armeno was tied behind suddenly backed up, kicking out with its sharp hooves. One caught her in the hip and she recoiled, grunting with pain and scrambling backwards out of the way. The horse kicked again, snorting at her unfamiliar presence.

"Control that beast!" she commanded, staggering to her feet and clutching at her hip. She pulled up her jacket to reveal a dark bruise already forming. From the ground Armeno gave a laugh, pushing himself backwards out of the way of the horse's hooves and rubbing at one cheek with his bound hands where her nails had cut him.

"Oh that's funny, is it?" Nox shrieked, enraged. "Shame it'll be the last thing you find amusing before you join your dear girlfriend in death." She wrenched her sword out of its scabbard, he eyes burning with anger as she pointed it at the elf.

"What have we here then?" Botsu, ever one to appear when she wasn't wanted, suddenly flitted down from the trees, tapping the end of her tail on the side of the sword as she hovered in the air. "Ssseemsss like you've found a toy." She turned to look at Armeno, her gaze cold.

"Out of the way, snake, he's not a *toy* for long." She drew her hand back, the point wavering. Botsu gave her a slinky smile, dropping her coils around Armeno's neck.

"Oh come come, you're just going to kill him like *that*?" she snapped her tail along the elf's face, making him flinch away from her cold touch. "Let me have sssome fun with him firssst." A malicious smile crept onto her face as she stroked her tail slower

410

across Armeno's face this time, ignoring his attempt to shake her free.

Nox stared at her for a moment, then quickly drew away her sword from the elf's throat. "You'll leave me be?"

"Oh darling, you don't like my company?" Botsu's voice took on a dejected tone, but her eyes mocked. "That sssaddensss me. No matter, I can have much more fun with thisss one anyway."

Nox rolled her eyes, stalking away to swing herself back onto Tamarisk. "You can have your play when we make camp tonight." She turned abruptly to the mercenary that had assumed the role of leader over the others, "What weapons did he have?"

"A sword, a bow and quiver of arrows, and two daggers, Commander," he replied. Nox raised one eyebrow.

"Where are they?"

The man started, pulling the weapons from where he had stashed them on his saddle, no doubt in order for him to take them for his own. She inspected them then belted Armeno's sword around his waist and slung the bow over one shoulder.

"These are good weapons- too good for *you*." She gave the man a pointed look. "Elven quality. Looks like you've become quite the benefactor for me, elf." She gave him a sly smile before looking up at the trail.

"Time to ride." She kicked her heels against Tamarisk's sides, galloping after the tail end of the army without waiting, leaving the group she left behind to settle the horses and pull Armeno to his feet once more.

She spurred Tamarisk on until the horse was foaming at the mouth and she had to slow. Her new weapon clinked against her side, reminding her of its true owner. Why had he followed behind? What did he want? Her anger started to cool as she made distance between them, gradually being replaced by guilt- she had left the man at Botsu's mercy, a fate terrible even for one who had insulted her so badly.

When night fell and they made camp, Nox tried to keep as far away from where she knew Armeno was being held, not wanting to be anywhere near either him or the venomous dragon. She managed to keep to herself for a few hours, but when it came to making her rounds of the troops, she couldn't avoid them any longer.

The venomous dragon had ordered the elf tied to a tree, his arms pulled tight behind him. His head flopped down onto his chest, long black hair covering his eyes.

The dragon herself had taken up her usual place around his shoulders, her inky tongue flicking lazily as she whispered into his ear. The edges of her mouth curled up as he tried to ignore her.

"You thought you could sssave her? Ha, that makesss me laugh. Why, I bet you couldn't even sssave yoursssself." She flicked her tongue, seeming to pause for a moment in thought. "But why would ssshe want to be sssaved? Not like there'sss much to sssee in you, isss there?"

Armeno turned his head away, shaking it slowly to try and slide her off his shoulders, but she just snapped the end of her tail under his chin, pulling it up so they were looking at each other, eye to eye. "What'sss it feel like, knowing you're ssstill alive, and ssshe's no more than the dussst under your feet?"

Armeno's eyes flickered from side to side before they dropped, defeated. The dragon's smile widened. "Oh, that hurtsss, doesss it? Knowing you'll never sssee her again. Ssshe'll never know how much you loved her."

"Leave me ALONE!" he suddenly roared, he eyes blazing with anger. "Just… leave me alone."

"But we're having ssso much fun," hissed Botsu, stroking the end of her tail along his face. "We can reminisccce for hoursss, there'sss nobody to ssstop us." She leant in closer, her voice hardly more than a whisper. "And nobody to hear you ssscream either. There'sss nobody that caresss about a little lossst elf and his little lossst love. But if you don't want to talk about it, then maybe we can find sssome other entertainment."

Suddenly she twisted her tail, flicking it so the blade that ran down one side cut through the elf's jacket, leaving a thin red line along his skin. He hissed in a breath.

"Hurtsss?"

Nox, watching from the shadows, turning away as the dragon flicked her tail again, cutting a line across Armeno's cheek. She walked away, turning once as a shout echoed through the air, then ran.

When Tamarisk's pale coat shone through the darkness near her path she slowed, walking up to the horse and brushing her hand down his nose. The stallion snorted, flicking his ears back in distaste and backing away. He was still saddled and she worked her way around to his side, pulling at the buckles until the saddle slid free into her arms, then onto the ground with a clatter, the contents of the saddlebags that Nox hadn't dared look inside lumpy with displaced items. She sighed and sat down, regarding the packs momentarily before furiously setting to and tugging out everything that they contained.

Most of it was just useful items- cooking equipment, a dagger, gloves, matches- nothing that really reminded Nox of Static. She packed the items into a pile so she could add them to her own meagre stack of belongings before pulling off the roll of bedding that the sorceress kept behind the cantle of the saddle, untying the knots that held it tightly together. A thick blanket unrolled itself across her lap. Twisted into the thicker fabric were the lighter folds of an emerald green cloak.

She shoved it off like it burned, recoiling. It wasn't quite the same as the other cloak that Static had worn, this one lighter and made with a smooth fabric, but it was still firmly *hers*. She stared at it for a moment, then shaking her head to dispel her sudden reluctance, took hold of the garment and shook out the creases.

The longer Nox looked at it, the more *wrong* it felt that she had it. Although it was quite late, and she knew that the army would be moving as soon as it was light, the Felixis felt wide awake. She packed all the items away in the saddlebags again, leaving the cloak in a little heap to one side, along with a few

415

slightly soft apples that Tamarisk started to tuck into, munching heartily.

"Hungry are you?" whispered Nox, holding out another apple for the horse. He snuffled at her fingers, finishing his mouthful before taking another bite. Faintly she wondered whether Botsu had left Armeno alone yet, but didn't really want to go and investigate. She lay down on one side, watching the horse hunt for more food.

Despite lying down, she still couldn't sleep and after a few minutes sat up again, rubbing her eyes in frustration. Tamarisk had lain down on his side and blew a warm huff of air at Static's old cloak, making the fabric rustle. Nox frowned at it, then picked it up in one hand and climbed to her feet, heading towards the food carts.

She stealthily pinched a loaf of bread and a wineskin from one when she reached it, tucking them into her armful and making her way to where the elf was. She stopped a little way away, peering through the darkness to see if the snakelike form of the venomous dragon was still keeping Armeno company. It seemed not. *Gone off to torment someone else*, she thought wryly before winding through the last few trees to crouch in front of the elf.

"Armeno?" she whispered, glancing over the elf's face. She couldn't tell whether he was awake or asleep, his black hair covering his face. If he looked in a bad state before, dusty from travelling, now he looked terrible, thin cuts from Botsu's blade crossing his cheeks and more slices through his shirt, cutting the fine cloth into ribbons. She winced as she pulled a little of the fabric away from his side, revealing fresh wounds, then flinched away as he moaned and shifted.

Nox hardened her expression as he blearily looked up, sliding away a little. He blinked a couple of times, scrunching his face up in pain, then saw Nox and narrowed his eyes in a glare.

"Come to gloat too have you? Go ahead." He tugged at one of his arms, trying to free it from its bonds but quickly gave up. He leaned his head back against the tree, watching Nox down the length of his nose.

She dropped her eyes to the floor, sitting before she reached for the bundle she had in her lap and unwrapped the cloak from around her stock of food. "I thought you might be hungry," she said quietly, looking up to meet his cold gaze.

There was a pause as he watched her, then he finally spoke. "Why are you helping me?"

Nox shrugged. "I don't know," she said simply, picking up the loaf of bread and breaking it into two, offering him a little. "Nobody else will care if you die. You might not get a chance to eat for a couple of days."

"You don't care," he muttered. She gave an exasperated sigh and sat forwards, shoving bread in his mouth as he opened it to speak again

"Oh just eat, before you start making me wonder why I'm here. Wonder any *more*." She glanced around, looking to see if they were being watched, then fed the elf more bread and a little wine out of the flask when he had eaten.

When it was all gone she shook out the cloak again and threw it over Armeno's front like a blanket, getting to her feet. "This was hers. But you probably knew that." She turned to go, padding softly away.

"This doesn't change anything," Armeno called in a low voice after her.

"I know."

She disappeared into the night, leaving Armeno alone to ponder why the Felixis had come to find him. He shifted against the tree slightly, trying to lessen the pull on his shoulders.

A small breeze stirred the leaves above him and he looked up, a faint star just visible through the canopy before he closed his eyes and tried to sleep. Painful memories managed to seep their way into his dreams, making him shake his head this way and that, before a new dream slipped in between the old.

It was dark. He sat up slowly, squinting to make out the source of the dull hushing noise that filled the cave he was in. There was a sudden flash of light, then right in front of him, within touching distance, sat Static, a faint smile on her lips.

He reached out a tentative hand to touch her cheek, but she was like mist, his hand passing straight through. She turned her head to one side, the smile fading.

"We always knew you would outlive me," she said quietly, reaching out to touch his hand. He felt nothing, just the wind. "I'm only human, and you're an elf."

Armeno shook his head, opening his fingers so she could slip hers in-between. "A few more years..."

She suddenly sat forwards, cupping her other hand around his cheek. "Things change. We started in battle." There was a glimmer of colour on one wall, two figures on horseback whirling around each other, the vague drawings almost lifelike in their movements. It was them, their first meeting on the beach near the Azure Caves many years before. "Things are never the same at the end." The figures suddenly halted their battle and fled, only to discover themselves in the middle of a war. A figure fell on one and it disappeared in a cloud of smoke, leaving the other alone. Armeno's face crumpled in sorrow and he tore his gaze away. She regarded him sadly, then leant forwards to whisper in his ear. "You know, the end is never really the end." Her lips brushed his, soft like a cloud, then she seemed to fade, her last words whispering through the air.

"I'll be waiting..."

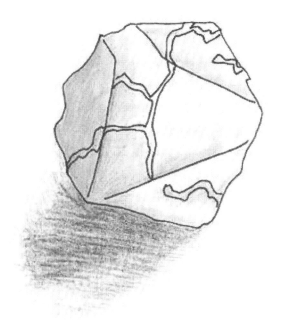

19
TARZ. A PLOT.

"I ne'er thought I'd see t'Ever Bridge."

After spending the night at Jiluria, the lash dragons had set out after the defenders that had docked from their ships the day before, catching up by midday. What had just been Racksom defenders had become an army, the guards of the port town having joined those from Racksom, and others soon expected, with word of the imminent attack on Tarz being sent to many of the cities and towns across Mirrahl.

The lash dragons, along with Liesk, Lutis and Foen, were walking near the back of the army, the rest stretching out in a long squiggly line in front of them. The Everplains ran in every direction, cut right through the middle by the same river that ran all the way from Quinsilla. In the very far distance the Amelle forest could just be seen as a dark green haze on the horizon, and closer, arching over the river, the Ever Bridge.

The Ever Bridge was like none other on the island, ancient even before the triblade dragon had plagued the land. As the lash dragons approached it they saw that twisted trees leaned across the gaping expanse of water, their branches reaching far across, the leaves that fluttered on them a myriad of colours. The bridge was made from curved stone blocks, the top a deceptively plain grey. Underneath though, it was like a different world, bright flowers growing in the many crevices in the jagged rock that hung down over the river. A few roots from the trees that stood like guardians twisted along the bridge, almost black amongst the brilliant yellow of the wood sorrel, the explosive pink and purple of saxifrage and nightshade and the deep waxy green of ivy in all the glory of summer. Bees buzzed from flower to flower, feasting on the sweet nectar the flowers offered, rolling in the pollen, completely oblivious to the army tramping overhead.

"It's beautiful," said Hone, her normally incessant chatter fading.

"Anyone who's e'er been here has always said t'same, but I'd ne'er thought I'd see it," said Aeron, smiling at the sight. "Once this war is over, I'd like t'come back here an' stay a while, not have t'gar somewhere."

"Well, you'll get that chance. To get back to the desert, the fastest way is back over the Ever Bridge and up the Everplains- unless you go through the Amelle forest, but it's pretty easy to get lost there, and there aren't many guides. I've heard that there are monsters there too, a black demon that prowls the forest, eating anyone it comes across," said Foen, wiggling the fingers of one hand in the air to scare the dragon. The sorcerer had managed to charm someone into giving him a horse, and had been studying a book in the saddle, but now stopped to admire the bridge with the rest of them.

"Maybe we'll spend a few days here on the way back then eh? That demon doesn't sound like much fun," said Lutis, clapping Aeron on the shoulder. The Elite looked at him in surprise.

"We?"

"Yep, I think I might head back to Kaionar with you lot- 'course, it'll probably take a while, what with your record for trouble," he winked at Hone, "But at least you're good company!"

It took four days for the army to march to Tarz from the Ever Bridge. The only report of Zartear's army was from far-ranging scouts, who told of the enemy heading for the city too, but crossing the Everplains much further north, buying the defenders some time to get to the city and start mounting defences.

Tarz was positioned so that the land around formed natural defences against any invaders that tried to attack, the Glacé mountains providing protection to the north and the river Tarz curving around the west of the city and cutting off any attack coming from the Everplains. Tarz itself was built on a hill, the buildings on the edges of the city shorter than those in the centre, all climbing towards the Jewel Tower at its very heart. The whole city was designed to resist any sort of attack- the perfect place to store the final jewel dragon.

The army didn't enter the city, instead making camp just outside its southern gate. Rolling prairies, like those in the Everplains, stretched out in front of the city down to the sea, little clumps of woodland breaking the meadows here and there. Only a few soldiers, those who had friends or relations in the city, entered it to stay with those they knew. Foen left the others for his sister's house, the woman living in the city- he promised that he would ask if they too could stay at hers, but the others had little hope that the erratic sorcerer would actually remember to inquire. It was getting late by the time Foen left for the city and the others started to set up camp, Neby lighting a fire while Echai and Hone prepared the little food they had left- a trip to one of Tarz' markets would definitely be in order the next morning. Aeron took himself off somewhere, which confused Tekek as she was given no order, until Echai set her to unpacking the blankets that they had brought with them to sleep on.

Their meal was short and quiet, Aeron returning halfway through with a very strange look on his face. When Liesk asked him why he looked so odd he just smiled, telling her there was nothing to worry about, and that they should all get a good night's rest.

The next day, to everyone's surprise, Foen hunted down the lash patrol and their friends to invite them to his sister's house. Aeron was doubtful that she would have enough room in her house for five dragons and three extra two-legs, but Foen insisted that they stay anyway. The sorcerer led them through the city, ushering them on when they were distracted by some attraction or another. None of them, not even Lutis, had been to Tarz before, and there was a world of things to explore.

His sister's house was reasonably large, and when they got to it, they found that she, like her brother, was a healer- although she was a witch, not a sorcerer, and could use magic. Standing next to each other, the two were very alike- she had the same blonde hair, cut short around her face, the same cheeky smile, and was even more petite than her brother. Foen introduced her as Risis.

"You're welcome to stay, just don't make too much mess." She shot Foen a look. "And please don't be up all hours of the night, I quite like my sleep."

Hone took an instant liking to the woman as she showed them around her house. The whole of the top floor was one big room, a window at one end looking out across the city. There was a balcony beyond that you could climb through onto. It was big enough for them all to fit into, and even had a couple of beds for Lutis and Foen to sleep in. Risis took Liesk off to another smaller room that she could use to have some privacy away from the others.

After a trip to the nearest market to stock up on food supplies, then eating most of what they had bought for lunch, Aeron called his patrol together.

"Ahreet, I have an idea. T'only problem it's not exactly… legal. So we're gonna have t'keep it quiet. Hear me out afore y'make any judgements.

"T'two other jewels were stolen easily, 'cause t'thieves knew right where t'look for them, it wherst jus' a matter o'getting' into t'Jewel Towers an' out again, right?"

Lutis nodded. "Easy as pie, those towers are like beacons."

"'Xactly. So, I say, let's make it harder for Zartear t'steal the third jewel. Lutis, you're gaarn t'steal the jewel first, an' replace it with a fake. Then, when Zartear flies in t'try an' take it, he'll take the fake, not t'real jewel." He paused, looking around at the group for their reactions.

There was a silence.

"It'll never work."

"Are we *really* going to break the law?"

"I bet Lutis can steal tha' easy!"

"Are you sure about this?"

"Yes… it's risky, but it might just work." Lutis' voice cut through the babble of voices, the man resting his chin on his interlaced fingers. "Of course, I can't just waltz up there and steal the jewel- I'm going to need a distraction, a fake jewel, a new pair of gloves- if I touch the real one then the dragon'll be released- and it'll have to be kept safe once I've stolen it."

"Y'think y'can do it?" asked Aeron, his expression grave. Lutis nodded.

"Course I can, I've already stolen one. How much harder can this one be?"

Echai shook his head, looking at the ceiling. "Oh, don't say that."

"Does anyone see any problems?" said Aeron, looking around the little group. There was another silence. "Good! T'work. Foen, you'd best get back t'your books, try an' find somethin' to stop t'other two dragons."

"Heh, don't you worry about me, I've got my sister on the case too." The sorcerer grinned and got to his feet, heading for the door. "Good luck!"

The Elite nodded, watching him go before turning back to the others. "Neby, Tekek, take some coins an' try an' find a jewellers, or some sort o'souvenir place. I bet y'can find a reasonable replica of t'jewel somewhere."

The two dragons dipped their heads, then climbed to their feet and headed for the door as Aeron gave out the rest of his orders.

"Hone, head into t'market an' buy a pair o'gloves. Make sure there're no holes in them- leather'll be best." The Elite smiled fondly at the dragon as she gave a little salute with one feather.

"I'll be back in no time!"

"You taught her tha', dids'eh Lutis? Echai, I need you t'head back t'the army an' get today's news. Make sure y'pick up any rumours gaarn 'round- we need ev'ry scrap o'information we can get. T'more notice we get tha' Zartear's army is approachin', the better. That way we can find t'best place t'hide t'jewel.

"Liesk, you're gaarn t'be t'distraction while Lutis swaps the jewels."

"What?" The question came simultaneously from both Liesk and Lutis. "I thought *you* were going to be the diversion?" continued Lutis, looking perplexed.

"Liesk has looks an' charm. She'll be a much better diversion than I'll e'er be."

Liesk gave him a horrified look as Lutis started chuckling, crossing her arms. "Men! You're all the same, even in dragon form." She flicked the end of Aeron's nose, making the dragon shrug wryly, then shot a haughty glance at Lutis, who tried to contain his laughter.

"Fine, I'll do it, but only because of the stakes."

Aeron smiled. "Thank you. For now, I s'ppose y'better gar an' help Foen look for his spell. I'm gaarn to gar an' see if I can get you two a pass f'the Jewel Tower."

"Ah, well Liesk, looks like you'll be the only one helping Foen then. Gotta go and check out the tower, make sure there's an escape route- just in case of course," said Lutis, stretching as he stood. "We're not doing this till tomorrow or later, right?"

Aeron nodded.

"Goodoh. See you later then!" He gave a cheerful wave and pulled open the door, clumping down the stairs two at a time.

"Looks like I've got a fun job then," grumbled Liesk, not looking forward to hours of pouring over books with the sorcerer and his sister.

For Liesk, the next day came too quickly. While Lutis was buzzing with anticipation, she just felt horribly nervous.

Aeron saw them off as they left Risis' house that morning. "Good luck," he whispered. "Don't get caught this time!"

"Didn't get caught last time!" Lutis whispered back with a wink, jauntily starting down the street. He tried to make light conversation as they headed for the heart of the city- the avian looked pale.

"Bet you didn't think you'd ever be doing this, eh?" he asked, sliding his hands into his pockets. He fiddled with the fake emerald in one of them, turning it between his fingers.

"Didn't think I'd ever see you again, after the mess you got yourself into in Racksom last time." She shook her head. "Don't you ever think of stealing from the thieves guild and coming back to my house to hide again."

"Did they come looking for me after I'd left?"

"Yes, they did. And they nearly found out you'd been at my place too- you and your pancakes!"

"Aww come on, you know you love my pancakes." He gave her a cheeky grin, nudging her in the side. "And you love having me around too, don't you?"

Liesk shoved him back, rolling her eyes. "Can't believe I'm still friends with you."

Lutis gave a laugh. "You make it sound as you want to be more than just friends. Well, I'm fine with that." He gave her a sly sideways glance, his grin widening as he saw her redden.

"I was thinking nothing of the sort!" she protested, pouting.

"Suit yourself. Want an apple?" He waved the fruit in front of her, having produced it from nowhere.

"Um… sure, an apple would be nice." She took it, taking a bite. "Where did you get this?"

"Off that stall back there." He pointed over his shoulder with his thumb.

"Lutis!" Liesk squealed, shoving the apple back in his hands. He grinned and bit into it, talking through his mouthful.

"What? Treat it like a warm up, keeping the ol' fingers light!" He offered it to her again, but she waved it away.

"No thanks, I'll pass on the stolen food."

"Wha'ever." He finished off the apple, tossing the core down an alleyway. "Okay, let's get this thing done."

The Jewel Tower was surrounded by an exotic fence, the only entrance to get to the tower itself being patrolled by four guards. As they approached one came forwards, frowning a little when Liesk and Lutis stopped outside the gate.

"This area is off limits to civilians. Turn back."

"We've got a pass." Lutis tugged a piece of paper out of one pocket, smoothing the corners flat before handing it to the guard. She scanned it, holding it up to the light to check the signatures were genuine.

"Fine. You need to show it when you go up into the tower. Make sure you're back down again before its dark, the staircase is pretty worn in places."

"Cheers." Lutis took the pass back as the guard unlocked the gate, locking it again behind them. There was another guard standing at the bottom of the tower itself, but the note proved evidence enough for him to let them past too.

"This is the fourth time I've climbed up a set of stairs like this, and they don't get any more interesting," grumbled Lutis as they ascended, peering at the staircase so he didn't slip.

"Just keep going," said Liesk from behind him. "How much further is it?"

"Dunno, can't see- oh wait, we're at the top." Light flooded into the staircase as it turned into the open windowed room at the top of the tower. A young man sat on the top step, looking bored, but when he saw Lutis he leapt to his feet, armour clanking.

"Who are you?" he asked, biting his lip with anxiety. "You're not going to tell anyone I was sitting down, are you?"

He was quite young, maybe twenty, and it was obvious that he couldn't have been a guard for very long, his armour shiny and new.

"We've got a note, come to see the defences up around the emerald." Lutis handed over the note again, then turned and started towards the jewel sitting on the table in the middle of the room. "This is it then eh? Doesn't look like much when it comes to it..." He peered at the gem, walking around the table once before stopping again, his back to the others.

"So, what sort of defences have you got up here then?" asked Liesk quietly, blinking innocently at the guard. He stuttered, stumped, then started to show her the magical wards that were set up in the window arches, explaining how they worked.

Blocking out the idle chatter of the other two, Lutis felt in his pocket for the fake jewel, tucking it into his palm. When he heard a lull in the conversation he quickly reached out for the real one, picking it up with his fingers and dropping the other in its place, pulling his hand away as soon as the swap was done and shoving it back into his pocket. The fake looked exactly the same as the real emerald- Neby and Tekek had done a good job. He inspected the jewel for a moment more, waiting for the siren that would give away their plot, then, when it didn't come, straightened up and turned to look at the others.

"That looks fine, shall we head-" He stopped mid-sentence, pulling a disgusted face. Liesk had her arms wrapped around the guard's neck, pulling him down into a passionate kiss. Lutis rolled his eyes, shoving his hands into his pockets.

"I'll see you at the bottom."

He started down the staircase, stopping halfway to drop the stolen gem into a small pouch, adding an extra layer of protection. He frowned at the innocent-looking object- it had been much too easy. So much for a challenge- obviously he would have to move onto even bigger game.

"She's coming," he said to the guard at the bottom of the tower, walking past without stopping. "Made a uh... a new friend."

Lutis walked straight back to Risis' house, the door opening before he knocked. They had been watching out for him from the balcony.

"Where's Liesk?" asked Aeron as he came to the door, peering into the street behind the thief.

"Still causing a distraction," replied Lutis, pulling the pouch out of his pocket and dumping it into the Elite's paws. "You're right, she's a much better diversion than you would have been."

"Y'got it?" Aeron grinned, picking the bag up by the drawstring and shaking it a little.

"Yep, easy. Mind your paws if you take a look, I suppose it'll do it's evil transform-y thing on dragons as well as humans." Lutis pushed the dragon aside, poking his head into the kitchen. "Is Hone around?"

"Aye, I think Foen was tryin' t'teach her 'nough words so she could help him with his books." He pulled a face. "Not sure he's havin' much success, he's not geetly patient. Lutis, you'd better keep a hold o'this, I've nowhere t'keep it." He passed the little bag back and Lutis shoved it into his pocket, tugging off his new gloves and cramming them in too as he started up the stairs to rescue Hone from Foen's spellbooks.

The Dragon Thief

20
EXPLOSIONS. THE ELVEN WARRIOR.

Over the next few days, reports of Zartear's army moving toward Tarz started to increase, and an attack was obviously imminent. The army that had organised outside Tarz' south gate was ordered into different divisions and training took up the warriors' days. More defenders were always arriving at the city, and, in-between training sessions, Hone would often climb to the top of a nearby hill to watch the little groups arriving at the city, sometimes with Lutis, sometimes with Tekek, sometimes on her own.

It was late afternoon when one such group caught her eye, a long triangular banner in bright yellow and black held high above them. She watched their advance a little further towards the city before getting to her feet and setting off at a run to meet with them, curious to know where they came from. She was sure she had seen a banner like that somewhere before...

When she got closer, she suddenly recognised not the banner, but the person holding it-it was Ebon, from Plurith! She gave a bugle of excitement, putting on a burst of speed.

"Ebon!" she squealed when the gryphon didn't see her approaching, making him stop and look around with confusion. A black and white head popped up behind Ebon, a grin stretching across the beaked face of Ink.

Hone! exclaimed the magpie dragon, taking to the air and promptly dive-bombing the lash apprentice, nipping at her wing in a friendly greeting as they tumbled onto the ground. *You rascal! How did you end up here? I thought you were going to come back to Plurith and say hi!*

Hone squeaked as Ink tweaked her wing, rustling her feathers and shoving the other dragon off. "Well, ista long story. I've been havin' all sorts o'fun adventures! An' there's gonna be a battle an' all... cannae jus' gar back t'the desert an' let Mirrahl get taken over by Zartear, canst I?"

Nah, can't do that. That's why we came- Ter's here too! said Ink, pointing a wing towards the others that had come from Plurith. Hone gave a bugle of excitement and leapt to her feet, giving Ebon a lick on the cheek before tackling Terrowin to the ground in greeting.

"Hi Ter! Howzah been? You an' Ink better come an' stay wit' us, Foen's sister's putting us up in her house, an' there's plenty space f'you too!"

"Hi lass. We're doin' good! Who's Foen?" He raised one eyebrow at the mention of the sorcerer, not having met him.

"He's a sorcerer! An' he's gonna stop t'triblade dragon!" Hone crowed, fluttering her head fins.

"Wot?"

"Oh! Y'don't know 'bout that either, djur? I'll get Lutis t'explain, he tells stories geet good."

He got out of going to prison then? chuckled Ink. Ebon, who was listening to the conversation, shook his head and looked at the sky.

"Thought he might wiggle his way out of that..." he muttered, but there was an edge of laughter in his voice.

Hone walked with the little group to the edge of the city, sharing her news and catching up with the others. It turned out that the 'demon' that Terrowin and Ink had gone to investigate was actually a rogue goblin- Hone presumed that it was one that had been part of the group that had chased them to Racksom, but had gotten lost in the forest and gone the wrong way.

When they got where the other troops were stationed Ebon went off to hunt down whoever was in charge and find out where to go, and get the latest news on Zartear's army. Hone dragged Terrowin and Ink to Risis' house, letting herself in by jiggling one claw in the lock of the front door.

"Lutis' been teachin' me how t'pick locks. Don't tell Aeron though, he'll have a gar," she whispered, giggling as she shut the door behind them before yelling up the stairs, "Oi y'all, Ter an' Ink are here!"

There was a muffled bang from upstairs, then a door flew open and Lutis staggered out in a cloud of smoke, followed by Foen, the sorcerer swearing at the top of his voice.

"Shit, I thought I had it this time! Why did you have to go and drop the bloody thing?" He gave Lutis a shove, dropping ash all over the floor. The sorcerer's normally blonde hair was black with soot, and spiked at the front where something had just blown up in front of him.

"Don't give me all the blame, Hone surprised me!" protested Lutis, pointing down the staircase at the dragon and brushing a little ash off his front before looking at the dragon. "What did you sa- Ink! Terrowin! Why're you in Tarz?"

"Sounds like the same reason as ye. Although... maybe not with the explosions. Wot are ye doin'?

"Apparently blowing up stuff," Lutis said ironically, coughing as more smoke billowed from the room. "Time to take a break?"

"No, I thought I had it that time!" said Foen again, waving a hand in front of him to disperse a little of the smoke as he disappeared back into the room- hopefully to open a window. "One more try?"

"Ugh, get someone else to help! Someone who can breathe smoke!" Lutis shook his head and ran down the stairs, grabbing his coat off one of the hooks in the hall. "Quick, let's get out of here before he gets you helping him too." He pushed the two dragons towards the door, looking over his shoulder to see if Foen had reappeared again.

As he pulled the door shut behind them, a frustrated shout echoed after them. "Lutis! Come back!"

~

A large map was spread out on the ground, showing the south of Mirrahl. Racksom and Tarz were clearly labelled, and someone had drawn a squiggling line between the two, marking the course that Zartear's army had taken through the forest and across the Everplains. The man himself leaned over the map, his grey eyes flicking over the page.

"Same as last time?" Nox also bent over the map, her eyes switching between the paper and the man. He nodded, sitting back.

"Yes. If our attack is expected, then doing exactly the same thing won't be."

"What about the city? I'm assuming the last jewel will release a dragon like the others. If it's as big as Xaoc, we could take the city."

"We are taking the city." Zartear permitted himself a small smile. "Then we'll take the rest of Mirrahl."

"The… the whole island?" Nox raised her brows- that wouldn't be possible. However, Zartear nodded.

"You sound surprised."

"I didn't think your plans were this big," she explained. "I thought we were just taking the main trading ports."

"You have no idea on the extent of my ideas."

"Going to enlighten me?"

He ignored the question. "We'll attack from the south. The west is protected by the river." He shot Nox a narrow look. "We take no prisoners. That includes the elf you've got tied up at the back of the army."

Nox paled. "How-"

"Do you not think I know what's going on in my own army?"

"No, of course not. I'll get someone to deal with him." She stood, brushing the dust off her trousers.

"Do it now."

She nodded and left him looking over the map. What more did he have planned? A nagging thought told her that, as his second in command, she should know his plans for the future... but he had never out-rightly told her his plans in the past. What was more worrying was that he might have told Xaoc instead- the dragon was looking like quite a threat to her command, now he had Botsu as an extra ally.

Getting rid of the elf was another problem. After secretly keeping him alive for a week and a half, the thought of killing him now just undid all her hard work. She pondered what to do as she walked, trying to work out a way to get him away without being killed, or caught herself.

She reached the elf faster than she would have liked, and had to cut her plotting short. Botsu had been keeping him company, as always, and at Nox's arrival leered.

"Come to sssee our friend again, have you?" The dragon cocked her head to one side, regarding the Felixis. "You ssseem to be ssspending an awful lot of time with him."

Nox scowled, glaring at Botsu. "Speak for yourself."

The dragon smiled, whirling into the air past Nox. As she passed, she whispered into the woman's ear, "I wasssn't the one who left him a presssent though, wasss I?"

She reddened with rage, curling her hands into fists as Botsu flew off. She watched the dragon go, then turned to Armeno, who was sitting on the ground watching her. Botsu had exchanged his thick woollen cloak for the silky green one, spiting him in any way she could, which included bringing up his painful memories of the past.

"Look," she said, sliding to her knees in front of him. "Zartear wants you dead. But... I can't let that happen, not after Static." She frowned, then pulled a dagger from her belt and stuck it into the ground behind his hands. "Cut yourself free and get the hell out of here. Head for the Everplains or something, but not Tarz."

445

Armeno narrowed his eyes, his fingers fumbling for the dagger. "You're not escaping that easily."

"Gods, you are stubborn aren't you?" She looked at the sky in frustration, then shook him once. "Get *out* of here. Get as far away from this place as you can." She rose to her feet, regarding him sadly. Botsu had hardly treated him well in the past week, and he was covered in thin cuts and dark bruises. "I'm sorry."

He watched her then shifted slightly, twisting his hand so that the dagger lay alongside the ropes that held his wrists together. She walked briskly off as he started sawing at his bonds. "Just wait, you'll be sorry."

There was a crack as one of the ropes snapped, then another, his wrists falling apart. He let out a sigh of relief, dropping his hands around to his front and rolling his shoulders, trying to work out the stiffness. His wrists were red raw from where the ropes had rubbed but he ignored them. He picked up the dagger- it was better than nothing- and climbed slowly to his feet, staggering slightly as white light danced in front of his eyes from dehydration. He put a hand on the side of the cart he had been tied to, rifling through its contents for anything that might have been useful. Nox had stolen his sword and bow, so he would have to make do with another for now, until he had the chance to get them back. Luckily the cart had all manner of provisions inside it and he helped himself, piling food and water into an empty sack, along with a light blanket. Luckily most of the mercenaries in the army didn't think he was good company, and he managed to fill his bag before a couple of soldiers walked nearby, deep in conversation.

He ducked behind the cart, hiding behind the wheel as they passed. It seemed they either were too thick to notice he was missing, or didn't know he was supposed to be tied up by the cart, because they walked straight past. He stole an extra loaf of bread out of the cart, filling his mouth before running, keeping low to the ground.

The plains near Tarz had little cover for the elf to hide behind, only the odd tree speckling the rolling meadows. When he made it over the first little undulation of the land he sunk to the ground, turning onto his belly and creeping through the grass to spy on the camp. Everything looked normal... nobody had discovered he had escaped yet, but that was bound to change soon enough. So, the army was heading for Tarz- he would too, despite Nox's warning words. Luckily it was starting to creep towards night, the sun sinking into the west and shooting burning rays in an arc across the sky, the chance of being spotted diminishing with every passing moment.

He rested for a while, eating a little more of the food he had stolen and healing his wrists, which ached the worst out of all his wounds. His limited magic gave out before he could move onto the others. Despite the danger he curled up to sleep for a couple of hours, tucking the green cloak tightly around him and burying his face in its folds as he waited for the sun to go down completely, before he headed further west towards the city.

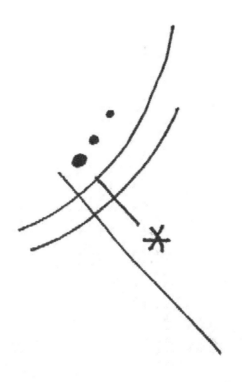

21
THE FINAL BATTLE.

The night was cold, colder than it had been for some time. Summer was starting to come to an end and autumn was creeping in, bringing chill winds from the Glacé mountains. In Tarz' pleasure gardens the trees were starting to lose their green, the leaves starting to darken to red and brown and fall to the ground, exposing the abandoned bird nests that were still tucked in their protective branches.

Watches had been allotted to those who had travelled to the city to fight, and Echai was sharing an early morning duty with Liesk. They sat together on the wall of the city, looking out across the plains. The defending army was a dark blot in the closest meadows, a few lamps flickering amongst the darkness here and there.

The avian yawned, stretching to try and stay awake, then broke the silence. "I would have thought they would have attacked the city by now."

"Maybe," said Echai quietly, taking his eyes off the plains for a moment. "Good for us, look at the swell of ranks we've had. I counted nearly a hundred more reach the city yesterday, and that was only during the morning watch."

"Gosh, that many? Zartear won't have a hope against us now. What do you think he's doing?"

"Collecting more followers? Healing their wounds- although I hardly think that's the case. Learning new magic? They could be doing anything for all we know."

"Could be collecting more followers I suppose… Zartear must be telling them some interesting lies to get them to follow him."

"What do you mean?" Echai sounded confused.

"Well, would you follow him if you knew a great big dragon was going to destroy everything at the end of it?"

"No, but so far it seems Zartear's got a pretty good hold on his dragons."

"We'll see. I wonder what would happen if someone else freed the last dragon." She looked at the sky, her eyes flicking between the stars of some constellation far above them. "Do you think power would be split between the two people that control the dragons?"

Echai looked at her in surprise, his eyes narrowing briefly. "That's not going to happen though, is it?" he said slowly. "The third jewel's safe, Lutis is looking after it."

"Yes, of course it's safe!" she laughed. "I was just interested, that's all. These jewels really are intriguing."

The lash Elite looked at her with a little doubt again, then out at the plains. Suddenly he gasped and leapt to his feet, leaning over the battlements to peer into the darkness. "There are lights in the plains. Look! Look!" He pointed into the distance with one claw. "It's Zartear, it must be, no reinforcements are going to be that big!"

"What? Lights?" Liesk jumped to her feet and peered into the distance, giving a little "Oh!" of surprise as she spotted the flickering of torches.

"We have to warn the army, quick! They'll be here by sunrise! Why didn't we spot them before?"

"They must have been behind some sort of hill or something. I'll head back to Risis' house and tell the others, you go down to the army and raise the alarm." She flared her wings, turning to jump off the side of the wall. "Oh, light the beacon too!"

The dragon nodded, running along the wall to where a large pile of tinder had been stacked. More beacons had been set up along Tarz' perimeter, and the watchers had been instructed to light the closest one if they saw anything. Echai bent down to the base of the pile and blew a little hot air. The wood smoked, but it didn't catch. Echai thumped the ground with one paw in frustration and tried again- the wood was wet! He didn't understand it; it hadn't rained in a week.

After a third try from a different angle he gave up- it was no use, the beacon would only smoke. He flared his head fins in annoyance and straightened, looking out towards the plains again-no, it was definitely an army approaching. He had to get the message out somehow... then he had it.

Filling his lungs with air, he let out the loudest bugle he could manage, the sound startlingly strident in the silence of the night. He bugled again, then ran, pelting down the wall towards the next beacon. Hopefully it wasn't wet too.

Halfway along the wall he met the next pair of watchers, heading towards him at a jog.

"What's going on? What was that noise?" asked one, who looked little more than a boy.

"That was me, there's an army approaching." He pointed out into the plains, but the angle had changed from where his own post had been, and the lights weren't visible. "You need to light the beacon, then spread the word."

"How come we can't see anything?" asked the boy, frowning in confusion at the dragon. Echai sighed.

"The angle's changed, there *is* an army coming. Light the beacon!" Echai patted him on one shoulder with his wing, giving him a smile. "Don't look so worried, it'll be fine."

The boy nodded, then turned to his companion. "Come on!"

As they set off on his order, the Elite's smile turned grim and he headed for the closest stairs, running to alert the defenders.

Dawn came only a few hours later, revealing the long lines of Zartear's army marching slowly across the southern plains towards Tarz. Echai had quickly spread the word amongst the defenders and now the camp was a frenzy of activity, tents being packed away and taken into the city, armour being donned and soldiers organising into little troops. Pennants fluttered above the warriors, the silver of Tarz, green and gold for Racksom, black and yellow for Plurith, even a pale white banner of Quinsilla fluttering to one side, and the purple of Didenne too.

The lash dragons stood under the Plurith pennant, having made their way onto the battlefield a while after Liesk had returned to the house with the bad news. Terrowin, Ink, Liesk and Lutis stood with them- they would fight together. Aeron had tried to persuade Liesk that she would be safer inside the city but the avian hadn't listened to him, insisting she would fight with the rest of them.

The Elite disappeared off with Echai, deep in conversation after the short argument. Lutis had gone off too, hunting for breakfast, and returned with a sack full of fruit, insisting that he had actually paid for the food. Liesk didn't quite believe him, but didn't press the matter. The two lash dragons returned as they were halfway through the food, Hone trying slices of each of the strange fruits to try and find one she actually liked. They each held an armful of dark metal, which turned out to be armour when they dropped it onto the ground.

"We found some dragon armour. There's not 'nough for everyone, but I thought we could split it up an' each wear a couple of pieces." Aeron pulled the tangle of metal apart, pushing different parts at each of his patrol members. "Cannae have my Elites gettin' hurt, canst I?"

As Aeron passed Hone a curved faceplate, the young dragon frowned, taking it tentatively. "Wotcher givin' this t'me? I'm not an Elite yet."

Aeron smiled, handing Tekek a pair of gauntlets for her front paws. "Hone, t'time has come t'make you an Elite. It's clear y'have all t'makings o' a great warrior."

Hone looked at him in incredulity for a moment, then a huge smile spread across her face. "Really?"

"Aye, really. 'Course, we're not in t'desert, so we cannae give you t'full ceremony, but you're still a fully fledged Elite." He unfolded one wing and a little pot dropped onto the floor, filled with sticky black paste. Picking it up, he scooped a little out with one claw and drew a pattern onto her shoulder. "Welcome t'the pack!"

She squealed with excitement, looking at the mark with unhidden pride. "Ista my special mark?"

"Aye, it is. It marks y'as an Elite o'my patrol. But y'knew tha' already." He winked, his eyes glittering with approval. "Now everyone, time t'armour up! We've got a battle 'head o'us."

It took a good hour to fit the lash Elites into their armour. One set was made for a large dragon, the other for a smaller one, so they had to swap many pieces around for it all to fit. The buckles that held the armour together were complicated, lots of different straps holding it in place so that the dragons could move easily. By the time they were finished, Zartear's army had come to a milling halt half a league to the south, forming a terrifying black line across the plains. There was quiet while the two armies regarded each other, then the horns of goblins started up from the enemy troops, sounding through the air. They were instantly overshadowed by the roar of the tribal battle blood as he raised his face to the sky. There was a moment of silence then the enemy army surged forwards, a wordless battlecry echoing through the ranks.

"Hold!" shouted a voice from the defender's side, magic making the word boom across the field. "Archers."

Lutis turned to watch as two lines of archers stepped forwards along the wall of the city, nocking arrows to their bows. They aimed them high into the sky, motionless until, "Fire!"

A fleet of arrows flew through the air, arching over the defenders before whistling down into the enemy troops, felling many before they even got close. More arrows shot through the air as the archers reloaded, then there was a screech as Ebon took to the sky at the head of a handful of dragons and two other gryphons, his navy blue feathers shining in the morning light. They headed high into the air, flying over the curve of the arrows.

"They've got rocks!" said Tekek, squinting into the sky. Another faint screech came from above as Ebon called to the others, then they released their burdens, dropping the huge rocks they had carried down onto the advancing enemy forces. A few arrows shot towards them from Zartear's side but they were much too low and they escaped unharmed.

A cry of victory washed through the defenders as the rocks crashed into the enemy, making great dents in the advancing forces. The Elites joined in the cry, despite not being able to see the success of the attack. They were standing a few rows back from the front, out of reach of the first wave of attackers that were soon to come their way.

Lutis gulped, his hand tightening around the unfamiliar short sword that Aeron had managed to find for him. With his other hand he reached into his coat pocket, checking that the emerald was still safe.

"Lutis, we'll fight t'gether," said Hone, who stood next to him.

"Okay... lets hope neither of us die eh?" He tried to joke, but the words stuck in his throat. He let out a tense breath, clutching at the blade. His stomach churned and he decided that having breakfast had been a bad idea- a very bad idea.

The ranks in front of them suddenly loosened as they ran forwards to meet the enemy, the sound of clashing steel and the frightened whinnies of horses filling the air. Hone gave a shriek next to him, laying her ears back as a mercenary kicked his horse towards them, sword drawn high, and bared her teeth, leaping in to attack. She ripped the man from the horse's back, her claws tearing through his light armour like it was cloth. Lutis ducked to one side as the horse galloped past, parrying the first attack that came his way, his heart in his mouth.

The lash Elites ripped a hole in the enemy forces that came at them, their sharp claws and bladed tails no match for the mercenaries' swords. Terrowin was fighting on Lutis' left, slashing out with his sword, Ink a little further off using her claws to dispatch those who dared approach her.

There was a scream overhead and a dragon flew past, spiralling through the air, it's tail smoking. It dived towards the ground, almost grazing the heads of those fighting below before it pulled up into the sky. Lutis ducked, swearing as a black arrow landed nearby, then dropped into a crouch as a goblin swung its blade at his head, stabbing out with his sword. It missed and the goblin parried it, almost wrenching the blade out of Lutis' hand. The man yelled and dived to one side, one of the lash Elites slicing out with their tail and cutting the goblin in twain.

"Thanks!" he shouted, hoping the dragon had heard him (whoever it was), and grabbed a shield off the floor, hoping he would do better stopping any attacks with it. A roar drowned out the sound of battle as Xaoc flew overhead, pursuing the first dragon. The tribal battle blood flapped almost lazily, the runes that decorated his wings glowing a menacing scarlet as he surveyed the ground below then let out a long hiss of flame, scorching both attackers and defenders alike, before turning up into the air to make another pass.

"Move, *move*!" screamed Aeron, the dragon turning and running for the city behind them. "Quick, he's comin' f'us!"

Hone ran past, then let out a frightened bugle as she saw Lutis and swerved towards him. He turned alongside her, running a couple of steps before jumping onto her back, hooking his arm around the spine between her shoulders. She looked around to check if he was safe, then put on a burst of speed as Xaoc coasted past, blackening the ground where they had been only moments before.

The Elite slid to a halt as they made it out of the tribal battle blood's range, looking back at the wake that it had left. Through the fire they could see the fighting stretching from right to left, and no victory in sight yet.

"Where's Ink and Ter?" shouted Lutis over the noise of the battle, pulling at one of Hone's ears to get her attention. "They were near us."

Hone searched for a moment. "I dunno! I'm sure they got clear."

Suddenly a flash of light shot through the fire, then one of the defenders nearby crumpled to the ground, felled by magic. Hone turned and ran again, dodging this way and that as more flashes of light came at them.

"Look oooout!" shouted a voice, then Ink came flying low overhead, Terrowin clutched in her claws. Lutis ducked as they grazed head height, Terrowin waving his sword and shouting a war-cry. There was another flash of magic, the ball of light hitting Terrowin right in the middle. His hold on Ink's paw slipped and he went crashing to the ground, falling like a rag-doll.

Terrowin! screamed Ink, diving to the ground to protect her friend from any more attacks, standing over him as she slashed out at a pair of mercenaries that stepped forwards to deliver a death blow. Lutis wrenched on Hone's wing, pulling her around in a circle back towards the others.

He jumped off the dragon's back as she attacked the two mercenaries with Ink, the two dragons working together to clear a circle around the fallen man. Lutis ran to his side, rolling him over onto his back. His shirt was blackened where the bolt had hit him, and still smoked.

"Ter? Terrowin?" Lutis asked, bending over his face to see if he was still alive. His hair ruffled slightly as the man breathed out, then he gave a hacking cough and opened his eyes, groaning in pain.

"Look out!"

Lutis twisted, slashing out with his sword at the soldier that had tried to creep up on them, slicing through her leg. She screamed and swung out with her sword but he blocked it and pushed her backwards, Hone catching her with the end of her tail and dispatching her quickly. Lutis turned back to Terrowin, dragging up his shirt to reveal the charred, burnt wound. Terrowin watched with glazed eyes, his shallow breaths suddenly interrupted by another barking cough.

"Ink!" The dragon appeared at his call, her black and white face streaked with scarlet. "Get Terrowin to a healer fast, he took a direct hit."

She nodded and hooked her front claws around Terrowin's arms, flaring her wings to take to the sky, but Lutis stopped her. "No wait, carry him on your back." Pushing away the dragon's grasp, he hefted the man into his arms then onto the dragon's back. He nodded at Ink and the dragon took off back towards the city on foot, dodging the attacks that came their way and calling for protection from the defenders.

~

Armeno had followed Zartear's army the day after he had escaped on foot, Velox still a captive with the other horses. It was dangerous, but he managed to keep out of sight, Static's emerald cloak providing camouflage against the green of the grass. When night had fallen he had cut in front of the army, joining the ranks of the defenders at an early hour, before Echai had sent out the signal to say that the army was approaching.

The elf didn't know that the others were in the city, or if he had, where they were, otherwise he would have fought alongside them. As it was he stuck to the edge of the defenders, keeping out of the way, hunting down a sword that he could use and some breakfast before returning to his post. The state of his clothes attracted some attention, but he covered up his ripped shirt with his cloak, disappearing into the crowds on the one occasion someone actually asked him about it.

When Zartear's army had attacked he had kept away from the main bulk of the fighting, uninterested in fighting faceless mercenaries. Instead he looked along the lines for the now-familiar form of Nox, and found her holding back from the first wave of fighters, letting the more eager mercenaries destroy the defenders' order before attacking herself.

As the two armies collided he concentrated on the battle in front of him, diving forwards when the first riders came his way. When one fell, pierced by an arrow through the chest, he dodged forwards, grabbing hold of his steed's reins and swinging himself up into the empty saddle. He kicked the beast into a canter, heading towards the middle of the fighting as the next wave of fighters surged forwards from Zartear's side, his eyes flicking between his opponents and the spotted horse that Nox rode.

"Armeno!" Someone calling his name shook him out of his fixed state and he looked up from the mercenary he had just impaled on his sword, wrenching it free.

"Look, look, it's the elf!" Tekek called, cutting down her opponent without mercy and waving a wing briefly to catch his attention. He saw the other dragons fighting nearby and turned the horse towards them, making his way slowly over.

"How are you here?" shouted Lutis, rolling under an attack and running for the elf. He got caught up with another opponent, blocking the sword with his shield.

"Long story!" he yelled back, riding his horse into the man who had attacked Lutis. The thief hastily retreated, returning to Hone's side so they could protect each other's backs. He ducked low over the mare's neck as Xaoc flew overhead again, spreading chaos. There was a sudden burst of heat as the dragon seared a line across the ground, setting alight everything in its wake.

Through the flames Armeno saw the familiar spotted hide of Tamarisk and spurred his mount on, leapt through the flames and dashed after the stallion. The mare squealed, her eyes rolling with fear, but Armeno kept her firmly in line, squeezing his heels against her sides.

The Felixis was easy to pick out in the fray of battle, Tamarisk's eccentric coat marking him amongst the darker coats of the other horses. Armeno rode forwards with a yell, his sword slashing out at her. She only just turned to parry it, the blades sparking as his slid down to her hilt. Nox's eyes widened as she recognised him, then dragged at her stallion's reins, trying to steer him away from Armeno.

"You let Kassie die!" he roared, stabbing out with his blade again. She dodged it, but only just, Tamarisk shying as the other horse came alongside and digging his heels into the ground.

"She was dying anyway!" shouted back Nox, blocking Armeno's attacks with her sword. "We couldn't do anything."

"I could have saved her. I could have!" His face contorted in anger, and, taking his sword in two hands, twisted the blade around Nox's, ripping it out of her hands. It flung away into the dirt, leaving her unarmed. Fear crossed her face and she vaulted out of the saddle, breaking into a run for the sword. As she bent to get it Armeno leapt off his own horse, swinging his sword. "That's MINE!"

Her hand closed around the hilt and she span around, driving it upwards towards the elf, but he flicked it out of the way, thrusting his own blade forwards, right into her heart.

She froze as the blade stabbed into her, her eyes widening and a little "oh!" forming on her lips as he wrenched it free, letting her drop to her knees. Time seemed to stand still as he stepped back, throwing the sword away from him and picking up his own, the sounds of battle turning into one dull roar around her. Her vision went black, one last breath gasping in her throat before she pitched forwards onto the ground, dead.

Armeno stood shocked for a moment as she fell, then gripped his sword a little firmer and turned to run after the horses, catching hold of Tamarisk's reins. He pulled the stallion to a stop, the horse whinnying in fear as he remounted, then turned the knabstrupper back towards where he had seen the lash Elites, hoping to fight nearby.

~

"Your coat's on fire!"

A frightened shout made Lutis turn, then realised what the person had said and looked down at the back of his coat, which was billowing black smoke into the air. He gave a yelp, dropping his shield and batting at it with his spare hand.

"Hold still." Liesk, who had shouted before, was now next to him and with one deft movement sliced off the bottom of his coat with the long spear that she held. The fabric dropped to the floor, a string of red cartridges spilling onto the ground. "What the-"

"They're fireworks, move!" shouted Lutis, taking hold of the avian's arm and pulling her along as the fabric smoked more. There was a *pop!* as a cartridge exploded, then another, something that whizzed suddenly catching alight and streaking after them, hitting Liesk square in the back and sending her tumbling to the ground.

"Liesk! Are you okay?" Lutis stopped, doubling back to offer the woman a hand. She shook her head and looked up, blinking, before her lips curved into a cruel smile and she grabbed her spear, pointing the tip at Lutis' throat.

"Give me the emerald," she snarled, her voice distorted. "Now."

He backed up, dropping his sword in surprise as Liesk rose to her feet, her weapon still aimed at him. "What? What do you mean?"

"Give it to me!" Her voice rose into a shriek and she jabbed out with her spear, ripping the front of Lutis' coat.

"You… you *traitor*!" he cried, the truth rushing over him like a wave. "You've been working against us all along!"

Liesk gave a high laugh, taking a step forwards and forcing Lutis back. "So, someone finally worked it out. Not before you blathered all your plans out to me though- thanks for that. You made my job *so* much easier."

"How... how long have you been working against us?" he stuttered, trying to buy some time.

"Oh, since those thieves came looking for you last time. They gave me a tip-off about Zartear's plans, and it sounded like the perfect way to actually get some power around here. But enough of that. Be sure to tell the others- if you live. Now, the emerald, *if you please*."

He gaped at her, astounded, then slowly reached into his pocket, the other hand raised into the air. His fingers fumbled for the little bag that held the jewel, trying to drag out the time. Maybe if he was slow enough, one of the lash Elites would come to his rescue...

"Come on, come on." Liesk started to become impatient, her free hand clenching in irritation. He reluctantly pulled the bag out of his pocket then suddenly threw it at her, hoping to catch her by surprise as he scrabbled on the ground for his sword.

She caught the bag, her nose wrinkling in anger at his ploy, then parried his attack with her spear, knocking his sword out of his grip with ease.

She tutted and twisted on the spot, slamming the blunt end of her spear into his head and knocking him to the ground. Pain exploded in his skull and he yelled, clutching at where she had hit him. Blood started to drip between his fingers, running hot along his cheek.

"Nice try," she said, pulling the string of the bag and tipping the jewel into her open palm. It lay in her hand, inert, then a bright golden light exploded from within it, blindingly bright. Her fist closed around the jewel and she swung her hand up into the air, giving a triumphant whoop.

A huge shockwave suddenly rippled out from the jewel, throwing Lutis backwards through the air and onto his back a few metres away. He screamed as he crashed to the ground, rolling over a couple of times before coming to a halt, blood dripping into his eyes. Groaning, he rubbed it away and sat up, spitting out more blood.

A huge dragon stood where he had been, its green scales glittering like jewels in the morning sun. It unfolded its great scaled wings and threw itself into the sky with one beat of them, rocketing up above the battle with ease. There was an unearthly scream as it caught Liesk in its grip, dragging her into the air.

"Retreat!" There was a shout from somewhere nearby as the dragon took to the air, then horn blasts echoed out from the wall of the city, calling back the defenders from across the battlefield. "Back to the city! The third jewel dragon has escaped!"

Lutis scrambled to his feet, rubbing at his eyes as he ran for the city. A horse whinnied nearby then Armeno cantered up, reaching out a hand to haul him up behind him. He stretched out his hand, catching it, but before the elf could drag him onto the horse there was a swishing nose behind him and he was suddenly tugged into the air by the back of his coat. A clawed paw grabbed one arm as he was lifted higher into the air and Armeno was pulled off the horse after him. Lutis gave a yell, writhing in the creature's grip to try and get free.

"Stay still!" shouted Ebon, the gryphon holding him tightly by the arm as they soared upwards into the sky. Armeno hung tightly onto his hand, reaching up to hang onto Lutis' coat with his other. The gryphon strained to lift the two men, his wings beating frantically at the air. "I cannot hold you like this for long!"

The gryphon didn't get time to settle himself as a frantic yell came from below. "Dragon!" shouted Armeno. "Battle blood!" Ebon took a brief look behind then dove for the ground, flapping to try and gain speed. There was a roar behind them, then sudden heat as the dragon turned to pursue them, belching flames.

"Let us up!" bellowed Lutis, bending his arm to swing Armeno up onto the gryphon between his wings. Ebon turned and the elf managed to clamber up, holding onto the beast for dear life.

"Hang on Lutis, I'm going to flick you, you'll land on my back!" Ebon looked down at the man then banked sharply upwards, throwing him out of his claws before Lutis could protest. He gave a scream of fear as the gryphon disappeared, the ground rushing up to meet him…

Ebon cart-wheeled in the air behind Lutis and came swooping back down underneath him, catching the man as he had said, banking swiftly to avoid the still pursuing Xaoc. Lutis' scream was cut off as he thumped onto the gryphon's back, throwing his arms around Armeno. They dived for the ground again, spinning to try and confuse the larger dragon. Lutis turned to look at it and saw him bank to the left, trying to cut them off.

"Turn right, NOW!" he shouted, tugging on the gryphon's feathers. The gryphon gave an indignant squawk and turned, narrowly missing Xaoc. His wingtip scraped over the dragon's side and infuriated the tribal battle blood even more. As they rushed overhead Lutis saw a figure crouched low over the dragon's back, fear knotting in his stomach- Zartear was flying with the great black dragon.

Ebon shot under Xaoc's tail, putting on a burst of speed as the dragon paused to try and locate them again. He dropped low to the ground, speeding through the city gates above the retreating forces, then slowed and turned to land on the city wall.

"You've got to get the rest of the army inside the city, the triblade dragon's about to form and there's no way we can stop it!" Lutis scrambled off Ebon's back, falling to the ground as his knees gave way. Armeno climbed off the gryphon too and pulled him to his feet, holding him upright until he could stand. "We've gotta find Foen, he's the only one who can stop Zartear now!"

Ebon nodded, breathing hard after his frightened flight before taking to the skies again, his blacked wings labouring. Armeno watched him go, leaning over the edge of the battlement as he saw a flash of colour below.

"The Elites are in the city. You go and find Foen, I'll get them and catch up," he said, before running for the nearest staircase down to the city level. Lutis nodded and started off down the wall, breaking into a run as he recognised where he was, not too far away from where Foen had said he would be. A few arrows shot towards the city from those opponents they had left behind and he was forced low, flinching when an arrow shot dangerously close by.

As he ran through a gatehouse, pausing for breath while there was protection from the enemy arrows, he saw Foen standing a little way off with his sister, the sorcerer clad in shining silver armour, and of course, trademark beige hat. He gave a grim smile and broke into a run again, shouting his name.

A shining silver barrier suddenly appeared in front of him and he crashed into it, dropping to the floor. He wrapped one hand around his stomach, winded, then squirmed as he felt the shield start to crush down on top of him, trying to work his way free of the magic.

"Wait, it's me!" he gasped, throwing out one hand to stop Risis from condensing her shield further. The pressure stopped, then lifted.

"Sorry, I didn't recognise you!" she said, starting forwards to help him to his feet. "You're all covered in blood."

"This is a war, what do you think I'd be covered in, daisy chains?" he snapped, trying to regain his breath. She pouted, hurt.

"The third dragon, it's been released. Who set it free?" demanded Foen, stepping forwards to shake Lutis by the shoulders. "You were supposed to protect it!"

"It was Liesk, she's a traitor. You've got to do something!"

The wizard paled. "Liesk? But... she was on our side!"

"No, she wasn't."

"You can explain later. The potion, it works! When the triblade dragon forms, keep back and try not to die." Foen rolled up his sleeves, producing a little vial from his belt and shaking it in front of Lutis with a grim smile.

"Uh, thanks?" he said, looking out at the abandoned battlefield. The dead and dying littered the plain, the two huge dragons flying high above, a few smaller defender dragons fleeing for the city before they were noticed.

"Lutis!" A gleeful shout came from the guard tower, then Hone bowled towards them, fluttering her wings. The dragon was in one piece, apart from a few scratches and scrapes, the rest of Aeron's patrol following.

"Hone! You're all still alive!"

"'Course we're still alive silly, we're Elites!" She gave him a quick feathery hug, then followed his gaze towards the dragons that still flew the skies. "This ista then, eh?"

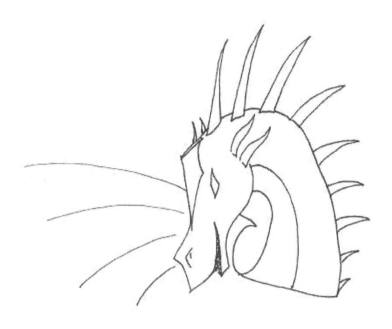

22
THE LAST STAND.

Liesk screamed as the dragon's claws cut into her arm, his every wing-beat wrenching at her shoulder until her whole arm was burning like fire. He seemed to hold no interest in her at all, his golden eyes scanning the ground for treasure. He suddenly swooped low to the ground, diving to inspect a glittering object that called him down to the battlefield. On his first dive her feet hit the ground, the impact jarring through her body as she was dragged a short way, then was pulled back into the air. The second time she lost her spear as it was ripped from her hand when it hit the ground, the rough wood ripping through her hand. She screamed again as splinters wedged themselves into her skin, blood leaking from fresh cuts.

"Khaan!" called a thunderous voice, making the dragon turn. Xaoc flew towards them, the tiny figure of Botsu curled tightly around one of the horns that curved back from his face.

"Xaoc. Released after so many years." His voice was low and hoarse with years of forced silence.

"Hello, my daaarling," hissed Botsu, uncurling herself from her vantage point and twirling through the air towards the hoarder dragon. "You brought a sssacrifice. How thoughtful."

"She was the one who summoned me," Khaan growled.

"Ssshe will do nicccely." The venomous dragon hovered in front of Liesk, her forked tongue licking between her lips.

"Sacrifice?" squeaked Liesk. "I summoned you! You can't harm me!" Beside those of the dragons, her voice was pitiful.

Xaoc gave a laugh, the sound like thunder. "We work for nobody."

"Traitorsss have their usesss. Yoursss isss finished!" crowed Botsu, her eyes gleaming as she regarded the avian, then she turned away. "Xxxaoc, do the honoursss?"

Khaan suddenly released his grip on Liesk's arm, sending her plunging towards the ground, tumbling over and over in the air. She tried to force her wings open, but she was falling too fast and they flapped uselessly. Screaming, she tried to right herself, battling to open her wings again. Xaoc gave a roar, then his scorching flames engulfed her completely.

Like a falling star, she crashed lifeless to the ground, a few dark feathers wafting up into the air before catching alight and burning into cinders.

The dragons took no notice of the dying girl, Botsu shooting the other two a victorious look as tendrils of dark magic started to twist around their bodies, binding them together. There was a flash of black, concealing the three, before it cleared and a huge black dragon exploded into view.

The defenders on the wall looked out with horror as the dragon twirled through the air, three heads belching smoke and fire down onto the battlefield below. Everything about it was unnatural-two pairs of wings, the coloured runes that covered its body, a long curling tail and no back legs. It gave a roar, drowning out all other sound, then turned towards the city, intent on razing it to the ground.

"Oh crap," squeaked Lutis as the dragon headed towards them, gripping his sword a little tighter. Hone patted him on the shoulder with one wing.

"It'll be ahreet, Foen'll stop it, ne'er fear." She gave him a smile, watching the dragon twirl through the sky. Lutis gulped, hardly reassured.

"Are you okay?" Neby asked softly from beside him, looking anxious. "You're very pale. Is that all your blood?"

Lutis looked down at himself, tugging at the front of his coat where it was glued to his shirt. The blue fabric was stained with a mixture of mud, ash and blood in turn, and was ripped in a dozen places. He didn't want to know what cuts and bruises he was getting under it all.

"No, I don't think it's all mine. I'm alright." He gave her a weak smile but the dragon didn't look convinced. She started to protest, telling him to go and seek shelter, but Aeron cut her off as he addressed them all.

"Everyone, get in a circle around Foen an' Risis. Tha' dragon's bound t'come our way sooner or later. Distract it, attack it, set it on fire, do whista can t'protect Foen- he's t'only one who can stop it."

The Elites did as their leader asked, Aeron and Echai standing in front of Foen and Risis, Neby, Armeno and Tekek to the right, and Hone and Lutis to the left. More warriors were filing onto the wall further along, those with bows shooting into the few enemy forces that swarmed outside the city. Inside the gate, battle had broken out as the defenders tried to force back Zartear's pursuing forces, fighting to close the gate.

The triblade dragon flew the length of the city wall, shooting past once before angling up into the sky and turning back on itself, fire shooting from its three mouths as it came back down on the city. To his side, Lutis saw Foen down the little vial of potion he had made, flexing his fingers experimentally as magic coursed through his veins, starting to read the spell that would separate the three dragons.

As if it knew something was threatening it the dragon stopped in mid-air, one head scouring along the wall to find its opponent. Two purple eyes fixed on the group of lash Elites, then the other two heads looked their way too, green and red eyes staring them down.

"Comin' this way, get ready!" Aeron shouted, flicking his tail. It dived towards them, a roar rumbling from one head before another shot a wall of fire at them, the third head adding more flames.

A shimmering silver barrier leapt up to deflect it, arching overhead briefly before it cut out as fire licked over its surface. Risis gave a tiny exclamation of surprise as the magic took its toll on her, then the witch collapsed to the ground in a dead faint as the dragon swept overhead. Armeno ran to her side and scooped her up in his arms, then ran for the gatehouse. He deposited her inside, checking she was still alive before returning to the wall.

The dragon curved back up into the sky, bearing down on them from above. The Elites scattered, Echai pulling Foen to safety as it scorched the wall with more fire, turning the stones black as it swooped over. Its tail smashed through the battlements as it headed out over the plains, sending rubble crashing to the ground below. As it coasted in a circle to attack again, the lash Elites gathered around the sorcerer, trying to protect him.

It came at them again, slower this time, hovering in front of the wall before its front claws caught at the battlements, carving long scratches into the stone. Aeron screeched a war-cry, ran forwards and leapt for the middle head, his patrol following suit. His front claws caught under it's scales, ripping them away as he clawed his way up its neck. It roared, trying to shake the Elite free. Echai attacked too, growling and whipping his tail across the dragon's nose so he left a long slice through its scale.

"You've gone too far, pitiful beassst!" snarled another of the heads, jerking forwards. Its jaws closed around Aeron's middle and ripped him off, throwing him onto the walkway. The third head gave a screech as golden light started to curl around it, Foen's spell taking effect.

Aeron cried out as he slid across the wall, leaving a track of blood behind from where the dragon's teeth had cut him. Hone screeched his name, abandoned her attack and started to run to protect him, but the head that he had attacked locked its sights onto him, and, opening its maw, blasted a hot jet of white fire at the Elite.

"NO!" screamed Hone, shying away from the flames until they died, then she leapt towards where Aeron lay. His tail-blade flopped across his face and she pulled it away, the breath catching in her throat. Behind her, Echai leapt off the triblade dragon too, running to her side.

Aeron opened his eye, fixing for a moment on the two dragons' faces. His scales had been scorched black and his wings were little more than smoking ruin, lying limply by his sides, not one shadow of their former splendour remaining.

"My son... an' daughter..." he whispered, his last breath rasping in his throat as his eye slipped shut again.

Hone shook her head in denial, one paw tentatively reaching out to touch the Elite on his shoulder. "Aeron? *Aeron*? Da-- Daddy?" A tear dripped along her muzzle, glinting as it fell onto his matt scales.

Echai gave a scream of grief and turned to attack the triblade dragon again as Hone bent over Aeron's body sobbing. It was coated in golden tendrils of light, its heads twisting up to roar at the sky as it started to change. A figure leapt from the dragon's back as it changed back into three, catching at the edge of the parapet.

Foen stood in front of the dragons as they reappeared, a steady stream of magic running from his hands around the hoarder dragon. It gave a roar of anger, the light enveloping it completely before it disappeared and a green emerald dropped to the ground. He dived for the jewel, wrapping it safely in a cloth before the dragon could be released again by accident.

Xaoc took his companion's bad luck as a benefit for himself and shot up into the sky out of the reach of the city's defenders. Botsu dropped a couple of feet as she readjusted to being small again, then her eyes fixed on Armeno, hissing. The elf had been thrown aside by the triblade dragon, and hurriedly stood as the venomous dragon came towards him

"Ssso, you essscaped!" she fumed, her tail whipping through the air behind her. "I would sssay we could have sssome more fun, but I'm bored of you!" She bared her fangs and lunged at the elf with a hiss, flattening her wings against her sides.

"Me TOO!" he shouted, swinging his sword through the air. It sliced the venomous dragon in half as she sunk her fangs into his arm, black blood gushing from her middle as her separated tail thumped to the ground. He screamed as she bit, her powerful venom sending fiery pain shooting up his arm, then wrenched her away, the dragon dead before she hit the ground. He gasped, dropping his sword and clutching at the wound before falling too.

"Armeno!" Lutis saw the elf go down and ran towards him, but an arm hooked itself around his boot and sent him crashing to the ground. The rider of the triblade dragon dragged himself onto the wall- Zartear pulled his broadsword from his back as the thief scrambled to his feet, parrying the first blow with his shortsword. The impact jolted up his arm and he staggered backwards, wrenching his sword free.

Zartear attacked, his broadsword swinging through the air to try and knock Lutis' sword out of his hands. He parried it again, adding his other hand to the hilt of his blade. Zartear scowled and pulled his blade free, driving his hilt forwards into the thief's ribs.

Pain exploded up his side as the sword slammed into him and he staggered backwards, his breaths coming shallowly. The man stepped forwards, slicing his broadsword downwards in a long cut, wrenching Lutis' sword out of his hands as he held it high to try and stop the blade. He cried out as the tip of Zartear's broadsword sliced its way from the palm of his hand to his elbow, hot blood seeping through his wrecked coat from the long wound and dripping onto the ground.

He jumped backwards, but tripped on his fallen sword and fell to the ground, more pain lancing across his ribs. Zartear gave a cruel smile and brought his sword round to point at Lutis as he scrambled backwards, leaving a trail of bloody handprints as blood coursed down his arm. He swung the sword to deliver a final blow but a screech from beside him stopped him in his tracks and he looked up, distracted. A red and purple blur leapt out of nowhere, crushing Zartear to the ground. He gave a furious shout, trying to get free of the Elite.

Lutis crawled a little further back then his arms gave way, black tingeing the edges of his vision. Someone shouted his name as his head cracked against the ground, then he felt cold hands pressing against his arm. A blurry face floated into view, then everything faded slowly away.

23
RECOVERY.

A chill breeze blew across the southern plains, autumn firmly on its way. The sky was dark, great pillar-like clouds seeming to make the world that little bit smaller. Sheets of rain washed across the landscape, blowing in waves as the wind pushed it this way and that.

A little way away from Tarz, on a small hummock of grass, the four remaining members of Aeron's patrol gathered, feeding a huge bonfire that refused to be quenched by the rain. The flames flickered high into the sky, wrapping greedy tendrils around the wood that they added. Echai helped Hone lift a huge trunk onto the pyre then the two stood back as it crackled, steam hissing from the cracks in the bark.

"Pa would be pleased," said Echai, staring at the flames. Hone sniffed beside him and he pulled her close, wrapping his wings around her.

"He wanted t'gar back to t'Ever Bridge," she said, tears running down her cheeks unchecked. "Now… now he ne'er can."

"He's with the stars now," Echai said quietly. Tekek and Neby joined them, the sandy coloured dragon burying her head in her friend's shoulder and sobbing freely. "Pa was the best patrol leader, and always kept us safe. None could have done a better job."

"I miss him," gulped Hone, looking up at her brother. His face was half-lit by the flames, his green and blue scales almost the same as their lost father's, apart from his purple feathers that marked him as different.

"We all miss him," said Tekek, her normally dreamy voice bleak. "It'll be strange, going back to the desert after all this. Echai, you'll lead us now, won't you?"

The dragon nodded slowly. "I suppose we'll head back to Racksom in a couple of weeks time with Foen… pick up Doan, if he wants to come with us, maybe stop off at Plurith on the way back. Then we'll head up to the desert mountains, tell Aeron's old pack what happened…" He tailed off, not used to taking charge. Over the next few months he would have to grow a lot to cope with the responsibilities of a patrol leader.

"I'm not comin' with you," said Hone suddenly, rubbing away her tears and looking up. "I… I don't think I can face t'desert without Aeron there… An' I think my place is here now."

"What? You have to come with us!" exclaimed Tekek. "You can't not come with us!"

"I don't wanna."

"Are you sure?" asked Echai. Hone nodded, her mind made up.

"I cannae come back with you. One day I will, but not now." She untangled herself from Echai's embrace, stepping over to Tekek. Neby looked up from the purple and red dragon's hug, her eyes rimmed with red. "It's not 'cause I don't like you, 'cause I do, you're like fam'ly. But right now, I think I need t'be away from t'desert." She looked at the pyre nearby, the flames still licking at the sky. "I ne'er knew Aeron was my real fam'ly, 'till t'very end…"

Neby nodded, understanding what the young dragon was trying to say. "Just because he never told you, doesn't mean he didn't love you."

"I know," Hone said sadly. She knew that for a lash dragon to have more than one child was looked badly upon, and Aeron would have lost his standing as a patrol leader- maybe even his standing as an Elite.

"Do you want to go back to Risis' house?" asked Echai. The young Elite nodded, taking one last look at the pyre before setting off at a run down the hill and heading back towards the city.

~

The rain battered down on the houses of Tarz, washing away the summer dust. It made a quiet pattering sound on the roof of Risis' house, creating a gentle music in the long room at the top of the house. It was quiet enough not to wake the man sleeping in the bed furthest away from the window.

There was a curious *'meow?'* as Risis' cat padded into the room, ignoring the two other occupied beds as he padded over to the third. He bunched his legs then leapt onto the bed, his soft silver tabby paws silent on the covers as he padded forwards, hunting for the warmest spot. The man didn't wake, breathing quietly as he slept, his brown hair ruffled across the pillow and sticking up in tufts from under the bandage around his head.

The cat peered over the bed then tried one paw on the man's chest, deciding that it was the most comfortable spot to sleep in. He woke with a yelp, flinching as the cat pressed on his broken ribs. It hissed and leapt off the bed, tail thick like a bottlebrush. He watched it saunter off and leap onto the next bed along, its occupant's long ear identifying the person as Armeno. The elf shifted slightly as the cat woke him too, stroking one hand slowly along the cat's back and making it purr in contentment.

"Lutis! You're awake!" A surprised cry came from across the room and he turned his head. Risis was sitting on the other bed with Terrowin, the short witch's cheeks red with embarrassment as she pushed the man's arm away from her waist. "Let me um... I'll go and get Foen."

She started to slide off the bed but Terrowin wrapped his arms around her again, holding her back. "Oi'm not done with ye yet though!" he complained. She batted at his hands and pulled them away, her cheeks reddening further.

"I'll be back in a minute," she said, giving him a kiss on the nose and disappearing out the door.

"Ye better be lass!" He gave a cheeky grin, looking at Lutis again. "How ye feelin' mate?"

"Not good," he mumbled, trying to sit up. Even the little movement made him puff for breath, and his left arm wobbled. "What happened?"

"Ye looked pretty bad when they brought ye 'ere," said Terrowin, grimacing. "Apparently ye took on Zartear! Wot were ye thinkin' mate?"

Lutis frowned, trying to remember, then groaned. "Oh god, yeah…"

"Good thing we've got that sorcerer on our side. Ye would 'ave died if it weren't for his quick thinkin' an' magic. Patched ye up a bit."

"I don't feel patched up," replied Lutis, rubbing at his head. He winced as he felt bandages, patting them lightly. Terrowin gave a short laugh.

"Not surprised, ye should 'ave seen the state o'ye when they brought ye 'ere." He pulled a wry face. "Ye ain't lookin' much better now if ye ask me."

"Oh thanks, that just makes me feel *so* much better," he grumbled, pulling the bed sheets a little higher. Someone had undressed him and it was chilly without a shirt on. Pain shot up his left arm and he quickly stopped, gulping when he saw that his forearm was swathed in bandages. "What did you say happened to me?"

Before Terrowin could speak the door flew open and Foen ran into the room, an eager look on his face.

"You *are* awake!" he crowed, a wide grin stretching across his face. "I thought it was just a ploy to get me up here for a rainy-day picnic or something."

Risis tutted from behind him and pushed past, handing the sorcerer a bag that clinked before going to curl up on Terrowin's bed again, shaking her short curls out of her face. Foen grabbed at the bag as it started to slip through his fingers, lugging it over to Lutis' side and dropping it onto the floor.

"How do you feel?" he asked, dragging up a chair and rifling through his bag.

"Really crap. What happened?"

"After the triblade dragon split back into three, I managed to trap the hoarder dragon in its jewel again. Armeno slew Botsu, but she bit him." He shot the elf a worried look, but he didn't look up. "I tell you, I've had an interesting time having to look after the three of you, all trying to die on me." He tutted, then continued, "Zartear managed to jump off the dragon somewhere in between, and I think he came after you."

"Yes, I remember that..."

"You're lucky it be alive. He broke two of your ribs and sliced all the way along your arm. Not to mention all the other cuts and bruises you've got- there were splinters of wood in your face, what made them?"

Lutis frowned, trying to recall the memory. "I *think* Liesk hit me, but I'm not sure... everything's a bit blurry," he admitted.

"I'm sure. Well, Hone'll be pleased to see you awake again. And as you are, I'm going to change your bandages, stay still." He took hold of Lutis' wrist, making him stretch out his arm as he started to peel away the bandages. Lutis watched him as he slowly unwrapped them, wincing as he saw the state of his arm.

A long red slice ran from his palm all the way to his elbow, raw and angry-looking against his pale skin. A line of neat stitches held the two sides together. He tried to pull his arm out of Foen's grip but the sorcerer gave him a whack on the hand, pinning him down while he hunted in his bag for more bandages. "Bloody hell..."

"You just wait until you see the state of your side," Foen said wryly, pulling out a roll of bandages with a little "aha!" and replacing the old ones. "Don't put too much weight on that arm, I don't want it to start bleeding again. You lost enough blood as it is."

Next he checked on Lutis' ribs, sucking in a disapproving breath when he saw that his skin was still cut and bruised a dark purple. "What have you been doing with yourself, I don't know," he muttered, poking at his side. Lutis yelped, shuffling away from his touch.

"Ooh, I hope Zartear's rotting in a cell somewhere, that hurts like hell."

Foen pulled a face, his eyes flicking to Lutis' face briefly. "Bad news I'm afraid. Hone managed to get him away from you, and we thought we had him, but the tribal battle blood appeared and we had to flee- Zartear escaped."

Lutis swore, scowling. Foen shrugged his regret and started applying a cream to his side, telling him to stop squirming when he tried to escape the sorcerer's cold hands.

When he was finished Foen disappeared down the stairs for a short while before returning with a tray of food, plonking it in front of Lutis. "Eat up, can't have you dying of starvation after rescuing you from the brink. Oh, and your coat's here." He pulled the dirty garment from out under the bed, holding it up. It drooped in sad tatters, completely ruined. "Hone was adamant that I didn't throw it away, said that you kept stuff in your pockets. Can you empty them so I can chuck this thing away?"

Lutis sighed, taking one corner in his hands. The fabric was black with dried blood. "I've had this coat for six years now."

"Looks like you'll be needing another one," said Foen, laying it over his abandoned chair, then swapped beds to check on Armeno. "Now elf, what are we going to do with you, eh?"

Lutis suddenly found himself hungry and attacked the food. Foen had even thought to bring up some water- strangely thoughtful for the normally absent-minded sorcerer, but he supposed he was so used to looking after other people, it was just something he always *did* remember to bring. Rain poured down the window, the wind whistling under the eaves of the house. A few leaves twisted through the air, one blowing against the glass panes and sticking flat.

He was almost finished with his meal when Ink padded into the room, licking her lips clean of red juice. The magpie dragon gave a squeal of excitement when she saw Lutis was awake, promptly bouncing over to his side and setting her front paws on the bed.

Ooh, Hone'll be pleased to see you're awake! she said, giving him a friendly lick on the hand. The dragon smelt sweet- she had found a punnet of strawberries down in the kitchen. Lutis ruffled her head feathers, pleased to see her in one piece.

"Where is that ol' lashy? Off with her mates and left me all alone?"

The smile dropped off Ink's face, her words hesitant. *No... they've gone to lay Aeron's deathfire.*

"...Deathfire?"

He died in the fight against that big dragon. Lutis, I'm sorry. It's the one time she's left your side in the past two days.

Lutis stared at her in disbelief then shoved away the tray of food, his eyes dropping to the ground. Ink stuttered more apologies before escaping over to Terrowin's bed, hiding underneath his blankets.

He slid back down the bed, turning over onto his side so the others couldn't see as he mourned the lash Elite. He slipped into a doze after a while, still tired from the battle. Risis and Foen disappeared off downstairs, the woman taking his unfinished tray of food away with her, leaving Terrowin talking quietly with Ink.

When the door creaked open again he didn't look to see who it was, assuming it was one of the two siblings returning to check on them again. There was a sniff, then light footsteps padded over to Terrowin's bed.

"I need someone t'talk to-" started Hone, her wings drooping, dripping water onto the floor from the tips. Lutis looked up at the sound of her voice, turning over and pushing his way up the bed again.

"Don't I get a hello?" he asked, rubbing his eyes with his right hand. The lash dragon turned, her head fins flaring in surprise when she saw the man was up.

"You're finally awake!" she exclaimed, leaping over the foot of Armeno's bed as she rushed to his side. The elf looked up, turning to look at the dragon as she scrambled over the end of his bed. One of his ears was slightly bent at the end, where Botsu had shifted the splint that had held it straight and made it heal at an angle instead, but his cheeks were no longer criss-crossed with cuts from the dragon's torture. "You've been asleep f'days."

"I know, I'm sorry," he said, leaning over to give her a hug. It hurt, but the dragon was hurting too. "I'm so, so sorry."

"I cannae believe he's gone," she mumbled, her voice cracking. "Out of everyone, Aeron? He was my Daddy, an' I dinae even know 'till the end…" She squeezed her eyes shut, tears welling up at their corners again. He took hold of her paw and helped her climb up onto the bed, pressing his face into her damp scales. She wrapped her wings around him, making a purple tent where they could grieve away from the world.

They sat in silence for a few minutes, then eventually broke apart, the dragon curling up across his legs and watching him silently. He wiped away a few tears, pushing the hair out of his face.

"How are the others?" he asked quietly.

"At t'pyre." She stretched out her front legs, laying her head on her paws. Lutis frowned and pushed her nose aside, running his fingers around the white bandage along her right leg.

"What did you do?"

"Zartear cut me with his sword. He was gaarn t'kill you, so I had t'stop him."

"You're so brave." He stretched out his left arm alongside her leg, matching their bandages together. "Look, we're the same."

She nodded. "I'm staying with you. T'others are gaarn back t'the desert without me."

"Are you sure? All your life, you've wanted to be an Elite. You're giving that up?"

"I'm still an Elite. I'm just... not with a patrol. Not with a patrol o'lashes. You're my patrol now."

PRONUNCIATION

Aeron- AIR-ron

Armeno- ARM-ay-no

Botsu- BOT-sue

Doan- DOUGH-an

Ebon- EB-on

Echai- EK-kai

Foen- FOE-enn

Hone- HOE-n

Khaan- KAA-n

Liesk- LEE-esque

Lutis Passal- Leu-TIS PASS-al

Neby- NEH-bee

Nox Arise- Nox Ar-ISS

Risis- REE-sis

Tekek- TEK-eck

Terrowin- TERR-oh-win

Xaoc- ZAY-oc

Zartear- ZAR-tear

ACKNOWLEDGMENTS

Wow, I've finally got to the end! Of course, I couldn't have done any of this without help- There are so many people to thank, and I've probably forgotten a few here, but everyone who helped, I'm eternally grateful. Emily, you're a great editor- thanks for putting up with my random plot-explosions and supplying even more random plot ideas. Also, for being a Lutis fangirl, that just makes you even cooler. Apollo, for being Lutis' other fangirl, supplying those gorgeous pictures of Xaoc and Ink, and generally being there to plot with- oh, and for being allowed to use Ink and Terrowin! They really are quite the pair.

Thanks to Tasha, who was always around on skype at the strangest hours to rant at, and for all the pep talks. Couldn't have done it without you buddy!

My friends Eldarwen, Zayzay and Artemis, for letting me use their characters (Xaoc, Zartear and his "smarmy git smile" and Armeno), and also supplying random writing advice, the lovely picture of a lash dragon (thanks Zay!) and giving time outs from novel/school stress. Arty, thanks for demanding chapters off me every day- you made me keep writing even when I was bored of it! But for the next one, please don't give me a huge plot idea halfway through writing again, that took forever to add! But, I love it all the same.

Thanks also to Echoingscreams, for the picture of a goblin. You're the #1 person to turn to for advice on goblins (something I'll need in the future, no doubt).

Of course, big thank you to Aero, who did the amazing front cover art. You're awesome!

Thanks to Millie, who managed to pervert many, many plot bunnies, and spawn even more!

Max, thanks for reading the whole thing through! You were the first person to (who hadn't got a character in it), and picked up some mistakes that I hadn't even thought of. Cheers!

My final thanks really must go to my long-suffering characters, who I put through a lot. Probably too much. But hey, you're all still in one piece, right?

10894552R00288

Made in the USA
Charleston, SC
14 January 2012